T0285296

Praise for Susan Petrone's previous novels:

Throw Like a Woman:

"While, on the surface, this is a novel about a woman battling to make her way in the man's world of professional baseball, debut author Petrone presents a stirring and humorous story of a woman doing considerably more than that — trying to rediscover herself, provide for her family, and perhaps find a little love along the way."
— *Booklist*

"Someday there will be a woman who plays Major League Baseball. And when it happens, I suspect it will be an awful lot like Susan Petrone's fun *Throw Like a Woman*. Susan knows baseball and so the novel — and her hero Brenda Haversham — crackles with authenticity. You can hear the pop of the ball hitting the catcher's mitt."
— Joe Posnanski, author of *The Soul of Baseball*, NBC Sports National Columnist

The Super Ladies:

"Book clubs of America, uncork the wine and settle in for a great discussion. *The Super Ladies* is big fun!"
— Mary Doria Russell, author of *The Sparrow, A Thread of Grace,* and *Epitaph*

"Very enjoyable read! This book was fun, quirky, different, and realistic — even with their 'super powers' it still seemed realistic! Like if this ever did happen in real life I would imagine it would be exactly like this."
— *Wall-to-Wall Books*

The Heebie-Jeebie Girl:

"The simple, desperate act that opens *The Heebie-Jeebie Girl* quickly turns complicated and dangerous. Susan Petrone has penned an open-hearted love letter to a still-proud city whose mills and bars used to operate around the clock, where jobs are scarce and people dream of hitting the lottery. A novel of magic and miracles, contrition and forgiveness, it's fitting that its hero, who can pick lucky numbers out of thin air, is named Hope. As Youngstown itself says: 'Some cities will chew you up and spit you out. Not me.'"
— Stewart O'Nan, author of *Snow Angels* and *Last Night at the Lobster*

"A series of unfortunate events weave together the complex and beautifully-rendered lives of an old man, a young girl, and a reluctant villain in this heartfelt page-turner set in 1977 Ohio. Petrone deftly blends suspense, fantasy, and family turmoil to paint an unflinching portrait of America's Rust Belt at its tipping point. If a city like Youngstown could talk, this is the story it might tell. I couldn't put it down!"
— D.M. Pulley, author of *The Dead Key* and *No One's Home*

The Musical Mozinskis

Susan Petrone

THE
ST▪RY
PLANT

The Story Plant
1270 Caroline Street
Suite D120-381
Atlanta, GA 30307

Copyright © 2023 by Susan Petrone
The Library of Congress Cataloguing-in-Publication Data is available upon request.

Story Plant hardcover ISBN-13: 978-1-61188-373-2
Story Plant e-book ISBN-13: 978-1-945839-79-5

Visit our website at www.TheStoryPlant.com

First Story Plant Printing: January 2024

Printed in the United States of America
0 9 8 7 6 5 4 3 2 1

For anyone who ever felt like they didn't fit in.

SING FOR YOUR SUPPER

Vincent Mozinski could grab music out of the air. He would reach out, grab the beat, and cup it in his hand, as though listening to it for a moment in private. Then he'd shake it — one–two–three–four — and throw the beat back out into the world for all to hear and for his children to see. It was something of a party trick. In performance, with an audience of strangers, it was akin to the flourish of a magician's theatrics, because Vincent knew the audience couldn't see what he saw. At home, in front of his family, there was the added intrigue of seeing the music. Seeing the beat, seeing the music, is just something everyone in the Mozinski family could do.

Do you know how music in cartoons is always signified by little musical notes floating through the air? Those notes are real. This mutual ability to see music — to see the notes in the air — is what started the Mozinski clan in the first place.

Vincent met his future wife in a music store on a lonely Wednesday afternoon in 1961. He was a 25-year-old jazz pianist wasting time before a gig smoking cigarettes and shooting the breeze with the owner while tinkering around on the old, beat-up piano in the back of the store when a lovely young woman around his age came in for some small purchase. The woman in question walked over and stood next to the piano, which Vincent was playing to within an inch of its life. This was not the first time a woman had stood by a piano to watch him play. Vincent always maintained that music is a magnet that attracts all matter of organic compounds. No less than the mating dance of the blue-footed booby, extravagant musical flourishes are a courting ritual used by most members of the Mozinski clan.

7

Vincent was coaxing a joyful noise out of the piano. More importantly, he was pulling a delightful profusion of notes from the depths of its soundboard. They tumbled out of the piano hard and fast, sparkling and spinning, a constant stream of triads falling over eighth notes jumping over dotted thirds in one big, beautiful mass. The notes resembled the way snow looks when it's swirling in the wind at twilight, when you can see each individual snowflake catch the light in its own way.

Vincent was not unaware of the presence of a beautiful but as-yet-unknown woman standing to his left, intently watching him play. He watched the notes stream over her as they poured forth from the piano. When he stopped, he gave the keys an extra flourish and the remaining notes sprang up higher than the rest, bounced off the ceiling, and slowly settled on the young woman, the fortunate notes dropping gently on her shoulders or getting tangled in her hair, the not-so-fortunate landing gently on the dusty floor by her feet.

At first, Vincent thought he had merely encountered another ordinary woman who enjoyed hearing a reasonably attractive man play the piano exceptionally well. After he stopped playing, he turned to look at her and saw the notes from the music he had made falling gently onto a stranger. This might have been the end of their acquaintance had, at that very moment, the woman not lifted up her hands and her arms to catch some of the tinkling notes as they fell around her. Like a woman standing in a summer rain after a drought, she caught the notes in her hands and smiled at them as they slipped through her fingers and drifted lazily to the ground, as though their fall from the grace of floating had been softened by the mere touch of her hands. When Vincent realized that there was standing in front of him a woman who could see music as he did — and who was a real dish to boot — he stood up, introduced himself, and proposed to her on the spot.

His exact first words were: "Hello, would you marry me?"

"It might help if I knew your name," she replied.

"I'm Vincent Mozinski," he said, and immediately presented his driver's license and Musicians' Union card (AFM local #4) as proof of his identity.

"Hello, Vincent Mozinski," she replied. "My name is Grace Klinefelter. Thank you for your proposal. Before I can even think of accepting, I need you to hear me play."

The music store's owner, who knew Vincent well and the young woman only as an infrequent customer, had watched this encounter with curiosity. For although he sold sheet music and instruments and instructed others in music and appreciated music in all its forms, he could not see music and thus had no idea why this young woman had been grasping at thin air and why one of his regular customers seemed so delighted by her doing so. Nonetheless, he pulled the best violin he had off the wall and handed it to the woman to play. While neither Grace nor Vincent can agree upon what he was playing on the piano when she walked in — he always insisted it was a Joplin rag while she was positive it was a stride version of "All of Me," they both agree that the first piece Grace ever played for her future husband was the allegro from Bach's Sonata No. 1 in G Minor for solo violin.

She stood a few feet away from him and began to play. As she played, she observed the stranger who had just asked her to marry him. At 26, with perfect pitch and a figure to match, Grace Klinefelter had been proposed to before, but never so quickly. Then again, she had never met anyone who appeared to be able to see music the way she saw music, but she had to be sure. Vincent had seated himself on the piano bench for her performance then, as the opening notes hit him, he stood and took two steps toward her. The notes approached him tentatively, dancing back and forth like a shy dog approaching a stranger. Vincent stood with his arms at his sides then slowly reached out his hands. Grace's music moved a little closer, and yet he stood motionless, his hands and arms open and welcoming. Grace continued playing, wondering, letting her music decide. Finally, in one immediate gesture of absolute trust, the notes pouring forth from her violin swirled around Vincent's feet, then encircled his legs, his waist, his arms and hands, his chest, his head, until he was completely enveloped in the spiral of notes she had made. Grace watched this as she played and knew that if her music could trust this man, then she could too. She finished the piece, brought the violin down from her chin, and said simply, "You know what? I think I will marry you."

After that, they devoted their lives to music and to the creation of more musicians. Their first-born was a girl, Clara, born in early December 1962. This first infant felt like a gift and a science experiment and a mystery. They fed her and loved her and played music for her, hoping that she carried within her the genes of music making. One day when Grace was playing with the baby, she sang. First, she sang "Hush Little Baby" to her, more colloquially known as the mockingbird song. Infant Clara gazed back at her with intense, hazel-brown eyes. It appeared she was listening, although who can tell with babies? Then Grace sang just the first note, a middle C, a simple *laaaa* that anyone could imitate. And baby Clara did, although it came out more like a *baaa*. But she was on pitch. Note by note, Grace sang the first few notes of the song to the baby, just a simple *ba*, with a simple progression, C−A−A−B−A−G−G. Her child echoed back each note with a perfectly on-pitch *ba*. It couldn't be a coincidence.

Emboldened by Clara's innate skill, over the next ten years Grace and Vincent produced five more children. The alarming frequency with which they procreated led to speculation that the couple did not practice birth control. Both Grace and Vincent were good Catholics and claimed that they used the so-called "rhythm method" of birth control but, as Vincent was a jazz musician, the rhythm was syncopated.

In the early days, when they had a growing family of small children, Vincent and Grace supported themselves by entertaining wealthy people in wealthy homes as they ate meals that cost enough to feed a family of eight — their family, in fact — for a week. Vincent played the piano, the accordion, and the clarinet. He was also a crooner, much to the delight of many a wealthy wife. He was, as they say, dreamy. Grace was primarily a violinist, although she had played trombone in her high school marching band and still knew her way around the old T-bone. As Grace Klinefelter, she played in orchestras and ensembles. As Grace Mozinski, she shifted her focus to birthing and raising more musicians and playing in string quartets on weekends.

Every one of the Mozinskis could play an instrument or two or three. The children played any number of instruments — the drums, the harp, the saxophone, the guitar, the violin, the piano, the cello, the bass, the trumpet, and, of course, the ever-present recorder. Vincent started everyone on the recorder because it's relatively simple to get a sound out of it, even for a toddler. And make no mistake, Vincent started his children playing as soon as they could hold the recorder and blow. His favorite joke was that if one of his children couldn't read music by the time they were eight years old, he'd put that kid up for adoption. It's the kind of joke you can safely make when you have a house full of children who play music as well as you do. A house full of, let's face it, prodigies. Like any parents, Grace and Vincent had no idea who their children would grow up to be, but they had hopes. And biases. When most parents were handing their children rattles, Grace and Vincent were handing their children maracas and shakers and cabasas. Just in case. Just to encourage whatever latent talent might be there. The music came to their children when they were in their cradles, leaving an indelible mark.

As the oldest, Clara strived to set a good example for her younger siblings by giving them much to live up to. She mastered the reading of both the treble and bass clefs before she could read the English language. She played the violin at three, the piano at five, and finally settled on the harp, or rather, the harp settled on her.

As Clara passed through the toddler stage and into school age, her mother looked at the child's long, curly brown hair and stated: "Clara has the look of a harpist." Clara wasn't sure about the harp at first. Her first instinct had been for something louder, like a brass instrument or even a woodwind, but from the first moment she sat down behind a troubadour harp at age five, Clara knew she was meant to play that instrument. Her hands moved easily and quickly over the strings, almost as though they were born knowing how to play it. Grace and Vincent murmured that she was a natural. They were right. When it came to music, they almost always were. Clara moved up to a full-sized harp at age 11 and played her first gig at a garden party for wealthy wives who oohed and aahed over the angelic little harpist with long, curly hair. They tipped her $20.

There was almost constant sound in the Mozinski house. Even after everyone had gone to sleep, there was a faintly distinguishable undertone of music in the house, like the hum of a refrigerator from another room. Music eventually dissipated into the air, but in bright light, one could sometimes pick out a few stray notes floating aimlessly through the house in the same way you might see dust motes floating through your living room on a sunny day. The notes from particularly heavy pieces — especially those written in minor keys — seemed to linger.

Susan Petrone

Someone always needed to vacuum after a ballad. Vincent insisted that one night, arriving home after a late gig, he spotted three entire measures of "Tuxedo Junction" still floating above the roof, a song that his older sons, Ellington and Bix, had been practicing earlier in the evening.

All seemed fine in the family until the birth of their sixth child. This youngest child, a girl named Viola, arrived approximately 20 months after her immediate predecessor, Thelonious. As they had with all of their other children, the family placed a child-sized mallet in her hand almost as soon as she could grasp it. Unlike their other children, however, this new infant did not immediately begin beating out simple rhythms on the wood block in front of her. They didn't expect the complicated 5/4 time that Ellington, the second-born, began beating out at the age of 14 months. It was clear from the outset that El was born to be a percussionist, but everyone had hoped their new bundle of joy could at least manage something in common time. She didn't. Not yet anyway. No one worried too much about it. After all, Viola was still a baby, and babies develop at different rates. Plus, the family had more pressing matters at hand.

Vincent gave music lessons and played out nearly every night. Grace took on the bulk of the childcare and housework, but on weekend afternoons, Vincent would mind the children while Grace played weddings and parties with her string quartet, sometimes two or three gigs in one day. If both parents had a gig, Clara was enlisted to babysit her younger siblings. Despite their hard work, money was, as they say, tight. Late at night, after the children had gone to bed, Grace and Vincent would talk about what bill to pay and what bill not to pay and how to make the remaining balance in their checking account dance like Ginger Rogers and Fred Astaire.

Whether or not the family was poor at that time depends entirely upon your definition of the word. The children never went to bed hungry. They were housed and fed and clothed. However, the quality and quantity of said housing, food, and clothing varied. The electricity was shut off once or twice. Temporarily, of course. And the gas company came to shut off the gas two days after Allegro's sixth birthday. It was the year Allie had the flu on her birthday. The three older children were at school, Vincent was off teaching music lessons, and Grace was home with one sick kid and two little ones. After lunch, Grace made cookies, nominally helped by Viola, who was not yet two and ate enough raw cookie dough that she no doubt developed an immunity to salmonella.

Sick or not, Allegro was in the room she shared with Clara practicing scales on the violin while Theo was practicing piano. Like all of his older siblings, he was using the beginner piano books that featured drawings of little elves with letters on their stomachs who introduced the notes. By the time the book got to Thelonious, it was held together with Scotch tape and one singular, courageous staple. When the children practiced like this, with one on one floor of the house and one on another floor or in another room, sometimes the notes would intermingle on the stairs. On that day, Theo's music had wended its way up the stairs and into Allegro's room as though it was asking her music to play. It was a long way, so not all of the notes made it, but if he played *forte*, enough notes made it up to Allie's room to play with her notes. She occasionally threw in a *forte* phrase just to mollify her younger brother.

Allie didn't hear the doorbell, but she noticed that Theo's music had stopped abruptly. Unlike most families, the Mozinski children didn't practice under duress. Playing music was a favorite activity. If Theo had stopped playing, it was a likely sign that the first tray of cookies was out of the oven. It turns out they were, and were being consumed by two men in blue East Ohio Gas Company shirts who were sitting at the kitchen table with Allie's mother and Viola and Theo.

"Hi, sweetie," her mother said, as though nothing was amiss. "How are you feeling?"

"Better," Allie said warily.

"I'm so glad. The next tray of cookies will be out in two minutes, and you'll get first pick."

"We ate a whole tray," Theo said. He looked a little too smug about this. If there hadn't been two strange men in the kitchen, Allie would have smacked him. Conversely, if there hadn't been two strange men in our kitchen, there would have been enough cookies for her.

"I'm sorry, little lady," one of the men said. He was a rotund black man with a moustache and a kind smile. "I didn't mean to eat your cookies."

Allie caught her mother's eye for a split second. Long enough to realize that the situation called for decorum. There were would be no smacking of younger brothers at that time.

She made herself sound extra cheerful as she said, "That's okay. There are more coming." Her mother would never know just how much saying this sapped Allie's six-year-old self-control.

"There certainly are," her mother said. "Thank you both for letting me finish baking."

"Of course. And thank you for the cookies," moustache man said. He glanced over at his partner, a younger white guy who didn't look much out of high school.

"Yeah, thanks a lot. These are delicious," the younger one said. Given the amount of crumbs on the small plate in front of him, Allie guessed that the majority of cookies from the first tray were now in his belly.

There was an uncomfortable silence that was thankfully broken by the timer on the old gas stove announcing that the next tray of cookies was ready to come out. It took young Allegro a moment to piece everything together. She was in kindergarten, but she could already read. She could certainly read the word "gas" on the men's shirts. And she knew that the stove and the furnace used gas because her father was always complaining about the pilot light going out. Things started to click in her young brain. "Can I do the cookies?" she asked.

"Actually, if you're feeling better, I was thinking you and Theo might want to play for our guests while the rest are baking."

It was clear that this was what is known in the trades as a command performance. Their mother commanded; the children would play. Theo needed a little coaxing to perform — not much, because he was a bit of a drama queen even at three — and the two children led the men from the gas company into the living room where the family's old upright piano lived. Allegro fetched the violin and bow from her room and went first, playing Minuet by Boccherini. It was a fairly standard piece for a younger violinist, but the guys from the gas company didn't know that. They sat next to each other on the sofa and were suitably impressed. Viola wandered in while Allie was playing and leaned against the easy chair. She didn't say anything — she was shy and a toddler to boot — but she clapped enthusiastically and cried "Yay!" when Allie was done.

"Wow," moustache man said. "You're very talented."

"Thank you." Allegro saw that Theo had opened up the beginner book with the elves and was about to play a song about something called a Kangarooster, which is just as insipid as it sounds. "Excuse me," she said to her little audience. "Don't play that," she whispered to Theo and quickly started looking through the music books and sheet music stacked on the piano.

"Why not?" Theo's response was not whispered.

"One moment, please," Allie said over her shoulder. To Theo, she whispered "It needs to be something a little more special."

"You mean harder?" he whispered back.

"Yes," Allie replied as she found what she was looking for. It was a book of simplified classical pieces that she was pretty sure Theo had seen before. He ought to be able to play it. She opened it to Grieg's "Morning Mood" from *Peer Gynt*. It was ridiculously watered down, with the left hand playing only one note per measure almost the entire way through. "Here, play this."

"I can't," Theo said in a voice bordering on whining. "I wanna play 'Kangarooster.'"

"This is the same thing," Allie snapped. "You can do it. You're a Mozinski. Take a look while I introduce you." She turned around to the gas company guys with a broad smile and saw that her mother had joined the audience. *If Mom wants us to put on a show,* Allie thought, *then that's what we'll do.* "Thank you so much for that warm response," Allie said in a voice that almost exactly matched what she had heard her mother say while watching her perform at a garden party the summer before. "You just heard Minuet by Luigi Boccherini. He was Italian. Next, Theo will play Edvard Grieg's "Morning Mood" from *Peer Gynt*, Opus 13. Edvard Grieg was from...?"

"Norway," her mother said softly.

"He was from Norway. And Theo and I are from Cleveland, Ohio. Obviously. Are you ready?" Allie asked her little brother.

With a terrified look, Theo gave a quiet "Yes."

"Great," Allie said with a big smile. "Take it away, Theo." She stepped aside and hoped that he had had enough time to look at the music. He had, and gave a passable performance. It wasn't up to Mozinski Family

Birthday Solo standards, but it served its purpose. When Theo was done, the men from the gas company applauded and stood up.

Moustache man did the talking for both of them. "Thank you for the wonderful performance and for the cookies."

"Thank you for the extra time," Grace replied. "The last two trays will be done in just a couple of minutes. You can go down to the basement and do whatever you need to do." She hadn't sung this, but Allie could almost see her mother's words hanging in the air between her and the men who had come to shut off the gas. Viola hadn't been looking for attention, but Grace scooped her up anyway and the youngest Mozinski snuggled against her mother's shoulder creating a wholesome tableau. It had the intended affect.

Moustache man looked over at his partner and raised his eyebrows just a little. The younger guy shrugged and looked almost as clueless as Theo and Viola. Allie, on the other hand, was in awe of her mother's powers of manipulation. "Ma'am, we're just going to put down that we were unable to gain access to the gas main and were not able to complete the shut off," moustache man said.

Grace's face changed in an instant. It reminded Allie of just how pretty her mom was. She wasn't entirely sure what moustache man meant, but it was clearly good news. "Thank you so much," her mother said, and it looked like she might even have tears in her eyes.

"Now this doesn't fix everything," moustache man continued. "It just delays it a day or two."

"We will get the bill paid pronto. Thank you again from the bottom of my heart."

After she had walked the gas company guys out of the house — still holding Viola — Grace plopped down on the sofa. Allegro and her younger brother cuddled up on either side of her, none of them saying a word. Allie felt like they had all suddenly become members of a special club that the rest of the family knew nothing about.

Later that day, after everyone else was home, Allie heard her mother singing the old Rodgers and Hart song, "Sing For Your Supper," as she folded laundry in the basement. For the first time but not the last, Allegro Mozinski realized she had done just that.

BOB'S CARS
(to the tune of "Goober Peas")

Vincent's regular gig was at the Statler Hotel in downtown Cleveland four nights a week (Tuesday through Friday from five to eleven). He was fortunate to live in a time and place where most hotel bars still had live entertainment. If they hadn't, his family might not have eaten, or he would have had to get a real job, and Vincent swore up and down that real jobs were for squares, not artists. People went to the Statler Hotel bar after work not because they were staying there but because Vincent Mozinski played a mean piano. Long ago, he learned that letting would-be Sinatras and Streisands sing along helped fill up the tip jar. One of the regulars was a man named Gregor Karpenko who had become something of a friend. Gregor and his family immigrated to the United States from Ukraine after the war and ended up in Cleveland. Gregor was only nine when he arrived, but quickly grasped how things worked in his adopted country. In modern parlance, you might say Gregor Karpenko knew how to hustle.

The first time Vincent mentioned Gregor was during a family dinner on a Monday evening. Most families hold Sunday dinner as sacrosanct, but there were often gigs to be played and money to be made on Sundays. Just as theaters are dark on Mondays, so was Vincent's booking calendar. The grocery store wasn't even open past six on Mondays.

"I met a really interesting fellow at work the other night," Vincent began one Monday evening.

"What's his name?" seven-year-old Bix asked. Other than music, people were one of Bix's favorite things.

"Gregor Karpenko. He's Ukrainian."

"Is being Ukrainian what makes him interesting, or does he have other things going for him?" Grace asked from the other end of the long kitchen table. She was holding six-month-old Viola on her lap and feeding her applesauce while simultaneously keeping an eye on Theo in the high chair next to her.

"He absolutely does. Very smart guy. His family came here after the war when he was a kid. He learned English first and translated everything for his parents..."

Ellington looked incredulous. "How come his parents don't speak English?"

"Because they're Ukrainian."

"What is that?"

"Someone from the Ukraine. It's in the Soviet Union," Clara said. She had been on a Rachmaninoff kick of late and the residual learning had seeped in.

"Woo-cwane," Theo said.

Theo had recently turned two. While most of the family was impressed that he had paid attention enough to even attempt the word "Ukraine," four-year-old Allegro did not give out participation points and corrected him, saying "No, 'U.' U-crane."

"Ooo-cwane."

"Better. You need to practice."

"I don't think Theo will have too many occasions to say the word 'Ukraine' in the near future," Grace said. "His time might be better spent practicing scales on the recorder."

"Or learning his letters," Clara added.

Grace gave her eldest an approving nod as she echoed "Yes, or learning his letters."

"Actually, we might all learn more about the Ukraine because I invited Gregor to join us for Thanksgiving."

Grace was used to having her husband occasionally bring home strangers. These were typically other musicians who needed a home-cooked meal and would participate in a low-key jam session in the living room afterwards. And she was not averse to taking in stray humans for holidays, but Thanksgiving was three days away. It didn't seem to be asking too much for a little more advance notice. She sighed inwardly. Like all great performers, hiding how she really felt in front of a crowd was second nature, and at this point, their offspring constituted a crowd. "That sounds great," she said with a smile. "What exactly does Gregor do?"

"He brings people together."

"What kind of people?"

"Oh, you know, business people."

"What kind of business?"

"This and that."

"The fact that you don't know makes him sound borderline shady."

The five older children followed their parents' conversation back and forth, tennis match-style. Baby Viola was still focused on applesauce. "What's 'shady' mean?" Ellington asked.

Vincent looked expectantly at his wife. Why not let her answer the awkward question?

"You know how trees give shade from the sun?" Grace said. Ellington nodded. "If something is shady, it means that it isn't out in the open. It's obscured. Possibly illegal."

"Wow..." said Ellington. He looked impressed. All of the children looked back at their father, even the baby.

"But Daddy's friend is *not* like that."

Bix broke the silence by saying "Well, that's a relief."

It wasn't exactly clear how Mr. Karpenko brought people together or how he made a living doing so. What the family knew is that he preferred Cole Porter to Nat King Cole, piano to saxophone, and routinely dropped a sawbuck in the tip jar on the piano at the Statler Hotel, so somehow, somewhere, he was, as Vincent put "making some scratch."

On Thanksgiving, Gregor Karpenko arrived on time — just after the Klinefelter grandparents arrived from Youngstown but before Grace put out the relish tray. Grace's first impression of him was of a big man with medium length, sleek, dark hair, and a bushy beard. He reminded her of a beaver, sans the oversized, front teeth. Did she like him? Not especially, but by the end of the day, she could honestly say that she didn't dislike him. He was polite and moderately amusing, and despite his somewhat broken English, made the traditional "you are what you eat" turkey joke to the children. He even managed to have a polite conversation with her father about cars; at least, it appeared to be about cars. She was so busy cooking and keeping children from fighting or making messes that she didn't have much time to pay close attention. What she didn't hear was Maarten Klinefelter raising his voice, which he typically did when he disagreed with someone.

To all outward appearances, Gregor had been a perfectly unobjectionable dinner guest. This was fortunate, because over the next few months, he became a frequent dinner guest as well. He was always polite and helped clear the table. After dinner, Vincent and Gregor would retire to the small sun room off the living room that Vincent called his office. It was there that the two men worked on projects that Grace called schemes. The schemes all seemed to focus on ways to enhance Vincent's career by having him sit in with or record with or meet some musician who was playing in town. Call them what you will — project or scheme — none of them panned out.

Then one night, in the spring of 1975, Vincent came home on a Thursday night from his gig at the Statler Hotel and said to his wife, "What would you think about having the kids sing on a commercial?" It was close to midnight, and Grace was already in bed, somewhat worn out from meeting the homework, food, bath, and bedtime needs of six children. She didn't quite hear him the first time and, with a yawn, asked him to repeat it.

"Gregor is producing a radio spot for a car dealership, and they want some kids to sing on it. I'm going to play on it, so we'll all be together."

Grace had questions: All of the kids? What were they going to sing? When was this happening? Where? Did it pay anything? But at 11:49 on a Thursday night, the first words out of her mouth were "Gregor is a producer?"

"Among other things, yes. So, what do you think? Good idea?"

"Uh, yeah, sure. If they want to do it. They can each choose to sing or not."

"Agreed."

"And I'll say right now Theo and Viola are too young."

"Sure, sure, absolutely," Vincent said as he unbuttoned his shirt. The prospect of playing for a commercial — even a one-off radio spot for Bob

Barlow of Bob's Cars — felt like the beginning of something good. If it required their children's voices, even better.

The next morning at breakfast, Vincent asked the children if they would like to cut a demo for a commercial. The answer, unsurprisingly, was yes. For 12-year-old Clara, the idea of cutting a demo sounded obscenely mature. She was wise enough not to say anything to any of the kids at Coventry Elementary School. After all, her father had proposed other ideas that didn't work out, even before Mr. Karpenko became a regular dinner guest. There was the time he was going to record an album and go out on tour for four months with his old jazz trio. Mr. Roy the drummer and Mr. Mike the bass player even showed up a bunch of times to rehearse, but then they stopped coming around and her father didn't go anywhere. And there was no record, only a reel-to-reel tape sitting among the other tapes and albums in the cupboard of the console stereo. Since her father's friendship with Mr. Karpenko, there had been talk of another commercial — this one for Severance Center shopping mall — and talk of opening their own nightclub that would offer jazz five nights a week. Those things hadn't happened, either. It wasn't until the entire family trooped down to a small recording studio in downtown Cleveland that Clara actually believed the commercial might happen.

At that point, Viola was still a toddler and Theo was four, so they waited in the lobby with Grace. Only the four older children and Vincent crowded into the recording studio. Before they went in, Vincent looked at Clara, Ellington, Bix, and Allegro and gave last-minute instructions. "Do your best and sing what you're told. I'll be in the studio too in case you're feeling shy or need any help, okay?"

"Okay," they replied, although they were not and they did not.

Gregor was waiting in the studio to greet them along with a thin, sallow-skinned man introduced as Mel, who would be their sound engineer. Gregor handed each of the children a sheet of paper with the lyrics to the jingle. "Can you all read?" he asked. If the youngest one could read, it stood to reason that all of them would be able to read the Bob's Cars jingle.

"Of course," Allie replied. She was only six, but already reading at an eighth grade level and made no attempt to hide her disdain that Mr. Karpenko had insinuated that she couldn't read.

"Okay, I sing the song to you, then you sing it to me, yes?" Gregor said.

"Okay," the four children said in a chorus that may or may not have been in two-part harmony. Gregor didn't seem to appreciate this.

He sang the Bob's Cars jingle, which was an embarrassingly simple ditty that blatantly stole the melody for the old folk tune "Goober Peas." The lyrics were to the point:

> Bob's Cars, great cars, at the price you like.
> Goodness, you'll find great deals, new or used with Bob's.

It was uninspiring.

Clara typically wasn't the type of girl to rock the boat, but she had been cautiously excited at the prospect of cutting a demo for a commercial. She was savvy enough to know that a demo was short for demonstration; it wasn't a guarantee. What if Bob Barlow from Bob's Cars didn't like the commercial because the lyrics were so bad?

"Excuse me, Mr. Karpenko? Are those the final lyrics?"

Gregor paused. He had not expected questions from this quarter. "Yes, these are the words you will sing. Is there problem?"

"Well, I guess they just seem a little...Is uninspired a word?"

"Clara, my job is to write jingle. Your job is to sing jingle. It is not your job to be critic for the lyrics," he said.

Behind Mr. Karpenko's back, her father sat at the piano. He looked at Clara and put a single index finger to his lips.

"I'm sorry, Mr. Karpenko," Clara said immediately, and put on what she hoped was an apologetic and conciliatory expression.

"Apology accepted." He gave all four children a quick once-over, as though waiting to see who would be the next smart aleck. He and Clara both looked at Ellington expectantly, but even El was momentarily silent. "Okay, now I sing it again, then you sing it the way I sing it."

Clara glanced over at her younger siblings, who looked ready to go. "Actually, I think we have it, sir," she said. Truth be told, she couldn't bear to hear him sing it again. He wasn't necessarily off key, but he wasn't entirely on it either. And watching the anemic little notes fluttering aimlessly through the air bordered on the painful.

He looked skeptical but said, "Okay, you sing."

Clara, Ellington, Bix, and Allegro sang the jingle a capella, exactly as Gregor had sung it, albeit on pitch. Ellington missed one or two words, but that was to be expected. Ellington sometimes had problems with focus. "Good," he said when they were done. "Again."

They sang it a second time exactly as he had sung it to them. This time word-perfect as well as pitch-perfect. When the children were done, Gregor nodded and gave a little smile. "Very good. Would you like to be singing it while your father plays?"

"Sure," the children replied, because singing along with the piano while their father played was one of the primary ways the family amused themselves on the days when the electric bill hadn't been paid and the television wasn't working.

Vincent played the intro to the jingle on the piano in the corner of the studio, but Bix raised his hand even as Allie started singing. Ellington and Clara waited. Bix's question was fairly obvious.

"Excuse me."

"What is it, Bix?" Gregor asked.

"You said you want us to sing it exactly like you sang it. Does that mean you want us to sing it in E-flat, the way you sang it, or in C, the way our dad is playing it?"

Although he had been a guest in their home numerous times for the past year and a half, Gregor Karpenko hadn't had much occasion to really get to know the Mozinski children. To be honest, the kids had mostly ignored him as well. As time went on, Gregor got to know each of the six children better. The one thing you could say for him at that moment is that he was smart enough to leave well enough alone when he was in over his head. "Sing in the key your father plays," he replied.

"Okay," Bix replied brightly.

Ellington rolled his eyes. Vincent didn't see it, but Clara did. She gave El's ankle a little kick and shot him a "Behave" look.

The four children sang the Bob's Cars jingle as though they were performing "Goober Peas" at Carnegie Hall. They added four-part harmony on the last two notes without being asked. And they held the last note just long enough, no breaths, and cut the note at the same time on their father's nod. It was the most impressive first take since Johnny

Cash recorded "A Boy Named Sue." They ignored Mr. Karpenko's direction because he was half a step behind the beat. When they were done, Clara caught her father's eye as he looked over from the piano. Above his head, she could see the music she and her siblings had made dancing in the air, bright and sparkly. Her father smiled, and she knew they had done well.

That was the last the children heard about the commercial for two weeks. Clara was glad she hadn't mentioned anything to her friends. It would be embarrassing to have yet another disappointment. Then her mother made all six children sit down in the living room before dinner and tuned the family stereo to a radio station that they normally didn't listen to. Vincent was already at work, playing piano at the Statler, but he had written down the station and the time to listen. The six children were scattered around the living room — some sprawled on the sofa, some on the floor, little Viola toddling from one sibling to another. Her mother wouldn't say why they all had to be there. To Clara, it felt like the Walton family gathering around the radio to listen to whatever people listened to back in the 1930s. They heard two men talk about the news. Then came a commercial for Coca-Cola. And a commercial for a bank. And then Clara heard a piano playing the melody to "Goober Peas" and heard her voice and those of her siblings singing the Bob's Cars jingle. In all the changes that were to come, all the successes and countless times Clara would hear a recording of their family, not one of those moments would ever match the joy and excitement and pride she felt the first time she heard herself singing the Bob's Cars jingle on the radio.

There was something about the children's voices — these particular children's voices — that struck people in just the right way. People listened and the music lingered with them. All through the spring of 1975, Clevelanders found themselves inadvertently singing the Bob's Cars jingle while doing the dishes or pulling out the lawnmower. Little kids would try to imitate the four-part harmony on the last notes, throwing their arms out to the side and belting their own off-key rendition of the jingle. This was all to the benefit of Bob Barlow and his car lots, who hired the family to record a second radio spot.

Gregor came into the Statler Hotel bar on a rainy Tuesday evening a few days after the children recorded the second commercial. Because he had acted as the booking agent, a portion of the check went to him. It was a slow night, and Vincent was experimenting a little, playing a few melodies of his own composition or changing up the tempo or the left hand on some well-known tunes. As Gregor entered the bar, Vincent had just started "Sophisticated Lady." Knowing his friend's taste, he kept it simple and traditional.

Gregor got a vodka gimlet and then headed over to the piano. He was always an appreciative audience, even if he couldn't see the music. When the song ended, he said "That is the most saddest song in the world."

"It can be," Vincent replied. "But you can always make it swing." With that, he launched into the song again, this time paying tribute to the old Art Tatum stride version he had listened to dozens of times. "See? Now it's more 'Syncopated Lady,'" he said.

Their conversation turned to plans. Vincent and Gregor always had plans. "Do you and Grace play together sometimes?" Gregor asked, taking a sip of his drink.

"Once in a while. Not since we had all the kids, though. Too hard to find a babysitter." One of the regulars came into the bar, a younger guy named John who worked nearby and whose last name Vincent could never remember. He did remember that the guy liked the Beatles and shifted into "Let It Be." The melody seemed to fit the mood of the evening. Vincent watched as the music made its way over the baby grand, past the round faux wood and metal tables and chairs, and over to the bar. It was always a little kick to watch the notes travel across the room, even if he knew no one else could see them. He was pretty sure the kids could see them. At least they all looked in the right place whenever he played at home. John was at the bar but turned around and raised his glass. On slow nights you had to cater to the regulars or you'd end up with an empty tip jar.

Gregor took a long, contemplative gaze at the bottom of his glass, as though trying to decide if he wanted another, and then said "Too bad the children can't play like you and Grace. They sing so nice."

"What are you talking about? They play."

"How do you never told me this?"

"How have you never asked?"

"They do not play music when I am at your house."

"Oh, well they play. Clara plays harp, Ellington plays drums, Bix plays trumpet, and Allie plays violin, like Grace."

"Oh." Gregor looked disappointed. "They don't play any other instruments?"

"They all have a secondary instrument. Piano, guitar..."

"There, there! Guitar is good. Teach them guitar. Make them into a band."

Vincent had never considered forming a band with his children. After all, he was the breadwinner. But they were talented and liked to play, at least it seemed like it. He had always led his own band. If it was a band made up of his own children, there wouldn't be any question as to who was in charge. "I'm sure they could do it..." he said thoughtfully as he hit the last chord to "Let It Be."

"If you and the children have a band, I will find places for you to play. I promise this."

Gregor Karpenko was true to his word. He managed to book the family to perform at the city's Fourth of July celebration that summer, billed as The Musical Mozinskis. They were one of several bands scheduled during the day at a stage set up near Edgewater Park. There were food vendors and fireworks after dark. The Musical Mozinskis were the first act. It was not the ideal placement, but it was still a gig. Their first gig. The lineup was Vincent on keyboards, Bix on lead guitar and vocals, Allie on rhythm guitar, Ellington on drums, and Clara as a reluctant bass player because, as Vincent said more than once, "Harps don't play rock and roll." Her mother told her that the bass holds everything together, but Clara suspected this was just to placate her. Clara had no idea she'd be playing bass almost exclusively for the next six years.

The kids were still working on mastering their new instruments. All but Ellington, who had been playing drums since he was four. The Musical Mozinskis' repertoire was not big. They played "This Land Is Your Land" because it was patriotic, "Here Comes the Sun" because everybody likes the Beatles, not just John from the bar, and the old Pete Seeger song "Black and White" because it had been a big hit for Three Dog Night a few years earlier. Vincent and Grace thought the combination of songs would make the band stand out. It did.

Clara and her friends liked to make fun of a local television variety show called *The Johnny Banks Talent Hour*. She and her friends were 12, so making fun of things was one of their hobbies. Even though they routinely derided the show, they watched it religiously every Sunday evening. The performers were mostly cutesy little kids whose parents believed they were the reincarnation of Shirley Temple or older men who thought they were a long-lost member of the Rat Pack. Every episode featured at least one dance duo or someone juggling plates or knives or a magician. The level of talent on the show was not exceptionally high. When her father announced that The Musical Mozinskis would be performing on *Johnny Banks*, Clara protested. Which is to say that she asked "Do we have to?"

"Yes," Vincent replied. They had just finished a two-hour rehearsal on a Sunday afternoon, working through The Jackson Five's "ABC" because, in 1975, any band made up primarily of children was obliged to do a song by The Jackson Five.

"That show sucks, Dad," Ellington said.

"No, it doesn't. It's a great show." Their father sounded frighteningly upbeat about the whole thing.

"Most of the people on there aren't very good, so we'll be the best," Allie said as though the entire thing had been settled. And it was.

Clara wasn't sure what she expected after they performed on the Fourth of July. She had hoped she'd be able to concentrate on the harp again. Instead, her father made her, Ellington, Bix, and Allie learn some new songs. She didn't think too much of it at the time. After all, music was what her family did. Some of her friends' families went skiing or played softball or watched movies together. Her family made music together. But none of her friends' parents made them do embarrassing things. Well, Denise Lobachek's parents made her whole family wear matching T-shirts when they went to amusement parks so it would be easy to find each other if they got lost, but that wasn't nearly as embarrassing as going on *The Johnny Banks Talent Hour*.

The one good thing about having her parents always be broke is that they didn't go out and buy matching costumes for the band. Instead, Grace told them all to wear jeans and their favorite white shirt. That, at least, was all right. It made them look like they belonged together without actually having to match.

Clara didn't dare tell any of her friends that her family (well, most of her family) was going to be performing on *Johnny Banks*. Everybody had heard the Bob's Cars commercial — you couldn't get away from it — but that was on the radio. You couldn't *see* them perform. Clara did her best to keep people from watching *Johnny Banks*. The evening the show aired, she even called Jennifer Mitchell when it was on because Jennifer always watched it and was a blabbermouth besides. They weren't even friends. She might have kept Jennifer from seeing *Johnny Banks*, but apparently everyone else in the seventh grade saw it. The funny thing was, on Monday at school, a couple of people said they had seen her on TV, as though that in itself was an accomplishment. And when a trio of the popular girls sang "A-B-C" as they walked by her in the hallway, they didn't seem snotty. Over at the elementary school, Ellington said nobody was stupid enough to bother him, plus Mary Lynn Sewicki, the hottest girl in sixth grade, deliberately bumped into him in the hallway. Hard. A small gaggle of fourth and fifth grade girls followed Bix around like he was a curly-haired Shaun Cassidy. Down in the second grade, Allegro suggested to her teacher that they show an encore presentation of *Johnny Banks* as a special school assembly. It was almost as though people thought it was cool that they had been on television, even on stupid *Johnny Banks*.

After the show aired, Clara's mother said they had received more calls and postcards than any other act that had ever appeared on *The Johnny Banks Talent Hour*. All through the winter and spring, The Musical Mozinskis were invited back on the show a second, third, and unprecedented fourth time. And then the Bicentennial happened.

BACK IN THE U.S.A.

Was it Gregor Karpenko? Was it Johnny Banks? It wasn't clear who connected The Musical Mozinskis to the national Bicentennial Celebration. Rumor had it that one of the producers was visiting family in Cleveland, saw the family on *The Johnny Banks Show*, and thought the children were "adorable." They were. Talented, small children singing and playing instruments are adorable, and the Mozinski family had a steady supply of them.

Gregor Karpenko was listed as the band's manager when the family was picked as one of five amateur musical acts from across the country to perform in a nationally televised two-hour special the following summer to celebrate America's Bicentennial. Vincent and Grace signed the contract, but Karpenko was the one who rented a bus and drove the entire family and all of their instruments to Washington, D.C., for the taping. The young kids looked at it like a vacation. They would be driving six hours and spending two nights in two hotel rooms so they could play one song.

Theo and Viola were still deemed too young to perform, but Grace was not about to miss the family's first national television appearance, so the entire family went. When they arrived in D.C., Vincent and the boys settled into one hotel room while Grace and the girls took the other. As they were getting settled into the room, Viola was jumping up and down on one of the two double beds, chanting "I feel so good today" over and over, which was part of the first line of the song the family would be performing the next day. As Viola sang — at least what amounted to her singing, it sounded more like screaming — Clara spotted a few stray notes flying around the room. It wasn't not music, but it wasn't quite music either.

Clara and Allie were wearing matching denim skirts and white shirts for the performance, and were both very careful to get their clothes out of the suitcase and hung up so they wouldn't be wrinkled. As she was fussing with her shirt and the hanger, Allie sneered over at Viola.

"You're off-key. It goes like this," she said and sang the entire first line. The notes that flew out of her mouth were neat and clean, as though they had been printed on the air. "See?" Allie added, motioning to the notes.

Viola looked up at the space above Allie's head. "What?" She looked confused.

Allie sang the first line of "Back in the U.S.A." again, pointing at the notes above her head and getting increasingly annoyed that Viola seemed unable to see them. Clara watched the whole thing but somehow couldn't make herself speak or move to stop it. Viola was only three. Clara didn't think it was fair to expect so much from her, even though she had watched her other siblings at that age and younger sing passable renditions of "How Much Is That Doggie in the Window?" just so they could gaze at the notes they had made. It was only when their mother came out of the bathroom to find Viola near tears and Allie practically screaming that Clara was able to find her voice.

"Leave her alone, Allie," Clara said at the same time Grace marched over, put a hand on Allie's shoulder, and turned her around to face her.

"Allegro Mozinski, stop that this instant."

"I was just trying to help her."

"No, you weren't. And you and I both know it."

Since her mother had Allie in hand, Clara went over to Viola and picked her up. Feeling the weight of her youngest sibling in her arms and Viola's tears on her neck made Clara feel momentarily brave. Their mother gave Viola a kiss on the forehead, then took Allie into the hallway for a "talk," so Clara was left alone with Viola for a moment.

"Whas Allie looking at?" Viola asked.

"Nothing."

"Whas she looking at?"

"Just...music," Clara said finally as she put Viola back on the bed. It was bad enough that Allie had been teasing her. Clara didn't want talk more about the music that Viola apparently couldn't see. It wasn't fair. Instead, she asked "Do you want to jump some more? We can pretend it's a trampoline."

Viola gave a couple little half-hearted jumps then stopped and looked at Clara. "How you see music?"

"Um, I don't know. Some of us just do. You'll be able to do it when you're a little older," she replied. "And I won't let Allie tease you again."

"Okay. Thank you, Clara. Wanna jump wid me?"

Clara did. They jumped on the bed and then jumped back and forth between the two beds and their mother didn't even get mad when she and Allie came back in.

The next morning, the family was called for rehearsal at eight-thirty. They had breakfast in the hotel, and then Mr. Karpenko would meet them in front of the hotel to drive to the rehearsal and sound check.

"Are we getting paid for this gig?" Allie asked as the older children were walking through the lobby after breakfast.

"*We* aren't," El said. "But Mom and Dad are. And I bet Mr. Karpenko is."

"Hey, we don't need to talk about this now," Vincent said. "Don't worry. I've got everything taken care of." He was pushing a cart with all of their instruments, but he managed to put one hand on Bix's shoulder. "Let's get ready for tonight. Bix, are you ready?"

"Uh-huh," Bix said quietly.

"Don't forget to move your head."

"Uh-huh."

"You're gonna be a star, little buddy."

"Uh-huh."

The family was singing "Back in the U.S.A." by Chuck Berry. They had rehearsed the song 212 times in the past month. Allie had counted. Bix hadn't. But it was enough times that he had mastered the iconic two-string Chuck Berry riff. It's a simple progression — C to F7 to C and back again. It's the same riff even as the chords change. He'd played it plenty of times. It was a blast to play. Every time he started hammering that riff, it made him feel as though he was an airplane about to take off. Still, he was nervous. National television was a far cry from *The Johnny Banks Talent Show*, and he was the front man.

Bix let Clara catch up to him so that they were positioned to sit together in the wayback of the van. Their dad and Mr. Karpenko were talking in the front, and Ellington and Allie were talking about something that probably wasn't important. "Are you okay?" Clara whispered to him.

"Yeah," he replied, looking out the window.

"Nervous?"

"A little."

"You'll be fine."

They all knew what their dad meant when he told Bix to remember to move his head. They were playing a Chuck Berry song. It is expected when playing a Chuck Berry cover that the lead guitarist do the duckwalk in homage to Mr. Berry. There are two variations. The more difficult version has the guitarist squatting and holding one leg out in front while hopping forward. Or the guitarist can crouch down to a squat and duckwalk across the stage. This classic option requires the guitarist to also move his or her head forward and backward like a duck. Both moves are ideally made while playing a guitar solo. Either option is a challenge, especially if you're a 10-year-old holding a full-size Kay Kelvinator hollowbody guitar.

Vincent desperately wanted Bix to do the duckwalk. He had, in fact (in private), ordered him to. Truth be told, the entire family wanted him to do it, because what could be more memorable than a cute, curly-haired, 10-year-old boy singing and playing Chuck Berry and doing the duckwalk? The Bicentennial Celebration wasn't a competition, as the kids had repeatedly been reminded, but they watched television. They knew that the millions of people watching were going to judge each of the acts from the privacy of their own home, the same way the Mozinski kids did whenever they watched TV. Bix wanted them to be the band people liked best. It was just a lot when he realized being the best act primarily depended on him.

During the rehearsal and sound check, they had a chance to check out the other performers. The opener was a college chorus from a big southern university. There were about 30 of them, wearing black robes with carmine trim. During the sound check, they sang a too-slow version of "America The Beautiful." The harmonies were tight as a drum, but the song sounded like a dirge, the notes somberly marching in the air above their heads. They were serviceable but not memorable. The Mozinski siblings watched from the wings since they would be performing right after the chorus. Their equipment was set up behind the choir's risers, hidden by a black curtain.

"No competition there," Ellington said.

"No competition there," Allie echoed.

"The opener is always vanilla," Vincent said.

The Musical Mozinskis were performing second that night, presumably because the band was primarily made up of children. It was assumed they would attract kid viewers who weren't going to stay up too late. When they called her and her family onstage for the sound check, Clara's stomach was turning somersaults. They had performed at an outdoor concert before, and they had performed on television, but not at the same time. And not on the National Mall for the country's 200th birthday. She closed her eyes and took a few deep breaths, trying to stay calm. The only people in the audience at this time were a handful of VIPs. The performers were permitted to sit in the first few rows of folding chairs to watch when they were done with their sound check. As the sound guy tested first Bix's mike, then her father's, hers, and Allie's, she saw the entire university chorus file into the folding chairs to watch. They were no longer wearing their robes, but they all had the straight-backed, clean-cut look one associates with a more conservative bent. Clara thought they all kind of looked alike.

Once they checked the sound levels, the family ran through "Back in the U.S.A." It was only a rehearsal, but her father and Mr. Karpenko told the kids to put their hearts into every performance, so they did. At least Clara did. She remembered to smile. Bix even did the classic duckwalk. They sounded great, and the university chorus in the first couple rows clapped when they were done. As they moved off the stage to go out front, the family passed by one of the other bands who were waiting in the wings. She had heard they were from Detroit and were called The Hi-Tones. They stood out because they were the only performers who weren't white.

"Hey little man. You get around pretty good on that guitar," one of them said to Bix as they passed. He was medium height and trim, wearing hip-hugger white pants that flared at the bottom and a snug, bright red shirt. The word "groovy" popped into Clara's head the moment she laid eyes on him. Next to him, her outfit felt dumpy. Next to him, most of the world looked dumpy.

"Thank you," Bix replied, but his smile looked forced.

Clara tried not look over her shoulder at the groovy guy as she went down the stairs. As soon as they sat down in the third row of seats, she tried to see if she could spot him in the wings. If she was too obvious, Ellington or someone would tease her about it later and ask if the groovy guy was her new boyfriend. As if. He was way too old for her. Clara had managed to go through the first 13 years of her life without a major crush. She had just started paying attention to the teen magazines, but crushes on movie stars and pop stars didn't count. She didn't know them. The boys in her school were, quite frankly, gross, not groovy. That she was sharing the same space and the same air as someone as glorious as the guy in the red shirt was a revelation. She was smitten.

Her reverie was broken by her father saying to Bix, "You forgot to move your head."

"Sorry."

"It's not a duckwalk if you aren't moving your head like a duck."

"I know. I'm sorry."

On the other side of Bix, Mr. Karpenko settled back into his metal folding chair. "You do the duckwalk tonight, yes? With the...?" and here he moved his head back and forth like a giant, bearded mallard.

"Yes, sir. Absolutely."

"Good boy."

"I can do the duckwalk," Allie piped up from where she was sitting on her father's other side. "It's easy. Let me do it."

"Allie, I know you can, but this is something the lead guitarist needs to do. On this number, Bix is the front man."

"But I can do it..."

"Rhythm guitar doesn't do the duckwalk," Ellington said, like Allie ought to know this.

"Shhh," Clara said. The sound guy was done testing the mikes for the next group, a string quartet, and she saw the first violin sit up straight and give the others the look that means *Are we ready?* "They're starting."

The string quartet was from California and was called Big Sur Strings. The only words Clara could think to describe their music was "breathtaking." They played George Gershwin's Lullaby for String Quartet, and she was so overcome that she almost forgot to breathe. Even Allie stopped talking and fidgeting to listen. When they were done, she glanced over at Mr. Karpenko, who was sitting next to her. He appeared to dab at his eyes.

"Did you like it?" Clara whispered to him.

"Is very nice, but it is not Prokofiev."

"I like Gershwin."

"Eh," Mr. Karpenko replied. Over the years, Clara would learn that "Eh" was Mr. Karpenko's way of letting you know that he didn't think much of something but was too polite to tell you.

"They're really good."

"Yes."

El, Bix, and Allie looked as worried as Clara felt. "Yes, I know they're great. Don't worry," their father said. "Most people have pedestrian tastes. They'll change the channel during the classical music."

After Big Sur Strings, there was a three-piece folk band that played "This Little Light of Mine." Between the two of them, Grace and Vincent had only amassed a handful of folk music records in the family collection, but Clara still knew the song. The folk band was bouncy and cheerful, which seemed to be the primary point of the concert. And their bass player played an upright, which she had asked for when her father suggested she play bass in the family band. Plucking vertical strings felt more natural, but her father nixed the idea.

"What did you think?" Clara asked Mr. Karpenko when the folk band was done.

"Eh."

There was one more band after the folk musicians — the same band they had seen going backstage earlier. The Hi-Tones. From the first chord of "Dancing In The Street," it was obvious they'd be the band that everyone remembered. There were six of them onstage — guitar, bass, drums, keyboard, trumpet, and saxophone. The groovy guy who'd spoken to Bix earlier was the lead guitarist and singer. He looked even more attractive onstage than he had backstage, like a flower that had just gone into full bloom. There were a bunch of college-aged girls from the university chorus sitting nearby. Most of them were clearly just as taken with the lead singer as Clara was and were much closer to his age, but when he sang the line "Every guy grab a girl," Clara wanted to believe he was looking straight at her. He was that kind of front man.

Clara had heard the song plenty of times before on the radio and at home because their mother listened to Motown as often as she did classical. The other musicians didn't sing backup; instead the horns hit the same fills as the Vandellas did for Martha Reeves on the original song. It made the interplay between voice and horn sound like a genuine conversation.

"We need a horn section..." Ellington murmured as they watched. Clara suspected they would need a lot more than a horn section to equal that performance but kept her mouth shut. There was no use being a Negative Nellie.

She was so engrossed in staring at the groovy guy that she didn't hear her father say "Come on," or notice that he and the others were already standing.

"They need you onstage again," Mr. Karpenko said. "To get ready for finale."

All of the acts were supposed to sing "This Land Is Your Land" as the finale. The producer kept reminding everyone that they would all be waiting backstage and that no one would be sitting in the audience during the performance. Every time he said that, he looked right at the Mozinski children, as though he thought they'd be sneaking out into the audience because they were kids. Vincent thought he should have been more worried about the college choir. Four of them didn't even make it onstage for the finale soundcheck. There were 30 of them with only one director and an assistant who looked exhausted. There was no way Vincent was going to let his kids run wild. There was too much riding on this performance.

There was only one microphone for the Mozinskis. Vincent stood back and let the four children take it. "People will want to see you, not me," he said. "Don't feel too bad. Those kids from the university only got two mikes for all of them." It was true, the university chorus was crowded around two microphones, boys at one, girls at the other. The ones in the back might as well not have bothered.

The Hi-Tones still had their instruments, and the folk band brought their instruments out for the finale, even the upright bass. In what was clearly a case of age discrimination, the producer told the Mozinski kids not to bring their instruments onstage for the finale. As the four of them stood waiting in front of the microphone while the sound crew checked the levels on each of the other mikes, Ellington said "This is stupid. I don't want to sing," and wandered back to the drummer for The Hi-Tones. "I'll be right back," Vincent whispered to his eldest and went off in search of Ellington. Clara put one hand on Allie's shoulder and one on Bix's shoulder. They would stay put.

After the soundcheck, they went back to the hotel, where Grace, Theo, and Viola were playing in the pool. Clara thought the littler kids had gotten the better end of the deal. They had a couple hours for sightseeing, but only a couple because her parents thought all the kids should rest before the performance since they would be staying up late. It's one thing to be forced to take a nap when you're three, it's quite another when you're 13. Clara was too nervous to rest and laid awake for 45 minutes in the double bed next to Allie, who seemed to be able to fall asleep anywhere.

They had dinner at the concert — there was a tent with a buffet and tables for all the performers. Even though her mother and the little ones weren't going to be onstage, the family ate together. Clara was so nervous she couldn't eat. She noticed Bix didn't eat anything either. Her father said "Don't forget," to Bix probably half a dozen times. Everyone knew what he was talking about.. Right before they went onstage, Mr. Karpenko reminded her to smile while she played. The university chorus was making its sad and plodding way through "America The Beautiful" as he said, "You must look like you enjoy yourself. If you have fun, the audience has fun."

"I know," she mumbled. "Why don't you tell Ellington that?"

"The drummer, no one cares if he smiles. Out front, you must smile."

"I don't hear you telling Bix or Allie to smile."

"Allie always smile, and Bix has other job to do," Mr. Karpenko whispered. He raised his voice just a little so the others could hear him. "Go out and become famous," he said.

That was when Clara realized just how much her parents and Mr. Karpenko had invested in this performance, why she had to smile and charm, why Bix had to do the duckwalk. They needed people to notice their performance, and this was, perhaps, their only opportunity.

In between acts, a newscaster named Alan Mumford, whom Clara never watched because she found the news boring at that age, and an actress named Alice Dimitri, whom she had seen in two movies, talked a little about the Bicentennial and each performer. Hearing Alice Dmitri introduce her family made Clara feel like she had gone to another planet. How could she reconcile the fact that she had seen and heard Alice Dimitri in real movies at the movie theater, and now Alice Dimitri was saying her and her family's names, and she and Alan Mumford were talking about how talented and how young The Musical Mozinskis were, and then the curtain rose and she was onstage.

The audience in front of her was much bigger than any audience she had ever performed for. Plus, there were four cameras. *The Johnny Banks Show* only had two. The number of people watching at home would be in the millions. It was more than Clara could comprehend. The producer had said to sing to the audience in front of them and let the cameramen do the rest, so she focused on the first few rows of the audience and tried to ignore everything else. She kept a smile on her face from the moment the curtain rose to the end of their song and hoped it didn't look terrified.

They covered "Back in the U.S.A." as Chuck Berry originally recorded it, with both a piano solo and a guitar solo. After the first verse, her father took his solo. Clara knew the cameras would zoom in on him, focus on his hands and the piano keys, or maybe his face. The verse — his solo — was only 18 seconds, but it was 18 seconds of performing for a bigger audience than her father had ever performed for in all his 40 years. Clara saw a hint of a smile cross his face as he went into his solo, secure in the fact that for the next 18 seconds, the world would be focused solely on him. She was glad for him. However, her father's moment of reverie lasted four seconds because Allie started doing the classic duckwalk during his solo. Two of the cameras immediately shifted their focus to get the little girl on rhythm guitar duckwalking. And yes, she moved her head back and forth.

Stealing focus during someone else's solo is the height of rudeness. No one had ever told Clara that — it was just a part of performance etiquette that she had figured out on her own. Maybe Allie hadn't figured it out yet. Or maybe she just wanted to show everyone that she could do what Bix couldn't or wouldn't do. Now that she had done the duckwalk, Bix had no choice. He sang another verse of the song then he took his solo and immediately squatted and duckwalked across the stage. He even remembered to move his head. In her ignorance or insensibility, Allie did it right along with him, like two guitar-playing ducks waddling towards each other in an image that would be carried on the newswires in the morning. The audience went crazy.

Afterward, Clara couldn't say how she knew that Bix was going to extend his solo for another verse. Anyone paying attention would have seen the annoyed look on his face that Allie was stealing focus from his solo the same way she had with their father's. But it wasn't Bix's face that clued her in. It was what he was playing. She heard it, felt it, and saw it. It was the first time she experienced that magic instant of recognition that there is no resolution to the verse, that her fellow musician has more to say. She understood that there was more to come. Her father heard it, El heard it. Allie didn't. Or couldn't. After how mean she had been to Viola the day before, Clara didn't feel too bad when Allie started playing the chorus while the rest of the band went back to the top of the verse so Bix could extend his solo. Maybe if she hadn't been doing the duckwalk she would have seen the shift in the notes floating above her head.

On the second time through the verse, Bix did the harder version of the duckwalk, the one where the guitarist sticks one leg out and hops across the stage on the other. By this time, Allie had given up on doing the duckwalk and was just trying to find her place in the song. Clara was positive their number got a much bigger, more enthusiastic round of applause than the university chorus had.

When they came offstage, Mr. Karpenko gave Bix a huge bear hug, said, "I knew you can do it!" and gave him a kiss on the top of his head. Clara's father put his hand on Bix's shoulder and said, "You done good, kid." He gave her and Ellington quick pats on the back and said, "Good work." All he said to Allie was, "We'll talk later." The stage manager shooed them out of the wings and back to the tent with the food, where Grace and the younger kids were waiting. The family went through the to-be-expected hugging and congratulating. Clara's mother gave her a big hug and whispered, "Well done. You held the whole thing together." The kids from the university chorus were already in there. They had already eaten all the desserts and most of the pizza from the buffet table. Clara didn't mind because The Hi-Tones were in the tent too, talking and laughing at the table closest to the big television set up in the tent so the musicians could watch the other performances. Clara noticed the lead singer was watching the Big Sur Strings' performance intently and wondered if he played any other instruments. She wondered if he might also be a fan of the harp.

Allie had wanted to stay backstage so she could watch the first violinist's technique from the wings, but the assistant stage manager kicked them out. Now that they were banished to the tent, Allie immediately gravitated to the television set to watch. There were a few empty chairs at one end of the long table where The Hi-Tones were sitting, so Clara followed Allie over and took a seat to watch. It just looked like she was keeping an eye on her sister, not on the lead singer.

Allie said a quick "Hi" to the guys from The Hi-Tones and asked the drummer, who was sitting closest to them, if she could sit there. The band were all wearing deep red shirts, but he was the only one wearing a T-shirt. It showed off his pecs and his biceps. Clara wondered if Ellington thought he'd end up that muscular from playing the drums.

"Of course," he said. "You kids did a good job."

"Thank you."

"Tough act to follow," the lead singer said. Clara tried not to blush. "You're making the rest of us look bad."

"Don't mind Harrison," the drummer said. "He's just mad he's not the youngest one here. He doesn't get to be the prodigy."

"I'm still a prodigy."

"Not a *child* prodigy."

Clara wanted to say she wasn't a child but realized in time that would be exactly what a child would say. Instead, she asked something she truly wanted to know. "How old are you?"

"Nineteen," Harrison replied. "How old are you?"

"Not 19," Allie said loudly.

This time Clara actually blushed. She wanted to kick Allie or tell her to shut up but knew that would be too immature. The only thing that saved her was the assistant stage manager coming to the door of the tent and telling The Hi-Tones to get their butts backstage.

Grace watched the evening's performances on the television backstage, but she gathered Theo and Viola to watch The Hi-Tones from the wings with the rest of the family. The musicians from Big Sur Strings and the folk trio stood nearby. She could see the university choir huddled in the wings on the opposite side of the stage and felt a surge of protectiveness, a feeling that her family was in a battle that it needed to win that night. She and the little ones stayed where they were as the rest of the family trooped onstage for the finale. She didn't mind not performing tonight. Truly, watching her four oldest children perform had been a delight. She wanted them to have more opportunities like this one. Vincent and Gregor had both grumbled that the Mozinskis were so far stage right they were practically off the stage. With so many performers onstage at once, it didn't seem to matter. The four children with Vincent standing behind them were nearly lost in the sea of other people onstage. They needed something to make them stand out. Grace looked down at four-year-old Theo and three-year-old Viola. Maybe the rest of the family needed two somethings to make them stand out.

Each of the acts was supposed to sing one verse of "This Land Is Your Land" on their own (except for the Big Sur Strings), and everyone would sing the chorus. As Clara, Ellington, Bix, and Allegro launched into their verse, Grace launched her secret weapon from the wings and changed the course of her family's collective future. The older children were singing "that ribbon of highway..." when the audience gave an audible "Oh" and broke into scattered applause as Theo and Viola wandered in from the wings. Theo was keeping time with a wood block, while Viola was doing the jumpy-jerky, joyful dance endemic to all tiny children. No one noticed that she wasn't on the beat. When people wrote and talked about the Bicentennial Celebration the next day, they wrote and talked about The Musical Mozinskis. They had stolen the show.

BACK IN THE U.S.A. REPRISE
(alt. B side: "Back In Cleveland")

Each of the children practiced every day, sometimes with their parents instructing, sometimes on their own. Once the family came back from Washington, D.C., Grace thought it prudent to jump start Viola's musical education in earnest. As she had with the other children, she started with the recorder. It's the classic beginner instrument because it gives an immediate return on investment — anyone who can blow can make a sound with it. Grace showed Viola the correct armature and finger positions. Whereas after a few minutes or so of playing around with the recorder, all of her other children had been able to pull off a passable rendition of, say, "Mary Had a Little Lamb," Viola just sat there happily tooting away note after unresolved note. When Grace sang *do, re, mi, fa, so, la, ti, do* and encouraged her youngest child to play it after her, Viola simply said, "I like hearing you sing, Mommy," and resumed her tuneless tooting. It was painful to see the stray notes struggling vainly out of the recorder, hovering for a moment, looking for any companions, then dropping like bricks. The floor around Viola was littered with crinkled, half-formed notes, like the corpses of so many dead mayflies. She appeared not to see them.

Grace wasn't worried. Viola was Viola — funny and sweet and smart as a whip. Maybe she just needed more time. Grace told the rest of the family not to worry, repeating the phrase "She's a late bloomer," often enough that the other children believed it. And things were starting to happen for the family. Vincent and Gregor rarely discussed how all of their deals came about, not even with her. Grace typically found out about things shortly before the children did. In the case of the family's first recording, she found out at the same time. A few weeks after the Bicentennial Celebration, the family was sitting down to dinner on a Monday evening when Vincent asked if the children would like to record a single.

Monday dinners almost always included the entire family and were almost always some variation on kluski noodles because it was an inexpensive way to find something all six kids would eat. Ellington had a piece of a noodle hanging out of his mouth as he asked, "A record?"

"Please don't talk with your mouth full," Grace said, trying not to let her annoyance at her husband seep into her voice.

"Or with food hanging out of it," Clara added.

"Yes, a record. Well, a single," said father.

"Would it be on America's Top 40?" Clara asked.

"Maybe. If it's successful."

"Okay, I'll do it!" Allie said, as though the rest of the family had been trying to convince her. She no longer shared a room with Clara but still spent a lot of time in her older sister's room, listening to whatever she was listening to on the radio. Grace always thought it was because she didn't like sharing a room with a toddler, but perhaps it was because the younger girls didn't have a radio.

"So Gregor got the backing?" Grace said. The last she'd heard about this was that Vincent and Gregor were sending out demo tapes.

Vincent smiled the big smile that had made women swoon back in the day. "Yep."

"What's backing?" Theo asked.

"Money to make the record."

"Wait, we have to pay to make a record?" Ellington said. "Are we ever gonna make any money doing this?"

"Don't worry about that. Your mother and I will take care of it. And I've already talked to Gregor about 'Groovy Twosie' for the B side," he said pointedly to Grace.

This was good news. "Groovy Twosie" was one of the songs Grace had written. Using one of her originals for the B side meant the family would be earning royalties instead of paying royalties on one of the songs. It was the first song she'd written since music school — just a fun, somewhat silly pop song. In the greater scheme of things, one little B side song credit didn't mean anything, but that didn't mean she couldn't be happy about it. Grace nodded and said, "I don't know about the rest of you, but I'm really excited. You're going to record a single!" Somehow getting their mother's approval made the whole idea of recording a single seem like more fun. Ellington even stopped complaining about not getting paid.

Vincent and the four older children recorded the single at the same studio where they had done the Bob's Cars jingle a year ago. The A side was, of course, "Back in the U.S.A." Vincent and Gregor wanted to capitalize on the success of the Bicentennial performance.

Clara spent most of her free time listening to the radio and worshipped at the altar of Casey Kasem's American Top 40 every week. The idea of a record she had played on making it anywhere near the charts, the idea of Casey Kasem ever uttering her name, seemed like one more of her father's grandiose failed plans. Except his last couple of plans hadn't failed. She spent her time rehearsing "Groovy Twosie" and practicing harp. Now that the family had been on national television, her parents had more gigs, and she'd been hired to play for a wedding and a baby shower. It paid far more than babysitting, so she was happy to spend her free time playing music.

The single was scheduled to come out in November. A couple weeks before the release date, Vincent asked the four older children if they would all like to take a trip to Hollywood to sing on a television show. He might as well have asked if they'd like to eat ice cream for dinner. Of course they wanted to fly on an airplane for the first time in their lives and stay in a hotel and appear on *The Tonight Show* Starring Johnny Carson. Actually, Clara and Ellington were the only ones who had ever heard of *The Tonight Show*. Their mother occasionally let them stay up late enough to watch it. They gave Bix and Allie the low-down on Carson.

Only the five of them went — Vincent, Clara, Ellington, Bix, and Allie. Mr. Karpenko was there too. He didn't stay in the hotel with the family, but he was there for the recording. Clara felt like he was always around. Mr. Karpenko wasn't a good or bad part of her life. He was simply a part of it now. They were scheduled to perform "Back in the U.S.A." in order to promote the single. It was a thrill when Clara heard her father say that to one of the producers, because it made them sound like professionals. She knew a professional was someone who was paid to do something, while an amateur was someone who didn't get paid. She wasn't sure what, if anything, their family was being paid for playing on *The Tonight Show*. But she had been paid to play music — more than once. She wasn't sure about her younger siblings, but she was a professional. At least a professional harpist.

Up to this point, they hadn't traveled much. Really, not at all. There were too many children to afford any prolonged vacations, certainly not anywhere outside the range of the family station wagon, which was the only vehicle large enough to transport all eight Mozinskis. The farthest they ever went as a family was a couple of trips to visit Vincent's family in Indiana and regular holiday jaunts to the Klinefelter grandparents in Youngstown. None of the children had ever been on an airplane, but when Clara looked out the airplane window as the plane took off in Cleveland, flying to Los Angeles to appear on *The Tonight Show* felt completely normal, as though this was how she was supposed to live.

Clara always thought *The Tonight Show* was recorded live and was just on late because of the time difference. She was surprised to learn they'd be recording the show during the afternoon. They flew in the evening before and had dinner in the hotel. The next day, a car picked the family up and took them to the studio. When an assistant at the studio seated all five of them in a row of chairs in make-up, the only thing Clara could think of was Dorothy and her friends getting cleaned up in the Emerald City before they met the Wizard of Oz. It certainly felt as foreign as Oz. She was, of course, Dorothy. Of her siblings, she'd peg Ellington as the Cowardly Lion — lots of bluster and complaining but decent at the core. Bix would be the Tin Man because he was always kind. Her father would be the Scarecrow, because he was always the one thinking up new plans. And Allie? *Wicked Witch of the West*, Clara thought.

"What are you giggling about?" Ellington asked from the next chair.

"Nothing," Clara replied.

"Sweetie, I need to do your lips. Please stop moving," the make-up woman said.

"It's the only time Dad'll let us wear lipstick!" Allie called from two chairs over.

One of the assistant directors, a slight young woman with brown hair cut like a boy, came up to Vincent's chair and asked for the correct pronunciation of their last name.

"Mo-zin-ski," Vincent replied carefully. Clara waited for her father's standard joke on the family name. "'Moe,' like from The Three Stooges, 'zin,' like zinfandel, and 'ski.' Just think of The Three Stooges drinking wine while skiing."

"Which is what it's like living with six kids," the four children added along with him. Clara used to think this joke was funny, but now it just seemed juvenile.

The assistant director gave a polite chuckle. "Well, I guarantee I'll never forget how to pronounce it," she said.

"Just make sure Ed gets it right," Vincent said. He sounded kind of rude, but Clara knew better than to say anything to her father. Instead, she just concentrated on enjoying how good she looked with the lipstick and a little bit of make-up. The make-up lady had said, "Just enough so you won't look washed out on camera." It turned out just enough was just right, and she hoped it wouldn't all wear off by the time they went on. The five of them, along with Mr. Karpenko, were sent to the green room to wait until it was time to sing "Back in the U.S.A." Everything felt clean and overly organized. El asked if he could meet Doc Severinsen, who led *The Tonight Show* band.

"Negatory, El," their father said. He was sitting on one of the two cushy sofas in the green room, reading a copy of the *LA Times* he had picked up in the hotel lobby. Allie was sitting next to him, resting her head against his arm. It looked like she was taking a nap.

"Why not?"

"Because the guests don't bother the band."

"I'm not gonna bother him, I just want to meet him..."

"It's not in the plan."

"But..."

"No."

Clara was reading a book for English class because her mother told them to bring homework on the trip so they wouldn't fall behind. El slammed his math workbook onto his lap and pretended to look at it. Clara glanced over at Bix. He momentarily lifted his eyes from his social studies workbook and then wisely went right back to it. Clara went back to her book. She and her brothers were on the sofa catty-corner from her father, while Mr. Karpenko was alternately pacing back and forth or sitting in the green room's sole easy chair.

"Maybe you meet Doc next time," Mr. Karpenko said to Ellington.

"What next time?" El asked. "Are we doing this again?"

"Are we?" Bix echoed.

"Do the song very well, and I will make sure you come on again."

"Gregor, don't make promises you can't..."

Mr. Karpenko interrupted her father with a *Tch tch tch tch* sound. It was a low B, and the eighth notes hung briefly over his head. For some reason, it made the children giggle, mainly because they knew Mr. Karpenko couldn't see it. "I do not offer what I do not deliver, Vincent." Here he turned to address Ellington directly. "Ellington, you will meet Doc Severinsen, just not today. Okay? All of you, I want you should play very well today. You do that, and I will make more good things happen for you. Deal?"

"Deal," El and Bix replied brightly.

"I always try to play well," Clara said, "but, yes, deal."

They did play well. Allie's catnap agreed with her, and she didn't steal focus during her father's solo. She and Bix had cooked up a little dueling duckwalking bit, and the audience loved it. Johnny Carson loved it. They were only supposed to do the song, but when they were done, Johnny said, "Why don't you all come over here and say hello?" Vincent sat down in the chair right next to Johnny Carson, while Ellington, Bix, and Clara squeezed onto the sofa next to Ed McMahon. Vincent's instincts as a showman never failed. He picked up Allie and placed her on his lap to enhance the cute factor.

Mr. Carson — their father had been adamant that the kids call Johnny "Mr. Carson" if they met him — asked the family to introduce themselves. Everyone looked at Clara because she was the oldest, so she said, "I'm Clara. I'm 13."

"Ellington. Age 12."

"Hi, my name is Bix. I'm 11." When he added "As of last week," it got a little chuckle from Mr. Carson.

It must have been because Ellington gave his full name, but Allie said, "I'm Allegro, and I'm eight and a half." The entire room was charmed.

"You have a big family," Johnny said.

"We have more at home," Allie replied.

This got a good laugh from the audience. "Is everyone in your family a musician?" Johnny asked.

Allie paused. "I think so."

Every family has its private jokes. They can range from burnt toast to prodigious farting to a love for buttered peas. These jokes are kept private because to make them public would invite pain. No one outside the family needs to know who can't cook or who suffers from flatulence. But there on *The Tonight Show*, Vincent made the #1 Mozinski Joke in public for the first time. "If they can't read music by the time they're eight, we put them up for adoption," he said. Johnny Carson and Ed McMahon cracked up, so Vincent kept going. "We've lost a couple of really nice kids that way, but the family business is the family business."

"So, it looks like you passed the test," Johnny said to Allie.

"Of course."

After Johnny composed himself, he asked Vincent "Now did they all take lessons or did you teach them or are they just a bunch of little musical geniuses?"

"All of the above," Vincent replied with a smile. "I've made my living playing jazz piano for years. My wife, Grace, is a classically trained violinist..."

"She taught me," Allie said.

"Grace pretty much has all the string instruments covered, and I do the brass and woodwinds. And piano. Between the two of us, we've been able to teach them what they need to know. And they're all incredibly talented kids."

"He said *geniuses*, Dad," Bix injected. There is a reason Vincent and Grace had made him the front man. Bix was not a shy child, and he had excellent timing.

"Musical geniuses and smart alecks," Vincent replied.

"Do you all play other instruments?" Mr. Carson looked right at Clara as he asked this, so she answered first. In the future, the children learned that all group questions were expected to be answered in order of age.

"I also play the harp," Clara said.

48

"I can play clarinet and saxophone, but I prefer percussion."

"Guitar and piano and trumpet."

"Violin."

"Do the younger ones play anything yet?"

"We start them all on the recorder and piano," Vincent said. "It gives them a firm base. It looks like Theo has gravitated toward the cello, but we're not sure yet. Some people think you shouldn't start music lessons until the child can read, so you aren't fighting two learning battles at once, but music isn't just an intellectual exercise. It's a deep part of being human. It's not just something you learn, it's something you feel — that everyone feels."

"That is beautiful. And I must say that you have a lovely, talented family."

"Thank you."

"Will you come back and visit me again?" Johnny asked Allie.

"Yes, because Ellington wants to meet Doc."

Johnny Carson chuckled. "I'm sure that can be arranged. Thank you to The Musical Mozinskis for joining us. Their new single is out November 19th. We'll be right back after this break."

And that was it. Johnny Carson waved goodbye to the family as an assistant ushered them offstage. The car that drove them to the studio deposited the family back at the hotel, where they packed, washed the make-up off their faces, and got right back into the car to go to the airport. Allie lamented that they didn't even have a chance to play in the hotel pool.

The single did well enough that The Musical Mozinskis recorded an entire album. It included the two tracks from the single, plus a bunch of catchy covers like "ABC," "The Loco-Motion," "Come Go With Me," "Let The Little Girl Dance," "Snap It Up," and a couple of originals. Privately, Vincent called the covers bubble gum. Grace reminded him that bubble gum-chewing girls had made stars out of everyone from Saint Frank Sinatra to Elvis Presley and perhaps he should be less dismissive of the tastes of girls and young women.

At home, the kids went to school and practiced. Grace and Vincent still gave lessons and played gigs. Clara also played the occasional harp gig because she was young enough that being a teenaged harpist was a novelty. The first album came out in the spring, and even though it didn't make huge stars out of The Musical Mozinskis, it sold well enough that kids at Roxboro Middle School either wanted to be Clara's friend or to make fun of her. There didn't seem to be any in-between. By the end of eighth grade, it was no longer a problem, because their parents had a contract for a musical variety show and moved the family from Cleveland to California.

SNAP IT UP

The concept for *The Musical Mozinskis Variety Show* was simple — a family of musicians moves to a new city and builds a new life that includes a surprising number of musical interludes. Future television scholars would laud the show for its quasi-metafictional premise. The show was supposed to take place in the family household, so there would be a simple family-oriented plot for each episode, but the bulk of the show would be the young Mozinski children "practicing" (i.e., performing) music with famous friends dropping by the house to perform with them. It was set to begin production in August and start airing the Wednesday after Labor Day, 1977. Everything happened very fast. The family had about a month to pack and move into a new house in Altadena. To varying degrees, each of the kids expected the new house to be big, like a mansion. After all, they were going to have a television show on a major network. They could be forgiven for thinking their family was suddenly rich. The Altadena house turned out to be smaller than the one the family lived in in Cleveland, and it was only two stories. It was the first time any of the kids had seen a stucco house and clay tiles. The six of them stood on the sidewalk in front of the new house, just staring.

"What kind of trees are those?" Theo asked.

"Palm trees," Clara, El, and Bix said at the same time.

"They don't look like the ones at home."

"That's because they're tropical," El said.

"What's tropical?"

"They have to be warm. If you planted a palm tree in Cleveland, it would die in the winter."

"I like the roof," Bix said.

"It's red," Viola added, in a tone that suggested she thought all roofs should be red. "It's pretty."

"Those are clay tiles," Clara said, as though this was a priori knowledge instead of something she had heard their parents discussing two weeks earlier.

"I liked our old house better," Theo declared.

"Yeah, me too," El added.

Allie gave a world-weary sigh. "I'll reserve judgement until I see the inside," she said.

Vincent came over and picked up Viola, then put a hand on Theo's shoulder. "It's nice, isn't it?"

"Yes," they replied. Contrary to standard group responses, the children didn't reply in harmony, which should have clued him in that some of his offspring were not pleased with the house or the move. They didn't have much time to miss their friends or their old house because the show became the all-consuming focus of the family's collective life. They would essentially be playing themselves — a big family that plays music. Because the children would be working during the day, the studio was required to hire a tutor who would run several hours of "show school" each day.

Like most television shows about families, the set was designed to look like a living room. In most living rooms, the focal point is a television or a sofa. The set for *The Musical Mozinskis Variety Show* had a sofa and two easy chairs, a coffee table, and bookshelves — filled equally with books and sheet music — but the focal point was a performance space marked by two music stands and a baby grand piano. It slightly resembled the living room of the old homestead in Cleveland, only larger and with newer furniture and a steeply upgraded piano. Vincent joked that's how you knew the show was fiction — up until this point, the family only ever had an upright.

The first episode centered on the family moving into the new house. The opening number was a piano and violin duet between Vincent and Grace on a near-empty set that started out as Bach's "Air on the G String" then morphed into a leisurely version of "Sweet Georgia Brown" that slowly increased in tempo, allowing Grace to show off her jazz violin chops. They are interrupted by all six children running in the pretend front door of their pretend new home. There was the thinly veiled plot of the family moving in — the obligatory alliterative wordplay about Bix's boxes and how Ellington's drum kit practically needed its own moving van and whether Clara's harp actually took up more room — plus some snippets of songs as they unpacked various instruments and objects.

Each of the children would carry in a box or two and then get distracted by the instruments and music as they did so. The entire family would eventually end up having a jam session. The first musical guests were scheduled to be The Madelines, the girl group who hit it big with the song "Snap It Up" in 1962. The Musical Mozinskis' cover of "Snap It Up" from the first LP had also been released as a single and topped out at a respectable #82 on the Billboard charts. The Madelines were supposed to play neighbors who hear the music and come over to welcome the family to the neighborhood. They would of course end up joining the family in singing "Snap It Up" for the finale with the family acting as backing band.

"Snap It Up" was the perfect song for the closing of the first episode because it had something that pleased everyone. Ellington loved playing it because the skipping, syncopated beat let him show off a little. Allie liked it because it was the first time her father had let her sing lead. Bix liked it because it gave him a break from singing lead. Clara liked it because it was fun to sing. The lyrics were simple:

> *Snap it up (right now)*
> *To the left (right now)*
> *To the right (right now)*
> *Snap it center, to the sides,*
> *Snap your fingers to the skies.*

The dance that went along with "Snap It Up" never became as popular as the song itself, mainly because some people aren't able to snap their fingers (but just about everyone can do a version of "The Twist" or the "Mashed Potato"). If the dance had taken off, The Madelines might have been more than a one-hit wonder, and the producers might not have been able to afford them.

The show's director, Don Kilgore, had a very specific vision for the show. The day after the family first met him, Ellington remarked that the tall, mostly bald Kilgore did not look like he knew what he was doing. Their father said that Don Kilgore had a resume as long as his arm and they should be honored to be working with him. Clara looked at her own long, slender arms, which were long enough to wrap around a full-sized harp, and wondered how many sheets of paper Mr. Kilgore's resume took up.

On the second day of rehearsals, they ran through "Snap It Up," sans Madelines, with what had become the standard family band — Vincent, Clara, Ellington, Bix, and Allie. There was minimal crew on set because they weren't taping, but when they finished, the crew applauded. Kilgore didn't.

"What about the rest of them?" he asked Vincent, who was still seated at the piano.

"The rest of who?"

"Grace and the little ones." He looked over at Stacy, the assistant director. "Where are the other two?"

"I think they're with the tutor," she replied carefully. Stacy always chose her words with care, especially when speaking with Mr. Kilgore.

"Get them." He walked onto the bright lights of the set and approached the piano. "Vincent, I thought we agreed we'd have the whole family for 'Snap It Up.' Where's Grace?"

"This is the lineup we had on the recording."

"New rule: everybody plays on the final song, every episode."

This was the first of many times the children observed the show hierarchy in action. Vincent took a moment, nodded, and said, "Understood. I'll need to write out new arrangements."

"That's why you're the music director."

By this time, someone had found Grace and recovered Theo and Viola from the tutor.

"Ellington," Grace said, even though she was addressing the room, "you've always said we need a horn section. Maybe that's what we need for 'Snap It Up.' Bix, Theo, and I will play trumpet, sax, and trombone."

"Then we have no lead guitar," Ellington said.

Allie gave an annoyed "Hello?" and pointed to herself. "I can do it."

El gave a little snort. "Sure you can."

"Stop it," their father snapped. "I'll write out the new arrangements. It'll be fine."

"What about this one?" Mr. Kilgore said, motioning to Viola, who had crawled up onto the piano seat next to their father.

"What *about* Viola?" Grace said in a tone that would have made any rational adult reevaluate their intended response.

Don Kilgore wasn't always tactful, but he was rational. "I'd really like to have Viola play on the closing number."

"She's four," Vincent said.

"She's still emerging as a musician and hasn't settled on an instrument yet," Grace added.

"Can't we just give her a tambourine or something like the little girl on *The Partridge Family*?"

As soon as Mr. Kilgore mentioned *The Partridge Family*, Clara laughed and immediately turned it into a cough. It might have worked had all of her siblings not done the same thing. Actually, Bix gave more of a "Ha!" and Ellington made sort of a puking sound, but the effect was the same. Even Viola giggled. Vincent threw a few pages of sheet music in the air, but it wasn't clear if he was annoyed with his children or his director. He lit a cigarette, which the children recognized as his way of momentarily giving up.

Kilgore looked around at the Mozinski children. "What's so funny?"

Allie, who had never bothered to hide her disdain for anything or anyone, said, "They don't actually *play* their instruments."

"Only two of them can even sing. It's all fake," Ellington said.

"They're not really a family," Theo added. "Our mom told us."

Kilgore looked over at Grace as though it was her fault that *The Partridge Family* didn't feature actual blood relatives. She was standing by the piano and had picked up Viola. Again, any rational being would tread carefully when Grace was holding one of her children. "*The Partridge Family* is a scripted show about an imaginary family. That isn't a secret," she said. "But if you'd like Viola to play tambourine on this song, I think that would be fine. What do you think?" she asked Viola. "Do you want to play tambourine on 'Snap It Up'?"

"Yes," Viola replied with a vehement nod of her head. "I can do it. I'm a Mozinski."

"Yes, you are," Grace said to her. To Mr. Kilgore she said, "Well then there you go, Don. The whole family will play the finale." Her voice was so pleasant that you couldn't imagine anyone disagreeing with her.

After spending the week rehearsing with just their family, taping the first episode in front of a live studio audience induced varying levels of stage fright. Knowing that there would be an audience was worlds different from actually having an audience. Clara and Bix stood just outside the sightlines, hiding in the wings, watching the comedian who was hired to warm up the crowd tell weak jokes.

"Are all those people really here to see us or do they just want to watch a television show get recorded?" she whispered.

"Maybe both. Or maybe they just like The Madelines." Ever since the Bicentennial performance, Bix seemed impervious to stage fright. "Are you nervous?"

"A little." Bix was one of the few people in the family you could admit being nervous to without him using the information against you at a later date.

"The audience for *The Tonight Show* was bigger than this. You were great then," Bix said.

"Yeah, but that was a year ago. We didn't know enough to be scared. And this is Our Show. What if something goes wrong?"

"If somebody blows a line, we'll stop and do another take." The idea that anyone in the family would hit a clinker while playing was unthinkable.

Their conversation was interrupted by their father, who put a hand on Bix's shoulder.

"Guys, move back," he hissed. It was difficult to tell if he was angry with them or not. "The audience shouldn't see you until we get introduced."

Clara obediently took two steps backwards. Bix merely said "Sean the cameraman said we'd be fine if we don't go past the yellow line," and stayed put.

"You're standing *on* the yellow line," his father said. "Move back."

Bix gave a barely audible sigh, which came out as a faint G-sharp over his head, and took half a step back.

Their father looked out onto the set. "That's better," he murmured and sauntered on set as the comedian introduced him. Vincent said hello to the audience and introduced Grace. Then they both called out the children's names. As always, they went in order of age. Don the Director had told them each to run onto the set as their name was called. When her father called her name, Clara ran.

Viola played tambourine on "Snap It Up," but there was so much going on that most people didn't notice she wasn't entirely on the beat, and if they did, she was little and cute and dancing with one of The Madelines, and nobody cared.

ABC

he Musical Mozinskis was, at heart, a musical variety show, but every
episode had a tenuous plot thread that held the songs together, such
as moving into the house, starting a new school, and, in a family of
musicians of varying ages, teaching the younger ones how to read music.
This family ritual was captured on film in Season 1, Episode 4, when
Vincent sat Viola down at the piano with an apple, a paring knife, a piece
of paper, and a pencil. He drew a picture of a circle on the piece of paper.

"This is called a whole note," he said.

"That's a circle," Viola said proudly, pointing at the circular whole
note on the paper in front of her.

"Yes," Vincent said. "A whole note looks just like a circle. Just like the
apple, see? Now a whole note gets four beats. One—two—three—four," he
said, tapping out a steady four count on the edge of the piano. Vincent
Mozinski was generally acknowledged to be a human metronome.

"One, two, three, four. One, two, three, four," Viola chanted happily
as her father attempted to explain the concept of a half note and quarter
note to her by drawing them on the paper and cutting the apple in half
and then into quarters. Viola ate the apple with him, just as his five previous children had done at their first music lesson, but it was clear that
the concept of whole and half notes was, at best, sketchy in her mind and
inextricably tied up with fruit. The writers threw in a few jokes like "Is
there a note for a triangle?" and "What hand are you supposed to eat the
apple with?" which was followed by Vincent playing a boogie-woogie
bass line with his left hand and eating an apple slice with his right, then

switching, then playing with both hands while a giggling Viola fed him another slice of apple. It was, as Don Kilgore said, television gold.

The five older children watched the rehearsal from one corner of the studio, far behind the cameras. They were all looking for the same thing. When their father wrote the circular whole note on the paper, he played a middle C and held it for four beats. When doing this same exercise with his first five children, each one of them had looked up at the air above the piano where the big, fat whole note was hovering. They all knew that the notes they created, the ones that shimmered in the air when they played, were always more beautiful, more vibrant than the notes on the physical page. It seemed like the note written on the page was the only one Viola could see. Just to be sure it wasn't a mistake, they all watched Viola while their father played the boogie-woogie. The notes literally danced along in the air above their father and Viola's heads. All she had to do was look up. Her siblings watched Viola as she watched her father's hands on the keyboard, oblivious to the music that was dancing just above her head if she could only see it.

Each of the Mozinski children had a different take on the family's move to California. Doing the show was fun — everyone was in agreement there. But having to move across the country in order to do the show was tough. And being together virtually all the time was even more difficult. Ellington, for one, was not a fan. The first couple months of the show were great. Everything was new, and he wasn't sick of show school yet, although to be fair, Ellington had never been of fan of school in any form. He had learned enough to know that his life had been turned upside down. As an adult, he'd explain to friends that most people in show business spend their whole lives trying to get on *The Tonight Show*. By the time he was 13, he had been on it twice.

The first time The Musical Mozinskis played *The Tonight Show* it seemed like an adventure or a game. Vincent told them to play Chuck Berry. Ellington and his siblings went out and played Chuck Berry like little champions. Ellington could honestly say he hadn't been nervous that first time, he'd been more interested in trying to meet Doc Severinsen, with whom he was admittedly obsessed. Doc had the greatest job in the world — he led a tight band, got to pick what he wanted to play, plus he was a sharp dresser. They didn't meet Doc the first time around, but Mr. Karpenko had promised he'd make it happen if they went on the show again. In the space of a year, Ellington realized he'd moved to California, had an album with two Top 100 singles, and was starting a weekly variety show. His life was so different that it seemed like Doc should be excited to meet him, not the other way around. The family was doing all kinds of publicity leading up to the premiere of the show, but the ratings were low for the first three episodes. Before the fourth episode aired, the family appeared on Carson again.

The fourth episode of *The Musical Mozinskis* was about the children starting at a new school, and they were playing the old Jackson Five tune "ABC" as the finale. Their cover of the song on the first album had cracked the Top 40 at number 38. Playing it on the show was a no-brainer. As a tie-in, they played it for the second appearance on Carson. As a music director, Vincent's tastes ran toward pop songs. Usually, Ellington would look at the song lists and think *Bubble gum. Oldies. Safe crap.* "ABC" was one of his father's few good picks.

El frequently made suggestions. For instance, he would ask something like, "Dad, what if we played something from Steve Miller Band? Like 'Jet Airliner'? Kind of ties into the family moving across country?" His father would respond with something like "We already did the moving storyline in the first episode."

"What about 'Rock'n Me Baby'? The show could be about Mom trying to get the little kids to go to sleep?"

At this, Vincent put his arm around Ellington's shoulder, gave him a pat that sure felt condescending, and said, "Son, I hate to break it to you, but that song isn't about rocking babies to sleep."

El decided to let his father bask in his *Father Knows Best* moment. At 13, he was already alarmingly aware of the song's subject matter and had even attempted the act once or twice (the rocking had stalled at second base), but there was no need to let Vincent know any of that. Ellington Mozinski wasn't a great student academically, but he was smart enough to keep his mouth shut on certain subjects. It wasn't as though he was asking his father if they could cover Zeppelin's "The Lemon Song," which would be awkward with a 12-year-old lead singer, but not every song has to be about puppy love and sunshine and flowers. El just wanted a little variety.

On the day of *The Tonight Show* taping, Karpenko and Vincent grabbed Ellington, Clara, Bix, and Allie off the set and hustled them over to The Burbank Studios. The first time on Carson, they had nothing to lose. Now they had a network show to save. *No pressure, kids. Just save the family farm,* Ellington thought.

He remembered everything about The Burbank Studios from the first time. The green room looked exactly the same as it had a year earlier. All the changes were internal. The first time on the show, Grace made the children bring their homework so they wouldn't fall behind in school. The second time, she made them bring their scripts so they could run lines for the taping of the show on Friday.

As soon as they entered the green room before the show, Vincent immediately said, "Run lines," so they did. For a while. But then their father and Mr. Karpenko walked out of the room for a cigarette break. The moment they were gone, Ellington dropped his script on the floor and said, "We don't have to do this if they're not here."

"Yes, we do," Clara said.

Allie nodded in a way that Ellington thought made her look like a bobblehead. "You were terrible at rehearsal yesterday," she said.

"What are you talking about? I was tight."

Allie gave an annoyed sigh like she was some old lady. "I'm not talking about when we were playing. I mean your lines. You don't know your lines."

Bix was as good a side man as he was a front man. "To be fair, the script also sucks," he said. "What does it matter if El says, 'I'm just worried the school won't be big enough to contain my cool,' or 'I don't think the school is big enough to contain my cool'?"

Allie goes "Because I'm supposed to say, 'I'm just worried the school won't be big enough to contain your ego.' If you mess up your line, it messes up *my* line."

"You could always try *improvising*," Ellington said, which cracked Bix up and annoyed his younger sister even more. Honestly, it was always so easy to get Allie mad sometimes it wasn't even fun.

"Shut up."

Despite Clara saying "Would you two please stop fighting?" Allie threw her script at Ellington. By the time Vincent and Mr. Karpenko came back, the script pages were all over the green room floor, Ellington had a bruised shin where Allie kicked him, and he and Bix were tickling Allie's feet and sides, which they had found was pretty much the only way to subdue Allie once she started hitting. Granted, she passed out from laughing one time when they were tickling her and everybody freaked out and blamed Ellington, so he tried to go easy on her.

Vincent was furious. "What the hell is going on in here?" he said. Ellington and Bix had Allie pinned down on one of the sofas while they were tickling her. Vincent grabbed one of Ellington's arms, pulled him away, and snapped "Leave her alone."

"She's okay. See, she's laughing," Ellington said. It really seemed like the punishment didn't fit the crime, especially because Bix had been tickling Allie too, but you didn't see their dad practically breaking Bix's arm.

"We were just tickling her," Bix added.

Vincent knelt down in front of Allie and asked "Are you all right, sweetie?" Allie totally played it up with a couple of deep breaths and a little sniffle like they actually hurt her or something, but then she nodded and said, "Uh-huh. I'm okay," like she was some brave little soldier.

Ellington was pretty sure it was all an act but didn't have any time to think about whether or not Allie was faking being hurt because, as he put it later, this is where it got nuts. His father stood up, turned around, and said, "I'm so sorry. I think they're a little wound up about being on the show. They normally don't act like this."

At first Ellington thought he was talking to Karpenko, then he realized that Doc Severinsen was standing in the doorway of the green room. Doc F-ing Severinsen. And he was wearing a blue sport jacket with a screaming neon lime green tie and looked like a million bucks, and there El was beating up his younger sister. All he could say was "Oh wow."

"It's okay," Doc said more to Vincent than to the children. "I was a boy once too. And I have kids." He walked into the room and over to the sofa where they were all clustered. Predictably, Doc approached Allie first, shaking her hand and saying "It's very nice to meet you, Allegro. I know Johnny's excited to have you back on the show." El figured he was lying to be polite, but Allie got herself together in an instant and said, "Thank you. I'm excited to be back," and sounded like she was nine going on 35. As much as she could be annoying, his sister Allegro was a born professional.

Ellington felt a momentary ping of annoyance when Doc turned to talk to Clara next, but then realized Doc was just being old-school polite, talking to the women first. "Clara, I'm so glad to meet you," he said.

Clara was maybe a little gushy but polite and said, "Thank you. It's very nice to meet you too. I mean, in person. I've watched you on the show so many times, I feel as if I already know you."

Doc gave her a broad smile and said, "That's the idea. Be friends with your audience. The longer you stay in this business, the more you'll understand it." Clara just sort of nodded because what are you supposed to say to that? "By the way, you play a mean bass line, young lady."

"Thank you." It seemed like Doc held Clara's hand longer than was absolutely necessary but let go a second before it got creepy. Then he turned and said, "Bix! Good to see you. Named after one of my favorite trumpeters of all time."

This was one of the few times in recorded history that Bix Mozinski did not have a clever reply. In awe, he murmured something like "Mine too."

Doc, being the perfect host, said, "I understand from your father that you also play trumpet along with guitar? That's great."

"Yeah, I do. I love jazz."

"Good man. So do I," Doc replied with a little wink and gave Bix a friendly pat on the shoulder. "Looking forward to hearing you later." Finally, he turned to Ellington, who was still so starstruck that he didn't even bother to think *It's about time.*

"Hi, I'm Ellington," he said and reached out to shake Doc's hand because it was freaking Doc Severinsen and it might not be a bad idea to leave him with a better impression than some kid who beats up his sister.

"Oh, I know who you are, Ellington. Good to meet you."

Doc Severinsen knew who he was? It was almost enough to make Ellington shit his pants. Almost. He managed to keep it together and said, "Good to meet you too." Then he blurted out the first thing that came to his mind: "You played with Buddy Rich."

"Oh yeah, he's an old friend. You like Buddy's playing?"

"Who doesn't? He's amazing."

"Very true. Very true. Well, you keep playing and practicing. That's how Buddy got to be Buddy."

"I will. Thank you for coming to talk to me. I mean, to us." Doc ostensibly came in to meet all of them, but Ellington had been the one to ask to meet him. It felt like the meeting was for him and him alone. It's not like Allie cared who he was.

Doc made a little small talk with Vincent and Karpenko before leaving. He was probably in the green room with them for all of eight minutes, but they were eight of the best minutes of Ellington's life. After he left, he thanked his father for bringing Doc in, and Vincent replied, "It was Gregor."

His father wasn't normally that generous, but with Karpenko standing right there, Ellington supposed he had to be. Ellington and his siblings thanked Karpenko, who merely replied, "Is my pleasure. I know you are a very big fan."

And then, because Vincent seemed to love telling Ellington he had done something wrong, his father said, "In the future, when you meet somebody at his level, talk about *his* work, not who he's played with." El was flying high enough that he didn't even bother giving a smart-alecky reply. He just said, "Yes, sir," and kept smiling.

Meeting Doc Severinsen was like a shot of adrenaline. It made Ellington feel a little more powerful, a little more cocky. He decided to liven things up. "ABC" has a drum break at the bridge. On the original Jackson Five recording, it's right before Michael Jackson shouts "Sit down, girl! I think I love you." After Doc left the green room, Ellington got to thinking, *Instead of a drum break, why not take a full solo?* Why not make it different? He wasn't sure exactly who he wanted to impress. Maybe Doc Severinsen, maybe the studio audience. Girls. Everybody. If you're going to play, why not make it count?

Ellington wasn't stupid enough to suggest a solo to his father, who seemed to think he invented music. Why ask only to get shot down? Clara had good chops. She'd hear it. The only person who would need a heads-up was Allie. While he grudgingly admired her impeccable technique, she lacked spontaneity. The family's dirty little secret was that if the music wasn't written out, Allie couldn't play it.

His father and Mr. Karpenko were occupied at one end of the green room in conversation with one of *The Tonight Show* producers who'd wandered in. While they had gotten more savvy about the industry, they weren't quite the wheelers and dealers they pretended to be. The family wasn't Jackson Five-famous or Osmond-level famous, but they were doing well for being managed by two guys who were in over their heads.

Ellington pulled Bix and Allie over to the farthest corner of the green room to talk. Clara kind of glanced over at them but didn't seem too interested. She concentrated on picking up the pages from their scripts that were still scattered all over the floor.

El tried to keep everything casual and just said, "Hey, at the drum break, I'm gonna take a solo."

"Cool with me," Bix replied, like it was no big deal.

When Vincent and Karpenko were "talking business," his children could have lit a bonfire in the green room and they wouldn't have noticed. They certainly didn't hear Allie hiss, "I'm telling."

"Oh come on, you are not," Ellington replied. "At the drum break, just stop playing for an extra verse."

"How do I know when to come back in?"

"It's just an extra verse. You'll hear it."

Allie looked like she was trying to come up with the best insult she could on short notice.

"You'll see it," Ellington added. He knew she could see the music, even if he wasn't exactly sure she saw it the same way he did.

Allie still looked skeptical, so Bix said, "I'll give you a signal." This was why Ellington pulled Bix into the conversation in the first place. Bix was good at talking people into doing things they didn't think they wanted to do.

The Musical Mozinskis were scheduled in *The Tonight Show's* first half hour because underage children performing on a show that aired at 11:30 p.m. generally didn't go on after midnight. Honestly, most of the teenyboppers who wanted to see the dreamy Bix Mozinski sing probably weren't allowed to stay up that late anyway. Their slot was three minutes and 15 seconds for the song and, if they were lucky and Johnny was in a good mood, two and a half minutes to sit and chat and promote the show. Vincent had drilled that into his children's heads.

Ellington sang secondary vocals on "ABC" because Vincent decided it would be weird to have a grown man and a boy essentially singing to the same girl. This one good idea from his father seemed like the musical equivalent of a blind squirrel finding a nut.

Musicians typically look at each other while they're playing to see who's going to solo, if they're taking another verse, if it's time to wrap things up. Not the Mozinskis. Bix never had to turn around to communicate with Ellington, none of them did. He could see what they were playing. From his vantage point at the back of the band, Ellington could see everything. He could see the notes in the air, the music that he and his family were creating. When the family played together, the music lined up as though it was written on a staff, like they were all literally on the same page. Ellington found it an awkward adjustment when he got older and started playing with other musicians. With other people, the notes were a little more jumbled, like they didn't want to fit together. If somebody was off the beat or hit a clunker, then their notes were off to the side or looked shriveled or deformed. Ellington never really thought of it as reading the music, it was just something that was there and made sense. Everything he played was right in front of him.

They entered the stage in dim light, during the first commercial break after the monologue. Ellington hadn't really paid attention to the monologue. He knew it was always jokes about politics or something equally boring. But he'd heard the audience laughing up a storm. It sounded like they were in a good mood. There was a moment when they were waiting for the floor director to usher them onstage, when Ellington thought he might not take the solo, when it seemed like a dumb idea. The second guessing was the matter of an instant. He heard his father whisper "Knock 'em dead" to Bix and his sisters, who were standing in front of him holding their instruments. The keyboard and drum kit were already set up onstage. Ellington held one drumstick in each hand, alternately tapping first his left then his right hand against his thighs. Then Vincent turned to Ellington, who was standing behind him, and whispered, "No mistakes, no funny business." Ellington didn't have a chance to defend himself, because the next moment they were quietly walking on stage and getting set. After Carson introduced them, the lights would come up to reveal the band and they'd go right into the song.

The break on "ABC" starts with the crash cymbal. Then Bix was supposed to yell "Sit down, girl! I think I love you!" Ellington could feel his father and Clara waiting as he started in on the cymbal. Instead of yelling the line everyone else was expecting, Bix turned sideways and took a couple steps backward. It was the standard gesture for the front man when the drummer takes a solo. Ellington noticed that Bix deliberately turned his back to Vincent and Allie, probably so he wouldn't have to deal with any of their father's dirty looks. Clara stopped playing on the break, and for a second, Ellington could see her right hand poised above the bass strings, waiting to go back in. She heard the change maybe even before she saw it, put her hand down, and took a step back. He'd always known she had good chops.

Ellington kept the crash cymbal going and counter-pointed it with a hard eighth-note pattern on the bass drum and high toms. Then he eased off the cymbal but kept up the bass pattern and put in a series of tom fills, alternating the sticking, left to right on the way down, right to left on the way up. He realized he was sampling Ringo's one and only drum solo, from the song "The End" on *Abbey Road*. Since he was already sampling the Ringo solo, Ellington figured he might as well finish it off. He also realized his sister Allie didn't listen to the Beatles and would have no idea when to come back in. Ellington could only hope that Bix figured it out. He must have, because he walked up to the mic and said loudly, "Are you ready, El?"

"NO!" Ellington yelled back in between tom hits.

Bix waited a second then yelled it again: "Are you ready, El?"

"NO!"

When he got to the part where he was beating the crap out of the floor tom, Bix yelled one last time, "Are you ready, El?"

This time Ellington replied with a loud, "YEAH!" and slipped back into the song.

Bix skipped the "Sit down, girl" part altogether and went right into the "Shake it, shake it, baby," part. He even remembered to sing "Dance with me, baby," because the producer and their mother had thought that singing "shake it" wasn't appropriate for a 12-year-old to sing. The first time they performed that song, Bix was nine. When he sang "Shake it" then, everybody thought it was cute.

They finished the song a little over time, but Johnny Carson still invited the family to come over to the couch to talk. Without even thinking about it, the children sat down in the same order they had the first time on the show, the way they always ended up siting, oldest to youngest from left to right, with the youngest sitting on the lap of whatever parent was part of the interview.

Ellington decided it was worth having his father get pissed off at him because after they got settled on the couch, the first thing Johnny Carson said was "That was quite a solo, young man."

"Thank you," Ellington replied as politely and humbly as he could, even though Johnny Carson had just complimented him, and Doc Severinsen was over in front of the band and gave him a little nod and a thumbs up, so it was kind of hard to feel humble right at that moment.

Ellington's small moment of glory was marred by his father saying "It certainly was." Vincent Mozinski wasn't the kind of father who spanked. He was far more subtle. Ellington figured he and Bix would get the silent treatment for a few days and then, maybe three or four weeks from now, if one of them were running late, their father would make some pointed remark about using up valuable time. Ellington had gotten used to his father's punishments. He didn't care about Vincent's silent treatments because sometimes it was nice not to have to hear his father griping at him. Ellington realized long before his father had that taking away television or electronic games wasn't really much of a punishment in their house. Vincent had raised a houseful of children whose favorite activity was playing music, and taking away rehearsal time would be killing the goose that laid the golden egg.

The first time the family appeared on the show, Johnny Carson had taken a shine to Allie. This was not an isolated occurrence. The Mozinski children were talented, but it didn't hurt that they weren't bad-looking either. Grace and Vincent joked that their baby factory had two standard models: straight, dark hair and blue eyes (Ellington, Allegro, and Thelonious) or curly, medium-brown hair and hazel eyes (Clara, Bix, and Viola). The combination of looks and talent made for an almost irresistible attraction for most adults. Allegro Mozinski had learned early on how to take advantage of it.

Johnny put his elbows on his desk and rested his chin on his hands, speaking directly to Allie. "Thank you for coming back to visit me."

"Thank you for having us back," Allie replied. She sounded sweet but not saccharin. The Mozinski children always made fun of little kids on TV who tried too hard.

"I understand that you and your family have a television show now."

"Uh-huh. It's called *The Musical Mozinskis*, and it's on Wednesday nights at eight-thirty."

"Airing on this network," her father added. She didn't mind her dad stealing focus because promoting the show was the whole point of why they were there.

"That was a good promo. You know, I think we could hire you to do Ed's job," Johnny said. Ed McMahon gave one of his trademark laughs even though it wasn't that funny.

This was one of those setup lines that Allie lived for. Adults still assumed she was an idiot because she was a child and a girl besides. Her biggest challenge was watching her tone. Allie was careful to sound as polite as possible as she replied, "No, thank you. I'd rather play music."

"Okay then. Looks like your job is safe, Ed," Johnny said, to another big guffaw. Making Johnny and Ed laugh and putting them in a good mood was her job. As expected, Johnny turned his attention to her father and asked, "Now Vincent, tell us a little about the show. Is it a variety show? Is it a sitcom?"

"It's a little of both."

"So it's a varietycom."

"I like that."

"You've created a new concept in television. The varietycom."

"A little bit, yeah," Vincent said and gave the producer-approved blurb: "*The Musical Mozinskis* tells the story of a family of musicians who move to a new city and are trying to make music while remaining a close-knit, loving family. There's plenty of laughs and plenty of great music, with some really special musical guests. It's a lot of fun to make and a lot of fun to watch."

"Well, that sounds wonderful. Are all of you having a good time working on the show?" With that, he finally looked over at the older kids. Bix and Ellington looked at Clara. No one minded that Clara was always expected to answer first, because it gave them a little time to think before they had to talk.

"It's great," she replied.

"How do you like living in California?"

"It's pretty. And I like how warm it is."

Ellington jumped into the conversation saying "I like getting to play music and not having to go to school."

"No school?" Johnny asked.

From her vantage point on her father's lap, Allie could tell that their father didn't even glance over at Ellington, but she could feel the chill emanating down *The Tonight Show* couch. "They go to school on the set," her father said.

"Oh yeah," El said, like he was trying to cover his tracks. "We go to show school with a tutor. I just like not having to spend the whole day there."

Of course you don't. Ingrate, Allie thought.

"Do you want to be a musician when you get older?"

"You mean do I want to *stay* a musician? Absolutely." Allie couldn't believe how stupid and, frankly, rude, her brother was being. She could tell their dad was already mad at him, so maybe Ellington figured Dad couldn't get any *more* mad. It wasn't the best logic, but she understood it.

"And what about you?" Johnny Carson asked Bix.

"Who me?" Bix said, and he managed to sound genuinely surprised that anyone was asking him a question. "I'm still trying to decide what I what I want to be when I grow up. Either a musician or an astronaut."

"An astronaut? Really?"

"No, I'm just kidding. Outer space scares me. Guess I'm stuck with musician," he replied and got a big laugh.

"And my friend Allegro here has already told me she wants to continue playing music, is that right?"

"Yes, I'm planning on being a concert violinist."

Johnny gave her a semi-impressed nod, as though nine-year-old girls weren't supposed to know that concert violinist was even a career option. "Wow, so not just any violinist. A concert violinist," he said. "You want to be the headliner."

Allie merely nodded and said, "Yes," which was clearly the only acceptable answer.

"Well, I for one am glad you all want to keep playing music, because you are an exceptionally talented family," Johnny said. "And make sure to tune into *The Musical Mozinskis*." He looked at Allie and asked "When was that?"

"Wednesday nights at eight-thirty," Allie said, on cue and with the proper level of cute.

"Wednesday nights at eight-thirty on this network." He shook Vincent's hand, thanked them for coming on the show, and the four children walked off the set and right back to the car so their father and Mr. Karpenko could take them back to their soundstage and back to work.

When the ratings started to go up, Karpenko maintained it was because *The Tonight Show* was great publicity. The producers said the show had just needed to find their audience. A small but vocal contingent (Ellington and Bix) told whoever would listen that it was because of El's solo on "ABC" because it proved that the Mozinskis weren't just another big family that sang. They could play.

BRIDGE OVER TROUBLED WATER

Somewhere during the fall of the first season, it occurred to the writers that Clara was a teenager and would, in fact, be turning 15 in December. This realization instituted two additions to the show: some truly horrible surly teenager jokes and the Birthday Solo. It was traditional in the family to give a solo performance in the living room on one's birthday, starting at age eight. It had become something of a family rite of passage. Playing as part of a group didn't count because it's far less stress-inducing. The Birthday Solo was a way to showcase one's growth as a musician over the past year, to challenge. On the show, it was a way to differentiate *The Musical Mozinskis* from *The Osmonds* and *The Jacksons* and all the other variety shows because the children played multiple instruments in multiple genres.

For Clara's 15th birthday, the writers recreated the family Birthday Solo on the living room set. The tenuous plotline of the episode was Clara arguing with her mother over being able to stay out late with her friends. This portion of the episode was entirely fictional because Clara didn't have any friends in California. The family had moved and gone straight into work on the show. Clara went to school on the set with her younger siblings and wrote letters back to her two best friends in Cleveland, so the idea of arguing with her parents over non-gig-related curfews tested Clara's limited acting skills. Still, she did her best.

When they rehearsed the argument scene with her mother, Don the Director told Clara that she was "wooden."

"I don't profess to be an actress, Mr. Kilgore," she replied. "Couldn't I just play my solo? I could do two pieces instead of one."

They were on the kitchen set with the crew, who were working to get the camera angles right and the lighting right, but Kilgore crossed through the no-man's-land that separated him and the cameras from the set, stopped in front of Clara, and put a hand on each of her upper arms. Even though they were surrounded by people, if her mother hadn't been standing next to her, Clara would have felt uncomfortable.

"Look, Clara, I know you aren't an actress. You are, however, an incredible musician."

"Thank you," she replied automatically, even though he was just getting started.

"When you're playing music, don't you ever...feel things? If you're playing a sad song, don't you feel sad too?"

"Sometimes."

"Or if you're playing a loud, fast song, doesn't it kind of perk you up?" Clara nodded, aware of where the conversation was going. "Can you pretend that this scene is like a loud, fast song that's getting you all riled up?"

"But a loud, fast song doesn't necessarily equate to anger, just energy. Usually, I feel happy."

"Okay." Kilgore stood up straight, removing his hands from her upper arms. He looked over at Grace, who was still waiting by the fake stove. Even though her musicianship exceeded that of her husband, the writers consistently had her doing "mom" things on the show, like cooking dinner or folding laundry. "Grace, help me out here."

Grace sighed and took a few steps over to her eldest child. "Clara, do you remember the last big talk we had before we moved?" Clara remembered but didn't say anything, so her mom added, "The talk where you told me and your father that you didn't want to move to California?"

"Yes," Clara replied quietly. She could feel everyone on the set watching, listening to the conversation. They didn't all have to know that she didn't want to be here. Clara spoke as carefully as Stacy telling Mr. Kilgore that Camera 2 was on the blink or that there were no more donuts. "As I recall, I merely asked if we could film the show in Cleveland so we wouldn't have to uproot the entire family by moving across the country."

Her mother lowered her voice a little, a small consideration for which Clara was grateful. "As *I* recall, you were very upset with me and your father because we had made a decision that we thought was best for the family, but you disagreed with it. Do you remember how you felt then?" Clara nodded. "I know it's hard to pull back a painful memory, but that's part of acting. Go back to that same emotional place where you were when you argued with me about moving but say the lines in the script. Can you do that?"

"I think so."

"That's great, sweetie. Okay, Don. Let's try this again," Grace said to Kilgore.

Clara tried thinking about the conversation — well, argument — she had with her parents before they moved. She tried remembering just how angry she was that they were pulling the entire family out of their home and out of their school and away from friends and how frustrating it was that they wouldn't even listen. When they ran through the scene again, Clara felt some of that same anger, and Mr. Kilgore and her mother told her it was much better.

On the show, she was supposed to go to her room and start playing the harp. For her Birthday Solo, she was playing and singing a version of "Bridge Over Troubled Water" arranged for solo harp. The sequence was supposed to look like she angrily runs to her room and works out the arrangement on the spot, when in reality it took her mother two weeks to create the arrangement for her. When her father made her learn bass because "There's no place for a harp in popular music," she had been determined to prove him wrong. With her mother's help, she was going to.

Clara had always thought the lyrics were the singer speaking to someone else. She loved the song, but singing it felt hollow because she wasn't anyone's bridge over troubled water. She wasn't a rock or a consolation for anyone. There's a line in the song about easing your mind when friends can't be found. That line always hit home because there had been so many times since they moved when Clara felt that she didn't have any friends. The first few months in California had been busy but lonely. There were moments when she wished she never suggested the song because singing that line made her unbelievably sad. It wasn't until the day they taped the episode and she was singing in front of the studio audience that she finally understood the song.

Clara and her harp were center stage with the family seated in front of her, the same way they would be if she was doing a Birthday Solo at home. As she sang the line about friends that can't be found, she glanced over at her mother and their eyes met. That's when it all made sense. Her mom was the one who always comforted her when she was feeling down and, as the song said, eased her mind. She was Clara's bridge over troubled water. She sang the rest of the song directly to her mother. When she finished, she thought she saw a small tear rolling down her mom's cheek. It could have been a trick of the light, but Sean on Camera 2 caught it too.

WIPE OUT

Ellington didn't lie to Johnny Carson; they really did go to school every day on the set, but it was akin to the one-room schoolhouse on Little House on the Stinking Prairie with just the six of them. He was inordinately proud to say he didn't learn much. He didn't have to, because he already had a job playing music. If the children weren't at the studio rehearsing for the show, they were home practicing. Monday morning meant a table-read for that week's script, then they'd have show school for a couple hours, go over blocking and staging, then more show school. The rest of the week was show school, rehearsals, and show school. The show taped on Friday evening, even though it didn't air until the following Wednesday. On the weekends, they practiced. That was their life, every single week.

Vincent didn't lie either. At least not about the show. *The Musical Mozinskis* really was sort of half variety show, half sitcom. Every episode had a thin plot that was really just an excuse for the family to perform some moderately related songs.

The executive producer of the show was a chunky, older white guy named Fritz Baker. The first time Ellington heard his name, all he could think of was *Fritz. As in 'The amplifier is on the fritz'? As in 'broken'?* When they started the show, he and his siblings thought Don the Director was the boss because he told them what to do each episode. After a few episodes, they realized that Fritz was in charge of the writers and the one who decided on the direction of the show. The first season, Ellington thought the direction must have been "Keep the show on the air so Karpenko can pay off the car note on his new Porsche," because there was no way Mr. Karpenko could have afforded that sweet ride back in Cleveland. After that, the direction seemed to be "Bring on more cute little Mozinskis to keep the show on the air." It seemed like the family was good on that front because they had Theo and Viola in reserve. Midway through the first season, Fritz started talking to Vincent and Grace about ways to introduce each of the kids. Focus groups showed that there were so many Mozinskis that audiences couldn't remember all of their names.

Whether or not you were a fan of the Birthday Solo depended on who you were. Competitive personalities like Ellington and Allegro thrived on it. Bix feigned apathy, but he loved showing off just as much as his father. Clara would have preferred keeping it a family-only tradition. Theo and Viola didn't have an opinion — at least not an opinion that counted — because you weren't expected to perform a Birthday Solo until your eighth birthday. Clara claimed this indicated at least some level of sensitivity on the part of their parents. Ellington always countered that it just meant their father had a healthy fear of Child Services. After Clara inaugurated the Birthday Solo, Ellington figured he'd be next, because his birthday was in February.

The family had three weeks off from doing the show around Christmas and New Year's. The children still had to practice for a few hours every day, but not having to go the studio or learn lines or go to show school felt like a vacation. The family's first house in California was in Altadena, a Spanish stucco claptrap that they had rented sight unseen when they got the contract for the show. The three boys shared the largest bedroom in Altadena. When Ellington complained and asked why they couldn't afford a bigger house, Grace told him they went smaller and cheaper to hedge their bets because they didn't know if the show would get cancelled.

On New Year's Day, the three boys were in their room racing slot cars that Bix had gotten for Christmas. Ellington was going on 14 and his newfound love of David Bowie and the New York Dolls were at odds with his father's musical choices for the show.

"There's no way Dad would let you do a Bowie song," Bix said. His car kept pulling ahead of Ellington's, but every time Ellington tried to pass him, he'd take the turn too fast and the car would go flying off the track.

"I know that. Bowie's stuff isn't drum-heavy anyway. It'd just be nice to do something a little different from all of the old man's cheesey crap. Like I was thinking about "Sing Sing Sing." He could do an arrangement for trumpet, trombone, and clarinet — you, Mom and Dad..."

"What about me?" Theo asked.

"What about you?"

"The horn section needs a saxophone," he said quietly.

"Maybe. Anyhow, Clara could still play bass, she could even play the upright, which she totally loves."

"That's not a bad idea," Bix says. "It'd give Dad a chance to channel his inner Benny Goodman."

Ellington hadn't thought of it quite like that, but it was a good idea. It was no secret that Vincent liked to show off.

The entire time they were talking, Theo was driving his car around the track super slowly. Ellington had lapped him eight times already. Theo was concentrating on his car and didn't even look up when he asked, "What about that surfing song with the drum solo? I can't remember the name of it."

Bix and Ellington asked, "What surfing song?" at the same time because it wasn't clicking. Then Theo scatted *ba-da-da-nana-nana-nana-nana-nana-nana-nah...*

Ellington was only half listening because Theo was seven and when does a seven-year-old have a good idea? He merely said, "That's the *Batman* theme," and lapped him again.

Bix said, "Oooohoohoo...wipeout!" in a voice that mimicked the lone vocal at the top of The Surfaris' one-hit wonder and Ellington realized what song Theo was talking about. It was actually a pretty good idea. He looked over at Theo and his car went flying off the track again. "'Wipe Out'?" Ellington asked as he got up to grab his car out of the corner. "I hadn't thought of that."

"That's what it's called? I didn't know," Theo said. "On the show you could pretend that you want to learn how to surf and Mom and Dad say no, and then you play the surfing song." The whole time he was speaking, he was watching his car while it crawled around the track. He might have been the slowest, but his car never once left the track.

"That's not a bad idea," Ellington said, and you'd think he just told Theo he won a million dollars or something. Theo smiled broadly, sat up a little straighter, and said, "Thanks." Ellington couldn't believe how simple that kid was sometimes.

"Plus, if you play "Wipe Out" then I can channel my inner Dick Dale," Bix said. Bix wasn't as bad as their father, but it was no secret he liked to show off a little too.

"Yeah. And it's the kind of song Vincent would pick."

Ellington figured he'd talk to Vincent after dinner, when his father might be in a receptive mood. Grace's Dutch heritage meant that the family always made *olliebollen* on New Year's Day. She said it was a Dutch tradition. Ellington loved that the name literally meant oil ball, because who doesn't like fried dough covered with powdered sugar? He could never figure out why his father didn't like them even though their Mozinski relatives made pretty much the exact same thing at Christmas and Vincent ate those. Did his father just prefer those because they were Polish and from his family? That seemed stupid because fried dough is fried dough, and fried dough is good. After dinner, Ellington scarfed down three *olliebollen* for dessert and then went off to talk to his father about his Birthday Solo.

In later years, most of the family agreed that the best thing about the place in Altadena was a small room in the back of the house that had two walls of windows. Normal people who weren't full of themselves would call it an office. The fact that Ellington's father called it a composing room just went to show you how annoying the guy could be. The baby grand the family bought after they arrived in California held a place of honor in the living room.The composing room was entirely their father's domain and held a Moog Polymoog Synthesizer that Vincent used for writing out music for the show and two bookshelves filled with stacks of music books and sheet music and fake books. There wasn't much in the way of furniture for sitting — just the bench by the synthesizer. The permanent features on top of the Moog were an ashtray, a hard pack of Marlboro Red cigarettes, and his father's Zippo lighter, plus alternating piles of sheet music and an assortment of Palomino Blackwing pencils of varying lengths. The most distinguishing feature of these soft black pencils was the super-cool rectangular eraser that slid in and out of a thin aluminum holder. The younger kids were forever taking the pencils so they could play with the erasers. Ellington had done the same thing when he was little, even though it pissed off his father to no end because he claimed that Blackwings were the only pencils he could write music with.

Ellington wasn't known for his manners, but he figured it couldn't hurt to be polite since he was sort of asking his father for something. He stopped in the doorway and even knocked as he asked, "Hey Dad, can I talk to you?" injecting as much Wally Cleaver into his voice as he could.

His father looked up and said, "Of course," but didn't put down his pencil. Ellington figured he had two minutes, tops, to make his case.

"What are you working on?" he asked, because why not start out with a little small talk? It's what his mom would have done.

"Something we might be able to record this summer," Vincent replied.

"Cool." Ellington knew the family was supposed to cut a new album during summer vacation, but if there were any songs for it, nobody had told him. It seemed like a good idea to cut to the chase because the clock was ticking, so he nonchalantly said, "I just wanted to ask you about my Birthday Solo."

"Your what?"

Vincent heard him. Ellington didn't stutter and nobody ever needed to ask him to speak up. His father just liked making him work.

"My Birthday Solo," he repeated. "I figured since Clara did hers that it was going to become a regular thing. You know, instead of just doing the Birthday Solo for the family we'd do it as part of the show. The whole 'family of musicians' thing..."

He was starting to babble, which doesn't help when talking to a tough audience. His father was just sitting there at the Moog, pencil in his right hand, giving him this blank look. Finally, after a suitably dramatic pause, he said, "You already had a solo this season."

"No, I haven't."

"What do you call the little stunt you pulled on Carson a couple months ago?"

And there it was, he'd walked right into his father thinking he was freaking Perry Mason. Still Ellington didn't give up, saying "I played a drum solo as part of a song. It wasn't on the show."

Vincent went off on a long "How would it look if you got two solos this season and everybody else only got one?" rant, and every time Ellington tried to say "No, I didn't," his father kept repeating, "You already *took* a solo." Finally, his father said "To be honest, I'm not sure the audience is ready for an unaccompanied drum solo," and gave an overly hearty, fake-sounding chuckle, like they'd been having a nice father-son chat. Then he said, "Go wash your face. You've got powdered sugar on your cheek." That was it. He told Ellington he had work to do and kicked him out of the room.

Bix told Ellington to forget it, but he was probably just happy Vincent left him alone. Their father was like an elephant — piss him off once and he would never forget it. Ellington considered his situation. His father was already mad at him. In fact, it could be argued that his father was constantly mad at him. At least it felt that way sometimes. It wasn't like he could get more angry, which is why when Christmas break was over and they were back at the studio, Ellington decided to go over his father's head.

Like all of the Mozinski children, Ellington had only ever talked to Fritz the Producer at the meet-and-greet before the first table-read where they all had to introduce themselves, and Fritz said he was a big fan of the drums. Whenever their producer talked to them on the set, he spoke to them as a collective, like "Hey, how's everybody doing today?" and "Who's ready to make some music?" He knew all of their names and the instruments they played, but Fritz directed all conversation to the unholy triumvirate of Mom, Dad, and Karpenko. He didn't really know the kids individually. Ellington decided to change that on the first day back after break when he went to the writers' room.

The writers' room was in another building. Ellington kind of knew where it was because they passed it on the way to the commissary. It wasn't that hard to find. A couple of people looked at him twice, like they weren't sure he belonged there, but *The Musical Mozinskis* was doing well enough in the ratings that the security guard in the writers' building looked at him and said, "You're one of those music kids, right?"

"Yeah," Ellington replied.

"What instrument you play?"

"Drums."

The guard nodded and said, "Yeah, yeah, you're real good, man," and let him in the building. Piece of cake. A building directory with a black background and white plastic letters was posted on the wall by the elevator, like in the medical building back home where their old family dentist was. He found the room number and walked up to the third floor. The door to their writers' room was half-open and Ellington could see four or five people in there. He gave the door frame his signature marcato knock — three raps, quiet loud quiet — and poked his head in the room.

He had always imagined the writers' room was like a living room with a bunch of typewriters, but it was just a conference room with a long table and a bunch of chairs and a couple of windows. Way more boring than he'd thought. Almost pathetic. There were three little metal desks along the walls, spaced a few feet apart like they didn't want people copying off of each other. Ellington could never remember the writers' names except for Jerry, who was only in his late 20s and already balding and who was always telling lame jokes that even Viola thought were stupid, and she was only four. Jerry was in the room along with Fritz and a few other guys.

"Hi, I'm Ellington Mozinski," he said, even though they had to know who he was because they were forced to watch the show every week.

The five of them sat there staring at Ellington for a minute, then Fritz stood up and switched into what seemed like Overly Happy to See You Mode. Ellington would have sworn Fritz's voice went up three steps as he said, "Hey there, Ellington. Good to see you. To what do I owe this surprise visit?"

Even if Fritz was probably about five seconds away from calling his parents, Ellington figured that since he was there, he might as well talk. For a brief instant, he regretted not bringing Bix along with him because of how good he was at schmoozing people. Then he thought *Screw it. I can do this.*

Ellington walked a few more steps into the room until he was standing at the head of the long table. He put his hands on the back of the closest chair and went right into his pitch: "So I had this idea for the show. You know how Clara had a Birthday Solo? My birthday is next, on February 22nd, and I was thinking we could do an episode where I want to learn how to surf and my mom and dad say no, and then we have some nice come-together, touchy-feelie moment where I realize they're just concerned for my safety, and then I play "Wipe Out" for my Birthday Solo." Fritz and the four writers just kept staring at him, and Ellington honestly wasn't sure if he was being clueless or they were. "You know the song 'Wipe Out'?" he added, because maybe they didn't know. They were writers, not musicians. "Big drum solo. Iconic." Jenny the Tutor had taught him enough that he sort of knew that the word "iconic" meant kind of classic, something everybody knew. It seemed like a description the writers would like.

Fritz looked at Jerry, then at one of the other guys and kind of tilted his head to the side, just enough to show that maybe he liked the idea, but all he said was, "We'll think about it, Ellington."

"But it's a really good idea," Ellington said, trying not to sound too desperate. Desperate didn't get things done.

Fritz sighed. "I'm not saying it's not a good idea, but we need to see if it would fit in with the larger trajectory of the show. Do you understand what that means?"

"Yeah," Ellington replied. "I understand." He understood enough — they were gonna to be dicks about it.

"Thanks for sharing your idea with us. We will definitely consider it."

There wasn't anything else to say except "Thanks," and try to walk out like they didn't just shoot down his idea because he was a kid. As Ellington walked down the hall, trying to figure out who to ask next, he faintly heard one of the writers start scatting the iconic "Wipe Out" guitar riff *ba-da-da-nana-nana-nana-nana-nana-nana-nah* and realized they liked the idea after all.

Two weeks later when Vincent told Ellington, Bix, Allie, and Clara that they needed to start rehearsing "Wipe Out" because Ellington would be playing it for his Birthday Solo, he acted surprised. His father was not as good at not acting pissed off. You can easily get used to having someone be constantly annoyed with you if it doesn't really affect you. His father might have been the music director, but that wasn't the reason people tuned in to the show. As long as Ellington didn't piss off Kilgore or Fritz, he was golden.

RAGE OVER A LOST PENNY

When Ellington claimed that the ratings went up because of his solo on *The Tonight Show*, everybody said it was just a coincidence. When he said that he was the one who made the Birthday Solos a regular thing on the show, the other kids knew it was true. Sure Bix and Theo gave him the idea, but he was the one who talked to Fritz and made it happen. Whether or not the Birthday Solos were a good thing depended on who you were and how large your ego was. Regardless of how you felt about it, after "Wipe Out," the Birthday Solo became an expected — and popular — feature on the show. The show's design didn't allow for long plot arcs or extensive character development. What kept viewers tuning in was the music. The Birthday Solo offered anticipation, even a little mystery, as the studio's publicity team made it clear that the children selected what they would play. This wasn't entirely true, but who cared? The Birthday Solos rarely occurred in alignment with someone's actual birthday. For instance, Allie's birthday was in March, but the writers put her birthday episode as the Season 1 finale, five weeks after her real birthday. As Mr. Karpenko frequently said, "Eh, is show business. Sometimes you must pretend."

Vincent would give the children the arrangements for the songs they'd be playing on the show a couple weeks in advance so they'd have time to rehearse, but they wouldn't get the script for the episode until the table-read. Allie had been practicing two pieces for her first Birthday Solo: Bach's Sonata No. 3 for solo violin and on piano, Beethoven's Rondo Capriccio in G Major, also known as *Rage over a Lost Penny*. Her older brothers teased her that she got to play two pieces because she was their dad's favorite. Every time one of her siblings said something like this, Allie brushed them off, saying something like "No, I'm not. Dad's favorite is Dad."

Any parent who feels the need to proclaim frequently and publicly that they don't have a favorite child is, unfortunately, lying. Allegro was indeed Vincent's favorite. It wasn't because she was the least trouble. That honor would have gone to Clara. It wasn't because she possessed the greatest multi-instrument talent. Bix and Theo both exceeded her on that front. It wasn't because she was the sweetest. That was Viola. It wasn't a shared love of jazz. The family's not-so-secret secret was that Allie couldn't jam. Her uncluttered, organized mind was never able to let loose, to unwind, deconstruct, and put a melody back together. It was one of the few concepts that eluded her. Because she didn't understand jazz and couldn't play it, she didn't like it. Ellington had far more in common with their father in that regard. Where Allegro and Vincent overlapped was in their ambition and focus. In his middle daughter, Vincent saw a mirror of his own desire for success.

The plots of *The Musical Mozinskis* were admittedly weak — they were simply hooks to hang the music on. Even so, the writing team outdid themselves in mediocrity for the episode around Allie's first Birthday Solo. The kind-of plot was young Allegro trying to decide whether she wanted yellow cake or chocolate cake for her birthday. In the end, Grace saves the day by making a double cake — half yellow, half chocolate. That was it. That was the big dramatic plot. With music. And bad jokes, mostly from Jerry, who was the only writer to stay on the show all four years. Allie thought that fact alone was a huge indicator of Jerry's level of talent.

At the table-read, the family, Don, Fritz, and Stacy the AD would sit around a large rectangular table and read the script out loud, each person reading their part and Stacy reading stage directions and filling in for anyone not present, such as the musical guests, who only showed up on taping day. The writers would sit in a few extra chairs in a ring outside the table.

Allie was excited going into the table-read for the final episode of Season 1. She'd been waiting months for a chance to truly demonstrate her playing. The Bach and the Beethoven were ready. She was ready.

Then they got to the part about the cake. At first it seemed kind of cute in a Storyline B sort of way. The episode opened with a scene with her parents where she's supposed to get upset about the cake because she can't choose. Then she talks to her siblings, and Bix, Clara, Theo, and Ellington play the old The Lovin' Spoonful tune "Did You Ever Have to Make up Your Mind?" She had heard them practicing the song with Theo on rhythm guitar in her place. Allie's character was just supposed to sit and pout the whole song, which honestly wasn't going to be that hard. Then she got to the Act II climax heart-to-heart talk scene with her mother in which her character is genuinely agonizing over whether to choose yellow cake or chocolate cake and realized there was no Storyline A. This was it. Her entire first birthday episode was about cake.

She glanced across the table at Ellington and Bix, who were not doing a very good job containing their laughter. Clearly, even the densest members of her family thought it was stupid too. She looked up and said to the table at large, "I'm sorry, but I can't do this."

Her parents both looked at her, then at each other, then at Fritz. He was staring right back at them. Finally, Fritz asked "What do you mean, Allie?"

Allie gave a little sigh. She knew what she had to say wasn't going to be popular, but you can't make an omelet without breaking a few eggs. "I can't do this script," she said. "This decision simply isn't that important."

"Birthday cake is very important," Fritz said. "Especially to a 10-year-old."

"Not this 10-year-old," Allie replied.

On the other side of the table, Ellington faked a cough to keep from laughing. Bix patted him on the back as though El really was choking. No one else said anything, they just looked back and forth between Allie and Fritz. Then Bix said, "I think what Allie means is that the whole cake decision seems out of character for her. That's not who she is."

During the four years of the show, Fritz the Producer only showed his anger in front of the cast twice. This was the first time. He spoke very slowly and deliberately. "Out of character? The writing team and the producer determine your character on this program. That character is reflected in the script."

Allie could see Fritz was getting angry, but she had no desire to back down. This inane script did not depict her accurately. "I thought we were playing ourselves," she said, and realized she might have accidentally raised her voice just a little. Who cared? Growing up with Ellington and Bix had taught her to be prepared to fight at any moment.

Everybody was quiet for a second, then her mother said, "You're all playing an interpretation of yourselves. Remember that this is still fiction. It's make-believe."

"It's not fiction. The show is about our family. We're playing *ourselves*, using our real names, and *I* don't agonize over yellow cake or chocolate cake."

Given a few more minutes, Grace might have been able to smooth things out. Her peace-keeping effort was derailed by Vincent, who snapped, "Allegro, enough." It was the same tone her father had used with her at the Bicentennial after she duckwalked during his solo. Allie was not a fan of backing down, but she knew a lost cause when she saw it. "Sorry, Fritz," her father said. "All of the kids will follow the script and do their parts and deliver a great season finale." Allie was sure she didn't imagine the extra emphasis he put on the word "all."

It felt like the Great Oz had spoken, but the tension around the table was still high. Bix broke the silence by saying "You know what's nice, Allie? Since the episode is all about you trying to make a choice, you get to do two solos instead of one."

Clara joined in. "That's true. I only got to do one."

It was sweet to have her siblings try to make her feel better. And a little patronizing. Mostly patronizing. Ellington give a little jump and Allie figured Clara must have kicked him under the table because he said, "Yeah, I only got one solo too. And I had to share it with doofus boy." He elbowed Bix as he said this. Bix elbowed Ellington. He elbowed Bix back. Bix responded with a punch and the fight was on until their father broke it up. Usually, her brothers were merely annoying. This was one of the few occasions where Allegro was just the slightest bit grateful to them for causing a distraction. If she were up against her father or even Don the Director, she would have kept fighting. They were weak. Fritz had the clout to shut her down. *We're the only family I know where the only way to stop a fight is to start another one*, she thought.

Since Theo was playing rhythm guitar on "Did You Ever Have to Make Up Your Mind?" Fritz decided that Viola had to play on it too in order to round things out. The youngest Mozinski had been safely relegated to tambourine for all finales. It was her musical safe haven. Grace had asked Ellington to keep an eye on Viola because the tambourine was a percussion instrument and you didn't say no to Mom. Ellington didn't like having to play babysitter. He always told Viola to stand in the back near his drum kit and lightly tap the tambourine whenever she saw his foot hitting the bass drum. That kept her marginally on the beat, although on playbacks he never actually heard the tambourine. He never bothered to ask her about it. Everything else on the show was pretend, why not Viola's playing?

The final scene of Allie's birthday episode had the entire family crowded around the kitchen table to sing "Happy Birthday." In a classic "Why not do both?" move, Grace cut the cake to show that it was half yellow and half chocolate. Don made them run through that part of the scene at least 20 times in rehearsal to get El and Bix to act surprised without them doing pratfalls in faux shock.

Having the entire family sing "Happy Birthday" to Allie took the place of the standard finale. In true Mozinski fashion, they sang it in three-part harmony. Ellington and Bix usually stood next to each other during family events. This was make-believe, so Don positioned Ellington next to Viola. It was the first time he had stood close enough to his youngest sister to hear her sing. Viola was off. Not just a little bit but really off-key. Ellington could see the music hanging in the air in front of him, the entire staff showing everything his family was singing, and off to the side were these sad little notes flopping around where they didn't belong. The audience was singing along too, so nobody really noticed unless their last name was Mozinski. Allie definitely noticed. Ellington watched as Allie's cheeks started to flush a pink and her eyes turn a darker shade of blue the way they always did when she got angry.

After the show taped, there were usually fans waiting around outside the soundstage. If there were, the whole family was obliged to go out and sign autographs or take photos. Ellington didn't mind signing autographs. It was like Doc said — make the audience think you're friends with them. Plus, sometimes there were girls around his age who wanted an autograph or a hug. He definitely didn't mind that.

The Cake Episode, as it would be referred to for the next 40 years, was the final episode of the season. There was no question that the entire family had to go out and sign autographs afterward. Ellington thought the crowd seemed bigger than normal. It looked like half the studio audience was hanging around to meet them. Karpenko and a couple of guys from the crew were around to run interference. Karpenko was supposed to be their manager, but El never saw him actually do anything that seemed useful except for keeping the littler kids from getting smushed by adoring fans.

Ellington was standing back-to-back with Bix, signing his name on whatever piece of paper somebody shoved into his hand. Having strangers tell you they love you is a total rush, so he had never minded signing autographs. At the beginning of the season, the studio tried to make the fans get in line, but it never worked. The working strategy was to divide and conquer. The family paired off in different spots, so instead of one huge mob there were scattered bunches of people. It made for decent crowd control. Ellington was out there signing and smiling and shaking hands for about half an hour. After a while, the crowd started to thin out, and he could see his mother and Viola standing a little ways away from him and Bix. Allie and Clara and Vincent and Theo were farther away. The studio had stacks of 8x10 glossy black-and-white photos of the entire family that they gave out after the show. Ellington was signing a small stack for a group of five girls. They were the last people waiting for him and Bix. There were two women who looked like they might be a couple of their moms talking to his mom and Viola.

One of the girls talking to Ellington was really stacked, even though she was probably only his age, so Ellington was liberally doling out the hugs. He was getting in one last squeeze when the two moms walked over. One of them was saying to the other one very loudly, "That little one is so cute. And I love how they have her sing off-key."

"Oh, I know," the other mom said. "It's adorable."

Ellington wasn't sure how to react to what the woman had said. It was true. Viola did sing off-key, but somehow hearing some stranger say it annoyed him. Bix put a hand on his shoulder and said to the girls,

"Sorry, we need to go." He managed to pull Ellington away from the girl with the good rack and over to where Karpenko was standing with their mother and Viola. Karpenko had one hand on Viola's shoulder. Ellington thought he looked like a big, hairy Ukrainian guard dog.

"She heard," Bix said quietly and went over to Viola and took her hand. "I'll walk in with you guys," he said and the two of them went inside with Karpenko. Ellington been so distracted by girls and boobs that he hadn't noticed the rest of the family was already gone. The two guys from the crew were shooing stragglers away, so it was just him and his mom left.

"You want to go in?" he asked.

"Yes," his mother replied, but she wasn't looking at him. She was looking over his shoulder, past him, at the two moms and the group of girls. Ellington had seen his mother upset and exasperated and even angry. Often at him. But he had never seen this "I-will-destroy-you" look before.

"I can't believe I signed an autograph for that bitch," his mother said. "Come on," and she led the way back into the studio. There was nothing else to do but follow her. From then on, Viola only mouthed the words. Ellington never heard her sing again.

LAZY DAY

There were times when Bix Mozinski felt like everything in his life came back to the Chuck Berry duckwalk. When he thought about it — and he did so often — he realized that if he hadn't done the duckwalk way back during the Bicentennial special, his and his family's lives might have unfurled very differently. No one would dispute that they were talented children, although there were times when he had felt less like a child and more like a performing monkey. Even as young kids, they were good enough for people to watch without changing the channel. Having a cute, curly-haired ten-year-old do the duckwalk though, well, that had been a game-changer. It made them stand out.

When he was older, music journalists and fan bloggers would speculate that Vincent Mozinski was just transferring all his musical aspirations onto his children. More specifically onto Bix, who grew up hearing his father privately claim that he had made the children famous. Bix never disputed his father's considerable talent, but it really seemed like his dad got that one bass-ackwards. If it wasn't for his children, Vincent Mozinski would never have been successful. Bix didn't fault his dad for pushing him to practice. He didn't fault his dad for making him the front man. But he sure as hell faulted his dad for what happened with Viola.

By the end of the show's first season, the family was legitimately famous. Especially Bix. The front man almost always gets the bulk of the attention. He hadn't had too much of an opportunity to enjoy or even think about his new fame. In later years, he felt like he ought to put air quotes around the phrase "child star." It didn't seem like they were stars at all. He was just playing music with his family. It didn't really dawn on

Susan Petrone

him that maybe his family had become different until the summer after the first season of the show.

The little house in Altadena was in a neighborhood that turned out to be mostly older people. If there were other kids living nearby, Bix never saw them. Then again, he was rarely home except to sleep. Everything important took place on the soundstage or at the recording studio. His parents bought the Pasadena house as soon as they found out the show was being renewed for a second season and the family moved that spring. Pasadena felt a little more like home. There were other families with kids. The neighborhood looked different from where they had lived in Cleveland. The trees and the architecture and the layout of the neighborhood all looked different, but the feel was the same. There were other houses with kids living in them. And it was summer and he didn't have to be at the studio all the time. Bix and his siblings still had to practice every day, but it seemed like he'd have at least a little bit of time to explore the neighborhood and maybe even make some friends.

The houses in their new neighborhood seemed to fall into three categories: modern, with lots of flat facades and right angles instead of peaked gables; stucco, in what his mom said was Spanish style; or bungalows. Their new house was a classic Craftsman bungalow but big, five bedrooms and a full basement. It was bigger than the house in Altadena, but not as big as the one back in Cleveland. That one had been built in 1926 and had six bedrooms, so that only two of the children had had to share a bedroom. The Cleveland house was a big wood and brick center-hall colonial, with dark varnished wood floors and trim. Bix always thought it'd fit in well in an old MGM movie. It was also drafty and impossible to heat, and his parents had bought it for a song when they got married in 1961. Almost all of the houses in their old neighborhood were similar. The Pasadena house reminded him a tiny bit of their old house back home. Sometimes Bix had to stop himself and remember that home was now here in California, not Cleveland.

All of the Mozinski children learned to play piano on the beat-up old upright with the C above middle C key that always stuck. The piano had a place of honor in the living room of the house in Cleveland but didn't make the move to California. Grace placed an ad in the *Cleveland Press* and sold it for $50 the month before they moved because they

92

needed to make a deposit with the moving company, but the advance check from the network hadn't arrived yet. Vincent counted the chickens before they hatched and ordered a baby grand piano to be delivered to the Altadena house. Bix loved the new piano. He actually stepped up his practicing once he didn't have to deal with the stupid sticking key. He didn't love it when they moved to Pasadena and his father ritualistically demanded that the baby grand be the first item brought into the new house. The entire family was standing in front of the Pasadena house, waiting to start carrying in boxes and suitcases and grumbling about their dad while the movers unloaded some chairs and boxes and other small things and set them on the front lawn. Bix could almost have dealt with this until one of the guys from the moving company referred to the baby grand as the first piece of "furniture," and his dad actually thought it necessary to correct him.

"It's an instrument, not furniture," his father said in a tone so grandiose it seemed he expected the movers genuflect to the piano. They didn't; they just moved it in the house.

The family taped the last show of the first season on a Friday in late May. Not only was taping done for the summer, so was show school. Everybody passed to their next grade — even Ellington — so Bix thought they'd finally have some time to just hang around and enjoy summer vacation. The house in Pasadena had an in-ground swimming pool, which was a huge selling point as far as he was concerned. The only people he knew who had built-in swimming pools were rich, because in northeast Ohio, you can only use a pool four or five months out of the year. It seemed like half the houses on their new street had one. The morning after the last taping, all six children went out to the pool. They didn't plan it — they just all wanted to do the same thing at the same time. Bix had loved going to the neighborhood pool back in Cleveland Heights, but Viola and Theo were both too young to remember that. They were making up for lost time. Viola had just turned five, but she could already dog-paddle almost as fast as Allie could swim. Even though they were only half-moved into the new house, Grace came out and played in the pool with the children too. Up until that day, Bix didn't know she could swim — really swim. She demonstrated the breast stroke for the kids, and once Ellington had stopped giggling about the word "breast," all six of them tried to learn it. His mom stayed outside with them almost the entire day. The only time she went inside was to make lunch. Their dad was somewhere inside, working on music or unpacking or something.

The only pool furniture they had were two plastic chairs and a chaise lounge that had been left behind by the previous owners. Pool furniture was far down on the to-do list. Around three in the afternoon, Bix was lying on a towel next to the lounger, kind of half on the concrete by the pool and half on the grass. His mom was on the lounger. He thought she was asleep but she rolled onto her side and looked down at him on his towel on the ground.

"Do you want to switch places, sweetie?" she asked. "I've had the lounger long enough."

"No, thanks. I'm fine." Truth be told, Bix did want to switch but felt like she deserved to be comfortable. His mom was easily a better musician than his dad, but she generally stayed in the background, playing whatever arrangements their dad wrote and keeping everyone in line. It seemed like she ought to get something nice once in a while.

"You're very sweet. Thank you," his mom replied, and Bix could have sworn she knew what he was thinking. She sat up and adjusted the lounger so she was sitting up. The first thing she did was a quick scan to make sure everybody was okay. They were. The other kids were playing Marco Polo in the water. Viola had a little blow-up floatie ring around her waist because she wasn't tall enough to keep her head above water even if she was standing in the very shallowest part of the pool. Clara was staying close to her too, just in case. "You can go and play, if you want. You don't need to keep me company," she added.

"I like hanging out with you." This was true. Sometimes just being in the same place as his mom made him happy. Bix always thought of this as one of her superpowers, right up there with her ability to write a catchy pop music bridge.

"Well, thanks," she replied with a big smile. "I like hanging out with you too." It looked like she was satisfied that nobody was drowning, and El and Allie weren't even fighting, which was as close to perfect as their family was going to get, so she settled back in the lounger. "Nothing to do but be with you..." she murmured.

"On a lovely lazy day," Bix said in a sing-songy voice as he stretched out on his towel. He wasn't sure where those words came from, but as soon as he said it, his mom sat up again.

"You know what? You take the lounger. I have some work I need to do inside."

"You sure?"

She was already standing up and wrapping her towel around her waist, even though they'd both been baking in the sun long enough that her suit had to be dry. "Positive." She squatted down and gave Bix a kiss on top of the head. "Thanks for the line."

For one glorious weekend, they didn't have to do anything. Bix practiced, and his mom made all of the children at least start unpacking the things in their rooms, but mostly he stayed out in the pool with his siblings. Then on Monday morning, his dad said they were having a family meeting in the living room. There were still boxes and stuff piled all over the place. The grand piano was there, of course. No matter what house they lived in, the piano went in the living room. So did the old dark green sofa and matching easy chair from the Cleveland house, along with the six-foot-high dark brown bookshelf that held music theory books, a musical dictionary, an encyclopedia of music history in four volumes, sheet music, and fake books, plus random art books and novels and books that somebody in the family didn't like enough to keep in their room but didn't want to get rid of either. The bookshelf was only half full at this point because nobody had felt motivated enough to try and organize it.

Bix had just eaten two bowls of Lucky Charms and all he wanted to do was go out and play in the pool or maybe take a bike ride to explore their new neighborhood. He and Ellington were sitting on the sofa making sure that everybody else knew they were bored and didn't want to be there. Clara was sitting next to them until El farted. Then she said, "You're disgusting," and sat on the floor next to Viola. Theo had been squished into the end of the sofa, but now he spread out a bit.

"Boys only," he said proudly.

Allie was hogging the easy chair that was catty-corner from the sofa. She rolled her eyes and said, "Pigs only."

"Oink," Ellington burped.

Bix managed to burp out a solid "Piggy" and they both burst into laughter.

"Guys, enough, all right?" Dad said. He and their mom were by the piano going over some hand-written sheet music.

Theo tried to burp "Sorry," but he'd never been able to burp on command, so it sounded more like a cough.

"Loser," El muttered.

"Can you all be quiet, please?" Their dad stood in the middle of the living room while their mom sat down at the piano. They all shut up. "I have some really exciting news."

"Are we getting a puppy?" Viola asked.

"No."

"Then I'm not excited."

"This summer, we are recording our second album." No one said anything because they already knew they were going to be recording a new album. That wasn't a surprise, and it wasn't really exciting anymore either. "We're also going on tour."

Clara, Allie, and Bix said, "What?" at the same time El said, "You're kidding," and Theo said, "Really?" and Viola said, "Everybody?" A tour was definitely a little more exciting.

"Not a big tour. We're just doing a handful of dates in August — three weeks, 14 shows, most of them at beautiful outdoor venues."

"Why are you just telling us this now?" Clara asked. She was generally quiet, but she was also the oldest. Bix was happy to let her take on the role of chief negotiator because Ellington always made their dad mad and the other kids were too young.

"This is plenty of notice — it's not like we're leaving tomorrow. We didn't want to say anything until everything was firmed up. Now we have a lot to do before the tour. The new album will be half covers, half new material. Your mother and I have some great new songs to play for you. We're going to be rehearsing the new stuff over the next seven weeks, and we go into the studio at the end of July."

Bix was grateful Clara actually paid attention in show school because apparently she was the only one who could figure out dates in her head. "Wait, seven weeks?" she asked. "The end of July is like seven weeks from today."

"Yep!" their dad replied and looked way too happy about it. He was greeted with what you might call a chorus of disapproval.

"So basically, our summer vacation lasted two days," El said. Their dad opened his mouth to say something else but Mom stood up and put her hand on his arm to stop him.

"Everybody," she began, "please don't worry. We'll make sure you all have time to do other things this summer. We'll have fun." She half turned her head to Dad. "Should we tell them where the tour is going?"

"Why not? We're doing a couple of dates here in California, but most of them will be in the Midwest. The last show of the tour will be in Cleveland. At Cain Park Amphitheater. And we'll stay there a couple extra days so you can see your grandparents and some of your old friends."

Now this was cool. Bix wanted to see his two best friends, Michael Winchester and Tom Shea. They had written him one long joint letter, and he sent them each a postcard with pictures of Hollywood on them, and his mom let him call them during Christmas vacation, but that was it. Bix wasn't big on writing letters or talking on the phone. Now he'd be able to see them in person. And Cain Park was actually near where they used to live. He hoped they might be able to go by their old house too. When they moved out to California the year before, everything seemed rushed, like they didn't really have time to say goodbye. Now he could. He was thinking and saying all this to Ellington who was talking at the same time. Everyone was talking and no one was listening because going back home for a show was pretty cool. The family meeting was derailed until their dad played a loud A minor with a diminished 6th chord on the piano that looked like a storm cloud over his head and they all settled down a little bit.

Their parents didn't even give them time to think about seeing their old friends because they wanted to play the new songs for the album. There were seven new songs and four covers. Their mom wrote five of the new ones while some hired gun had written the others. Bix's favorite was one of his mom's called "From the Bottom to the Top" because it had a great beat that he knew Ellington would be able to do all sorts of funky things with. It seemed like it would be fun to sing, too.

The first three covers were okay, then his dad launched into the opening chords of "One Fine Day" on the piano. Bix dug how it opened, with the C alternating with A minor. It made him sit up and listen. His mom sang lead with his dad doing the *shoo-be-doo-be-doo-be-doo-be doo-wop-wops*. Bix had heard it before on the radio and liked it as far as he liked girl songs.

"You're gonna want me for your girl?" he said when they were done. "I'm not singing that."

"You're not singing it. Clara's going to sing lead on that one."

Everyone all looked over at Clara, who was sitting on the floor with Viola playing Cat's Cradle with a long piece of yarn while they listened. Clara had a great mezzo-soprano voice. When she was 10, she sang and played "Danny Boy" on the harp on St. Patrick's Day and it made their Grandfather Klinefelter weep buckets, and he wasn't even Irish. Bix knew she could crush the vocals but thought his parents were making a big mistake because Clara didn't have the personality or the desire to front the band, not even on one song. His older sister looked at their dad like he had just told her she was going to eat a live cockroach.

"I am?" she asked.

"Yes!" their dad said, standing up from the piano. "We want to make sure everybody gets a chance to shine. And then next season, you'll sing it on the show."

"Do I have a choice?"

"Just sing it," Bix and Ellington said at the same time.

"Did you know it's one of Fritz's favorite songs?" Vincent added.

"No."

When Clara didn't say anything else, Allie piped up. "If Clara doesn't want to do it, I'll sing it."

"Well, you'll sing *on* it..." their mom started to say.

"Yes, you'll do backup," Dad added. "And in a few years when Viola's a little older, I can see the three of you doing all sorts of great girl groups covers. Maybe even an old Andrews Sisters' tune." He turned back to their mom and asked if she wanted to play the last song. If he had looked at Clara and Viola, really looked at them, he might have seen how worried they both looked, even if it was for different reasons.

"I have to play this one," his mom said as she sat down at the piano. "The lead sheet is still half in my head and the other half is illegible."

Their dad gave a little bow and a flourish with his arm like a ringmaster introducing the flying trapeze artist and said, "Ladies and gentlemen — and Ellington (Bix snort-laughed at that) — I give you Grace Klinefelter Mozinski."

"This is called 'Lazy Day,'" his mom said, and Bix could swear she gave him a little wink. As she played the arpeggiated opening chords — C, F-minor, G, C — it suddenly it felt like he was lying on a raft in the middle of peaceful lake on a warm, sunny day. It sounded like pure bliss. And then she started singing:

> *Nothing to do but be with you on a lovely lazy day.*
> *Worries seem to slip away on a lovely lazy day.*

If Bix hadn't known where the song came from and when she wrote it, he might have thought it was a love song. As he listened, he realized it was her love song to him and his siblings. To her kids. He wondered if maybe he wasn't the right person to sing this one, that maybe his mom ought to sing it.

His dad was accompanying her on the old acoustic guitar that Bix had learned to play on, just strumming along and doing a little harmony on the chorus. No matter who or what he was listening to, Bix saw the music as notes in the air like they were written neatly on a staff. One of the few exceptions to this was when he listened to his parents play music together. There was something about the particular combination of her music and his that made the notes kind of dance back and forth, as though their music was flirting with each other. Listening to them play "Lazy Day" for the first time, Bix watched as those graceful arpeggios from his mother mingled with the simple strummed chords from his father in what seemed like a delicate little dance. He figured if he ever met someone whose music mingled with his like that, he'd probably marry her too.

Vincent wasn't lying when he said they were going to start rehearsing that day. He had apparently found the copy machine at the local library even before they found the nearest grocery store, because he handed each child a photocopied stack of arrangements. Bix noticed his stack of music was thicker than everyone else's, which meant he would be playing on every track. Theo's pile of music was the smallest, but he was still only seven. He could play a passable rhythm guitar and saxophone, but his primary instrument was the cello. No matter how prodigiously talented Theo was on cello, their father didn't see a place for it in pop music. Bix looked through the music quickly, just seeing how many songs they had him singing lead on. Around him, his siblings were rifling through their music too. Bix looked up to ask his dad when they'd get the sheets for "Lazy Day" and noticed Viola had scooted away from Clara and was sitting by herself near the half-emptied boxes by the bookcase. Her hands were empty.

"Vincent?" his mom said, and for a second it looked like she wanted to kill him. For an instant, Bix almost agreed with her. "You forgot something."

His dad looked around and saw Viola. She was hugging her knees and staring at the floor in front of her, not meeting anyone else's eyes. The other children stopped what they were doing and looked up from their music. Their dad didn't have anything else in his hands. Bix didn't see another pile of sheet music on the piano. There was obviously no music for Viola. For a moment no one moved, no one spoke. His mom was still behind the piano, but she moved their father out of the way and quickly walked across the room and knelt down next to Viola.

"You are playing on this record. I want you on tambourine. I want you singing back up. And I have a couple of ideas for 'Lazy Day' and 'From the Bottom to the Top' that I want your help with. I know you're still learning to read music, so I'm going to work with you on your parts, okay?"

Viola looked up and said quietly, "Okay." It felt like his mother had just broken some evil spell. Bix didn't even realize he'd been holding his breath, but now that Mom had matters in hand, he took a slow, deep breath. It was the only thing he could think to do. Nothing else seemed right. And for the first time, he didn't know what to say to help make things better. If it had been any other of his siblings, they would have been flat-out crying. Even a five-year-old Ellington would have screamed and cried if he'd been left out. Viola didn't, she just sat and watched. All Bix could do was sit and marvel at his baby sister.

LAY DOWN SALLY

There were plenty of times that summer when Bix wished he could trade places with Viola. She had free time that the rest of them didn't. Bix wanted to get to know their new neighborhood, maybe start making some new friends, but how do you make friends when you're in the studio or rehearsing? You don't. In later years, he joked they were socially stunted. At 12 going on 13, he just said that his dad wouldn't give them a break. The only thing that saved the summer from being a total wreck was his mom negotiating with Dad and Karpenko for all the children to have two afternoons a week where they didn't have anything scheduled — no practicing, no rehearsals, no recording. The first free afternoon they got, Bix and Ellington took their bikes out for a ride around the neighborhood. Their mom had mentioned that the local junior high was only a few blocks away, so they decided to explore that. Even though he knew he'd probably never go there, Bix wanted to see and maybe daydream what it'd be like to go to regular school again, or to go anywhere with other kids again. The younger kids wanted to go with them, but honestly, who wanted a seven-year-old and a five-year-old tagging along on a bike ride? Their mom promised to take them to a park with a playground. Even Allie seemed interested in that, and Clara said she wanted to be alone. Bix figured she felt the same way about hanging out with him and Ellington as he felt about hanging out with Theo and Viola.

Ellington had gotten a ten-speed bike for his birthday in February while Bix still had the chopper style bike with a banana seat that had seemed incredibly cool when he was 10. Two years later, it was too small and, frankly, looked stupid. El was way faster on his new bike and kept flying down the street ahead of him. He'd get a block ahead then double back to Bix. It was embarrassing. It wasn't like their parents couldn't afford a new bike. It was just a matter of having somebody notice he needed one and taking the time to get a new one.

They were riding in the street, and Bix almost got run over a couple times because he couldn't get out of the way of a car fast enough. It was almost enough to send him to the sidewalk. Almost. Only little kids rode their bikes on the sidewalk. It took them about half an hour to find the junior high because they got the name of the street wrong. The school took up one huge block, half of which was a rectangular playing field with a backstop and bleachers for baseball at one end and goal posts and bleachers for football at the other end. Five guys were messing around on the football field. There were two girls sitting in the bleachers, half watching the boys and half talking to each other. Bix and Ellington biked by, not too fast, not too slow, and tried not to stare too much. Seeing other kids around their age who weren't their siblings was a novelty.

"What do you think?" El said and started to slow down. "Let's stop."

"No, keep going," Bix replied and started to pedal faster.

"What is wrong with you?"

"Nothing. Let's just go around the block." It wasn't necessarily nerves that made Bix want to ride around the block instead of talking to the group of kids. He wanted to talk to kids who weren't related to him even more than he wanted a new bike, but he wanted to get the lay of the land first. The other side of the block had a parking lot and a basketball court. That side looked like the place where school buses and parents dropped students off, and the houses over there were just a little bit smaller, like nobody wanted to live that close to a school parking lot. Living across the street from a sports field seemed like it would be noisy, but the houses on the front side of the block were bigger and a little nicer. The parking lot side reminded Bix of their neighborhood in Cleveland. The playing field side reminded him of their new neighborhood.

Bix hadn't thought about the fact that they probably looked more conspicuously dorky riding around the block and then stopping than if they had just parked their bikes and gone over to talk to the other kids in the first place. There was a tiny side parking lot right next to the infield with a "Staff Only" sign posted on it. The second time around, he and Ellington pulled their bikes into that lot and walked them down the third base line of the baseball field and over to the football half. The distance hadn't seemed far until they actually started walking towards this group of strange kids; then it seemed like they were walking forever. The girls sitting on the bleachers could clearly see them coming. The guys were running all their plays to the goal post nearest them, so he and Ellington would have to walk right by them.

"This was a dumb idea," Bix said.

"No, it's not." El said. "Meeting new people is a great idea." They were close enough now that the five guys playing football stopped mid-huddle. One minute, the three guys playing offense were planning their next play, the next minute, they were staring at the two brothers. The two guys playing defense were on the 20-yard line. Now they had stopped and were standing motionless, watching their approach. Originally Ellington had been making a beeline to the girls, but now he half raised his right hand. "Hey, how're you doing?" he called. One of the guys on defense kind of waved back but the kid next to him gave him a backhanded slap on the shoulder and the guy put his arm down.

Ellington gave a little shrug. He laid his bike down in the grass and walked over to the two girls on the bleachers. Bix wasn't sure what else to do so he dropped his bike next to Elligton's and walked right along-side him. All the kids were all around El's age — probably 14 or 15 — the girls too. Bix tried stand as tall as possible. Ellington only had about two inches on him, but he had broader shoulders and more heft while Bix kept hoping for a growth spurt. They were close enough to say hello to the girls. El said "Good afternoon" to the girls in a manner that sounded like he was trying to be smooth. Bix went with a simple "Hi." It wasn't what his mom would term "gallant," but it was friendly.

The guys walked over to the bleachers so it was the two brothers facing all of them. One of the guys had the lightest hair Bix had ever seen — almost white. "What do you want?" he asked.

"Nothing," El said. "We just moved in so we're just exploring the neighborhood. I'm El, and this is my brother Bix."

The kid with the white hair kind of laughed, except it came out more like a sputter in B-flat. Bix could see a ragged dotted half note above his head. "What kind of names are those?"

"It's short for Ellington. We're named after musicians," El added with just the right tone so it sounded like he might think it was stupid to be named after famous jazz musicians if these kids also thought it was stupid.

"There's a fashion magazine named *Elle*," one of the girls said dreamily, and Bix couldn't tell if she was saying it as an insult or if she wasn't sure that what she was saying was true. She had long dark hair so curly it almost looked frizzy, and she kept twirling one strand around her left index finger.

"Oh my gosh, are you guys on that show? The music show?" the other girl asked. Bix decided she was the cute one, and not just because she recognized them.

"*The Musical Mozinskis*?" El asked. "Yeah, that's us."

"I seen that show," one of the guys said. "You play with your sisters."

This was verifiably true, but coming out of this kid's mouth, it sounded like an insult. Bix spent most of his time around adults. Adults didn't scare him. Few things did. But a group of kids who were just a little older and a little bigger than he was made him wary. It was almost as though he didn't know how to talk to them. Suddenly the idea of saying very little seemed the wisest course of action.

The biggest guy of the group had actual shoulders and biceps. He looked like he could even be 16. Bix wasn't sure if he was Hispanic or just had a good tan. Nearly half the kids in their old neighborhood back in Cleveland were black, but the only Hispanic kids he knew were on *Sesame Street* when he watched it with Theo and Viola. It was one more new thing to figure out about his new life. "So, are you guys like TV stars?" the big guy said.

"No, we're musicians," Ellington replied.

"What do you play?"

"I play drums. He plays guitar and trumpet and sings."

"You come to serenade us?" This made the other guys laugh and the girl with the frizzy hair kind of giggle, so he kept going. "Come on, let me hear you sing something."

All of them looked at Bix expectantly, even Ellington. When he was little, he thought he ended up as the front man out of happenstance — Ellington was older and the more likely candidate, but having the drummer as the lead singer doesn't work because there's no focal point for the audience during live shows. Clara didn't have any desire to sing lead. Allie was too little when they started. Having one of their parents sing lead would have defeated the whole schtick of a band of children, so Bix was the one who ended up in front of the microphone. But standing there on the football field at Winslow Junior High in front of a bunch of strange kids who may or may not have wanted to kick his and Ellington's asses out of sheer boredom, Bix realized that his parents had made him the front man because he could do it better than anyone else. The only way he could explain it is that he couldn't ever remember feeling embarrassed. The only time he ever felt nervous before a performance was before the Bicentennial show. And once he nailed that, he knew he could nail anything. It really did always come back to the Chuck Berry duckwalk.

The first song that popped into his mind that he could sing solo a capella and not sound too bad was Clapton's "Lay Down, Sally," which had been big that spring. He sang the last two lines of the chorus, and when he got to the "I've been trying all night long just to talk to you" line, he looked right at the two girls. Not the one with the frizzy hair — he had a feeling she and the guy with the big shoulders were an item. He sang it to the skinny girl with the brown hair cut in a bob who blushed a little when he was done, the notes shimmering in the afternoon sun above her head like a halo. She was definitely cute.

The whole thing felt like an initiation. The guy with the shoulders kind of nodded. "Not bad," he admitted.

"You guys play football?" one of the other guys asked. He was the tallest and had been playing quarterback. He still held the football in one hand.

"Sure," Ellington replied and held up his hands. The guy tossed him the football and then took a few steps backwards. El looked down at the ball for a second then threw a respectable spiral back. Bix was impressed since it was probably the first time either of them had touched a football in a couple years. They had both played peewee flag football back in elementary school, although El played longer. All extracurricular sports stopped once their parents realized the children were good enough to be taken seriously. Once they started doing *The Johnny Banks Show* and other gigs back in Cleveland, there wasn't time for sports or clubs.

"Touch only," the quarterback said. "No tackling."

"Cool."

At first it seemed like these kids only wanted Ellington to play. That would even them up at three on three, plus they were all older, but they asked Bix to play too. Actually, it was more like they told him he was playing. There was no way he could say no and ever hope to hang with them again. They weren't playing an actual game — just kind of taking turns trading downs to see who could score. The tall guy playing quarterback said he looked like a halfback, so Bix joined the guys playing offense and Ellington became the third defender.

On the first play, the quarterback told Bix to run a post to the left. He had a feeling the ball was heading his way and not because he looked like he knew what he was doing. It was like them making him sing. Another test. The kid with the almost-white hair was covering Bix so closely he couldn't get open. The quarterback threw to him anyway and the kid with the almost-white hair knocked it out of his hands. They kind of hit shoulders but Bix didn't lose his footing and didn't fall. It was a small victory. On second down, the quarterback threw to the guy that Ellington was defending. The guy caught it but Ellington at least got the tackle, or what passed for the tackle. The quarterback went to Bix again on third and two. This time, he caught it, and for one bright, shining moment that lasted as long as a sixteenth note, he had the football in his hands, then the kid with the almost-white hair ran into him and knocked him flat on the ground.

The field was hard, and the grass so dry it felt like hundreds of little needles jabbing at his arms and legs. Bix took a deep breath and opened his eyes to see the kid with the almost-white hair standing over him. "Sorry, man." He didn't sound sorry.

Ellington came running over yelling "What the hell? You said this wasn't tackle."

"I didn't *tackle* him."

"Then why is he on the ground?"

"It was an accident."

"Maybe's he's just a little wuss," the guy with the shoulders said.

Bix was still lying on the ground. The grass was still hard and prickly, but the sun was deliciously warm. It wasn't so bad lying there. Then his older brother's face blocked out the sun. "You okay?" he asked.

"Yeah, fine. Just knocked the wind out of me," Bix replied and reached up for Ellington's outstretched hand with his left hand. He got to his feet and made sure to act as though nothing hurt.

"Nice catch, anyway."

"Thanks." He looked down at the football, which was somehow still in his hands. At least he hadn't fumbled. Now that he was up, he realized that his entire right hand hurt. Bix shifted the ball to his left hand and gave the right a little shake, hoping it was just a stinger.

Ellington took the football from him and tossed it aside. He didn't even bother giving it to one of the other guys. "Hold out your hand," he said. Bix did. Ellington took Bix's right hand and gently squeezed on different parts like he was one of the medics on *M*A*S*H* or *Emergency!* "Does that hurt?" he asked with each little squeeze.

"A little," Bix lied when El got to his right middle finger. It hurt like crazy.

"If you can't play guitar, Vincent is gonna kill you."

"Who's Vincent?" the quarterback asked.

"Our dad," Bix answered.

"He lets you call him by his first name?"

"He doesn't *let* me do anything," Ellington replied. "You probably shouldn't play football anymore," he said to Bix.

"Poor little rich boy can't take it?" the guy with the shoulders asked.

"We aren't rich," El said at the same time Bix said, "I can take it. I'm fine."

"Then let's play."

"Not him. He needs to protect his hands."

The kid with the almost-white hair kind of snorted. "Maybe you should *both* go back to your TV show and sing more faggy songs," he said.

Bix could almost see the anger rise up in Ellington the same way he could see the notes appear above a musician. Ellington took a couple steps toward the white-haired kid and said, "Shut the hell up."

"You gonna make me?"

Bix put his left hand (the hand that didn't hurt) on Ellington's shoulder. "Let's just go," he said.

"Yeah, you better get your brother out of here before he gets his ass kicked," one of the guys said.

"Come on," Bix said, a little more urgently. Ellington must have realized that getting into a two-against-five fight would be ugly. "They're idiots," Bix added sotto voce.

Ellington kind of half raised his arms in a dismissive gesture that wasn't as insulting as flipping the bird but not nearly as benign as waving. He took a few steps backwards, not turning his back on the guys. Bix was already by their bikes when Ellington yelled "Assholes!" and came running up shouting "Go! Go! Go!" He grabbed his bike and took off with Bix right behind. His old chopper was slow but it did better on the grass than El's ten-speed. By the time they hit the side parking lot, three of the football guys had almost caught up with them. They gained a little speed once they were on asphalt and managed to put some distance between them and the football guys. Bix was standing on the pedals, pumping his legs as fast as he could, his lungs and right hand screaming for mercy. The football guys yelled "You chicken shits!" like it would make them come back and fight. *So much for making new friends,* Bix thought.

His right hand was sore, and it hurt to hold a guitar pick for longer than he told his parents it did. He and Ellington were grounded for two weeks. And no more football — not that they would have played with those guys again. But no more anything, ever, that could hurt his hands. From then on, there was only music.

LET THE LITTLE GIRL DANCE

Going on tour with your family is like going on one of those family vacations in a movie where everybody is packed into the same car for hours on end. In the Mozinskis' case it was a tour bus — so there was more room than a station wagon and their parents didn't have to do any of the driving — but the effect was the same. Within four days, all of the children were sick of reading, word-search puzzles, playing I Spy and Punch Buggy, and each other. The performances were fun. The one thing that made everything worth it was the prospect of doing the show in Cleveland at the end of the tour and visiting old friends. Grace told her children it was a lesson in delayed gratification.

It wasn't a big tour — 14 shows over three weeks. The family got into a routine from the first show. One of their parents — usually Vincent — would do a telephone interview from the hotel in the previous city a couple days before the next show for the print media. Then the entire family would do some local radio or TV the day of the show. Karpenko had an elaborate chart for each date and the publicity and where they were staying. The adults didn't pass along many details, only what to play and when to play it. Every night, Bix looked down at the set list taped to the floor in front of his microphone and saw the same songs, usually in the same order. Sometimes his dad would feel a little frisky and open with "ABC" instead of putting it second. They always played "Lazy Day" and "From the Bottom to the Top" because those would be on the new album.

Viola and Theo didn't play on every number, but there were a handful of songs where their father had Clara play keyboards and put Theo on bass. At seven, he was already a respectable bass player. Viola stayed on tambourine. Every performance included a set of four songs with just the six children. Midway through every show, their parents always did a couple songs as a duet to give the kids a break and maybe show off a little bit. On this tour, they were playing the mashup of Bach's *Air on the G String* and "Sweet Georgia Brown" with Vincent on piano and Grace on violin. They had played it on the first episode of the show and it always went over well in concert because the audience reliably went nuts for a classical piece that evolved into a jazz violin piece. And no matter what order the songs were in, Bix knew at some point during the show he'd end up doing the duckwalk because "Back in the U.S.A." was expected and his dad said they couldn't disappoint the audience. Bix tried hard not to disappoint.

They had a family meeting an hour before every show to make sure everyone knew the setlist and, as Vincent put it, "to get everyone psyched up." Before the fourth show of the tour, in St. Louis, their father announced that they were switching out "Snap it Up" with "Let the Little Girl Dance" as the last song of the kids' set. "That'll give you a chance to go out and have some fun in the spotlight, sweetie," he said to Viola.

The old Billy Bland tune "Let the Little Girl Dance" had been on the first album. When they played it on the show the previous winter, Don the Director sent Viola and her ever-present tambourine out front to dance around with Bix. The studio audience ate it up.

The littlest Mozinski was sitting on Grace's lap on one of the chairs in the dressing room. She had been half snuggling, half looking as bored as the older kids by their father's ineffectual pep talk. When her dad said she had to dance out front, she glanced over at Allie. Allegro didn't say anything and didn't look at anyone, but she took the news of the song switch with an exasperated sigh and rolled her head back so she was looking at the ceiling.

"I don't wanna," Viola said quietly.

"Come on, it'll be great," Vincent said. "You had fun when we did it on the show, right?"

Viola, who hadn't yet learned how to lie effectively, replied "I don't know."

"Well, you'll have fun doing it tonight."

Grace whispered something in Viola's ear. Viola didn't say anything, but she turned and buried her face in their mother's neck. It looked to Bix like she didn't want to dance.

"We haven't rehearsed 'Let the Little Girl Dance' for like, a week. Maybe we should wait and try it in Iowa City?" Clara said.

Bix watched all this, a little unsure where his loyalties ought to lie. They had rehearsed "Let the Little Girl Dance" before the tour started, but Viola always stayed in back near Ellington and the drum kit. This was the first time they'd be doing it in concert. He looked over at his mom and Viola.

"I agree," his mom said. Her eyes met his and it felt like his mom was expecting him to say something.

"Yeah," he said then added, "I mean, we don't want to be under-rehearsed," because under-rehearsing was on the level of mortal sin in their family. Saying it to his dad was like waving a red flag in front of a bull.

"Fine, we run through it in soundcheck on Thursday and it'll close the kids' set for the rest of the tour."

Two days later, in Iowa City, they ran through the song three times during soundcheck. The third time through, Vincent insisted that Viola go out front and dance with her brother. "Do it like you did on the show," he said.

"I don't remember what I did," Viola replied.

Vincent squatted down to her level. It was the first time Bix could remember him doing something like that. Their dad was always Up There — larger than life. He didn't make himself smaller for anything or anyone. It seemed like a good sign that he was doing so for Viola. Honestly, Bix figured it was probably tough for her. Everyone else in the family had already claimed all the good instruments. It was like there wasn't anything left for her.

"You don't have to the same exact thing," Dad said. "Just dance however you feel."

"What if I don't feel anything?"

Their father had his back to Allegro, otherwise he would have seen her roll her eyes and sort of flop her entire body in a spasm of annoyance. Bix saw it. Clara was over behind the keyboard and Theo was standing next to him, cradling the electric bass while they waited to run through the song again. Neither of them said anything because it was just Allie being Allie.

"When you hear the music just move to it. Bounce around to the beat, okay?" their father said brightly.

"I'll try."

Viola did what she was told and bounced around to the music, sometimes on the beat, sometimes not. Bix tried to help her, reminding Viola before each show to "Do what I do," and then dancing a simple twist with her. Whether she would dance on the beat was a source of speculation for Allie and Ellington, who actually bet each other every night on whether Viola would find the beat on "Let the Little Girl Dance." Bix ignored it. As long they didn't say anything in front of Viola, it didn't seem to matter.

AIR ON THE G STRING

The tour bus was black and gray with "The Musical Mozinskis" painted in a jaunty script on each side in red letters. Viola insisted it was burgundy, not red. By the time the bus pulled into Cleveland the night before their final show, Ellington and Allie were no longer talking to each other, their mom wasn't talking to their dad, and Clara wasn't talking to anyone. Viola, on the other hand, was talking to anyone who would listen. She spent a lot of time talking to Mr. Karpenko, who told her stories about growing up in Ukraine. Bix had tried to be extra nice to her since Iowa City, and she held his hand as they walked into the Statler Hotel in downtown Cleveland. It was about 9:30 on a Thursday night, and even though they'd already stayed in a bunch of hotels, the idea that this would be the last one for a while felt a little overwhelming.

"Is this Cleveland?" Viola asked as they walked in the revolving doors.

"Yes."

"It says 'Statler Hotel,'" she said, pointing the sign behind the check in counter.

"Yep. You're a good reader."

"Thanks." She looked around the lobby. It wasn't impressive. "Why are we here?"

"Here in Cleveland? We have a gig tomorrow. And Grandma and Grandpa Klinefelter are driving up from Youngstown, and we're going to see some of our old friends."

"I know *that*. Why are we in a hotel? Why don't we stay at our house?"

"We don't have a house here anymore. We sold it last year, remember?"

"No. Nobody tells me anything," she sighed.

Bix led her over to some blockish-looking chairs at one end of the lobby. Mr. Karpenko was at the front desk getting everybody checked in and getting room keys. When Grace and Clara walked into the lobby, Bix caught his mom's eye so she'd know he had Viola.

The lobby's color scheme was primarily a faded peachy color and something that Bix thought looked like a light purple.

"It's puce," Viola said confidently.

"Puke?"

Viola giggled. "*Puuuce.* Puke would have more brown."

"When did you learn so much about colors?"

"I don't know. Around." Viola sat down on one of the peach-colored chairs and bounced her rear end on it twice. "It's not very bouncy, but it reminds me of Mr. Karpenko," she announced and stood up.

Viola frequently said weird things like that. Bix figured it came with being five. "So Mr. Karpenko isn't bouncy either?"

"Huh?"

"Why'd you say the chair reminded you of Mr. Karpenko?"

"Same color," Viola replied in a tone that said Bix ought to know this. Mr. Karpenko's hair was frizzy and dark — almost black. It didn't look anything like the chair. Bix didn't have a chance to ask her what she meant because Theo came over and started chasing Viola around the chairs. They were supposed to behave themselves in hotels, but they'd been sitting in the bus all day. Just standing up felt good. Bix started chasing Theo and Viola, making monster sounds. It was a lot of fun until their father came over and told them to stop horsing around.

"Why can't we play?" Viola asked.

"Mom said this is the same hotel where Dad used to play the piano. He probably wants to make a good impression," Bix replied.

Theo gave an exasperated sigh that sounded like *Guhhhh* and said, "He doesn't work here anymore, and now he's famous. How is being famous *not* a good impression?"

Theo had a point, but Bix told them they had to quiet down anyway.

The next morning at seven o'clock, the entire family played "From the Bottom to the Top" on a local morning TV show, and then all of them had to go to a radio station for an interview, even though Vincent did most of the talking. Bix figured the rest of them could have slept in. The show at Cain Park was that night, then they were supposed to have the weekend to catch up with their friends before flying back to California on Monday. Every interview used the word "homecoming," but Bix still didn't feel like he was home. It was just another gig. The only difference was the family was driving around town in a big van instead of the tour bus and he recognized some of the places they drove by.

His parents promised they would be able to go by the old house. This is what Bix had been waiting for. It wasn't necessarily that he wanted to live in Cleveland again, but he missed his old life. He had liked when they walked to school and hung out with their friends and just messed around on bikes or in somebody's backyard playing basketball or baseball. Tom Shea had a huge backyard and his parents had a tent, so they would have these great campouts there every summer. The summer he was 10, a bunch of girls from their school even walked over and talked to them in the backyard for an hour. It was kind of like having a boy-girl party. Cindy Carney had sat next to him the whole time and she never once said anything about him playing on *The Johnny Banks Show* or the Bicentennial special or anything. He liked that about her. She knew the names of six different constellations when all Bix knew was the Big Dipper. Then that fall they were on *The Tonight Show* and the first album came out and everything changed.

When his parents told him they would "go by" the old house, they hadn't mentioned that the entire family was going to be followed by a camera crew from a local TV station. Walking through the front door for the first time in a year actually gave Bix a little tingle in his belly. Not nerves. Excitement. It felt like the thrill he got before going onstage. The whole family walked into the living room together, and the news team got nice footage of Grace asking Viola if she remembered it and Viola saying she remembered the fireplace.

A younger couple with a three-year-old and a baby had bought the house. Bix vaguely remembered them from a year ago. They didn't look too happy about the camera crew either. The wife kept apologizing for everything being a mess, and Bix's mom kept saying that everything looked lovely. Bix thought it looked cleaner and more organized than it ever did when they lived there. The living room walls were the same dull beige they had been when they lived there, and the dining room had the same flowered wallpaper that his father and mother hung 10 years earlier and didn't notice was upside down until shortly before they moved. Some of the bedrooms had been painted. Clara's old room on the second floor was now occupied by the older child, a little boy who said "George" when Clara asked him his name and then said nothing else.

Going through the house being followed by strangers who were recording everything was uncomfortable, and Bix and Ellington peeled off from the rest of the family to visit their old room on the third floor. When he was little, Bix had what he called a sticker collection on the inside of the closet door. Most of the stickers were from Wacky Packages, those baseball-card sized stickers with product parodies like Frosted Snakes and Rice-A-Phoni. The pictures on the stickers were, as Clara and Allie had often stated, "totally gross," which was one of the reasons Bix and Ellington loved them. He stopped collecting the stickers when he was eight or nine, but kept the stickers where they were. It would have been too much work to scrape them off the door. When the two of them walked into their old bedroom, Ellington stopped and surveyed the boxes stacked two and three high at one end of the long room. It looked like the new family was using the room for storage. Bix went right for the closet door. When he opened it, the first thing that caught his eye was the Poop-Tarts sticker. He was pleased to see that it still made him laugh.

"Check it out," Bix said.

Ellington went over to the closet saying "Oh my God, are they still there?"

"Yep." The two of them stood for a moment, admiring the glorious array of disgusting stickers. Bix was about to say Poop-Tarts again simply because Clara and Allie always found that one particularly disgusting when he heard a noise by the door. He glanced up and was staring almost directly into the light from the camera.

"Don't mind us," the reporter said. "Pretend we aren't here." She was probably around their mom's age, only with way more make-up and fancier clothes. The camera man didn't say anything but kept the camera trained on them.

Bix stopped himself from saying anything else to Ellington. In his head, he could almost hear the annoying reporter doing a voice over about it later. Even the front man deserves to keep some things private.

"But you are here," El replied. "You want us to cry now or something?" Years later, when Bix settled into a steady piano gig at an upscale bar/restaurant in Chicago, one of the regulars told him that this footage showed up in a documentary about the family. The person also said that you can hear the camera man laugh when El says this.

"Come on," Bix said and walked out of the room. He wanted to say something like "Thanks for ruining the visit to our old house," but the camera was still rolling. He didn't want to give the camera crew anything, good or bad. Not when they were taking the visit to their old house away from him.

When they got back in the van to return to the hotel, Viola took the seat next to Bix.

"I didn't like that," she said.

Bix leaned closer to her. "Me either," he whispered.

"Those people live in our house." Viola sounded rather peeved.

"It's not our house anymore."

"I wish it was."

The show that night at Cain Park had sold out months before. The park was only a mile and a half away from the old house, and Bix remembered going sledding on the big hill at the far end of the park. The Klinefelter grandparents were in the front row along with a bunch of friends and old neighbors. The audience sang along and seemed to be having a good time. Bix wanted to enjoy himself, but for some reason he couldn't. Nothing seemed to be going the way he thought it would, and no one had said anything about when any of them would actually get to see their friends. Everything seemed like it was prescheduled and planned. He had kind of gotten used to that and reminded himself that they still had two days before they flew back. It made him feel like everything would be okay, then they got to the middle of the show.

They had just finished the kids-only set, and Bix was standing in the wings, watching his parents do their three-song set. He'd always loved watching his parents play. His mom and dad making music together was the one constant in their house. When he thought about it, his parents' music was what made him and his siblings. None of them would even be alive if it weren't for music.

His parents always ended their set with the "Air on the G String/ Sweet Georgia Brown" medley. When they started the Bach piece, his mom's violin sounded mournful. That was the only word Bix could think of to describe it. The notes were swirling around over her head like a cloud or an umbrella or the way he always imagined the Enterprise's force field on *Star Trek* would look. It was like she was encased in her own music. For as long as he'd been alive, whenever he watched his parents play together, their music intertwined, the notes moving together in the air above them. That night on the final show of the tour, it didn't. His father's music stayed above him. His mother's stayed above her. Separate. The music didn't mingle or dance.

He heard Clara behind him whisper "Something's wrong." He'd been so focused on the music that he didn't realize she was standing next to him.

"What do you mean?" he asked.

"You know what I mean. Look," she hissed. "They're playing together but the notes aren't together."

Bix realized this was a conversation he could only have with one of his siblings. No one else on Earth would understand. He had never thought of being grateful for his family before, but he was very glad to have Clara next to him to see what he was seeing and know he wasn't imagining it.

After that night, Bix watched more carefully whenever his parents played together. Music does different things when it's coming from an ensemble than when it's coming from a singular instrument or a duet. Sometimes he and Clara compared notes. He never realized how much she paid attention to their parents' music too.

One thing he wouldn't have noticed until Clara pointed it out was how few duets their parents did during the second season of the show. The first season, Fritz and the writers had thrown in a mother-father duet every third episode. Not so the second season. The children weren't involved in production decisions. Someone — usually Vincent — would tell them what they were playing and then they'd get the script. But they heard things. It was amazing what you could hear if you were paying attention.

Bix overheard his mom telling Fritz that she thought a Valentine's Day duet with Vincent would be a little cheesey. The Valentine's episode that season was about each of the kids getting a Valentine from their crush except Ellington. Fritz had said they were all playing "interpretations" of themselves but this seemed like they were pushing it. Bix privately found this plot hilarious because his brother Ellington never had trouble getting girls. The plot of the episode might have been unrealistic, but the writing team definitely had El's number because his character on the show was just as self-absorbed and hormone-driven as the real guy. His mom lost that argument with Fritz, so on that episode his parents ended up playing "My Funny Valentine" and Ellington did a solo of "It Never Entered My Mind" on the vibes because his birthday was close enough to Valentine's Day that the writers decided to combine it with his Birthday Solo. The vibraphone was a Christmas gift because Vincent thought it would be good for El to stretch himself.

That was one of only a handful of duets Bix saw his parents play that season. When he paid attention, he noticed the separation in their music. It wasn't a one-time thing. Their music didn't move together the way it used to. They still played well together, and they still sounded like they always did, but only if he closed his eyes.

GROOVY TWOSIE

Vincent Mozinski was generally acknowledged to be a top-notch musical talent. After all, he was the music director for *The Musical Mozinskis* and the mastermind behind the family's rise to fame. Vincent almost never made mistakes while playing. If he did, he was smart enough to play the clinker again, giving the impression that the false note was meant to be there. It was behavior that he wouldn't put up with in his children's performances, but as Ellington put it, "Vincent's a little sloppy."

Ellington didn't know what the word "derivative" meant, but he knew it when he heard it, like when the incidental music between scenes for almost every episode in Season 2 used the same chord progression as the chorus of the old song "Swinging on a Star." He heard it when song after song on each album featured the same line up, the same instruments, and the same limited dynamics. Whenever he asked his father if they could make some small change to a song — like adding a drum break or singular bass line — Vincent just shook his head and gave some platitude about audience expectations and lowest common denominators. Privately, Ellington thought his father was a hack.

His mom, on the other hand, turned out some pretty great work when she felt like it. Her arrangements had more depth, more complexity, more imagination. Ellington wasn't a big fan of the harp or of Simon and Garfunkel, but he had to admit that the harp arrangement of "Bridge Over Troubled Water" his mom did for Clara's Birthday Solo the first season was pretty cool. It certainly wasn't something his father would have ever thought of.

Everyone has their limitations — some more than others. Ellington was used to having his father pretend to know more about the music business than he really did. Once the show was established, El decided Vincent's greatest limitation was being a second-rate composer. There was something almost pathetic the way his dad used to sit at the piano with a stack of blank sheet music and a bunch of freshly sharpened Palomino Blackwing pencils and tell him and his siblings that they needed to be quiet while he composed. Even with all his dad's rituals and imposed household silent periods, he turned out boring stuff. His mother, on the other hand, would write catchy little tunes while she was cleaning the house or making dinner or changing diapers. If you needed proof as to who was the better songwriter, you only had to look at record sales. The ones his mom wrote were hits. The ones his dad wrote were filler.

His mom's first big song-writing win was "Groovy Twosie," which was the B side of "Back in the U.S.A.," the family's first single. They performed it on the show in Season 1. "Groovy Twosie" wasn't the first pop song Grace ever wrote, but it was the first one she ever played for her children. She introduced the song to them in the living room of the old house in Cleveland back when the only songs the family had ever recorded were for Bob's Cars. She played it through on the piano with Vincent improvising some harmonies on the chorus. The lyrics were simple but fun. Some would say silly, but they worked, even if they confused some of the kids at their first listen.

> *I was one and you were one*
> *But now we're two and it's a groove*
> *The grooviest twosiest you ever soosiest*

"Is 'soosiest' supposed to rhyme with 'twosiest' or 'grooviest'?" Clara asked.

"Yes," Grace replied. Clara smiled but Ellington looked dumbfounded so Grace added "Internal rhyme."

This was a bridge too far for Allie. "If 'soosiest' is supposed to take the place of the word 'seen,' it doesn't work. They don't sound anything alike," she said.

Ellington didn't want to give Allegro the satisfaction of being right about anything, but he had been trying to figure out why the lyrics sounded strange to him. "They don't sound alike," he said. "How's Bix supposed to sing it?"

"The same way Dad and I just did," Grace replied. "It isn't supposed to rhyme. It's supposed to be fun. Just sing it," she added to Bix.

"Just sing it" became a family mantra. It gave the Mozinski children faith in their mother's instincts and gave the family a place in the pantheon of great misheard lyrics of the rock era because people consistently wanted to call it "Groovy Tuesday" instead of "Groovy Twosie." Most of the Mozinskis would take the time to correct the line in an interview. Everyone but Allie stopped correcting people when The Hi-Tones covered "Groovy Twosie" in 1978 and it went to number 12 on the pop charts. The lead singer for The Hi-Tones, Harrison Melond, made the "Now we're two and it's a groove" line sound positively obscene.

The family hadn't seen The Hi-Tones since the Bicentennial Celebration, but once their cover of "Groovy Twosie" hit it big, it was a no-brainer to have them on the show. They were the musical guests for one of the last episodes of Season 2. The children suspected Fritz scheduled The Hi-Tones as guests because none of them was turning eight that year and they needed a ratings booster.

The family rehearsed the show Monday through Thursday and recorded on Friday evening with a live studio audience. The show aired the following Wednesday. Musical guests typically only showed up on Fridays for afternoon rehearsal and the evening taping.

All six children went to show school on the set every day. State law required they spend a minimum of three hours a day with Jenny the Tutor. Jenny was right out of college when she started and stayed with the show all four seasons. For reasons known only to her, she liked the idea of being in a one-room schoolhouse. The classroom was one of the few rooms with windows, which at least made it bearable. Ellington always said he hated her but Bix suspected that's because he had a little crush on her.

There were three dressing rooms on the show: family women, family men, and guests. Ellington and Bix had been loitering around the guest dressing room as much as possible because El wanted to run into Eddie

Gibson, The Hi-Tones drummer. As was often the case, Bix kept him company. Ellington seemed almost as excited about having them on the show as Clara was. Her crush on Harrison Melond was a poorly kept secret.

They had morning rehearsal of the scenes without The Hi-Tones, then all the kids were stuck in the classroom for two hours until the meet-and-greet lunch with The Hi-Tones. Fridays were always math mornings, which didn't help matters in the concentration department. Viola was almost six and had breezed through kindergarten and first grade and was starting second-grade work without any of her siblings noticing. She finished her worksheet early and wandered off without asking. Each of the children worked at their own school desk arranged in a half-circle. Jenny had a chair on wheels that she rolled around so she could work with each child one-on-one. She was finishing up with Ellington when she noticed Viola was gone.

Jenny looked around and asked Ellington if he knew where Viola was. This did not give her brownie points for brains, because everyone knew that Ellington could barely keep track of Ellington, much less Viola.

"No idea," El said.

"Did she say she was going to the restroom?" Jenny's voice kind of trailed off.

Clara looked up from her Algebra II lesson and said "She already finished her classwork. She'll be back."

"You guys know you need to actually be in the room doing your coursework in order for me to pass you, right?"

"You mean so you can keep your job..." Allie muttered.

"Isn't Viola like, a semester ahead already? It's not like she's going to fail because she took a long bathroom break," Bix said. Jenny didn't look convinced, so he added, "And we won't tell anybody she left." Bix liked Jenny. Anyone who was getting Ellington through high school was okay in his book. He didn't want Jenny to get in trouble for losing one of his siblings. Jenny always seemed to be worried about getting fired or losing her teaching license. This seemed like an unfounded fear because Bix was pretty sure they couldn't find anybody else who wanted to teach the six of them every day.

"Do you want me to go and look for her?" Theo asked.

"I'll go," Clara said, standing up.

"You just want to see if Harrison is here yet," Allie said and stretched out Harrison's name for an astounding four beats.

"I'm going to fetch Viola." It occurred to Bix that his sister Clara was not nearly as talented at lying as she was at music.

"Thanks, Clara. Please come right back. You know show days always go late and you're behind on instructional hours for the week. All of you are." Jenny looked right at El when she said that.

Bix tried not to laugh too loudly and looked back down at his prealgebra worksheet, which he actually kind of liked, and pretended to be hard at work. Clara had just stood up when Viola came running back into the room.

"They're here!" she squealed. Bix figured she was too little to remember when the family recorded "Groovy Twosie." They rarely listened to their own recordings at home because that was just weird, but he knew she'd heard The Hi-Tones' cover — it had been all over the place. Years later, as an adult, it was The Hi-Tones' funky take on the song that Bix always heard in his head, not the sugary pop original on which he had sung lead. "Sorry I took so long," Viola said to Jenny.

Clara was still standing by her desk about ready to jump out of her skin. "May I be excused for a moment?" she asked.

"We only have 10 minutes left," Jenny said. Clara kind of shifted her weight back and forth from one foot to another in an *adagio* variation of the I-have-to-pee shuffle.

"Can you hold it?"

"Not really. And I'm done," she said and held up her worksheet.

"Fine," Jenny said with one of those sighs that made you wonder why she kept such a lousy job. "Give me the worksheet. I'll see you this afternoon."

"Thank you!" Clara was out of the room in the space of a sixteenth note, so maybe she was a better liar than Bix thought. Once she was gone, the rest of children got restless, but Jenny actually kept them until exactly 12:15.

Cast and crew always had lunch with the musical guests so the first time they met wasn't at rehearsal. It was supposed to make things go more smoothly on set, but really was just an excuse for light socializing. Instead of going to the studio commissary, everyone ate at tables set up in an empty studio. When the rest of the kids got to lunch, Clara was already sitting next to Harrison Melond. Bix was feeling borderline chivalrous and asked Ellington if maybe they should go sit with Clara and Harrison. "Just in case," he said.

"Why?" Ellington looked as though he truly had no idea what Bix was talking about.

At 13, Bix was already fodder for teen magazines, but he hadn't done much more than kiss a few girls. He wasn't sure when Ellington found the opportunities to do all the things he said he did with girls, but he was pretty sure Harrison would do the same thing with their sister if given the chance. "I mean, Harrison's a lot older than Clara..."

"Clara's 16. Harrison's like 22. She's jailbait. Plus, he's *black*."

"What does that have to do with anything?"

Ellington shook his head like Bix was an idiot. "Forget it, I want to talk to Eddie."

As in most things with Ellington, Bix acquiesced, even if he wasn't sure why. Whenever he said "Okay" to his older brother, it always came out as "Oh-*kaaay*" with a slurred fifth.

Eddie Gibson was already sitting next to their mother with Karpenko seated across from them. It looked like Eddie was mainly focused on their mom. Bix wasn't surprised. He could admit his mom was pretty. And Karpenko kind of resembled a bear — too much fat and too much facial hair with bad breath. Who wouldn't want to sit with his mom over that? "Let's go sit with them," El said.

"Okay." Bix didn't mind doing what El wanted. Sometimes it got them into trouble, but that was part of the fun. They got some food and went over to the table. Ellington didn't say anything, merely plopped his plate on the table on the other side of Eddie and said, "Hi."

"Hey there, young man," Eddie said.

"Ellington, we are in the middle of something," Karpenko said. "Maybe you two talk later?"

"It's fine, Gregor. Have a seat, sweetie," Grace said and reached across Eddie to pat El's hand. It was kind of a far reach, but Eddie didn't seem to mind Grace getting that close to him. Bix was still standing next

to the table feeling a little awkward, so his mom said, "Both of you." It felt a little condescending, but he knew Ellington wanted to talk to Eddie about his ride cymbals and Bix didn't have anywhere else to sit. He sat down next to Karpenko, right across from his mom, Eddie, and Ellington.

"I was just asking your mother if she had any other tunes we might look at. Harrison has written a few songs, but I'm always on the lookout for fresh material."

"Cool. Hey, if I write some songs, can I send them to you?" Ellington said.

Grace looked surprised, like she knew this was a lie. Bix knew it was mostly a lie. He'd heard all three of the songs Ellington had written and knew that his older brother's song-writing skills did not match the sophistication of his playing.

Eddie nodded like he was impressed. "Absolutely. What kind of stuff are you writing? Rock and roll?"

"Umm...kind of a jazz-rock fusion thing. They're instrumentals." That part was true. As adolescent boys who spent every waking hour with their family, neither Ellington nor Bix had much to say lyrically. El was at least trying, which was more than Bix could say for himself.

"I'll be happy to give them a listen if you send them," Eddie replied, which Bix took as a polite way of saying "Get out of here, kid, you bother me."

"I'm writing songs too," Bix said. This was a bald-faced lie, but sometimes one just wants to be part of a conversation.

"Is that a fact?" Eddie asked. "You two collaborating on anything?"

"No," Bix and Ellington answered at the same time.

"But we're thinking about it," Ellington added too quickly. "Right?"

"Yes." Bix figured they were pretty obvious, but their mom and Eddie let them stay and talk. He liked that Eddie treated them like regular musicians, not children.

Ellington never sent Eddie any demos of his songs, but The Hi-Tones recorded three more of Grace's, including another Top 40 hit, "Why'd You Do That?"

When they recorded the show that evening, the studio audience went crazy when The Hi-Tones came onstage. They had gotten pretty big off of "Groovy Twosie." Their version was R&B/funk-inspired with just enough pop to make it mainstream. The pretend plot of the episode was that the Mozinski children ask The Hi-Tones to come and play "Groovy Twosie" as a surprise for their parents' anniversary, seemingly because they were a groovy twosome. Bix knew his parents' anniversary was in October and this was now March, but The Hi-Tones hadn't been available before. As Karpenko always said, "Is all pretend."

The episode was one of the few finales where the whole family didn't play. Grace and Vincent just watched while the six children played with The Hi-Tones. There were two drum kits set up, so Ellington got to play alongside Eddie Gibson, which had been one of his life goals since he was 11. Bix had fun playing with The Hi-Tones too. It felt freer, looser, than sharing the stage with his father.

The younger Mozinskis meshed well with The Hi-Tones. As he shared front man duties with Harrison, Bix watched their music align with his and with his family's. As they played, Bix noticed that the notes from Clara's bass were kind of hanging off by themselves and so were the notes from Harrison's guitar. Then on the bridge, Clara's notes and Harrison's notes started dancing together. This wasn't the usual way of musicians talking to each other while playing. This was different. This was Clara's and Harrison's notes having their own little conversation up in the air. For all the world, it kind of reminded Bix of what used to happen when his parents played music together. And his older sister looked happy, like she knew Harrison wouldn't always be too old for her.

MUSIC FACTORY

There's a lot to be said for growing up in a big family. Most of it negative.

Allegro Mozinski had her opinions about growing up in a large family and was generally only too willing to share them. The negatives included being required to share the spotlight; rarely receiving the undivided attention of one parent, much less both; the constant sharing of space, food, and clothing; and having the world compare you to your siblings or lump all of you together. No matter how she played — how well or how difficult the piece — there was always another sibling with another song coming right after her. For her Birthday Solo at the end of Season 2, she played Paganini's Caprice No. 24 in A Minor. Bloody Paganini, and her father barely noticed. Fritz the Producer just said, "Very nice." She was positive she saw an old man in the studio audience yawn at the end of the performance. Her mother said nice things about her playing, but her mother always said nice things about her playing. Her mother even said nice things about Viola's tambourine playing, so it wasn't like she could trust *her* to give an honest opinion. The only adult who showed a modicum of respect was stinky, hairy Mr. Karpenko, who said, "Paganini is wild beast, but you tame him."

To make matters worse, her father "celebrated" the end of the second season of *The Musical Mozinskis* by buying all six children matching blue work shirts. When they first started out, she and Clara had worn matching outfits for performances, but that was when they were little and still relatively unknown. At this point, the family was doing very well. For example, Allie knew that her parents would be grossing $135,000 per episode next season, and that wasn't factoring in income from record sales, tours, and merchandising (the idea that there were girls running around somewhere wearing T-shirts bearing her brother Bix's face was laughable). There was absolutely a generous costume budget, but her dear father still decided to go to K-Mart or some such hole and buy six blue work shirts for his children and presented them the day after they taped the final episode of Season 2 as though they were treasured gifts. Her mother insisted all the children try them on in the living room. Allie hated having to humor her father in this way, but she put the stiff blue work shirt on over her tank top and buttoned two buttons.

"We look like we just escaped from prison," she said as she tied the bottom ends of the shirt into a loose knot. It looked a little like Emmy Lou from *The Beverly Hillbillies*, but it was better than buttoning the entire thing.

"Or a chain gang," Clara added. Allie noticed Clara had done the same thing to her shirt.

"What's a chain gang?" Theo asked.

"They chain a bunch of prisoners together and make them work outside digging ditches and stuff," Ellington said.

"Chained together? Eeeww, how'd they go to the bathroom?"

"Sometimes they put long-haired homos on the chain gang too, just to scare them."

"Ellington! We don't use that kind of language in this house," their mom snapped.

El gave an exaggerated "Sorry," that clearly did nothing to appease their mom.

As usual, their father was single-mindedly focused. Sometimes it was a song, sometimes it was just the bridge, sometimes it was a meal. Today it was blue work shirts. "You all look great," he said.

"Mom, this is a little big," Viola whispered.

"You'll grow into it," Grace whispered back. "Listen to Daddy for a moment, okay?"

"It looks cute, Viola," Vincent said without really looking at her. "Now you're probably wondering why your dear old dad got you all these cool shirts."

"That's not exactly how I would have phrased it," Allie said.

Susan Petrone

"Well, my dear Allegro, you are partially responsible for the idea."

"Psyche!" Ellington said. He and Bix laughed. The shirts weren't as ugly on them because they were boys.

"What could I possibly have done to make you buy this shirt?"

"The other day you said something about how our family was like a music factory, and that got me thinking about the next album. We're going to call it *Music Factory*, and I was thinking you could all wear these shirts for the album cover photo."

When Allie had said it was like their family was a music factory, she was angry that they had another summer of rehearsing and recording and touring in front of them instead of an actual vacation. She certainly wasn't intending for it to be the title of their third album. She thought it was pretty pathetic that she understood irony at 11 years old, but her father and manager didn't.

"Doesn't the record company have a designer that does the album cover?" Clara asked. "Maybe they'll want to do something different."

"What if we had a picture of a factory on the cover?" Viola asked. "I could draw it."

"Instead of smoke stacks, it could have little musical notes coming out of it," Bix added. He wasn't against the blue shirts in principle, but the shirt was kind of itchy. And this shade of blue didn't look good on him.

"I like that. Good idea, Bix," Vincent said.

"Viola said it first."

"But you had the notes coming out of the smoke stacks...We can still use the work shirts."

"We don't have to use them," Allie said. But her father had moved on to another topic.

The blue work shirts were immortalized on the back cover of the *Music Factory* album. If used record places were still a thing, you could probably find one in the dollar bin. As soon as the photoshoot was over, Allie made sure to "accidentally" stain her shirt with spaghetti sauce so her father wouldn't be tempted to have them all wear the shirts on tour that summer.

Despite the blue work shirts and lack of fun, even Allegro admitted there were some perks to being a child star: She didn't have to go to regular school. She was frequently treated like royalty. The word "prodigy"

130

was bandied about frequently when she was younger, which was certainly a self-esteem builder. And most importantly, she learned early on that she could do almost anything she wanted because she was one of the family breadwinners. She and her siblings were responsible for the family's success. Her mother wrote most of their songs — and they were by and large quite good songs. Her father did the arrangements and sometimes played backup keyboards. But she and her siblings were the primary music makers. Allie had been only slightly exaggerating when she used the term "music factory" to describe her family.

By Season 3, they had the show formula down to a science. There were twenty-six 30-minute episodes, which translated into 22 minutes of actual show time. There were two or three songs every episode, the lineup of which varied based on the assumed plot, but the entire family played on the finale. That was holy law that had come down from Mount Fritz. Everyone over the age of eight got one Birthday Solo episode per season, plus there was the obligatory parents' wedding anniversary episode. The date of their anniversary fluctuated based on the whim of the writers, but the viewers didn't seem to notice or care. There were four special guest episodes per season. Each child could expect to feature in one additional episode per season beyond their birthday episode; however, they had little to no input in the plot. Sometimes it was embarrassing, sometimes it was merely ill-advised. Sometimes both. Take for example the "school candy sale" episode, in which Allie was presumed to be selling candy bars for the school Explorers Club. Not only had she not attended a regular school since age eight, Allie declared at the table-read that she was not a likely candidate for something called the "Explorers Club." The show's interpretation of their personalities bore little relationship to reality. Her protests went unanswered. In the episode, Allie was supposed to be selling candy door-to-door, which allowed Fritz to call in a number of favors and have C-list musicians answer the door as Allie tried to sell them candy. She wouldn't have minded so much if she knew who Sandy Staunton, Michael Rouller, or Bobby Tango and the Bumper Boys were. Neither did most of the studio audience.

The music on the show and on the Musical Mozinskis records was almost exclusively pop music. Allie insisted on playing classical for her Birthday Solos, but wasn't allowed to play anything even remotely challenging in a regular episode until after Theo's first Birthday Solo at the start of Season 3. For some reason, seeing the little boy with longer-than-usual hair play the prelude of Bach's Cello Suite No. 1 in G Major sent everyone into a tizzy. Allie thought it was illustrative of the rampant sexism on set and in their family. The only good thing was that it made it easier to throw in a few classical pieces in the future.

Allegro learned violin because her mother played violin, because the family already owned a violin, and the instrument would not need to be purchased or rented. Allie always took exception to the mythology that her parents had a gift for matching children with instruments as a polite exaggeration. Case in point, Clara and the harp. Clara's long, curly brown hair made her look like an angel as a toddler. If Vincent had a bit more creativity in him, he may well have rented her out at Christmas. Angels reportedly play harps, so by that definition, yes, Clara had the look of a harpist. What her parents always neglected to mention is that the original troubadour harp Clara learned to play on was acquired in a fire sale when a small college nearby was downsizing its music department. They bought the harp for next to nothing and then convinced Clara she was born to play it. Had there been a quarter-size cello available at the same price, it's just as likely they would have stated that she had the long limbs of a fine cellist. It was happenstance, not magic.

Allie played guitar out of necessity, not desire. When Gregor Karpenko and her father first cooked up a scheme to have the family play at the local July 4th celebration back in Cleveland, she was seven and didn't play guitar. She played violin, but Vincent needed a rhythm guitarist and taught her the chords to the three songs they played. Allegro learned them. Once you have calluses on your fingers from one string instrument, it's not difficult to learn another. Allie's fingers had been calloused since she was four. The electric guitar she played at that first performance was borrowed from a friend of her father who owned a music store. It was never clear to her whether the store's owner knew it had been borrowed.

The begging, borrowing, and, let's face it, stealing of instruments stopped when her parents signed the contract for the first season of *The Musical Mozinskis*. After that, it seemed as though Vincent purchased a new instrument every few months. Allie didn't complain because at the beginning of the third season, she was the beneficiary of a new violin. And not just any violin, but a Herbert Stengel from 1900 with a warm, rich tone. Allie had always practiced on Grace's violin because Vincent's unspoken bias against classical music on the show meant that her Birthday Solo was the only time she played violin on the air. Every other performance and recording was on the stupid electric guitar.

Allegro had been lobbying for a new instrument for years. After all, she was her father's favorite. Everybody knew that, even if he never came right out and admitted it. But whenever Allie asked, he gave her the line about classical music not being the family's primary focus. Apparently not even being Vincent's favorite was enough to score a new instrument, until it was. A few weeks before they started production on Season 3 of the show, out of nowhere, her father asked if she wanted a violin of her own so she wouldn't have to use her mom's. The answer, not surprisingly, was a resounding "Yes."

She got the violin on a Saturday in August, driving out to the rare instrument dealer with her father to pick it up. When they got home, the rest of the family gathered around to look.

"It's so pretty!" Viola exclaimed as Allie took it out of the case.

"Wait'll you hear it," her father said.

Allie ordered everyone to sit down so she could grace them with an impromptu recital. She had played the Stengel at the dealer's office, so she knew it was in tune. Allie raised the instrument to her chin and immediately went into Beethoven's Romance No. 2 in F Major. She didn't have it quite up to Mozinski family performance standards, but she couldn't wait to hear it coming out of the Stengel. The instrument didn't disappoint.

When she was finished, the other kids drifted out of the room, but Ellington stayed behind while Allie put the violin gently back in its case. She was going upstairs to practice but didn't want even the slightest risk of damaging the instrument. "So you're all excited about a *used* violin. At least when I got my vibraphone last year, it was new," Ellington said.

"It's not the same thing, idiot. Violins increase in value." Allie knew he knew this. Ellington was just being Ellington. In other words, an asshole.

"It's still secondhand. Somebody else thought it was junk and they got rid of it. You have someone else's 80-year-old junk."

"Does someone else's junk cost $8,000?" she asked.

Vincent had told her not to mention the price of the instrument to anyone, but the look on Ellington's face was worth more than any repercussions from her father. She knew the violin had cost more than El's vibraphone. It was delicious to rub his face in it.

"Eight thousand dollars? What the hell?" El blustered and stormed out of the room. Allie could hear him yelling for their dad as she calmly brought the Stengel up to her room to practice.

The house in Pasadena was big, but not so big that Ellington raising his voice in the living room couldn't be heard in the kitchen. Grace had gone into the kitchen to empty the dishwasher after Allie's impromptu recital on the Stengel. Even after three years and an extended contract from the network, she resisted hiring a maid or a cook. It didn't make sense to spend everything they earned, not when show business was so volatile and uncertain.

Two nights later, when she and Vincent were getting ready for bed, she casually asked about the violin.

"It was a good investment," Vincent said as he squeezed a bit of toothpaste onto his toothbrush. He added, "And it's a legitimate business expense. Lowers our taxes," as he began brushing his teeth.

Grace was sitting on the edge of their bed, watching him through the open bathroom door of the master bedroom. In Cleveland, Vincent had slept in boxers and an old T-shirt. Once they moved to California, he switched to pajama pants and no shirt. She hadn't quite been able to figure out this change in sleepwear. At 43, perhaps he just wanted to think of himself as a sexy California dad. Back in Cleveland, there had been a few times when she suspected he was cheating on her and one time when she knew he had. She didn't think he was messing around on her now. The way their lives were currently configured, they were bound at the hip. Cheating would take more planning and finagling of time and schedules than it was worth.

"I understand that it's a business expense. Just like the vibraphone, and the Venus harp, and Theo's Selmer..."

Vincent spit and said "That's a great-sounding horn, isn't it?"

"We've also bought six guitars over the past three years."

"To be fair, one of those was a bass."

"You know I love a Hammond B3 as much as the next person, and now I own one. Woo-hoo," she said, although she was pretty sure he didn't catch the sarcasm. "You bought me a new trombone..."

"Family horn section. You done in here?" he asked and turned off the bathroom light without waiting for a response.

"We're — correction, *you're* buying instruments faster than they will ever be played. We're instrument rich and cash poor."

"They're investments."

"You bought Viola a Gemeinhardt flute. She doesn't even play flute."

"She might as well learn on the best." Vincent walked over to his side of the bed and took off his watch. "You coming to bed or are you gonna stay up for a while?"

Grace was exhausted and very much ready for bed. Most days were like this. If they weren't taping, they were rehearsing, if they weren't rehearsing, she was writing songs, and if she wasn't writing songs, she was trying to maintain some semblance of order and a minimal level of cleanliness in their house. She flopped back on the bed, her legs dangling off the end, and stayed for there a moment, waiting to see if Vincent would do anything. A touch, a quick kiss on the forehead, or even just a word would be welcome. It felt like she was testing him without letting him know he was being tested.

There was silence in the room for a moment, then Vincent said, "Okay, nighty-night." He half sang the "nighty-night," as though doing so increased the level of affection. For half a second, Grace focused on the pair of slurred notes — F to G — that danced briefly above their bed before the light went out.

SLEIGH RIDE
(Not that one, the Mozart version)

Now that she had a superior instrument, Allie needed more opportunities to play it on the show. For that, she needed allies. She started with Theo because he preferred cello to saxophone the same way she preferred violin to guitar. She tracked him down in the boys' dressing room early in Season 3 during one of the few times when they didn't have show school and weren't actually on set. He was reading a book Jenny the Tutor had assigned him to read. Theo wasn't a great student academically, but he was diligent.

"Hi. I have a proposition," Allie said as she plopped down on the worn blue sofa next to him. The sofa was covered with the same itchy, burlap-like fabric as the sofa in the girls' dressing room but it was better than the chairs in front of the vanity. Those were metal rolling chairs with a thin seat cushion that was about as soft as a paper bag. Most of them had wobbly wheels. You'd think by this time they would have improved the furniture on set, but you'd think wrong.

"What's a proposition?" he asked.

Sometimes Allegro forgot that her brothers were musical prodigies, not necessarily scholastic ones. "A proposal," she said. "Like on *Let's Make a Deal*. I propose that we do a classical piece for the Christmas Special."

Theo made a dismissive little noise that sounded like *Pfft* and appeared as a B-flat above his head. "Dad'll never go for it."

"I found an arrangement of Mozart's *Sleigh Ride* for two violins, cello, and bass. So essentially Mom, me, you, and Clara. All of Dad's favorites."

He made the *Pfft* sound again, this time in F-sharp. "I'm not one of his favorites. You are, and maybe Clara, but that's it." Allie didn't challenge him on whether Mom was still one of Dad's favorites. They both knew what the answer was. She waited and let him think for a moment. "*Sleigh Ride*. Like Leroy Anderson's 'Sleigh Ride'?"

"No, Mozart's *Sleigh Ride*. German Dance No. 3. It's better. It's Christmasy because it mentions sleighs, but it's more challenging than playing more Barry Manilow or ABBA covers."

Theo thought for a moment. They all still felt the sting of the season premiere, which featured bell-bottoms and a cover of ABBA's "Waterloo."

"Good point. Okay, I'll do it if Mom and Clara do it."

"Done," Allie said with far more confidence than any 11-year-old with a limited chance of getting her way ought to have.

Allie knew Fritz and the writers wrote the episodes far in advance, but that was pretty much the limit of her knowledge around the show's inner workings. She wasn't entirely sure how far in advance things got written, but it was already October, so it seemed like she ought to get moving. She found her mother and Mr. Karpenko in the commissary having coffee and talking. They often discussed music because of their shared love for the classical canon. Allie told Grace her idea for a quartet playing Mozart's *Sleigh Ride* for the Christmas Special. Her mother was skeptical, but Mr. Karpenko must have been in a good mood because he said he would take care of it. Allie hadn't always trusted Mr. Karpenko, but he and her father were close. If anyone could convince the music director of *The Musical Mozinskis* to include Mozart's *Sleigh Ride* in the Christmas Special, it was him.

Vincent did all the musical arrangements for the show and would give them to the family a few weeks before taping, so they'd have time to rehearse. He typically sprang the choices on them at home. Allie thought it was so they'd have time to digest his pedestrian taste in music without making a scene in front of the producer or the crew. She wasn't sure if her mother was just humoring her, but she started rehearsing German Dance No. 3 with her, Theo, and Clara, who was only too happy to trade in the electric bass for a double bass for a change.

The Sunday after Thanksgiving, right after dinner, her father gathered the family in the living room and announced that the finale for the

Christmas Special would be a special arrangement of Leroy Anderson's "Sleigh Ride," with strings, horns, percussion, and jingle bells. He specifically looked at Viola when he mentioned jingle bells, because everyone knew her limitations, even if no one had the courage or decency to mention it. He started passing around photocopied sheets of his arrangement.

Allegro took the sheet music and looked at it for a moment, wondering if she had misheard her father. She hadn't. "What about Mozart's *Sleigh Ride*?" she asked.

"Oh sweetie, Mozart didn't write 'Sleigh Ride.' Leroy Anderson did." He kept saying "Lee-roy," like in the Jim Croce song "Bad, Bad Leroy Brown." Allie was already upset, and that didn't help. Situations like this were when her father's refusal to learn the classical canon went from quaint to annoying.

"Mozart did so write a piece called *Sleigh Ride*. Sometimes it's called German Dance No. 3. And by the way, it's pronounced 'La-roy' Anderson, not 'Lee-roy,'" she retorted.

Vincent gave her a blank look. "She's right, you know," Grace said gently. "It is 'La-roy.'"

"Gregor told me you wanted to perform 'Sleigh Ride,'" Vincent said.

The other kids started to snicker. All but Ellington, who actually burst into a genuine laugh. "Obviously there's been a little misunderstanding," Grace said as she stood up and placed a hand on Vincent's arm to calm him. Somehow, she managed to give El a small kick on the shin as she did so. Allie couldn't help but be impressed by this. "We'll talk to Fritz and clear it all up."

"So they're two different songs with the same name?" Viola asked.

"Yeah, dummy," Ellington said.

"Shut up, she's not dumb," Clara said and gave El a push on the shoulder.

"Why does everybody keep beating me up?" he said.

"Because you're a jerk."

"Yes, sweetie, the songs have the same name," Mom said to Viola. "As you can see, it's easy to mix them up."

"What if you played both?" Viola said. "Like what if that was part of the show, where Allie wants to play one song and you want to play the other one and then you play both? Like with the birthday cake?"

"That's a very good idea," Mom said. "What's the plot of the Christmas Special supposed to be?"

"Fritz said something about the younger kids not believing in Santa anymore and the rest of us trying to make them still believe."

"No!" Theo said at the same time Viola said, "But I don't believe in Santa Claus."

"What did you say, sweetie?" Grace asked.

"I don't believe in Santa Claus," Viola repeated.

"Yes, you do. Last year you even got a letter from him. I remember you were so excited," Clara said. She looked genuinely upset at the prospect of the youngest Mozinski not believing in a make-believe character whose annual journey is completely improbable.

"I remember. It looked like the same printing from Mom's typewriter, only in red. I didn't want to disappoint you, so I went along with it."

"Well, I think we've all learned something this evening," Grace said, and it sounded like she was trying to keep from laughing, whether at Viola or Vincent or both was unclear. She was right. Allie learned two things: one, Viola was a little smarter than she thought and two, if she wanted something done, she needed to do it herself rather than trust Mr. Karpenko. Or anyone.

Fritz and the writers liked the whole "Sleigh Ride" kerfuffle idea so much that they used it. Normally each child would get one extra feature beyond their birthday episode. That year Viola got three, because the Christmas Special was all about her, the child who couldn't carry a tune if it weighed two ounces and had a handle. Grace must have even mentioned the Christmas letter from the year before, because they used the "I didn't want to disappoint you" line. It got a huge laugh from the studio audience.

The entire episode was about Viola carrying around a set of sleigh bells and waiting to play "Sleigh Ride" at the end of the episode but having half the family say, "No, the *Sleigh Ride* we're playing doesn't have jingle bells in it," and the other half say "You just have to wait a little bit." It was, in modern parlance, somewhat meta. The writers went whole hog on the "cute little girl at Christmas" theme and even had Viola introduce each song, which is something they never did on the show. Allie found the idea that Viola was being featured in an extra episode annoying at best, but kept her mouth shut. At least she didn't have to wait for her Birthday Solo to play the Stengel on the show.

During the Friday afternoon rehearsal, a few hours before they taped, Don the Director got the idea to have Viola start playing the jingle bells midway through the Mozart. "It'll add texture," he said.

Grace tilted her head slightly in a way that, after two and a half seasons, Don ought to recognize as a sign she'd heard something ridiculous. But all she said was "It's not in the score, but we can try it."

"Excuse me, but I don't think Mozart needs any more texture," Allie added.

Viola was supposed to spend the song watching from one of the chairs on the living room set. She didn't move as she said, "I think it's better without the bells."

"Nonsense, come on over here," Don said. He gave Viola some simple blocking. "Okay, now when Viola starts playing the bells, Allie, I want you to say 'Not yet,' and then Clara says 'I like it.' Grace, you say 'Me too,' and Theo, you give a 'Me three.'"

"Are we supposed to stop playing to say these lines?" Clara asked.

"Yeah, sure, that's a good idea. Then just pick up wherever you left off, only with the bells."

"So we *are* adding the jingle bells to this piece?" Allie asked. "Even though it's not in the score?" This was getting out of hand.

"Yes!" Don with his trademark goofy smile. Fortunately, Allie didn't have to see it too often.

"Some orchestral versions of the German Dance No. 3 feature sleigh bells," her mother said gently. "Let's try it and see."

They tried it, and Viola was off the beat. Even Don the Director could hear it, and he was not known to possess any musical ability. He stopped them and they tried the piece again. The second time, Viola was off the beat but Clara flubbed a note and stopped playing before Don could stop them. "Sorry," she said. "Can we take it again?"

The third time, Viola was still off the beat. This time Theo flubbed an entire measure. "Sorry, I got lost for a second," he said. Allie was starting to think something was up. Theo and Clara didn't make mistakes. Not when they were playing.

Each time they started the piece, it was perfect. Then they did the silly business Don added with Viola interrupting and joining in on the bells. Every time they restarted, Viola was off, but Clara or Theo or even her mother would suddenly make a mistake so they had to stop, making it look like it was their fault, not Viola's. After a certain point, Allie couldn't take it anymore and exclaimed, "This is ridiculous! Why am I the only one who can play this without messing up?"

"Sorry, I haven't played double bass for a long time. Never actually," Clara said lightly. She sounded deliberately neutral.

"Viola, sweetie, do you want to play on this?" Grace asked softly. Up until that point, Allegro had hardly looked at her little sister. It was bad enough that she had to see the pathetic notes from the sleigh bells scooting around in the air, completely removed from everything else being played. But now Allie glanced over to where Viola was once again sitting on the living room chair, waiting for them to start playing again so she could do the stupid business with the sleigh bells that Don had told her to do. She didn't say anything but slowly shook her head. It was something of a revelation. Allegro had never suspected Viola knew that she was different from the rest of the family. She didn't necessarily feel more sympathetic towards Viola, but filed the information away for another day. She didn't have time to process it right then.

"Excuse me, Mr. Kilgore," Theo said. If he was calling Don "Mr. Kilgore," he obviously had a plan. The drama queen parts of his personality complemented the devious parts. "If we add sleigh bells to this piece, do we need to change the script?"

Moments like this were why Allie rarely had to see Don's goofy smile. "What did you mean, Theo?"

"Well, the whole first half of the show, we're telling Viola that one of the pieces has sleigh bells and the other one doesn't. But now we're saying this piece does have bells. If we add this bit, does this mean we have to change the script for the earlier scenes?" Making major changes to the script on show day required an act of God. It was, as they had all heard Fritz say, a royal pain in the ass.

"Should we call Fritz?" Grace asked.

One could almost see the sad, rusty gears in Don's brain turning as he said, "No, that won't be necessary."

Whether in rehearsal or performance, Allegro was always focused on her playing. She would look at the sheet music on the stand in front of her, at her fellow players, at the notes in the air above her, occasionally at her fingers, and sometimes she would close her eyes and look at nothing at all as she played, losing herself entirely to the music.

When they performed German Dance No. 3 in front of the studio audience that night, at the measure where Don had suggested Viola interrupt with the sleigh bells, Allie glanced over at her little sister. Viola was still seated on the chair in the corner, right where Don had told her to sit. Perhaps Allie wasn't entirely convinced that Viola would stay put. She did, though. Viola stayed in the chair, quietly holding the sleigh bells. At the point where Don had told her to start playing, Viola momentarily glanced down at the bells in her hands but didn't shake them, didn't make any noise at all. Allie caught the brief look at the sleigh bells. For a second, she felt sorry for Viola. Honestly, how pathetic was it to not be able to make music? The moment passed and Allie moved on. There were some challenging triplets in the closing measures that she needed to concentrate on.

FINALLY

Allie wasn't the only one who wanted to expand the show's musical offerings. One of the few things she and Ellington agreed on was that they wanted to play something other than saccharine pop music. To be honest, that was the only thing they agreed on, and that was only in principle. Allie wanted to play more classical; El wanted more jazz. Their father wanted better ratings. Normally Bix might have been an ally in the quest for musical diversity, but he was the primary beneficiary of Vincent's reliance on bubble gum music. Now that Bix was 14, the teenybopper magazines had declared him "crush-worthy." Allie found the entire idea of someone being "crush-worthy" to be both elitist and silly. In the end, he was still her big brother Bix: stinky and occasionally annoying and frequently in need of a haircut, although the curls were apparently one of his best features. Fritz told him to keep it shaggy.

In the spirit of the enemy of my enemy is my friend, Allie proposed an alliance to Ellington. During the height of the show's success, it was almost impossible to talk to Ellington or Bix alone. Whether at the studio or at home, if you had one, you had the other. Allie tracked them down in Bix's room one afternoon during the family's three-week break around Christmas and New Year's. Allie avoided El's room at all costs because it smelled like a goat pen and she could almost feel the presence of hidden *Playboy* magazines in every corner. The room Bix and Theo shared was a little less disgusting, thanks to Theo's obsessive-compulsive tendencies. Bix and El were sitting on the floor, leaning against Bix's bed, and taking turns playing a handheld electronic football game Bix got for Christmas. When Allie walked in the room, they both glanced over at her. Bix said, "Hey, Allie," in his usual friendly manner.

Ellington said, "What do you want?"

"I have a proposal."

Ellington just rolled his eyes, but Bix said, "For who?"

Allie resisted the urge to correct him with a "For whom?" She needed them. Instead, she said, "Both of you, I guess." She sat down on Theo's bed, which was a safe distance away on the other side of the room. "We both hate Dad's choice in music..." she began.

"Everybody hates his choice in music except Fritz."

"And the viewing public," Bix added. He had the game in his hands and was frantically pushing a button and saying "Come on come on" to the series of electronic dots on the screen in front of him. It seemed to Allie that he and Ellington were far too invested in the outcome of an imaginary football game.

"What if we present a united front?" Allie said. "Give him some song suggestions — ones where he can show off a little too."

Ellington actually looked up from the game. "Talking to Vincent won't work, but talking to Fritz might. It got me my first Birthday Solo."

"And all the other Birthday Solos," Bix added. "Here, your turn," he said, handing the game to Ellington.

"If you and Fritz are so buddy-buddy, why haven't you asked him if you can play more jazz?" Allie asked, although she suspected it might hit a sore spot. Part of her hoped it would.

"Fritz doesn't like me."

"He's been mad at both of us since we tried to put a leftover sandwich in the garbage disposal in the kitchen sink on the set," Bix explained.

"You do know that sink is fake, right?"

"I do now," Ellington said with a laugh.

"We knew then. We were just curious to see if it would work. I mean, water comes out of the sink so it kind of works."

"Okay, so I'll approach Fritz on my own, but I'll suggest interjecting a little more classical *and* more jazz," Allie said very pointedly. "In return, you two work on Mr. Karpenko."

"Karpenko?" Ellington scoffed. "You know he's scamming the whole family." He was now pushing a button on the game just as earnestly as Bix had been. That seemed to be the point of the entire pointless game.

"Are you saying you think he's embezzling?" Allie asked. "What makes you think he's stealing from us?" she added, because it looked like El might not know what embezzling meant.

"I can just tell."

"Be that as it may..."

"What does that even mean?" Bix asked. "Be that as it may?"

Allie wasn't entirely sure if she was using the phrase correctly, but that was information they didn't need. Especially not when she was outnumbered. "It's just another way of saying 'Anyway.'"

"Why don't you just say 'anyway'?"

"*Anyway*, why don't you two talk to Mr. Karpenko and tell him you want to play a classic, like 'All Of You' by Cole Porter?"

"Cole Porter? I'm sick of Cole Porter," Ellington said.

"Mr. Karpenko likes Cole Porter. And I think Miles Davis does too. He covered it on '*Round About Midnight*, didn't he?" she added in response to their blank looks. The cluelessness of her older brothers was a source of never-ending astonishment.

Ellington actually put down the football game. "Oh yeah, I hadn't even thought about that," he said.

Bix said, "I'm in," and took the game back from Ellington.

"Me too. What do you want to play?"

"Maybe some Schubert. Suggest it for Valentine's Day. People think strings are romantic."

"Done."

Allegro did not share with her brothers her opinion that they were as dumb as a box of rocks.

Allie and Theo played a Serenade by Schubert for the Valentine's Day episode, and the world did not end. At least not for them. It was, however, mortifying for Clara, but not because of the Schubert. The episode was all about her and the boy she has a crush on. In a stunning example of art imitating life, Fritz the Producer or the casting director or *some*one snagged Danny Daley as a guest star. If you aren't familiar with Danny Daley, you were clearly wise enough not to have been reading teen fan magazines in the late 1970s. He was one of the never-ending line of pretty-boy pop stars who had a hit song or two and whose pictures filled the pages of all the teenybopper magazines but whose actual talent level was in inverse proportion to their looks.

Clara had always listened to the pop stations on the radio and knew the words to every song in the Top 40 every week. In a normal family, her ability to play a song after having only heard it twice might seem freakish. In the Mozinski family, it was expected. She had a sizable crush on Danny Daley. Allie wasn't a fan, but had to admit he was classically good-looking in a heteronormative Eurocentric way. At 17, he possessed the wholesome California surfer boy vibe that caused young girls to experiment with self-pleasure. Allie had only anecdotal evidence for this. She did know that if you "accidentally" walked into Clara's room without knocking when she wasn't practicing harp, you might see her looking flushed and embarrassed and you might see the latest issue of *Tiger Beat* open to a photo spread of Danny Daley lying on the bed next to her.

Be that as it may, the show landed the young Mr. Daley as a guest star for the Valentine's Day episode. The thin excuse for a plot was that he was a boy at school Clara had a crush on but who doesn't know she exists, except that of course he does and likes her too. You might have seen this plot twist before. Danny's big hit that spring was "Wherever You Go," a song whose lyrics were borderline stalkerish by contemporary standards. In 1980, with a danceable beat and a cute boy singer, it was pop gold. "Wherever You Go" was going to be the finale of the episode, with the family band playing backup. Clara was fine with that. By that time, the family had played with a dozen guest musicians. It was the second song for the episode that gave Clara trouble, because how can you have a declaration of, if not love, then at least mutual crush, without a duet?

One place where Clara stood in sharp contrast with most of her siblings was her aversion to the spotlight. Allie could not ever remember a time when her older sister requested to sing lead. Ever. It was astounding when she thought about it. If you're going to be onstage, why not be the center of attention?

Clara and Danny had the big declaration of true love scene near the end of the episode. Jane Austen had initiated this trope 175 years earlier, but Mr. Darcy never sang a duet of "Finally" with Elizabeth Bennett to seal the deal. "Finally" was, of course, Danny Daley's first big hit, and it was as sappy a song as the title might lead you to believe. Clara knew the song forwards and backwards and had privately written her own arrangement of it for solo harp. Even so, she didn't want to sing it with him.

The standard schedule dictated that the family meet the guest stars for lunch on Friday, have an afternoon rehearsal, and tape the show in front of a live audience on Friday evening. Even the B- and C-list guests who appeared on the show couldn't be bothered to show up for the table-read. At least until Danny Daley and his agent.

The whole family had to be at the Monday table-read, along with Fritz and Don, and Stacy the AD, who read the stage directions. The writers would sit outside the inner sanctum, taking notes for rewrites. Clara was 16, but Grace and Vincent still wouldn't let her drive herself to rehearsals. Every day, the entire family drove together. On the morning of the Danny Daley table-read, all eight of them trooped into the room together and sat down. They were always together.

Allie sat next to Clara. They used to sit in descending order of age, the way they always did during group interviews, but lately she'd been avoiding Ellington because he was such an asshole. He didn't tickle Clara the way he did Allie, but he could burp and fart on command. He and Bix always sat together. Sometimes they let Theo sit with them, sometimes Theo stayed near her and Clara. Viola always sat next to their mother. Half the time there weren't enough chairs. Allie privately thought this was because none of the crew could count past 10. On the day of the table-read for the Danny Daley episode (Season 3, Episode 19, if you want to be precise), there was one extra chair at the table, right next to Fritz. Allie didn't think anything of it because no one ever wanted to sit next to Fritz or Don. They would always try to make awkward small talk or decide they needed to give one of the children "more screen time," which sounded good in theory, but typically meant something embarrassing. In short, they treated the children like children. Allegro, for one, found this offensive.

Just as they were getting settled, the rehearsal room door opened up and in walked a 30-ish white man in a decidedly expensive, bespoke suit. No one in a suit like that ever came near *The Musical Mozinskis'* set unless they were network executives. None of the family had ever seen this man before. He was followed by none other than Danny Daley in all his pubescent, surfer boy, heartthrob glory. There was a lot of noise in the room, so while Allie couldn't quite hear Clara's barely audible gasp, she clearly saw the slurred F in the air just above their heads and followed her gaze to the sight of Danny Daley and his agent shaking hands with Fritz on the other side of the table.

"He's here..." Clara murmured and grabbed Allie's forearm so hard it hurt. "He's here."

"Ow! Calm down."

Clara removed her hand from Allie's arm and took a deep breath. She had always been impressively talented at tamping down her emotions. Fritz did his overly jolly welcome and went around the table to introduce Danny to everybody. He even made Stacy get an extra chair for Danny's agent, because the agent was apparently too classy to sit in the outer circle peanut gallery with the writers. Fritz opened the read with his usual inflated sense of occasion, welcoming their "esteemed" guests. Then he went around the table and had each family member introduce themself. Fritz turned to Danny sitting on his left and said, "Would you like to start?" as though no one knew who he was.

Danny flashed a big sexy grin and said "Hi, I'm Danny Daley," while looking right at Clara. Allie kicked Clara's ankle under the table. Bix and Ellington kind of snorted back laughs. The entire exercise seemed like a waste of time. Danny's agent was named Ken. He oozed smooth. The Mozinskis might not have been as famous as Danny Daley, but he had to know who they were. About the only people Danny and Danny's agent wouldn't know were Don and Stacy. Allie watched as her parents politely introduced themselves. Viola just gave her first name very quietly.

"Hi Viola, I'm glad to finally meet you," Danny said, which was actually rather kind of him, because Viola didn't do anything on the show except look cute and mouth the words.

"Hey, I'm Ellington Mozinski." El always gave his full name.

"I'm Bix. How're you doing?"

"Hello, I'm Allegro." Allie was almost 12 and figured she was old enough to flirt with Danny Daley too, because why should Clara have all the fun?

"Allegro means *fast*, doesn't it?" Ken the Agent said.

"Lively," Grace said before Allie could respond. She and Viola were on the short end of the rectangular table, with only Vincent and the table's corner in between them, so Ken caught the full brunt of Grace's expression. Allie honestly hoped to never have her mother look at her like that, but was also a little curious as to why she was so angry, especially when her father didn't seem bothered.

There was an awkward silence and then everyone looked at Clara, because it was her turn to introduce herself. "Hello," she said, then added, "Oh, I'm Clara," with a nervous little laugh.

"It's great to meet you. I'm a big fan of your bass playing," Danny said.

Theo was on Clara's other side and simply said, "I'm Thelonious," although it was 50-50 whether Danny was giving Theo his full attention. Stacy and Don introduced themselves, then Fritz said, "And we're back to me!" as though this was somehow a surprise. They started the read, with Stacy reading the opening stage directions. Everything was fine until they got to the obligatory declaration of love scene. Throughout the episode, Clara laments the fact that her crush doesn't know she exists. The writers were so lazy that they even named the character Danny, although Fritz kept saying "The live audience is going to flip their lids when you make your entrance, Danny." The episode unfolded in a fairly predictable way. The rest of the kids tease Clara, which didn't require much of an acting stretch. Allie and Theo sneak in the Schubert. Their parents recite comforting platitudes appropriate for unrequited teenage loves. Clara comes home from school and has the standard heart-to-heart talk with Grace, then the doorbell rings and it's Danny Daley, the crush, standing there to deliver a Valentine and ask Clara out on a date. Clara and Danny sing "Finally," they kiss, Grace invites him to dinner, and then the entire family joins them onstage for "Wherever You Go" for the finale. The looming Sword of Damocles hanging over the table-read was the kiss written into the script.

The family always rehearsed the songs a couple weeks in advance of each episode, but never saw the full script until the table-read. Danny read his line: "Would you maybe want to go out to dinner sometime?" because the writers thought that in 1980, teenage boys still spoke like that to teenage girls they wanted to date.

Clara read her line: "Yeah, that would be great." They never performed any of the songs during the reads, so Stacy merely read the next stage direction: "They sing 'Finally' as a duet. As the song ends, they share a hesitant kiss," and all hell broke loose at the table. All three brothers emitted some sort of variation on the theme of "Holy crap!" Oddly enough, they all did it in G-flat. Viola gasped in a high C. Allie heard Clara gulp. Stacy saved the day by reading the next stage direction, "Grace enters from the kitchen," because the writers always had her entering from the kitchen. Grace calmly delivered her line, "Hello, I don't believe we've met," which was actually funny on a number of levels.

Not only did Danny Daley attend the table-read, he showed up for rehearsal on Thursday, which was both unnecessary and unprecedented. It was ostensibly so he could rehearse both numbers with the family. Allie had her doubts.

Normally if they weren't in a scene, Allie and her siblings were in show school or wandering around the studio lot, or in their dressing rooms, or the commissary, or literally anywhere else but on the set. The set was work. But when Clara and Danny rehearsed the "Finally" scene on Thursday, all of the other children managed to find their way to the set when they all should have been in show school. Jenny the Tutor must have been very lonely that day. Ellington and Bix sat in the last row of audience seats, as though they thought no one would notice them back there. They made enough noise that everyone did. Theo and Viola were younger but slightly stealthier. They stood on the sidelines, near Camera 2, which was operated by Sean, an older African-American man who had children of his own and never lost his patience when the kids bothered him.

Allie watched from the second row on the far aisle, house right. It wasn't a bad vantage point. Her mom was on set because she was in the scene, and her dad was on set because he was the music director with an inflated sense of self-importance. For the moment, she was at liberty.

Clara had been walking through the blocking of the scene all week with Stacy reading Danny's lines. No kiss. Not even pantomimed. Don started off by giving Danny his blocking and then they ran through the scene. Because all the music on the show was played live, not recorded, Clara was playing piano on "Finally." Allie thought this was one of the few times her father had a useful idea. As long as Clara had something to do with her hands, she could sing a solo. On "Finally," she and Danny traded verses and sang the third verse together. As a standard pop song, it only had three verses, all of which were lyrically uninspiring and slightly derivative.

They ran through the scene a few times, and when they got to the song, Vincent stopped them twice. The first time was because he thought Clara started the tempo a little too fast; the second time because he wanted Danny to give the slightest pause before the words "ready" and "steady" to punctuate the admittedly simplistic rhyme on a song that Danny had already sold 500,000 copies of with no pause before "ready" or "steady." They started the song a third time. Clara set the perfect tempo, Danny punctuated all the end rhymes like a champion troubadour, and when they got to the end of the song, Allie would have bet her Stengel that Clara would deliberately mess up again to delay having to kiss Danny Daley in front of everybody because she was so nervous. And she would have been out an $8,000 violin because Clara and Danny finished the song, gazed deep into each other's eyes, and shared a kiss that wasn't nearly as hesitant as the script called for.

"They got past that pretty easily, didn't they?" Ken the Agent had sat down in the seat next to Allie sometime during the rehearsal. She hadn't paid much attention to him. This was the first time he'd spoken. Allie wasn't really sure what she was supposed to say in response, so she just said, "I guess so." They had to keep their voices low because the rehearsal was still going on. Don was talking camera angles.

"I've been watching you," Ken said in a low voice. "Your violin playing is exquisite."

This was something Allie knew how to respond to. "Thank you," she replied. "I prefer the violin to anything else."

"You should be playing it exclusively."

"I wish."

"Have you talked to your parents or your agent about this?"

"I don't have an agent. At least I don't think I do. We have Mr. Karpenko. He's our manager. Him and my parents."

"Has Mr. Karpenko ever booked you for any orchestral or chamber music engagements?"

"Playing with an orchestra would be amazing, but none of us have ever done anything like that."

"How old are you, Allegro?"

"I'll be 12 next month."

"So young, yet so old..." Ken whispered. "Martha Argerich was playing piano concertos with some of the world's leading orchestras when she was younger than you are. Yo-Yo Ma played cello for President Eisenhower when he was a little boy. Why not Allegro Mozinski?" He was close enough that Allegro could smell his aftershave. Her father wore English Leather. She knew that because the bottle came in cute little wooden boxes that she used to fight Theo for when they were younger. Ken the Agent's aftershave smelled different. It smelled like money and opportunity. "Would you like to play a concerto with an orchestra?"

"Yes," she replied, and realized that she had been holding her breath the entire time he was talking because it sounded more exciting than anything she had ever done before.

"You're the most talented one in the bunch," Ken the Agent said as he leaned back in his chair and added almost as an afterthought "It's a shame they're holding you back."

He didn't say anything after that, they both just sat there quietly and watched Clara and Danny run through the scene and the song a few more times before lunch break. After that the family rehearsed "Wherever You Go" with Danny, but the entire time Allie kept wondering *Why not me?*

Her mother's first words when Allie told her Ken the Agent was going to book her to play a concerto with an orchestra were "Absolutely not." Allegro had expected this and was prepared. They were sitting in the commissary having something to eat before the last rehearsal of the day. Allie couldn't remember the last time her family had eaten dinner at home during the week. It had to have been sometime around Christmas. "Could you tell me what your objections are?" she asked politely.

"I don't want you galivanting around the country with a strange man. Plus, you don't even know if this will actually happen. I'm sure Mr. Osso was just making polite conversation."

Up until that point, Allie hadn't been entirely sure what Ken the Agent's last name was. She hadn't thought to ask. "He assured me that he could make it happen," she replied, although she was well aware that Ken the

Agent had made no assurance. At least not in so many words. She wasn't completely lying, plus using that phrasing with her mother made her sound convincing. "After all, he's Danny Daley's agent, and look at his career."

"Does Mr. Osso manage other classical musicians?"

"I don't know."

"Has he shown you a contract?"

"No," Allie replied. She realized that her mother was questioning her as though she were an adult. Allie typically appreciated this, except when doing so accentuated the fact that she wasn't one, in which case she hated it.

"You do realize that we already have a manager."

"Yes, but Mr. Karpenko isn't an *agent*..."

"I understand that. If you want to be released from your contract, then you would have to discuss it with Mr. Karpenko directly. And probably some lawyers. Are you prepared to do that?"

This was absolute rubbish, and Allie told her so. "They wouldn't let me talk to lawyers. I'm a kid!" she exclaimed. "That's why I'm asking you..." As soon as she said this, Allie realized she had pretty much made her mother's argument for her.

Allie typically didn't like to be touched, but when her mother placed a hand on her hair and looked right into her eyes, she didn't mind too much. "Allie, you're a brilliant young woman and a deeply gifted musician," Grace said. "My job is to keep you safe and to help you develop your talent. If Mr. Osso is interested in booking you in classical venues, he'll need to go through proper channels. I guarantee you he knows this."

"Are you the proper channel?"

"I'm one of them."

"Then why did he talk to me first?"

"I assume it was to see if it was something you'd even be interested in. And I'm sure because he knew you'd come and talk to me. May I add that I'm very glad you did." Her mother paused for a moment, like she was trying to decide how to say something or maybe whether to say it at all. "Sweetie, as you get older, more people may approach you, asking for something from you. Please, please, please talk me about it. And if anyone ever does or says something that makes you feel uncomfortable, leave the room immediately and come and find me. Do you understand?"

"Of course," Allie replied because she was not wired to admit she didn't understand something. It was kind of obvious her mom was talking about Ken the Agent. "I get it, we already *have* a manager."

"That isn't entirely what I mean, but...we'll leave that discussion for another day."

It still seemed like her mom was trying to tell her something else, but if it was that important then she'd just come out and say it.

Allie took a bite of her chicken cacciatore while she thought about all this. The problem with being a child prodigy is that you aren't able to dictate the terms of your engagement with the world. Adults, including parents, treat you like a short adult until they decide to pull rank. Then they treat you like a child. It was beyond frustrating. Allie made sure to daintily wipe her mouth with her napkin before saying "*When* Mr. Osso talks to you about this, please let him know that I'm very interested."

Grace took a thoughtful sip of her tea. Allie waited for her to say something. Going head-to-head in the dramatic pause arena with the person who had taught her the value of such a pause was a frequent exercise in the student trying to usurp the master. "*If* he speaks to me about it, I will," her mother said finally. Her reply was the conversational equivalent of the fat lady singing in the opera. Conversation over. The next time Allie saw Ken the Agent, she told him to talk with her father about booking her in classical venues. In retrospect, Allie realized she should have saved herself the trouble and talked to her dad in the first place. He was annoying in any number of ways, but he absolutely understood the importance of one's career path.

The Valentine's Day episode beat out every other show in *The Musical Mozinskis'* time slot. This was clearly thanks to Danny Daley, but it also meant more people than usual heard Allie and Theo play Schubert. Clara even got hate mail from crazed Danny fans because she got to kiss him on national television, which just goes to show you how petty teenage girls can be.

Allie kept her word to Ellington and Bix and talked to Vincent about including more jazz in the show mix. When she told him it would "add to our musical diversity," he replied that he was impressed by her vocabulary, which made Allie wonder if he had ever bothered to listen to her speak.

POMP AND CIRCUMSTANCE

The first episode of *The Musical Mozinskis* aired in September 1977, a month before Theo turned six. Viola was four. The two of them grew up on camera in a way their older siblings did not. When the older kids were rehearsing or performing, Vincent would give the smaller ones wood blocks or the ubiquitous tambourine so they could play with the rest of the family. Off camera, they practiced. The four older Mozinskis had gone to school and had friends and did normal things before the family hit it big. Theo went to show school starting in kindergarten, but he always wondered what it would be like to go to regular school. Life was all about music — learning it, rehearsing it, performing it — and always with his siblings. Occasionally, one of them would have a short-lived friendship with a counterpart child star on the studio lot, but those kids turned out to be just as messed up as they were.

Show school was a single room with the six Mozinski children and one tutor. It was a little like being homeschooled, except instead of being taught by one of their parents, they had Jenny the Tutor, who was fresh out of college the first season. Jenny was competent, although Theo didn't have any other teachers to compare her to until he was 10, which seemed like an awfully long time to live with substandard instruction. He suspected that Jenny the Tutor privately gave up sometime during the second season. To be fair, his brother Ellington had the intellectual capacity of a gnat, while Allie was borderline genius. You could say that the family traversed the full academic spectrum.

If there was a show-school fight, it was almost always between Allie and Ellington. Theo managed to stay out of most of the drama, at least for the first season, when he and Viola weren't regulars. On heavy rehearsal days, their parents used Jenny the Tutor as a sort of glorified babysitter. When the four older kids were on set, Jenny would sometimes just give the younger ones a few worksheets and call it a day. Other times they'd go for walks around the studio lot or play games. Jenny was the one who taught Theo and Viola how to play go fish and crazy eights and checkers. They did a lot of art projects too. There was time for it because Theo and Viola were the only two who routinely exceeded their instructional hours for the week. Stacy the Assistant Director had the crew put a few of their drawings on the set refrigerator for added authenticity.

Theo wasn't crazy about art class, as Jenny called it. It was mainly an excuse to draw or color or make things out of paper, but Theo always gave it his all because Viola liked it. He had to admit she was much better at drawing than he was. Whenever Jenny pulled out the construction paper or colored pencils, Theo made sure to get as excited as Viola did. It just seemed like she needed something to be good at because she was kind of an oddball. Theo knew he wasn't anywhere near normal, but sometimes Viola would say things that really didn't make any sense. For instance, the two of them would be drawing or playing a game and she'd say something like "Your voice is purple when you sing."

The first time she said something like that was near the beginning of Season 2. Jenny had him and Viola making jack-o'-lanterns out of construction paper. They cut orange paper into the shape of big pumpkins, then cut black construction paper into different shapes for the eyes and mouth. The pièces de résistance were the accordion-folded strips of orange paper that would become the jack-o'-lantern's springy arms and legs. The accordion folding was time-consuming business, and Theo was concentrating hard, folding the long strips of paper first this way then that. It took him a moment to figure out how to do it properly. Jenny had to show him twice, while Viola got it right away. Viola was pretty much useless as a musician, so he didn't feel too bad that she understood how to accordion-fold a strip of paper. He could play an arpeggio on the cello with a vibrato as quick as the flutter of a hummingbird's wings. In the greater scheme of things, he figured he had the more useful skill. When Viola said his voice was purple, he only half heard her.

"What?" he asked. This time he remembered to flip the strip of paper over to fold it the other way.

Viola had already finished one of her jack-o'-lantern's arms and was folding and flipping away on the next one like she didn't have a care in the world. "Your voice is purple when you sing," she repeated, as though Theo should actually know what she was talking about.

"I don't get what you mean."

"Your voice is purple," she said again, a little louder this time.

"Oh, okay," he said blankly. Theo wasn't trying to be mean. He always made a point of not teasing her — at least not about music. Losing in checkers was fair game. He had already kind of figured out that Viola couldn't see music the way he could — the way the rest of the family could. It was kind of sad that she was pretending she could, and she wasn't even pretending right.

Viola stopped folding and flipping for a second. "Just...forget it," she said.

He didn't think much about what Viola said; he was more focused on getting his playing up to the level where he could play something on the show beyond the finale. Theo gravitated toward the cello early on. It was the most sublime sound he had ever heard, even if he didn't know the word "sublime" when he was three and started lessons. He just remembered seeing the cello and liking the shape and the sound. It looked like the violin Allie and his mother played, only bigger. Maybe the attraction was just that little kid thing of wanting something big, but Theo chose the cello or the cello chose him.

The instrument had always felt like an extension of his body. Once Theo picked up the cello, everyone knew it would be his primary instrument. All of the children had a primary instrument and a secondary instrument. Grace and Vincent suggested a woodwind for Theo's secondary instrument. When they suggested the clarinet, he asked for a saxophone. It was the only time that one of the Mozinski children had flat out refused their parents' instrument suggestion. Theo liked the saxophone because it had panache. Theo didn't know the word "panache" either when he was five, but the saxophone made him feel like he could swagger.

With the lineup of the family band fairly set, it was obvious that Theo and Viola were looked at as the bench players, there to fill in the gaps. They were the farm system for the family business. Theo didn't focus on an instrument someone else in the family already played until Clara graduated from high school.

Show school had one overwhelmingly redeeming quality: each of the children could work at their own pace. Jenny the Tutor had material they were required to learn via the State Board of Education. When you're the only one in your grade, you don't need to wait for the rest of the class to get the hang of whatever it is you're were studying. At the start of Season 4, Theo learned that if you didn't fart around, you could get out of high school nearly a full year earlier than your show business-obsessed father expected. That's when he realized Clara would someday go to college and the family band would need a new bass player.

He'd heard Clara and Jenny the Tutor talking during show school the previous week, but it went in one ear and out the other. School was an afterthought. He thought they were talking about homework or something. He didn't think anything of it until Sunday dinner after the first show week of the season.

When he was very young and they lived in Cleveland, Theo vaguely remembered having family dinners on Mondays because nobody hires musicians for a Monday night gig. Once they moved to California and started doing the show, they typically had dinner at the commissary during the week. That's when their parents decided to make Sunday dinner a required affair. By the fourth season, Sunday dinner didn't quite have the emotional heft it that it used to. There was always someone who didn't want to be there. Either Ellington wanted to go hear a band somewhere or their father wanted to work on arrangements or Allie acted as though she literally would rather be anywhere else in the world. The main attraction was their mother's cooking.

Clara's GED bombshell could only have been detonated during this time slot. Theo admired how she mentioned she was graduating, but it came out as though she was asking him to pass her the green beans, which she actually did right after she mentioned taking the GED. It was quite the performance.

He passed the bowl of green beans over to Clara, all the while wondering why his mother was smiling and singing *baa-ba-ba-bah-baa-dah, baa-ba-ba-bah-baa-dah* to a tune he'd never heard before.

"What are you singing?" Ellington asked.

"It's called *Pomp and Circumstance*," Grace replied. "They play it at graduations."

"Taking the GED means Clara's going to graduate from high school," Allie said to Ellington.

"No duh. I knew that."

"Just checking. You seemed a little confused."

"I'm gonna take it next year, probably," he replied.

"Funny thing. Me too," Allie said. Through Ken the Agent, Allie had played concertos with four orchestras during the summer, which meant they could expect her to be more insufferable than usual until October, at the very least.

"So what does this mean?" Vincent said.

"It means I'm graduating from high school," Clara said.

"It means you won't have to go to show school anymore. Lucky," Bix said.

Ellington gave a signature "Oh!" like he had just discovered a diamond in the mashed potatoes. "We should do an episode about it so we could play Alice Cooper."

"Yes!"

Bix and Ellington shout-sang the first two lines of "School's Out" then quieted down once they realized that now was not the time.

"And I'm looking at colleges," Clara said.

Vincent paused for a moment then said, "Well, I'm sure a class or two here and there wouldn't get in the way of the taping schedule," and took another bite of chicken as though unilaterally deciding Clara's immediate future was all in a day's work.

While the other kids had their eyes on their father, Theo scanned his siblings. The optimistic ones like Viola and Bix seemed to be waiting to see if their dad would say anything else, the cynical ones like Allegro and Ellington looked incredulous because they knew he wouldn't. Theo looked to Clara and his mom at the other end of the table. The two of them exchanged a look and then his mom said, "Conservatories don't allow for part-time students."

"We have a contract, dear," Vincent said. "We, all of us, have a contract with the network."

"I never signed a contract," Clara said carefully.

"Your mother and I signed it on your behalf because you're minors."

"Until December." Clara said this so softly that it would have been easy to miss if this were a normal, free-wheeling Mozinski dinner table conversation instead of one of the most entertaining back-and-forths the family had witnessed since Allegro told Fritz the Producer that the choosing of a birthday cake flavor was not a compelling dramatic arc. Theo had never in his life heard Clara backtalk their father, or anyone really. Allie might have been Dad's favorite, but Clara was always the good girl. It was sort of a heady is-this-really-happening experience to hear her speak up for herself.

"Our entire family is under contract to the network, which means you are contractually obliged to attend all rehearsals and tapings for *The Musical Mozinskis.*"

"I wasn't talking about this year. Next year." And just like that, she was back to being Clara the Quiet.

LET'S GET IT ON

During Season 4, there was a very bad sitcom called *Family Way* that taped one soundstage over from *The Musical Mozinskis*. It was about a family with three teenage daughters, the eldest of whom gets pregnant. The entire family decides to raise the baby with her. Hilarity does not ensue.

The younger daughters were played two actresses named Valerie DelVecchio and Natalie Givens. They were 17 and 15, but played a little younger on the show. Theo was eating lunch with his brothers in the studio commissary the first time Ellington and Bix saw Valerie and Natalie. It was fascinating to watch his older brothers go from burping contest to on-the-make in the blink of an eye. He could almost see El puff out his chest and shake up his plumage like some dissipated bird going into a mating dance. Bix didn't seem to have to do anything to make girls drop their panties for him. Theo had never personally seen any female panty-dropping, nor was he at all interested in it. However, Ellington seemed obsessed with girls' panties and their removal and talked about it pretty much anytime there were no adults or sisters around so Theo got an earful all the same.

The teenybopper magazines always talked about Bix's hair, which was light brown and curly like Clara and Viola's, and his eyes, which were also brown, and in which a girl could apparently get lost. Ragging on Bix for his dreamy curls and soulful eyes was one of the few activities Ellington and Allie could agree on. Theo suspected that Ellington gave Bix a hard time because those magazines almost never wrote about him. Their publicist was always sharing photos and articles with his parents in order to justify her existence. The teen magazines focused almost exclusively on Bix. Theo was nine and too young to be regarded as crush-worthy. This was not a problem. He had already discovered he didn't want his picture in those magazines with all the pretty boys. He knew the magazines were supposed to be for girls, but he liked looking at them too.

Ellington was 17, which should have been prime teenybopper fodder. He wasn't ugly. At least Theo hoped not, because they shared the same dark hair and blue eyes as their father and Allie. If El was ugly, then he probably was too. And no one had ever called Allie ugly. The problem with Ellington was not his looks but his look. As Jerry of the writing staff put it, "In a regular high school, Ellington would be voted 'Most Likely to Stab You in Your Sleep.'"

While not even his mother would describe Ellington as cuddly, Valerie DelVecchio apparently liked noncuddly bad boy drummers. It didn't hurt that *The Musical Mozinskis* was going into its fourth season and Valerie only had a Flintstones vitamins commercial on her resume prior to landing *Family Way*. Dating Ellington Mozinski was a good move for her career-wise. The Mozinski brothers and the girls from *Family Way* first met up in October and were bona fide items by Christmas. Theo had a front row seat to his older brothers' first serious relationships. Every day in the boys' dressing room, Ellington would hold court on how far he had gotten with Valerie.

The three-week break around Christmas and New Year's put a temporary stop on all this because while both Ellington and Bix had been able to see their girlfriends during the break, they hadn't had any privacy. Doing the show week after week might have been a grind, but the combination of their two soundstages and an entire studio lot equaled countless corners and closets where they could be alone. After the table-read on the first day after the holidays, the boys had a short break before show school. Their mother sent them to the dressing room to study that week's script.

Theo walked in and immediately claimed one end of the ugly blue dressing room sofa before his big brothers got there. The sofa was scratchy, but it was still more comfortable than the metal rolling chairs by the vanity. Bix came in right after him and took the other end of the sofa.

"Looks like you get one of the crappy chairs," Theo said. He didn't often have a chance to get the best of Ellington, even if it was just about where to sit.

"Like I care," Ellington said as he dropped that week's script on the vanity. "I'm gonna go find the girls, you wanna come?" he added to Bix.

"Allie and Viola are probably already at show school," Theo said.

"Not those girls, idiot. Bix, you coming?"

"Natalie and I are meeting at lunch. And we have show school in like half an hour."

"Forget show school. I haven't gotten laid in more than three weeks."

Theo's sex education had ramped up considerably since his brothers started hanging out with the girls from *Family Way*. He knew that getting laid was another way of saying going all the way, which was sex and also how babies were made. The first time Ellington told him about the mechanics of the whole thing, Theo was sure he was joking. It was only when Bix corroborated the story that Theo believed it. According to Ellington, it felt amazing. Theo knew it felt pretty good to touch his own penis. While the idea of having someone else touch it for him was intriguing, the prospect of putting it inside a girl just seemed like one of the most ridiculous things he'd ever heard.

Bix was still on the sofa, that week's script in hand. "Why don't you just see her later when you have more time?"

"If you had ever actually got in Natalie's pants, you'd understand."

"I've gotten in her pants."

Ellington snorted. "You haven't *screwed* her. And until you do, you won't get why I'm going to find Valerie, bring her to that prop room nobody uses near the back of their soundstage, lay her ass down on the sofa that's in there..."

"I get it," Bix interrupted. "Geez, there's children present."

"I'm not a child!" Theo said.

"You don't need to hear this."

"Sure he does. We have make sure Theo doesn't end up some long-haired homo."

Ellington said this looking straight at Theo, who felt suddenly exposed. Homos were guys who liked other guys, which, according to Ellington, was pretty much the worst thing you could be. There were plenty of rock stars with long hair, like the singer from Journey and everybody in Mötley Crüe, so Theo was comfortable with his hair being down to his shoulders. The whole homo thing was another story. He had never told anyone that he liked looking at the teen magazines because he thought some of the boys in them were cute. It seemed like Ellington knew somehow.

"I'm not a homo," he said. And just to make sure that his brothers left him alone, he added "If there was a girl my age on *Family Way*, I'd tap her ass." He'd heard Ellington say this about some of the fans who hung around the soundstage door after the show taped. It didn't quite have the effect he wanted because Ellington and Bix burst into laughter.

"Come on, Bix," Ellington managed, "if you cut school for her, Natalie will know how much you like her. Theo will cover for both of us, right?"

Bix had stood up and both of his older brothers were now looking down at him expectantly. "Tell Jenny we had to go to wardrobe for costume fittings," Bix said.

"Okay," Theo replied. Truly there was no other acceptable answer.

Helping Bix go all the way with Natalie became his and Ellington's winter project. In order to achieve this goal, they played to their strengths. In late January, Bix told Theo that they were going to record a cover of Marvin Gaye's "Let's Get It On." Theo kind of laughed because he knew what that song was about. Granted the first time he heard it, he wasn't entirely clear on what getting it on entailed, but several months of listening to Ellington had wised him up. Theo definitely knew the song was on the List of Inappropriate Songs for *The Musical Mozinskis*. But if it was just the kids and no parents, then it wasn't really *The Musical Mozinskis*, it was just a Valentine's Day gift for his brothers' girlfriends, which kind of made it all right. Plus, he'd get a chance to play saxophone on a funky track. That was enough incentive to conveniently forget to tell his parents about the song.

The Mozinski siblings recorded "Let's Get It On" on a Saturday afternoon during one of the rare times when both their parents were out.

Grace and Vincent had always made a point of a monthly date night, although the definition of what constituted a "date" evolved over the years. That month, they had opted to go out to lunch and to do errands. Clara wondered what it would be like to have mundane, boring dates like that. All the times she'd gone out with Danny Daley last year, every date had been planned out to the minute. Danny hadn't been allowed to drive them himself due to insurance and safety concerns. At least that's what Ken the Agent said. Instead, Danny would always pick her up in a hired car with a chauffeur and they'd go out to dinner and then to a movie premiere or play or concert or somewhere where it paid to have Danny Daley be seen with Clara Mozinski and vice versa. The only time they were ever able to just hang out on their own and have a few hours to do whatever they wanted was the one time Danny came to the house when Clara was supposed to be babysitting Theo and Viola because everyone else was gone. She had to bribe those two not to tell their parents because they'd worry she and Danny would get up to some sort of unchaperoned mischief, which they did. The actual sex had been a little hurried, because Clara was worried one of the younger kids would walk in on them and because Danny wasn't as experienced as he let on. Still, Clara had done it, gladly leaving her virginity in the rearview mirror.

She had mixed feelings about participating in a recording whose sole purpose was to help Bix lose his virginity and felt like her time was better spent doing almost anything else. There was a lot going on. Ever since the performance at Cain Park during their first tour, she had kept one eye on her parents, tracking how they and their music interacted. Clara didn't care too much for herself if they stayed together. After all, she was starting college in the fall and wouldn't even be here if they split up. It just didn't seem fair to the little kids like Viola and Theo. Granted, she hadn't yet told her parents she'd been accepted to the Cleveland Institute of Music to study harp. That could wait until after the season finale. There was too much going on just now.

Clara made a point of being the last one to show up in the recording studio their father had built in the basement of the house in Pasadena. He justified the expense by saying it would allow the family to record good quality demos, even though it wasn't used all that often. Clara thought of it as one more example of conspicuous consumption. It seemed more like an excuse to spend a lot of money and acquire a lot of equipment. As usual, Viola wasn't playing, but she was there, lingering on the outskirts of whatever her siblings were doing.

"Hey Clara!" Bix said cheerfully. "I was just about to send Viola up to your room to get you."

"I'm not your errand girl," Viola said without looking up from the large pad of paper she was drawing on.

"You are no one's errand girl, sweetie," Clara said. To Bix she merely sighed, "Tell me why we're doing this again?" even though she knew perfectly well that the whole point of the song was so that Bix might convince Natalie Givens to dance the horizontal tango with him.

"So Ellington and Bix can have sex with Valerie and Natalie," Allie said.

"It's not like that!" Bix said at the same time Ellington was saying, "Maybe I already have."

"If you've already done it, why do we have to record the song?" Allie asked.

"I really like Natalie, okay? I want to do something special for her for Valentine's Day," Bix said, although it seemed like he was arguing with nobody.

"Why do you want to have sex with her?" Viola asked loudly. The others stopped and Ellington, Bix, and Allie burst out laughing.

"Oh honey," Clara said slowly, "sometimes older...teenagers — or adults like to kiss and hug. And sometimes they...touch each other. It's a way of showing the other person that they love them."

"I know that part." Viola put down her green colored pencil on the top of the mixing board and looked at Bix. "So does that mean you're in love with Natalie Givens?" Viola asked.

One of Bix Mozinski's most striking qualities was his incapacity to be embarrassed. Even with all five of his siblings staring at him, at least three of whom were thinking up any number of good insults, he didn't blush or stammer. He simply said, "It's a little too soon to use that word, but I have strong feelings for her."

"Are you in love with Valerie?" Viola asked Ellington.

"None of your business."

"That means he is," Allie said.

Ellington threw a drumstick at her, but only because she wasn't holding her guitar. Instruments were always protected. People were secondary.

"Can we just record this?" Bix said. "We need to get done before Mom and Dad get home."

"Fine," Clara said as she slung the bass over her shoulder. They did a rough run-through of the song, and it wasn't too bad for the first time. Bix nailed the *wah-wah-wah-waaah* guitar opening. Even if the overall result didn't have the funky aphrodisiac powers of the original, it was surprisingly respectable considering that two-fifths of the band had yet to reach puberty and most of those who had were still virgins.

After the first run through, Ellington said, "Bix, you need to give it more...oomph," and kind of half stood up behind the drum kit and gave a hard pelvic thrust on the *oomph*.

"El, I don't think Viola or Theo or, geez, any of us need to see that," Clara said.

"I'm just saying that it's, you know...baby-making music..."

"No. It's. Not," she said and didn't even care if she sounded like the mean older sister she had never been. Her brothers decidedly did not need baby-making music. She and Danny hadn't needed baby-making music in order to do the nasty. Not that her brothers needed to know that.

"Yeah, it is."

"Not for you two. There will be no baby-making. Viola, go 'la-la-la-la-la,'" Clara said, putting her hands over her ears to demonstrate.

Viola put her pencil down in frustration. "Why am I the only one not allowed to hear this?"

"Who here knows where babies come from?" Allie said, raising her hand. Viola and Theo looked at Allie, Bix, and El, who all had their hands raised, and then at each other, who didn't. They both shyly raised theirs. Clara figured the younger two learned everything they knew from listening to Ellington because Grace Mozinski didn't have The Talk with her kids until they were 12. If her mother wouldn't correct the information, she'd probably have to do it.

"When did you two learn this? Last week?" Allie said sarcastically.

"Leave them alone," Clara said.

"I'm just saying if either of them actually knows anything about where babies come from, they probably just learned it."

"It doesn't matter when they learned it."

"God, Clara, you act like sex is some dirty thing. Lighten up."

"Ellington, shut up," she snapped. The whole thing was getting out of hand. "Can we please just stop having inappropriate conversations in front of the little kids?"

"We're not little!" Theo and Viola said at the same time.

Bix gave them one of his reassuring Bix smiles. "Theo, Viola, I know you're not *little*, but this song does deal with some...mature themes. I think you can handle it, but we'll stop talking about it and just play, okay?"

"Okay," they replied.

"And please don't mention the song to Mom or Dad."

"Or Karpenko," Ellington added.

"Right."

"I can keep secrets," Viola said, and Clara could have sworn her baby sister was talking directly to her when she said this.

"We both can," Theo added. Clara was curious about what kind of dirt Theo had on Ellington, but knew this wasn't the time to ask.

"When we were sitting outside at the picnic table the other day, Natalie let me braid her hair and then she braided mine. She's cool," Viola said.

"You know, this recording is for Valerie too. Not just Natalie," El said. He was clearly annoyed that nobody was mentioning his girlfriend.

"Valerie is not nice," Viola informed Ellington. This was not news, but it was one of the rare times someone pointed it out.

"So what?" he replied.

"So why do you still want to have sex with her if she's mean?"

"Enough with talking about having sex!" Clara said. "You know what? I'm sick of this. I'm making an executive decision. I think all six of us should play on this. Viola too." The others looked from Clara to Viola in shock. When Clara added "And not tambourine," Ellington's jaw dropped low enough to hit his floor tom.

"Are you kidding?" he exclaimed.

Ever the diplomat, Bix added "I'm not sure we have time to redo the arrangements."

"Either Viola plays or I don't."

This was a bold gambit. Clara really didn't want to do the stupid recording in the first place. She figured Bix and Ellington would never agree to have Viola play on their little seduction song and she could just go on her merry way. It was, in theory, an easy way out of wasting an entire afternoon. The big question mark in all this was, of course, Viola.

Bix asked the question they were all wondering: "Do you want to play?"

Viola stopped for a moment. This was the first time any of them had ever invited her to play. She was always added in by one of their parents or Don the Director. "I guess so," she said quietly.

"Viola, you can read music, right, buddy?" From Clara, that question would have sounded condescending. From Theo, it would have sounded supportive. From Ellington or Allie, it would have sounded incredulous. Bix managed to make it sound neutral.

Viola looked a little defensive as she replied in the affirmative. Clara was pretty sure the answer was not entirely truthful, but she already felt bad enough for the kid.

"You know if you can't read music by the time you're eight, Mom and Dad will put you up for adoption," Ellington said.

Clara sighed. "That joke has never been funny," she said.

"Johnny Carson laughed at it."

"Shut up, Ellington."

"You said not tambourine," Bix said to Clara. "So what is she gonna play?"

Clara had been so sure Bix and Ellington would veto Viola playing on the track that she hadn't even thought about a possible instrument for her youngest sibling. She looked across the room and saw the over-priced, underused Hammond B3. "Viola, you're playing keyboards."

Bix and El gave her a stereo "What?"

Clara ignored them. "If I show you what to play, can you do it?" she asked Viola.

"I can try."

"Good enough for me." Clara sat Viola down at the keyboard and stood behind her. "Run through it again," she instructed. As they ran through the song again, Clara added a simple one-note-at-a-time keyboard part that echoed the bass line. She showed Viola exactly what to play. Viola copied her, playing it with one single index finger. "Watch me," Clara said. "If you aren't sure, I'll nod whenever you need to play a new note." The keyboard addition was beyond easy and didn't add much depth to the song, but it meant Viola was technically playing with her siblings.

They recorded the song on the reel-to-reel, then Bix and Ellington made three copies on cassette, one each for Valerie and Natalie and one for themselves. It is the only extant recording of all six Mozinski children playing at the same time, no parents, no tambourine.

4'33"

The season finale in 1981 coincided with Viola's first Birthday Solo. By this time, the Birthday Solos had become A Thing. Just as Donny and Marie had the little-bit-country-little-bit-rock-and-roll medley they did every week, *The Musical Mozinskis* had Birthday Solos. Back when Theo was about to play his first Birthday Solo, Mr. Karpenko actually pointed out a piece in *People* magazine's "What to Watch" section which read "Tune into *The Musical Mozinskis* as the next little Mozinski, Theo, makes his solo debut. Happy birthday, Theo!" Theo always thought the article should have added, "We're going to record you playing in front of a studio audience and then broadcast it to millions of viewers all around the country, but no pressure, little boy. Have a great anxiety-filled birthday!"

As the youngest, Viola was de facto the last solo debut, and the network's marketing team was making the most of it. The week before Viola's first Birthday Solo was scheduled to air, *People* ran a "What to Watch" blurb twice as long as Theo's.

Her piece was an overly simplified version of Beethoven's *Ode to Joy* on the piano. It wasn't an actual sonata or étude for piano by Beethoven. It was a Beethoven melody arranged and adapted by Vincent for, as Grace put it, young hands. The arrangement was watered down compared to what any of the other children would have played. Theo had a sneaking suspicion that his little sister wasn't cut out to be a musician, but it wasn't like he was going to say anything. Who would listen to him?

Vincent's arrangement called for the solo piano to be joined by other instruments — cello, violin, trumpet, timpani, harp, violin, and clarinet — one by one as each family member joined in. Technically,

Viola would fulfill the Birthday Solo expectation, but for most of it, she wouldn't actually be playing on her own.

Family legend had it that the Birthday Solo tradition started when Grace and Vincent first started dating. They got in the habit of performing miniconcerts on their birthdays and passed the tradition along to their children. The only kindness in the whole business was that the Birthday Solo ritual didn't start until one's eighth birthday. Even after the show started, every child still performed Birthday Solos at home. It was supposed to be a fun family activity, but over the years it became a cutthroat competition to see who could play the most technically challenging piece or who showed the widest range. Let's just say you wouldn't be caught dead playing some candy-ass version of "Twinkle, Twinkle, Little Star" on your Birthday Solo unless it was all 12 of Mozart's variations, and you'd better nail every trill and rising sixteenth note in the finale or you'd hear it about later.

On the show, each child got one piece for their Birthday Solo unless they were named Allegro, in which case they got two. On the show, the piece couldn't be longer than three minutes and 20 seconds in performance. At home, the children could play anything they wanted and as many pieces as they wanted — usually one for each instrument. Viola's birthday was in early May, so the timing was perfect for the season finale — The Littlest Mozinski Makes Her Debut. Fritz, Don, and Vincent anticipated a ratings bonanza. Because she had to perform on the show, Vincent insisted Viola perform the standard Birthday Solo at home as sort of a practice, the idea being that the family was large enough to simulate performance conditions while not having the pressure of an actual performance. Vincent only thought performing at home was lowkey because he never had the pleasure of having El and Allie dissect one of his performances.

Theo had heard Viola working with their mom on *Ode to Joy*, but the day before the family celebrated her birthday at home, she tracked Theo down while he was practicing in the room he shared with Bix. Bix and Ellington were out chasing the *Family Way* girls, so the house was relatively quiet. Theo heard three evenly spaced knocks on the bedroom door and knew it was Viola. She and Clara were the only siblings who knocked, and Clara's knock was consistently a legato–staccato–staccato–legato deal.

"Whatcha doing?" Viola asked as she walked in.

"Stevcik," Theo replied.

She nodded. The thing about Viola that always surprised Theo was how smart she was. She knew that Stevcik was the king of bowing exercises; she just couldn't play them to save her life. "Can I talk to you?"

"Sure." Theo was sitting on a chair in front of the music stand. He moved the stand over so he could see Viola, who sat down on the edge of his bed.

"Ellington has this idea to help me with my Birthday Solo," she said.

"What it is?" Theo asked.

"He said there's this song by a guy named John Cage where I don't have to play."

"Huh?"

"It's modern."

"Oh." Theo knew a lot about music by age nine, but the idea of a song where you didn't actually play seemed like some kind of weird joke. He considered the source of the information. Ellington was widely known as a ginormous jerk. "Do you think Ellington made it up?" he asked.

"No, I looked him up in the library. John Cage is a real guy and it's a real song. So do you think I should do it?"

"Do you want to play it?'

"It's the only piece I know I can play without messing up."

This sounded like the saddest reason in the world to do anything, but Viola was Viola. "Then I guess you ought to do it," Theo replied.

The family celebrated Viola's birthday at home on a Sunday, because there were no gigs and nothing show-related except rehearsals at home. Mr. Karpenko was there because he was seemingly always there. After dinner, the entire family trooped into the living room for Viola's Birthday Solo. The house in Pasadena had a huge living room that sometimes functioned as a performance hall. One half of the room had a sofa and chairs like a normal living room, and the other half had the baby grand and a couple of straight-backed chairs for performance or practice. It looked a lot like the set of the show, and Theo was never sure if the set had been designed to look like their living room or if the living room had been designed to look like the set. He just knew that's how his parents had arranged the furniture.

Theo noticed the sheet music for the simplified arrangement of *Ode to Joy* sitting on the piano. His mom and Viola hung back for a moment while everyone else got settled. He faintly heard his mother ask Viola "Are you okay?" and Viola reply "Yeah," in a voice that was softer than usual.

Grace kissed Viola on top of the head and walked to the center of the room. After 20 years of marriage, she had acquired the Mozinski reliance on tradition and exaggeration. She waited a few seconds while the rest of the family quieted down, then said, "Ladies and gentlemen, it is my great pleasure to introduce to you an incomparable, brilliant, eight-year-old who will perform an étude based on Beethoven's *Ode to Joy*."

"Étude my eye," Allie mumbled.

If Theo had been sitting close enough, he would have pinched her, but he was way over on the loveseat next to Bix, and Allie was on the far end of the sofa with Clara and Ellington. He couldn't hear Clara, but he saw her lips form the words "Stop it" to Allie.

Grace ignored the snide comments from the peanut gallery and merely said, "Ladies and gentlemen, I give you, Viola Mozinski."

Everyone applauded — even Allie, because she was not entirely without manners — as Viola calmly entered the living room and sat down at the piano. Theo's stomach did a little flip-flop as she raised the lid to reveal the gleaming black and white keys. He could almost see the huge jumble of notes piled up inside the piano, waiting for Viola to pull them out, string them together, and release them. He glanced over at his mother, who had sat down on the arm of the easy chair where his father was sitting. She was watching Viola intently. It seemed like he and his mom were both trying to will Viola to play well.

Viola poised her fingers over the keys and glanced up at the sheet music for *Ode to Joy*, but she didn't play it. Instead she said, "This is a piece by John Cage," placed her hands lightly in her lap, and held that pose. When Viola said it was a song where she didn't have to play, Theo didn't completely understand, but she really wasn't playing. He was beginning to think this was some sort of joke or prank on Ellington's part, but Ellington was perched on the edge of the sofa looking for all the world like he was listening. Except there wasn't anything to listen to. This wasn't music, this was silence. Theo sat politely, but whatever sympathy he had had for Viola before was starting to turn into anger. This was, to put it bluntly, a load of crap.

And then Bix burped.

It was a very small burp; if Theo hadn't been sitting next to him, he wouldn't have even heard it. Theo glanced over at Bix and both their eyes widened as they saw a dotted half note, perfect and shining, lingering just in front of his mouth. He never realized that his brother burped in A-flat.

Theo suddenly became aware of the sound of his own heartbeat, a steady larghetto in 2/2 time. It was a beat that he had never been fully aware of before and wouldn't have heard had Viola not been playing.

Over on the sofa, Ellington shifted slightly in his seat, and Theo heard the crack of his elbow as he moved. Theo glanced over at him and their eyes met over the tiny eighth note that sprang off his elbow. An F. Ellington gave a little smile and turned his attention back to Viola, who was still sitting motionless at the piano. She drew in a quick little breath — the same tiny sound you might make if you miss a note or a beat while playing. Above her head, there appeared a triplet of eighth notes — an arpeggio that mimicked her rising intake of breath. All around him, in what he thought was silence, Theo saw the sounds of his family, and that was its own kind of music.

Exactly four minutes and 33 seconds after she had sat down, Viola closed the lid of the piano. Theo started applauding immediately. So did El and Grace. Clara and Bix joined in enthusiastically enough, but Allie, Vincent, and Mr. Karpenko hesitated before giving half-hearted claps. Before she stood up, Theo saw Viola sigh, the hint of a smile on her round face. He couldn't hear the sigh, but he saw it, a shimmering whole note lingering over the piano as she stood up and took a bow.

The whole "John Cage Stunt" didn't go over well with Vincent. Among the siblings, the prevailing attitude was that Viola was the only kid who could have gotten away with it. Any of the rest of them would have caught holy hell. If Theo had ever needed proof that his parents were aware that Viola was a special case, musically speaking, this was it. Viola wasn't punished. The only person to get punished after the John Cage Stunt was Ellington. It wasn't difficult to figure out that he was the one who had encouraged Viola to play 4'33." Viola spent most of her free time drawing and looking at art books. She was not exploring post-war avant-garde composers. Ellington lost car driving privileges for two months, which meant he wasn't be able to drive around with Natalie DelVecchio looking for places where they could park. Viola got an unwanted Birthday Solo on national television.

ODE TO JOY

The week before the season finale was brutal. They rehearsed *Ode to Joy* 30 times a day, at least it felt like it. Theo could play the cello part with his eyes closed, except the one time he did, Don the Director yelled at him for being disrespectful. He wasn't trying to be disrespectful to Viola. But just because she was his favorite sibling didn't mean he was supposed to pretend she could play. He had to do something to keep from getting bored.

The show taped on Fridays before a studio audience, right after dinner. The first season, the season finale had been Allie's Birthday Solo, but the show wasn't always tied to reality. Allie's Birthday Solo had aired a month earlier. The so-called plot of the finale was Viola turning eight and being nervous about playing for her older siblings because she's the youngest. It was a little too much art imitating life even for Theo's young tastes. He didn't need to ask Viola how she felt about it, and the writers didn't need to stretch themselves with this one. The semiclever enhancement to the script was the addition of a teddy bear named Joy. Throughout the episode, Viola wonders if turning eight and being allowed to perform a solo means she's getting too old for teddy bears. The fact that she had never had a teddy bear in any previous episode wasn't important.

Every birthday episode featured a seeming problem that was solved by a heart-to-heart talk with Grace because Vincent could never quite pull off the warm and cuddly *Father Knows Best* vibe on camera. The plots of the show were formulaic. The birthday girl (or boy) would profess some secret fear to Mom or they'd have a run-of-the-mill parent-child argument — it alternated — and then the solo served as the resolution. For Viola's first Birthday Solo, a teddy bear named Joy plus *Ode to Joy* equaled dramatic resolution. For episodes like these, the other kids would do a number that functioned as either comic relief or a commentary on the Big Problem. They were their own Greek chorus. For this episode, the older kids played a cover of Elvis Presley's "Teddy Bear." Vincent had suggested the song when the writers pitched the Joy the Teddy Bear idea. Fritz and the writers loved it.

On the day they were scheduled to tape the season finale, Viola had not yet run though *Ode to Joy* without making a mistake within the first two measures. The rest of the family was supposed to join her onstage in reverse age order. Theo's chair was preset near the piano. His job was walk out with his cello and bow, sit down, and join in after measure 16. Viola just needed to play the melody through one time on her own, then the rest of the family could carry her.

On Friday afternoon, Theo sat next to Viola in the commissary for lunch. It was macaroni-and-cheese day, which they both loved, but today Viola didn't eat anything. She was sitting in between Theo and their mom, staring at her untouched plate of mac and cheese. Bix and Ellington were sitting with the girls from *Family Way.* Allie was sitting with Clara and some people from a sitcom called *Two Times the Fun.* Vincent and Mr. Karpenko were off making deals. They were very focused on keeping the music factory going.

"It's extra cheesy today. It's really good," Theo said. He wasn't great at starting scintillating conversation when he was nine, but he thought he should at least try to help Viola.

"Mm-hmm," she replied.

Their mom was having her usual salad. She looked over at Viola and asked if she was okay.

"Yeah."

Grace gently placed her fork on the side of her plate — the tables in the commissary never got cleaned properly and someone in the family was always getting sick until they learned not put place the silverware directly on the table — and put her arm around Viola's shoulder. It was kind of noisy in the commissary, so Theo could barely hear her ask "Do you want to do your solo?"

Viola's answer was even quieter, but Theo heard it. It was the saddest little "No" he ever heard before or since.

"I'll try talking to Fritz one more time," Grace said as she stood up. "I'll meet you back at the soundstage."

"Okay," Theo called after her. Watching the purposeful way their mother walked away seemed to perk Viola up a little bit.

"Do you think I'll have to play?" Viola asked.

"Not if you don't want to," Theo said. He almost added, "Don't worry, Mom will take care of it," but he didn't.

When Theo and Viola got back to the soundstage, there was a big argument going on in front of the living room set. Their mother was facing down Fritz the Producer, Don the Director, and their dad. Mr. Karpenko was standing off to the side, listening and watching. He had been made associate producer sometime during the second season. From what Theo could gather, that gave him half a vote. It really looked like this was a conversation the grown-ups should be having in private, so he and Viola held back behind one of the cameras, even though people on the crew were starting to come back in for the final run-through before they taped.

"She just needs the play the theme through one time. Sixteen measures," Vincent was saying. "That's all. Anyone can play 16 measures on their own."

"No, not everyone can do that. And no one should be forced to play if they don't want to," Grace said.

"Or if they are not capable of doing so," Karpenko added. Viola was standing next to Theo, but she took a little step backwards, away from everybody, when Karpenko said this. Maybe he was trying to help, but it just sounded like an insult. Theo honestly couldn't figure out if Mr. Karpenko was on his mom's side or his dad's side. It kind of seemed like everybody was on his dad's side.

"Grace, we are not changing the script and we are not changing songs. We can't. If you didn't want Viola to do a solo, you should have spoken up a month ago."

"I did, Fritz," Grace said. Theo could have sworn that his mother looked a little taller than her five feet four inches when she said this. It made him proud and glad that he was on his mom's side. "Do you not remember the conversation we had in February? And in January? And last year?" Fritz didn't say anything.

Vincent caught sight of Theo and Viola standing just outside the ring of adults and his expression changed. "Dear, I think you're over-reacting. Viola can play the *Ode to Joy* arrangement I did for her, right honey?" he added as he glanced their way. Viola leaned a little closer to Theo and grabbed his hand. For an instant, it felt weird to have her grab onto him, as though she thought he could protect her. He wasn't sure if he could, but put an arm around his little sister anyway. He almost said something but realized his father's love of hearing himself talk meant Viola didn't actually have to answer. "This is getting blown out of proportion. It's all going to be fine," he said a little louder than necessary, just so anyone from the crew was who eavesdropping wouldn't have anything to gossip about. He walked over to Grace with a big smile on his face and tried to take her hand. "Viola can do it. After all, she's a Mozinski."

Grace shook his hand off, said, "She's a Klinefelter," and walked off the set.

Theo didn't see his mother again until the cast introductions. The network hired a would-be comedian to warm up the audience before the taping and during breaks. There was a different comedian each season — Theo knew the guy this season was named Ricky Jay, but that was all he knew. He had learned pretty quickly not to get attached to people on the crew because they had a tendency to leave. Part of Ricky Jay's job was to introduce the cast before the taping, so the studio audience could see everyone in the flesh. The level of young female squealing always went up about 10 decibels when Bix was introduced. Their father referred to the girls as the frantic fanatics. Their mother often reminded their father that those frantic fanatics had helped buy the house in Pasadena. Usually, Theo found the frantic fanatics kind of comical. On this day, they were just annoying. Even after the introductions, they kept screaming and squealing. Theo wanted to ask his mom if Viola still had to do the solo, but it was noisy and busy and he didn't get a chance.

Theo was playing lead guitar for the first time on "Teddy Bear." That had always been Bix's role, but Vincent didn't want to complicate things by adding saxophone to the arrangement. Having Theo play guitar freed Bix to go into full-on Elvis Presley mode.

The five older Mozinskis were playing the song to Viola, who was curled up in the big easy chair on the living room set. When they rehearsed the song, Viola hadn't needed to be there. In fact, she had conveniently found excuses not to be there — she needed to be in show school or wardrobe or she was practicing her solo with her mother. As a result, Bix had played out during rehearsals, singing to whoever was watching on set. It wasn't until they got to the Friday run-through that Stacy the Assistant Director whispered to Grace that maybe having an older brother sing about wanting to be his younger sister's teddy bear was inappropriate. Grace merely replied, "That's Vincent's problem," and walked away.

Grace did everything the way she always did. She went out and smiled and waved during the introductions. She delivered her lines and hit all her marks. When she and Viola did the right-before-the-second-commercial-break-heart-to-heart conversation scene, it was perfect. Even so, Theo felt like something was wrong. His mom was there but she also seemed a thousand miles away. In musician terms, she was technically proficient but lacking in passion.

Fritz had always insisted that Bix's brown curly hair stay a little shaggy. That morning, however, the hair and makeup team had given him a slight haircut. It wasn't quite a pompadour, but when Francine in hair managed to tease out a dainty spit curl on Bix's forehead and wardrobe squeezed him into pants that were slightly tighter than a 15-year-old boy reasonably ought to be wearing on a family television show, it wasn't *not* a pompadour. When they taped "Teddy Bear" in front of the studio audience, the frantic fanatics went nuts. Theo tried to ignore it and concentrate on playing.

He didn't have a solo, but there were a couple of little fills and tags that gave him a chance to show off, not that anyone could hear the lead guitar or anything else over the screaming. Bix was channeling his inner Elvis, hip-jerking and emoting all over the place. It was almost too much to watch. Out of the corner of his eye, Theo saw his mother standing in the wings, watching, a big smile on her face. If she was enjoying it, maybe he could too. Theo thought maybe he was imagining her being distant. Then his father sidled up next her and tried to put his arm around her. She shrugged him off. It was subtle, just a little move of her shoulder to tell his arm that it wasn't welcome near her. That was enough for Theo. Still, there wasn't any time to talk to her backstage because when the audience was in the studio, Don was a stickler for keeping things moving.

Ode to Joy was the episode finale. Viola was supposed to carry Joy the Teddy Bear onto the living room set, put the bear on top of the piano, sit down, and start playing. Theo stood in the wings with his cello, waiting for his cue. Viola would play the melody through one time on her own — 16 measures. At measure 12, Theo would walk out to his chair, take a seat, and join in the second time through the melody, followed by the rest of the family, one by one. All of their entrances were from different parts of the set, so the others were waiting in different places. The only other person entering from his spot was his mom.

Don called "Action," and the studio audience hushed as Viola walked onstage, although there were a few audible "Awwww's" because the youngest Mozinski always had the cute factor. Viola carried Joy the Teddy Bear as if she had been carrying it her entire life. Even though it wasn't his scene, Theo had a slew of butterflies in his stomach. He had never heard her play *Ode to Joy* or anything all the way through without making copious mistakes. That didn't mean he wasn't hoping this time would be different. He said a silent prayer for a miracle that would make her be able to play like the rest of the family. Instead, she sat down on the piano bench, gently placed the teddy bear next to the sheet music, and waited.

It was a little like when she played 4'33" for her Birthday Solo at home. Theo took a deep breath and waited, willing his little sister to do something — even just playing the melody with one hand. Still Viola sat at the keyboard, not moving. The audience started getting restless. Theo half expected Don the Director to yell "Cut" when his mother kissed him on the top of his head and said, "I love you so much. Go out and play your part, okay?" then she walked out onstage.

Theo was pretty sure Viola wasn't expecting their mother to walk onstage. He sure wasn't expecting it. There was complete silence in the studio as his mother sat down on the piano bench next to Viola and gently placed her own hands on the keyboard. Then she started to play *Ode to Joy*. Theo wasn't sure what to do, but his mom had told him to go out and play his part. So he did.

At measure 12, Theo carried his cello and bow out to the chair that was sitting slightly downstage from the piano. He was seated and ready at measure 15. At measure 16, he started to play along, sharing the melody with the piano. Except the piano had stopped. Theo quickly realized he was playing alone. He didn't stop but turned his head slightly to the right and he saw his mother and Viola walking offstage. Viola was carrying the teddy bear. He didn't know at the time, but he wouldn't see either of them again for seven months.

He kept playing.

DE DO DO DO, DE DA DA DA

W hen her mom pulled her off the set, they walked to the dressing room, grabbed her mom's purse and their jackets, and headed for home. They weren't supposed to bring home costume pieces or props, but her mom told her not to change. Viola's costume was a green and yellow sundress that was really cute. It felt strange not changing, but if her mom said it was okay, then it was okay. Viola hoped this meant she'd be able to keep it. She did, however, leave Joy the Teddy Bear in the dressing room.

Her mother was quiet and quick as they walked through the back-stage corridors and down the wide hallway that led to the side exit of the soundstage. They didn't say goodbye to anyone, so Viola figured someone from the studio would try to stop them. Well, stop her mom anyway. No one at the studio had ever paid much attention to her. Her mother was walking very fast, and Viola was holding onto her hand for dear life and trying to keep up. They were maybe 20 feet from the exit door when Viola heard Stacy call her mom's name. It figured that they'd send her to track them down. Stacy always got stuck doing the dirty jobs Don and Fritz or the writers didn't want to do. Viola liked her because she treated everyone the same and was always nice to her and her siblings.

Her mom didn't stop walking as she half sang out, "Can't talk now, Stacy. Sorry!"

"Wait!" Stacy yelled. She was a quick runner and caught up to them just as they reached the door. "Please. You can't just leave."

"Watch me, my friend."

"But we're not done taping."

With her free hand, Grace motioned to Viola and herself. "We are."

"Where are you going?"

For the first time her mother stopped walking and looked at Stacy. "I'm taking Viola home."

She and Stacy looked at each other for a moment, then Stacy nodded. "I can see why you want to do that. I feel obliged to tell you that Fritz is coming after you."

Viola saw her mother smile for the first time all day. "I think we can outrun Fritz." She was right. A geriatric turtle could outrun Fritz.

"He said he was taking a golf cart."

"Thanks for the warning."

"You're welcome." Stacy looked down at Viola. "Good night, Viola," she said. "Don't tell your big brothers and sisters, but I've always thought you're the best of the bunch."

"Thank you," Viola said. She had always thought Stacy was cool, but now she liked her even more.

"See you next season," Stacy said.

"God willing and the creek don't rise, yes." Grace looked down at Viola. "Let's go," she added.

"What creek?" Viola asked as they exited into the wide alley that ran between their soundstage and the one next to it. This was the place where they would normally be signing autographs and taking pictures with fans after the taping.

"Heck, you might as well ask 'What God?'" her mother replied.

Viola thought about this as she race-walked her way alongside her mother. When she was really little, before they moved, Viola had vague memories of going to church with her family, but they hadn't set foot in a church since they moved to California. God was as much of an undiscovered country as the circle of fifths she sometimes heard her older siblings talk about.

The soundstages were long buildings close to the length of a football field. The alley between the soundstages opened up onto Century Boulevard, which was essentially a main road through the studio lot. Across Century Boulevard was another alley running in between more soundstages. Beyond that was the parking lot.

One of the things Viola would always remember about the studio was the motion, how there was always activity, always people moving — walking or driving or moving something or carrying or building something. It was like a little city all by itself, only with almost no cars but plenty of flatbed trucks and golf carts. Mostly golf carts. If anyone happened to notice that two members of the Mozinski family were walking toward the parking lot while their show was still taping, they didn't say anything.

"If Fritz is grabbing a cart..." her mom muttered. She looked down at Viola but didn't stop walking. "Sweetie, if anyone asks, I need you to pretend that you're sick."

Normally Viola was the type of child who would truthfully say "But I'm not sick." Normally. Right now, she didn't want to talk to Fritz any more than her mom did. Probably less. She just wanted to go home. She felt stupid and embarrassed and like she had ruined everything. It wouldn't be much of a stretch to say she was sick. "Got it," she replied. In that moment, it felt like she became her mom's partner.

Just ahead of them were two guys getting out of a golf cart by the side door of the opposite sound stage. They pulled three big black equipment cases out of the back and went inside, leaving the golf cart unattended.

"Come on," her mom said and started to run. Viola ran after her, unsure whether to be scared or thrilled. Maybe a little of both. Her mom was already in the driver's seat of the golf cart when she got there. "Get in, get in," Grace said, but not too loud. It was clear they were doing something that maybe they shouldn't be doing, but she was with her mom. By definition, that meant everything was all right.

The golf cart was dark blue and had the words "Mike's Millions" painted on both sides. It was the name of a sitcom Viola wasn't allowed to watch because the humor was "a little too adult." Viola asked if the cart belonged to that show.

"Probably," her mom said as she got the cart started.

"I hope riding in their golf cart isn't too adult for me."

"Touché," her mother replied.

Golf carts don't go very fast, but they're faster than walking. And faster than two guys can run when they come out of a soundstage and see their golf cart speeding down the alley. It was at that point Viola decided the whole exercise was more fun than scary. They were almost to Century

Boulevard when another golf cart came speeding out of the loading doors at the end of their soundstage. One of their crew members was driving it and Fritz was in the passenger seat calling her mother's name.

"Hold on," her mom said. "Stay with me. And remember, you're sick."

"Okay."

Fritz's golf cart started driving next to theirs. "Grace! What are you doing?" Fritz yelled.

"Taking Viola home. She's sick," her mom called back. It seemed like she'd be more believable as sick by staying quiet, but Viola held her stomach like she might throw up. It seemed more convincing.

Century Boulevard was the main artery through the studio grounds. It was always busy. Her mom stopped the cart to let a truck pulling a trailer go by. The trailer had a cutaway of a house sitting on it. If the camera angle was just right, you'd never know it wasn't part of a real house. Like their happy family and her musical talent and everything else at the studio, it was fake.

Fritz's golf cart stopped next to theirs. Fritz wasn't that stupid; he stayed in his cart in case he needed to give chase. "Grace, please come back," he called to them.

"I'm sorry, Fritz, but Viola really needs to go home." She sounded calm and concerned, as though she was picking her daughter up from school and talking to the school nurse.

Viola was still holding her stomach and trying to look sick, but she took a quick glance behind them and saw the two guys from *Mike's Millions* running up the alley towards them. "Mom," she said quietly, "I think Mike noticed we took his cart."

"And off we go," her mother said brightly. While it may not be possible to actually floor it in a golf cart, it is possible to take your executive producer by surprise and weave your way around another golf cart, a group of people on a studio tour, and two men in suits walking with a third man who may or may not have been a well-known movie star crossing Century Boulevard. Grace didn't slow down or stop for anyone, but she called "Sick kid, coming through!" to some guys in the next alley who were unloading lumber from a pick-up truck.

Viola's knowledge of the studio rules was rudimentary at best, but she knew you weren't supposed to leave golf carts in the parking lot. You also weren't supposed to wear your costume home or steal a golf cart from another show and yet here they were doing it, so who knew what rules applied at that moment?

They drove the cart right out to the middle of the parking lot to where her dad had parked the family van that morning. Grace calmly parked the golf cart in an empty space a few spaces away from the van. Viola jumped out of the golf cart as soon as her mother stopped and immediately climbed into the front passenger seat of the van.

"Kids ride in the back," Grace said as she turned the ignition key.

"Please? I never get to sit up front."

Her mom sighed. "Fine. Put on your seat belt."

For the first time in her life, Viola was glad her parents didn't let Clara or Ellington drive themselves to the studio. They always insisted the family arrive en masse in the ugly brown Volkswagen Vanagon. She knew they weren't exactly ditching the rest of the family with no way to get home. Everyone else would get home, they'd just have to find another way. And they still had to finish taping the show. Plus, it was the season finale, which meant most of the audience would hang around outside waiting for autographs. All of this would take a very long time. She wasn't in a rush to see them. Viola waited until they had pulled out of the studio gate and were on the road to ask, "Do you think everybody is going to be mad at me?"

"I'm sure they won't be, sweetie," her mother replied.

"I'll bet Ellington and Allie tease me."

"I won't let them." And the determined way her mother said this made Viola half believe it, although nothing had stopped her older siblings from teasing her before.

"Do you think Dad's going to be mad at me?"

"Of course not."

They drove in silence for a moment. Grace had always made a point of being honest with her children but here she was telling a half truth to her youngest. *Of course Vincent's going to be angry,* she thought. *Just not with*

Viola. Vincent would be furious. Everyone at the studio would be furious. Viola wasn't the one who had walked out.

She turned on the radio to fill the silence between her and Viola and to try and calm the thoughts racing through her mind. Every single one of the other kids would try and commandeer the radio if they were sitting up front. Viola was the only one who never seemed to care what was playing.

"Do you want to play DJ?" she asked.

"No, thanks," Viola said as she gazed out the window. Grace left it on the station they'd been listening to on the way to the studio that morning. The radio was playing The Police's "De Do Do Do, De Da Da Da." She kept it on because she admired the lyrical hook even as it parodied pop music's obsession with nonsense lyrics. One smash song like this would pay a lot of bills. She couldn't help singing along on the chorus and glanced over at Viola, who was still looking out the window. "Do you like this song?" Grace asked her.

"Uh-huh. It's got rainbow polka dots."

Viola occasionally said cryptic things like this. Ellington and Allie claimed she just did it because she couldn't see the music. Maybe she was just pretending. There was nothing wrong with Viola trying to emulate her older siblings. "Do you mind that I'm singing along?" Grace asked.

"No, I like the way you sing."

"Do you wanna sing with me?"

"No, I'm not a good singer," Viola replied. The matter-of-fact way her child denigrated herself was heart-wrenching.

Grace's hands gripped the steering wheel a little tighter. "Who told you that?" she asked.

"Everybody."

It was hard to tell whether Viola was sad or resigned. If she was being brutally honest, Grace knew that her youngest was not a great singer relative to the rest of the family, but that was admittedly a high bar. The other five were...unusual. Maybe Viola was the only normal one in the bunch instead of the other way around.

"I like the way you sing," Grace said. This was truth. What mother doesn't love the sound of her child's voice? When they got in the car, Grace's only goal was to get Viola off the set, out of the studio, and home. But now it seemed like Pasadena wasn't far enough away from everything that was hurting Viola. Grace started doing some quick time calculations in her head, mumbling half to herself "...at least an hour ahead of them, maybe more...get in, get out..."

"What are you talking about?" Viola asked her.

Best to clear the idea with the kid before committing. "How would you like to go on a trip? Just you and me?" Grace asked, trying to sound as casual as possible.

"Sure! Where are we going?"

"I thought we'd go see Grandma and Grandpa in Youngstown," she replied. "Doesn't that sound like fun?" Saying it aloud made it seem a little less crazy.

"Yeah." She could almost hear the wheels turning in Viola's brain. "Are we running away from home?" Viola asked.

Grace was quiet for a moment. This was exactly what they were doing, but her kid didn't have to come right out and say it. She took a quick deep breath and calmly asked, "Why do you ask?"

"I don't know, it just *seems* like it. Like in *From the Mixed-Up Files of Mrs. Basil E. Frankweiler*," Viola added.

"I love that book," Grace replied as she merged into the right-hand lane. They were close to their freeway exit. If they were going to do this, she would need to commit and get Viola's buy-in right now. "Well, we aren't going to live in a museum. We're just going to visit your grandparents. We're not running. We're just leaving for a bit."

At eight, Viola didn't make much of a distinction between "running" and "leaving." Both involved packed suitcases and going somewhere without the rest of the family. It was just a matter of the degree of urgency involved in the going. In books, sometimes the parents split up and got divorced and the dad left. Or the mom and all the kids went somewhere else. Her mom was only taking her, which sure felt like running away. It seemed like the show and their family and everything else was about to get turned upside down, and it was all her fault. Viola didn't bother saying anything because she was sure her mom would deny it. She just said, "Okay, let's go."

When they got home, her mother told her to go pack. "You can bring two suitcases," she said. "The bigger suitcase should be all clothes. In the second suitcase you can bring anything that's special to you."

"Anything?"

"Mmm-hmm."

This seemed like a reasonable deal. "What kind of clothes do I need?" Viola asked.

"Whatever one wears for a summer in Youngstown, Ohio."

"Is that like summer here?"

"Pretty much. Maybe a little cooler. The most important thing is, you need to be packed and ready in half an hour."

Viola just nodded and headed for her room. She didn't have any more questions. They were in a hurry, they were leaving before the rest of the family got home, and they wouldn't be saying goodbye. They were definitely running away.

The first suitcase was a piece of cake. Shorts, T-shirts, jeans, underwear, socks, a couple sweatshirts, two dresses that her grandparents had given her, sandals, and a pair of dressy shoes, just in case. She wore her sneakers and her favorite jacket over the sundress from the studio. If they were really running away, then it was probably hers for keeps.

It took her all of 10 minutes to pack her clothes. The second suitcase was harder. She looked around her room and wondered when she'd see it again. Viola's room was the smallest in the house, so whenever she and her mom did come home, she was pretty sure none of her siblings would have taken over her room. Somehow the idea that she could come back and have her room be exactly the same as it was right now was comforting. Leaving didn't make her scared or sad. It would have been nice to bring Theo with them, but mostly it felt like a relief. Going to her grandparents meant she wouldn't have to worry about trying to play music or fit in. She could just be herself.

She started packing the second suitcase.

Exactly 35 minutes after they stepped in the back door of the house in Pasadena, Viola and her mother walked out the front door to a big black sedan that was waiting to take them to the airport. They each had two suitcases, plus Grace carried her violin. As her mother pulled the front door shut with a little slam, Viola noticed she didn't lock it with the key. Then she realized her mom wasn't bringing her house key because they weren't coming back.

Grace had never been one to use the family's fame as leverage. She had never said "Do you know who I am?" to a concierge or maître d'. On the contrary, she made a point to stay under the radar. Most people didn't realize who she was until someone saw her name on a credit card. But when they got to the ticket counter at the airport, she didn't hesitate to use her television mom voice to say "Good evening, I'm Grace Mozinski, and my daughter and I need to get to Youngstown, Ohio, immediately." If the Delta ticket agent thought there was a family emergency, so be it.

Having a semifamous name and a credit card with no maximum limit can work wonders. Ninety minutes later, they were on an airplane. When they first came to California four years earlier, Grace had been unsure whether the show would do well and bought eight tickets in economy class. For this trip, Grace bought two first-class tickets and tried not to think about how the credit card bill would arrive at the house in Pasadena sometime in the next month and Vincent would have to pay it. She tried not to feel guilty. She had earned this money too. It was hers.

Somewhere over Colorado, Viola leaned on her arm and gave a little yawn. It looked like the long day was finally catching up to her. Grace looked at her watch and remembered she needed to set it three hours ahead.

"What are you doing?" Viola asked sleepily.

"I'm resetting my watch because we're going to a different time zone. Ohio is three hours ahead of California."

"How come?"

This was one of those questions where Grace understood the answer but couldn't think of an easy way to explain it. "Okay, when the sun is directly overhead, it's twelve noon, right?" Viola's non-committal "I guess so" made Grace feel like she'd dropped a few parenting balls. "So if the sun is directly overhead in Ohio and it's twelve noon, it's only going to be nine o'clock in the morning in California because the earth is turning underneath the sun like this." She tried to demonstrate using one motionless hand as the sun with the other hand tightly balled into a rotating fist.

"I'm not sure I totally get it," Viola said with a yawn.

"It doesn't matter if you totally get it right now. Just think of it as we're going into the future."

"Okay. Hello, future," Viola replied with a tired smile and settled her head against Grace's arm.

NOWHERE MAN

There were major differences between living with her siblings in California and living with her grandparents in Ohio. In California, Viola was the youngest child of a big television family. In Ohio, she was an only child. In California, she always felt like an afterthought. In Ohio, she was the center of attention. In California, there was always music coming from their house, made by seven of the eight people who lived there. In Ohio, the only music came from her grandparents' record player. The first few weeks they were there, her mother didn't listen to music at all and never touched her violin or the piano in the living room. She played games with Viola, and they baked with her grandma and worked with her grandpa in his garden or went to the park together, but no one made any music. It was kind of like being on permanent vacation.

There were days when her mother didn't want to do anything except stay in her room or take a long drive by herself. On those days, Viola stayed in her room and drew. Sometimes she listened to the radio and explored her grandparents' record collection. Most of the records they owned were old big band and classical, which seemed too much like what her family used to play. She ignored those.

It was no surprise that her grandparents owned every one of the Musical Mozinskis records, and Viola couldn't help but pull out *Lazy Day*, which had always been her favorite album cover. It featured a slightly grainy image of all six children relaxing in what looks to be the living room of a summer cottage. Clara is reading a book at one end of a long, somewhat beat-up sofa, and Theo is at the other, book in hand but staring off into space as though he's thinking. Ellington is lying on the rug, hands behind his head, feet crossed, taking a nap. Bix is sitting on the arm of a chair, lazily strumming on a guitar. Allie is on another chair, holding a notepad, chewing thoughtfully on a pen, as though she's putting final notes on her plan for world domination. Viola herself is off to the side, hardly in the picture. She's lying on her stomach in front of a large pad of paper, a box of colored pencils next to her, drawing away. Her grandparents had plenty of photographs of her and her sisters and brothers all over the house. Pictures on the wall were okay. Normal people had pictures of their family on the wall. Seeing herself and her siblings on the album cover was not okay. Viola hid all of the Musical Mozinskis records behind the other records on the bottom shelf of her grandparents' console stereo.

She looked through the rest of the records, and in the middle of the Dorsey Brothers and Glenn Miller and Beethoven she found a copy of *Rubber Soul* by The Beatles. It was the only record in the entire house that seemed at all interesting. Viola carried it down to the basement where her grandma was doing laundry.

"I didn't know you liked the Beatles," Viola said. "Wow."

"I'm sorry I can't say I'm a big fan," said her grandma. "Your mother gave it to us for Christmas when it came out. I guess she wanted to expand our musical horizons," she added with a laugh.

The album looked practically new. "Can I listen to it?" Viola asked.

"Of course. In fact, if you really like it, you can have it," she replied.

It didn't matter that she only got the album because her grandparents didn't want it. The record was now hers, and Viola kept it in her room, separate from the rest of the records in the house, because it was hers, and there wasn't much in the house she could say that about. Her favorite song on it was "Nowhere Man," because she felt like a nowhere girl. She and her mom were living with her grandparents, but it didn't feel like they *lived* there. It seemed like they were visiting. Everyone pretended that they were visiting, that this was just a temporary separation. Her grandma would say something like "It's so nice to have you here for the summer," or her grandpa would say "Now when you're back home, don't you take any guff from Ellington, okay?" The expectation was always that they would return to California. Maybe at the end of the summer, maybe at the end of the Musical Mozinskis tour.

Vincent called every day for the first week, sometimes two or three times a day. Grace talked to him. Viola did too, although it felt like neither of them had much to say to each other beyond "hello" and "how are you." Viola talked to her siblings too, mostly Theo and Clara. Sometimes Bix. The way Viola found out she wasn't going home — or rather, that home was no longer with the rest of the family — was from Theo.

Viola and Grace usually talked to the rest of the family on the phone in the kitchen. It was a pale yellow rotary phone mounted on the wall. Even though it had a long curly cord for the headset, you couldn't really sit down and get comfortable when you were talking on it. It wasn't good for long conversations. For that, Viola needed to use the light blue phone that sat on a little table in the hallway on the second floor. That phone had a long cord, long enough that you could bring the phone into one of the three bedrooms. That's what her mother did sometimes when she talked to her father. Viola usually just talked to her dad on the kitchen phone.

They had been in Youngstown for two weeks when Theo told Viola they were going on tour. "Where?" she asked.

"I'm not really sure," he said. Viola had always seen Theo's voice as a rich violet. When he sang or even just talked, it always looked like thousands of tiny violet-colored dots swirling around him. Theo had the prettiest voice to look at of anyone in their family, not that Viola had ever said this. She wasn't stupid enough to give Ellington or Allie any ammunition against him. They spent a lot of time together when they were little, partly because they were the youngest, and partly because Viola liked looking at his voice. On the phone, it wasn't the same. Theo's voice went right into her ear, into her head, and it didn't have any room to swirl around in the air. Viola closed her eyes and tried to imagine what she knew Theo's voice looked like. "You know how Dad likes to spring things on us at the last minute," he said.

"I remember," she replied quietly.

"They said it's going to be a lot of state fairs and stuff. It's a long tour. They said they added some dates because we aren't going to do the show anymore." This was news.

"You're not?" She couldn't bring myself to say "We're not" because she didn't feel like part of the "We" anymore.

Theo was quiet for a second, then he said, "No, the show got cancelled. I think because, like, variety shows aren't as popular anymore?"

"Oh. Sorry."

"I don't mind.

"When does the tour start?"

"Umm..." she heard Theo say, "Clara, when does the tour start?" Then he said to her, "In 10 days."

"Does it come anywhere near Youngstown?"

"I don't think so. I mean, I think Dad would've said if it was. So I don't know when we get to see you and Mom."

"I hope it's soon. I miss you."

"Me too. I miss you both." She heard him say a muffled "What?" then he came back and said, "Dad said I have to hang up now because long distance is expensive."

After they hung up, Viola went and found her mom, who was sitting on the steps of the front porch with a notebook and pencil. She was writing something, or at least thinking about writing something. At the moment, she was staring at the house across the street.

Viola sat down on the step next to her. "Hi," she said.

Grace rested the notebook on her knees, put an arm around Viola's shoulders, and said, "Hey, kiddo."

Viola cuddled up against her mom. It was one place where she had always felt safe. She took a little breath then asked, "We aren't going back, are we?"

Her mother looked at her as though Viola had uncovered a forbidden secret. "What makes you say that?"

"Everybody else is going on tour, but we aren't. Even if we went back, they wouldn't be there. There wouldn't be anyone to go back to."

"You miss your brothers and sisters," her mom said, not as a question but just as a statement of fact.

"Yeah."

"Do...you want to go on the tour?" her mother said carefully.

This was the hardest and the easiest question to answer. "No," Viola replied. She waited a moment to see how her mother reacted. When she didn't say anything, Viola asked, "Are you mad that I don't want to?"

Her mom held her tighter and said, "Oh sweetie, no! Of course not. Why would you think that?"

Viola didn't want to cry, but she couldn't help it. Once she started crying, it felt like all the words started to fall out of her. "Because that's what our family does, except I'm no good at it, and everybody knows I stink."

She was crying hard now, and her mom pulled her onto her lap, whispering over and over that everything was all right. She said it so gently, so lovingly that her voice turned from its normal pale yellow to a rich golden hue that wrapped around Viola. She wasn't singing, but she might as well have been.

TAKE FIVE

After the summer tour, what was left of The Musical Mozinskis returned to Pasadena to what Allegro referred to as House Testosterone. She had never been particularly close to either of her sisters, but now she found herself missing both of them.

When Clara informed their father that she had to leave the tour early because her classes at the Cleveland Institute of Music started on August 24th and she wanted to be there on the 22nd to have the weekend to get settled, Allegro was almost as furious as her father. She and Clara had shared hotel rooms for seven weeks all across second-rate venues and state fairs and never once did Clara tell her she was leaving. Angry as she was, she missed having Clara as an ally against the Ellington-Bix gauntlet. And she even missed stupid little Viola, who couldn't play but at least wasn't smelly, loud, or intentionally cruel, and was sometimes even funny. Not that she would ever admit she missed her sisters to anyone. That would be an admission of weakness, of need. One of the things Ken had told her more than once was how powerful her playing was, how strong she was. "Like a force of nature," he always said.

Whenever Allie stood onstage and saw the notes from the Stengel swirling overhead, leading the music of a full orchestra, it felt like she was a general leading an armed division into battle, like Prospero controlling the winds and bending the elements to his will. That was strength. A girl like that didn't miss her sisters.

The three weeks between her mother leaving and the start of the summer tour had been controlled chaos because no one wanted to do the things her mother had always done. Her father had, at least, made sure the garbage with all of the dirty take-out containers and leftovers got taken out. And he hired someone to come in and check on things and do some cleaning while they were gone. Even so, the house seemed dirty and stale when they finally arrived from the airport late on a Thursday afternoon. Her dad ordered pizza because there wasn't any food in the house.

"We'll have to hit the grocery store tomorrow," he said through a hefty bite of pepperoni pizza. Allie hated pepperoni but it was her father's favorite, so he always ordered it. "Maybe you can help me with that, Allie?"

Allegro looked up from her plate where she was carefully removing the offending slices of pepperoni without sacrificing any of the cheese and regarded her father across the dinner table. "Why me?" she asked simply. "Why can't Bix and Ellington go? El could even drive to save you the time and effort."

Before her father even had time to react, Ellington said, "Because grocery shopping's kind of a chick job. Maybe you should take Theo with you," he added and was the only one to laugh at his joke. Even Bix just shrugged and grabbed another slice of pizza. Theo didn't even look up from his food.

"Ellington..." their father said sharply.

"What?" El replied innocently.

Vincent just shook his head and sighed, like he didn't even think it was worth the argument. Allie looked from one to the other and figured her dad had to be tired. On a normal day, he would never pass up the opportunity to correct Ellington.

"You're such a troglodyte," she said.

"Just call 'em like I see 'em."

"Apologize to your brother," Vincent said.

"Sorry, Theo."

"Thanks," Theo mumbled. He looked like he would rather be anywhere else in the world at that moment.

"My God, the sexism in here is as pungent as the stench of cheap pepperoni," Allie said. Her father and brothers looked at her blankly. "I'm talking about the innate assumption that grocery shopping is women's work and the corresponding assumption that anything female is somehow inferior."

Her dad blustered through a lame apology, which Allie ignored. She made sure to tell him — not ask him — to keep the cleaning service. She knew the fridge would soon be filled with pizza boxes or Styrofoam containers holding decomposing leftover lo mein noodles or half-eaten hamburgers that no one would eat and no one would throw out.

The food situation in House Testosterone was only one of several challenges. There was also the laundry. Everyone's dirty clothes (with the exception of Ellington, who hadn't bothered to unpack) were sitting in a pile by the washing machine. Allie had resisted doing any laundry because it just seemed so obvious that her dad and brothers were waiting for her to do it simply because she was a girl. She finally threw in a load just of her things on Sunday afternoon because they were all supposed to be starting school the next day and she wanted to be ready. School had started three weeks earlier but the tour was extended once the show got cancelled as a way of making up for lost revenue. Allie hadn't attended regular school since third grade. In her opinion, sending them to a new high school three weeks into the school year was the worst idea her father had come up with since the bell-bottoms debacle of 1979.

Ken called her the same day to touch base regarding some potential winter concerts. He was the first to suggest Allie drop out of The Musical Mozinskis. Ultimately it was her choice, of course. Everything that happened with him was always her choice. Ken only ever made suggestions, discussed possibilities. When they talked, he nonchalantly mentioned that maybe there was a way for her to concentrate on her classical career. "I'm not saying a permanent break," he said. "It's your family, after all. But playing rhythm guitar behind Bix isn't helping your career. I would hate it if you weren't able to develop to your full potential."

Allie was a big fan of her own potential. Honestly, sometimes it felt like she was the only one who cared about what happened to her. When her mom took Viola to Youngstown, it had seemed like a temporary thing. It kind of made sense for them to go away during the summer tour. It wasn't like anyone had ever bought a ticket to a Musical Mozinskis concert to see *Viola*. She didn't even play. Not really. Originally, Theo did double duty, playing his own parts and filling in on Grace's parts on other songs. Her dad had had to redo some arrangements after Clara left, but the tour was easier without somebody having to worry about where Viola was during sound check or performances. In that respect, it made life simpler.

On the other hand, Allie had to admit that not having her mom on tour had been unsettling, but that was more a question of efficiency. She hadn't realized just how much her mom held things together and made sure everyone and everything was where it was supposed to be. Instead of her mom, they got Mr. Karpenko clucking around like a substitute mother hen who had never even laid an egg, much less hatched one. And it's not as if her father could be bothered with details like making sure the luggage got on the bus or that their dinner stop had a salad bar. Her mom had made sure everyone was happy. Or at least okay. Happy was reserved for being onstage, for making music. Everything else was just the stuff Allie had to slough through until she could pick up the Stengel again. Playing guitar didn't bring quite the same level of joy as playing the violin, but it wasn't all bad. There were precious minutes onstage where she'd look over at Bix and he would smile and come over and start dancing around her with his guitar. Sometimes she danced too. It was, for lack of a better word, fun.

Clara had always stayed firmly stage left, plucking away at the bass and looking like she didn't care if she was there or not. Allie sometimes thought no one could hate the family band more than she did, but the last few weeks of the tour, Clara wasn't even there. It was hard not to feel a little jealous. Having Clara at college, studying the one thing she loved more than anything else while Allie was stuck with all three stinky brothers and their father playing the same insipid songs for the umpteenth time just seemed completely unfair.

Whenever she complained on the phone, her mom would listen quietly while she talked and then tell her that the decision had to be up to her father. When she talked to Mr. Karpenko, he would just say something like "You can try all day but you never get milk from a bull, yes?" which she supposed meant Karpenko thought it was useless to ask her father anything. He wasn't entirely wrong — it was useless asking her father for anything — but that didn't help. The only person who actually listened *and* offered any helpful suggestions was Ken, who suggested she take a break from the family band and wondered if Allie could keep working with Jenny the Tutor instead of wasting her time at the local high school. She went right to work on both suggestions.

When Allie told Bix she wanted to leave the family band and asked for his help, Bix wasn't that surprised. After their mom and Viola and then Clara left, he figured the last female domino in the family would fall any minute. It was probably kind of tough on her being the only girl, and it was pretty obvious she hated just about everything and everyone.

Sometimes, when they were rehearsing for the new album, he and Ellington would start jamming, just banging away on a riff and a rhythm. Theo would usually join in too, even if he didn't seem to be having any fun. Allie never jammed with them. Neither did their father. Usually, Vincent would tell them to save it for their own time, even though Bix found the riff for "Better Wait" while they were fooling around during family rehearsal.

They were rehearsing a cover of "Goin' Back to Indiana" for the new album when Vincent stopped them, saying, "I still don't like that progression." He picked up one of the ever-present Palomino Blackwing pencils from the piano and added, "Take five, guys," which is a phrase no sensible band leader uses because smart-asses like Ellington Mozinski will invariably start playing the stop-start rhythm of the Brubeck classic. The final notes of "Goin' Back to Indiana" were still drifting into noth-ingness in the living room air as Vincent lit a cigarette and started to jot down an adjustment to the arrangement, momentarily oblivious to his children.

Allie said, "I'll be right back," and left the room. She didn't come back.

Bix listened to Ellington for a moment, watching the complex drum notation in the air as El started playing with the rhythm, driving it a little more aggressively. *Not all California jazz is cool...*Bix thought as he picked up his guitar. *Some of it's very hot.* He started in the original E-flat, playing the main Paul Desmond saxophone theme. He didn't look up from the guitar, but heard Theo reliably join in with the *do-pah de-pah do-pah* bass line. The second time through Bix started playing with the theme, and Ellington added a little harder drive to the rhythm.

Whenever Bix took a solo, it felt like he was unfolding a huge roadmap. Opening the melody and taking it apart was fun. No, not fun — it was joy in action. Splicing a song open was easy. Piecing it back together was the challenge. It was like trying to refold the map the same way you opened it, so that it was recognizable and whole again. This time he didn't feel like putting the melody back together. Instead, he kept coming back to the riff he had uncovered.

Bix heard the change in what Ellington and Theo were playing. They were following his lead. He looked up and saw the notes from the three of them enmeshed above his head. Everything fit as neatly as though it had been printed in midair. Why had he never noticed before just how tight and solid the music was when it was just him and his brothers? He started to think maybe Allie was right. She ought to take a break from the family band. Not only that, maybe his dad should too.

"Guys, let's get back to work," Vincent said.

Theo stopped playing immediately, but Bix and Ellington didn't. Bix wasn't usually one to disobey or ignore his father, but he wanted to explore this melody just a little bit longer because it felt like he was on to something. "Wait..." he said, not caring if it sounded rude. The one-word command seemed to fit the feel of what he was playing but didn't fit the rhythm. "Better wait..." he half sang. That fit. "Better wait till I'm done lovin' you..." he sang softly.

Theo started playing again and sounded downright apologetic as he explained to their father, "It's a good line."

SHE'S NOT THERE

E llington respected his father's musicianship. To an extent. Vincent could play, he just wrote boring arrangements. It had always been like this. Now that they were done with the show, Ellington thought maybe The Musical Mozinskis could branch out with more complex arrangements and fewer covers. His mom had sent him, Bix, and Theo each a new song as an early Christmas present. And Bix had written a couple of really good songs. "Better Wait," especially, was a solid single.

While his siblings were paying attention in show school, Ellington had been studying the competition. All the Osmond brothers not named Donny were second-tier acts at this point. Same thing with every Jackson not named Michael. Whenever a family band fell apart, one of them got a successful solo career and the rest of the family got second-class shit. They had to update The Musical Mozinskis before somebody decided Bix needed a solo album, and where the hell would that leave him?

They were only five months into the Post-Mom Era, but Allie had already left the band. Ellington wasn't sure how she'd done it. Something about Ken the Agent and Allie focusing on her classical music career. He didn't really pay attention when his dad talked about it. The details didn't matter. The important thing was that Allie didn't have to play with the family band anymore. Ellington wondered sometimes if Ken the Agent was going to sign Theo too, then he could corner the market on kid-classical-music prodigies.

Allie somehow managed to get out of going to regular school too. Jenny the Tutor came to the house three days a week to work with her. Sometimes Jenny helped Ellington with his homework too, which was good because regular high school was for the birds. He just needed to pass the GED and get out.

The other thing he needed to do was make a decent album with his dad and his brothers.

The day The Musical Mozinskis became The Mozinski Brothers was the day they recorded "She's Not There." It had been Ellington's idea to cover the song because it satisfied Vincent's '60s pop music obsession, but it was a much cooler song than most of his picks. It seemed like the best of both worlds until he saw Vincent's arrangement, which was so true to the original Zombies' performance that Ellington wondered out loud why they were bothering to record it all.

They were already in the studio and a day behind schedule, so every minute the boys screwed around was costly. Vincent and Mr. Karpenko had already said so about six times that day. When Ellington asked why they were bothering to record a cover that sounded exactly like the original, Vincent put his hand over his mic so the sound engineer in the control room wouldn't hear his hissed reply of "Because I'm your father and the band leader, and I know what's best." He removed his hand from the mic and said in his normal voice, "Let's try it again, Dave. The boys will give it a little more life this time, won't you guys?"

Ellington looked over at Bix from his spot behind the drum kit and nodded. Bix was always elected to break tough news to their father. "Dad, we were messing around with the song the other day," Bix began, "and I think we found an interesting take on it. More of a punk feel. Can we just play it for you?"

Vincent scoffed. "Punk like those guys who only know three chords and call themselves musicians?"

"You know, if you ever listened to new music maybe you'd like it," Ellington interjected. He knew he shouldn't say anything because Vincent never listened to him.

"I know what's going on in the music market."

"So do I, Dad. And I actually buy records."

Dave's voice came over the speaker from the control room, "Come on, Vincent. Let the kids have some fun."

"Dave, we're overbudget as it is."

"I wouldn't mind hearing their take on the tune. You said yourself there's something missing."

Ellington looked down so he wouldn't catch either of his brother's eyes. He knew he'd laugh. Having someone else call out their dad was just too perfect.

"Thanks, Dave," Ellington said loudly and looking right at his father.

"Fine. One time through. I'll listen from the other room," Vincent added as he left the studio. His head was barely visible through the glass wall separating the studio from the control booth. Dave was leaning forward in his chair, engaged and ready, while Vincent was leaning back, looking like he might take a little nap.

"Let's wake Dad up," Ellington whispered to his brothers. Even dorky Theo smiled at that.

Just as Ellington was about to count off the beat, Vincent's voice came over the intercom from the control booth: "What are you gonna do about the keyboard solo? Do you want me to sit in?"

"What? No, we're fine," Ellington snapped.

"Thanks, Dad, but this version doesn't have the keyboard solo," Bix added. "Let's try it again."

His father might have thought stopping them right at the count off would mess up their concentration. Ellington couldn't speak for his brothers, but the whole thing just fueled his anger. They took kind of a Circle Jerks take on their version, keeping the melody mostly intact but letting Bix practically scream the chorus and giving Ellington a chance to smack the shit out of his kit. Theo and his bass line were the steady undertone that held the song together. It was the most fun Ellington had had playing with his family in years, probably since "Wipe Out," and that was ages ago. When they were done, all three brothers turned to the window separating the recording studio from the control booth.

Dave spoke first, with a huge smile and a "That was some hardcore shit, guys!" Dave had been the studio engineer for *Music Factory* too. He had never, ever cussed in front of them before. That had to mean he really liked it. Dave turned to Vincent. "What'd you think?"

"Well, that's certainly a different interpretation," Vincent replied.

"It's *our* interpretation," Ellington said.

"I like the edge you guys gave it. What would you say to bringing down the hardcore vibe a notch and adding kind of a Buzzcocks, Go-Go's pop punk feel. I have some ideas."

"I'm good with that," Bix said.

"You just named two of my favorite bands, man," Ellington said. This was turning out to be better than he anticipated. If they could find a new sound, maybe they could become a different sort of band. After all, they weren't little kids anymore.

"Okay," Theo added.

Ellington watched for his father to say something else. Anything. Vincent slowly stood up. "Do you need keyboard on this?" he asked.

Ellington exchanged a look with Bix. With two multi-instrumentalist brothers, it was pretty clear what the answer was. "No, sir," Ellington replied. "I think the three of us can handle everything." He wasn't entirely sure why he threw in the "sir." He only ever called Vincent that when he knew he was in trouble.

"Fine. Do whatever you want with it," Vincent said and left the control booth.

The stay in Youngstown was always supposed to be temporary, but every time Grace thought about moving back to California, she found a reason not to. First her parents needed her a little longer because her mother was still recovering from knee surgery, then the tour was extended. Then Viola started school. Staying, deferring was easier than deciding. When the kids at Austintown Intermediate School learned that Viola Klinefelter was really that no-talent kid from The Musical Mozinskis with the teddy bear, things did not go well.

Grace went looking for a new school and found one, except it was in Cleveland. It was worth the move to make her kid happy. They were, at least, moving back to familiar territory. And the small private school was a perfect fit for Viola. Vincent called it "that hippy-dippy touchy-feelie school" but still paid half the tuition, so Grace didn't care what he called it. Among Viola's classmates at the Bellflower School were the children of actors, musicians, artists, politicians, and a member of the Dubai royal family. She was far from being the most famous or the weirdest child at her new school.

The Bellflower School was in University Circle, near the Cleveland Institute of Music, where Clara was studying harp, which was another point in its favor. Clara insisted on living on campus, which Grace supported because it seemed like perhaps they all needed a break from family togetherness. Vincent hadn't even wanted Clara to go to college, much less live in a dorm. It seemed like the only thing she and Vincent could agree on was that all of their children should be happy and have a chance to follow their dreams; they just disagreed on how each child was supposed to do so.

Grace found a four-bedroom house in Cleveland Heights that was small enough to be affordable and maintain but large enough to accommodate any of the other kids if they wanted to visit. "Consider it 3642 East," she said to Vincent on the phone, a reference to the street number of the house in Pasadena. She and Vincent still talked once a week, less now about whether Grace and Viola were coming home and more about basic parenting decisions: who was paying what tuition, which kids might be visiting at Christmas. Once in a while, Vincent might offer a half-hearted "When do you think you'll be coming back?" or Grace would answer a question with a "That's something we can pursue when we're all back together." They both knew what the answer was. It was just easier not to talk about it.

The first time Grace heard "She's Not There" as done by The Mozinski Brothers, she was home alone in late January with a cassette demo of the album that Vincent sent her. Actually, the handwriting on the padded envelope looked feminine — it was definitely not Vincent's writing. Maybe he'd hired a secretary. Maybe he'd found a girlfriend. Maybe both. Bix and Theo mentioned someone named Patty a few times on the phone, but they tactfully hadn't said anything when they visited at Christmas. Ellington opted to stay in California with Vincent for the holidays. So had Allie, ostensibly because she was preparing for a series of spring concertos.

Grace had written four songs for the new album the previous summer — one each for Ellington, Bix, Allegro, and Thelonious. The three she wrote for the boys were on the album, but the one for Allie, "Ask Me

If I Care," wasn't. Grace thought it had the potential to be an anthemic sort of break-up song, and she wrote the lyrics with Allie's biting wit in mind. If Allie only wanted to play classical and The Mozinski Brothers weren't going to record it, she'd need to find another home for it. There were royalties from The Musical Mozinski albums, but the checks weren't as big as she'd hoped. She and Vincent had never talked about finances. Initially he'd simply paid the credit card bill every month. Then he told her the bank had lowered the credit limit. Another time he said he'd maxed out all the credit cards that month because he'd invested in some new instruments. It seemed like most of their money was tied up in instruments. Grace quickly realized that she was better off with her own income stream. That meant playing and song writing.

As she listened to The Mozinski Brothers' new album, she thought about where she might send "Ask Me If I Care." Maybe to Eddie Gibson from The Hi-Tones. Maybe someone else. The new album had two songs written by Bix, "Better Wait" and "The Middle Brother." "Better Wait" was particularly good. She was no longer the only songwriter in the family. Just as she was starting to think the older kids might not need her, she listened to "She's Not There," which was the last track on the album. When she heard Bix's screaming vocals and Ellington punishing his drums and even Theo singing harmony on the chorus sounding older and angrier than she'd ever heard before, it struck her that perhaps she had left behind a bigger mess than she realized.

SOPHISTICATED LADY

This is what Theo knew: Nothing. Nobody told him a darn thing. He didn't know that Ellington had dropped out of high school. They were working with Jenny the Tutor again so he didn't have to go to regular school anymore. Two months of middle school had been more than enough to let him know he wasn't missing anything. One day, Ellington didn't come downstairs when Jenny arrived. Theo figured he took the same test Clara did and graduated. Nobody bothered to tell him otherwise.

He didn't know that their dad was actually dating Patty. She was supposed to be an accountant or something, helping him with taxes and business, which is why they had to get together so often. It was stupid Mr. Karpenko who told him that his dad was dating Patty, and that was an accident. Karpenko had called for Dad and said something like "I forget, Vincent has date. Tell him call me when he is back." Theo had gone up to Bix's room and asked point blank, "Is Dad dating Patty?"

Bix was sitting with his guitar trying to write a song that was half as good as "Better Wait," at least that's what he said. "Yeah," Bix replied without glancing up. "I don't know how serious it is, but they're definitely going out."

Theo was aghast. "How is that possible?" he stammered. "He's still married to Mom!"

Bix sighed and rested his hands on the guitar. When he spoke to Theo, it felt like the first time anybody in the house had looked directly at him in months. "Dude, they're separated," Bix said. Theo appreciated that he said this nice and not as though he thought Theo was an idiot. "It's like step one to getting divorced."

"Mom and Dad are getting divorced?"

"I don't know for sure, but you gotta figure it's gonna happen sooner or later. If Mom was going to come home, she would have done it by now. And it's not like Dad's in a big hurry to go to Cleveland and bring her back."

"He calls her a lot."

"Not that much anymore. And talk is cheap. He hasn't gone to see her."

Theo thought about this for a moment and felt like the biggest, blindest moron in the world. It was obvious that his mom wasn't coming back. It was even more obvious that his dad didn't care. Theo just hadn't paid attention. But it still would have been nice if somebody told him something.

If nobody was going to tell him anything important, then he wasn't going to tell them anything either. When he and Bix visited their mom at Christmas, she asked how things were at home. He just said "Fine." Ellington was almost always out of the house, so he wasn't there to call him a fag, and Allie was usually rehearsing somewhere, so she wasn't around to be mean. Things were mostly fine at home. His mom didn't specifically ask if they still had Sunday dinners together or if Dad spent time with him or if Theo was lonely. The answers to that would have been no, no, and yes, but Theo didn't volunteer any information.

When he and Bix got back to California, their dad asked them all sorts of questions about their mom, like how she looked and what the house was like. It seemed like their dad wanted to know more than Theo or Bix could tell him. Even if he somehow did know about his mom's inner workings, he wouldn't tell his dad. If his dad couldn't even bother to tell him that he was having some big love affair with Patty the accountant, then he wasn't going to bother to tell his dad if Mom was happy (he wasn't sure) or if he noticed if she was seeing anybody (Theo hadn't, then again, he hadn't noticed that his dad and Patty were dating either).

Once he realized nobody was going to tell him what he needed to know, Theo started watching and he learned a few things on his own. He knew that Allie wanted to do something called emancipation so she could move out of the house even though she was only 14. He knew that Ellington hated Dad, even though that wasn't a big secret. He knew he didn't hate anybody, but he felt better when he was with his mom and Viola than he did with his dad. It wasn't that his dad was mean, he just wasn't home that much. And now that The Musical Mozinskis had become The Mozinski Brothers, Dad didn't have to rehearse with them. It was like he didn't care if Theo or any of them were okay as long as they kept practicing.

When Theo told his father he wanted to move to Cleveland and live with his mom, Vincent's first response was "What about the band? You're letting down your brothers."

When Theo was five, Clara showed him the Top 40 singles list in the entertainment section of the *Cleveland Plain Dealer* and proudly pointed out "Back in the U.S.A." at #28, saying "That's us! That's our family." Ever since then, Theo religiously checked the Top 40 list, first in the *Plain Dealer* then in the *LA Times*. "Better Wait," the first single from The Mozinski Brothers' self-titled album, didn't make the Top 40. And the album was never in the Top 100 list. His dad always had copies of *Variety* lying around the house, so Theo checked that too, just in case. The only mention of his family he found in *Variety* was his dad being listed as the music director for some movie starring a couple of actors he'd never heard of. It didn't seem like The Mozinski Brothers were going to have much of a career as a band if they weren't selling any records, and Theo said as much to his dad.

"Theo, your job is to play music," his father said. "Leave the business part to me."

Theo was tempted to say "You're doing a lousy job of it." That's what Ellington would have said, although El would probably say "shitty." All Theo said was "Okay." Then he called his mom and told her he was moving to Cleveland.

They made him fly to Cleveland with Mr. Karpenko, who seemed to think he was Theo's entertainment rather than a chaperone. He wouldn't stop talking, sometimes asking questions and sometimes going on and on about how much he loved Theo's family and what an amazing journey they were all on. It was kind of sweet but kind of weird at the same time, like Karpenko was trying to make himself be a part of their family, even though he technically wasn't. At one point, Karpenko got up to use the restroom, leaving Theo alone in the seat. One of the flight attendants came by and asked Theo if he or his daddy would like anything to drink. It wasn't so much that she assumed that big hairy, stinky Karpenko was his father, it was the use of the word "daddy." He had never called his father "daddy." That was way too cuddly a word to use for his father, plus it sounded like the flight attendant thought he was a little kid, not a 10-going-on-11-year-old internationally known musical prodigy ("Lazy Day" and "I Know That You Know" had both charted high in Europe).

"That's actually not my father," Theo replied as politely as he could, then added, "He's my manager" because it sounded important.

"Oh, excuse me, sweetie," said the flight attendant, and Theo noticed she sounded a little like one of the characters from *The Dukes of Hazzard*. Her voice lilted and trilled in A-flat. "That's very impressive. Are you a little actor, honey?"

"I'm a cellist," he replied and liked how that sounded coming out of his mouth. Theo decided that's how he was going to introduce himself from now on.

Just then, Mr. Karpenko came lumbering down the narrow airplane aisle and eased himself back into his seat. When he thought about it, he had known Mr. Karpenko literally all his life. He was the only person not in their family that he didn't remember meeting. He'd always just been there. Maybe not part of the family, but also not not part of the family. Karpenko still talked to him the entire way to Cleveland, but it didn't seem as annoying. It was just Mr. Karpenko being Mr. Karpenko.

Getting Theo back was like recovering a lost gem. That wasn't entirely right. Grace hadn't lost Theo so much as she had temporarily abandoned him. If he was a little too clingy for a boy his age, it was partially her fault. Vincent wasn't a bad father, just an inattentive one. When she and Viola picked up Theo and Gregor at the airport, she gave her son a hug and then found that she couldn't quite let go. "Thank you," she said to Gregor over the top of Theo's head, which was kind of difficult, since he had grown at least another inch since she saw him at Christmas.

Gregor still had some family in Cleveland and stayed with them while in town, so Grace was surprised when he showed up at the house a week later. Theo had come home during spring break but was now attending the Bellflower School with Viola. The new house was a couple miles away from where they had lived previously, but both Viola and Theo were so young when they moved to California that it was all new. She had already seen how proud Viola was to be able to show her older brother their new neighborhood and to tell him about their new school. Theo's first day had gone well, and Grace was feeling like she could relax, that maybe everything was going to be all right.

She spent the first few hours of the day composing, and was now listening to Sarah Vaughn while she washed the kitchen floor. She wasn't expecting Gregor Karpenko ringing her front doorbell and peering in the beveled glass door like a grizzly bear peeping tom. Still, she was happy to welcome him in. Like it or not, he'd been a part of the family for years now. And it wasn't as though doing housework was her favorite task.

Gregor seemed more awkward than usual, and Grace saw he was holding a thick manilla envelope in his left hand. It suddenly became clear to her why he was there. Even so, she went through the motions of making him some strong black tea and put some nonstale cookies on a plate as though she didn't know he was there to do something that both she and Vincent had been too cowardly to do.

When they each had a mug of tea in one hand and a cookie in the other, it seemed appropriate to say "I have a feeling I know why you're here." Gregor didn't say anything as he handed her the envelope, but his dark brown eyes glistened above his bushy salt and pepper beard.

On the turntable, Sarah Vaughn started singing "Sophisticated Lady." As she looked through the divorce documents, Grace occasionally glanced up to study Gregor's face. He was listening to the record.

"I did not know this song has words," he said.

"It didn't originally. They were added later. Duke Ellington approved of them. More or less."

Gregor paused for a moment, listening to Ms. Vaughn sing about missing the love one had long ago. "Vincent play this song for me years ago. At the Statler Hotel," he said.

"Wow, that was a while ago."

"A lot happen since then," Gregor said with a smile. This was undeniably true.

They were both silent for a moment, again listening to the song. "Still the most sad song I ever hear in my life," Gregor said.

"Agreed." Grace held up the papers slightly and said, "I will sign these. I'm guessing Vincent asked you to bring them back?"

"It would be nice, thank you."

"It would be nice if my husband had the balls to talk to me about this in person. Then again, it's not like I'm the paragon of courage over here."

Gregor said, taking a sip of tea. "I'm sorry I cannot provide your husband with bigger balls." Grace laughed and almost spit her tea onto her lap. "And you did the bravest thing. You walk away and protected Viola." Gregor said.

"Thank you." Grace continued looking through the divorce papers. It looked pretty straightforward, with an equal distribution of assets and shared custody. "Have you looked at this?" she asked.

"No. Is not my business."

"I was just wondering, because it doesn't say much about the kids in here — four of them are still under 18. I'm not asking him for child support — I will find a way to take care of Viola and Theo. I have some income. Not as much as it was, but it's enough. The cost of living is pretty low here."

"The children will be okay."

"It's nice of you to say that but..."

"Grace! Do you not think I took care of this? I am your manager. I am *their* manager. They all have accounts. How do you say — trusts? Each child has a trust. Is Coogan's Law."

"Vincent said..."

"Vincent did not set it up. I do it. He signed the papers, but I make it happen. Fifty percent of everything the child earns goes into their trust. The law is 15 percent, but I say my English is not so good. I hear 50 percent, so that's what they have. The children will be okay."

"You're saying each of the children has a trust fund?"

"Is that what you call it? Trust fund? Yes."

"Even Viola?"

Gregor looked shocked. "Of course. She was on the show. She is listed on all the records. She gets her share. They all get the money at age 21."

"Can Vincent access it?"

"What? No. It belongs to them only."

For a moment, Grace found it hard to catch her breath. When they first went out to California and signed the contracts for the show, she let Vincent and Gregor take care of most of the paperwork. She signed whatever Vincent handed to her. She'd been focused on moving six children and a household 2,500 miles cross-country. Whenever she asked Vincent about the children's future, he would always brush her off, saying that the family was earning the money and he'd take care of it. She'd trusted him when it appeared she should have put a little more faith in Gregor Karpenko. "Thank you, Gregor, for looking out for my kids."

"Is the law," he replied with a smile. "And I have no children, so sometimes I pretend yours belong to me, too," he added and ate an entire Pepperidge Farm Chessmen cookie in one bite.

Things felt a little brighter. Even looking through the divorce papers didn't seem as heart-wrenching as it had a few minutes earlier now that she was assured all of her children had their own nest egg that Vincent couldn't touch. She still had the mess of papers in her hand and realized she'd probably put them out of order. "I should probably have a lawyer look through this before I sign," she said.

"Good idea."

In that moment, Grace made a decision. "And you're off the hook," she added. "I'm going to deliver the papers myself."

CALYPSO BLUES

Later on, Vincent would insist he told Allie, Bix, and Ellington that their mother was coming to Pasadena, but when Grace arrived at the house on a Tuesday morning during a tutoring session, Allie forgot her father had ever told her anything. She forgot that her mom had been gone for 10 months, forgot that she herself had opted not to go to Cleveland for Christmas, forgot that she repeatedly declined to talk to her mom on the phone, forgot that she hadn't read any of the letters her mom wrote to her, forgot that she was angry and lonely and feeling abandoned, forgot everything except that her mother was standing in the entrance hall of their house.

"Mom!" she said quietly but didn't move. Now that Ellington had dropped out of school and Theo moved, it was just her and Bix working with Jenny, and she didn't really care what Bix thought of her. He never used personal information as a weapon. Even so, she found she didn't want to stand up and go to her mother. Not yet anyway. Bix was already on his feet and somehow being hugged by their mother and she was not. That hardly seemed fair, except that Bix was always so bright and chipper and, for lack of a better word *nice*, that it was like *of course* he's getting hugged by Mom first. Bix liked everyone and didn't hold grudges. He resembled a dog in that way.

They worked with Jenny at the table in the large formal dining room. Ever since last summer, Allie and her mom had been separated by 2,380 miles. Now they were only separated by the living room. Bix was talking a mile a minute to Mom about Bix stuff, but he finally shut up long enough for her mom to look over at her.

"Hi Allie," she said.

For a second Allie felt like she couldn't catch her breath, then she managed a "Hi." Her mom took a couple steps toward her and stopped, like she was waiting to see if Allie wanted to come to her. And Allie did. One second, she was sitting in the dining room with Jenny the Tutor, the next second, she was hugging her mom and her mom was hugging her and they were both crying a little. As a rule, Allie didn't cry around other people. Bix was standing between her mother and the front door. Allie turned her head the other direction so he couldn't see any of her tears. The entryway had a vaulted ceiling with a wide curved staircase leading to the second floor. Allie was resting her head on her mother's shoulder and closed her eyes for a second because it felt nice to just be there with her mom, even if Bix might have seen her cry. She heard a derisive grunt and opened her eyes to see Ellington leaning on the railing of the landing at the top of the stairs.

"Ellington," her mom said, in that way she had where just saying someone's name made it sound as though she'd been looking for that person all her life.

"Nice of you to finally come back," he snapped.

Every time Allie thought about seeing her mother again, she imagined herself saying something equally sarcastic, albeit a little more cutting and clever. She hadn't planned on defending her mother, yet she heard herself saying to Ellington "At least she's here."

"Yippee. Some of us aren't going to cry about it."

Darn it, Ellington *had* seen her cry. She decided to ignore him; often that was the only thing that kept her from killing him. "How long are you here?" she asked her mom.

"A couple weeks."

"How come Clara and Theo and Viola aren't with you?" Bix asked.

"They all have school. Speaking of which — hi, Jenny. I'm sorry for interrupting your school day."

Allie hadn't even noticed Jenny the Tutor standing awkwardly just outside the little circle of her, Bix, and Mom. "That's okay. It's good to see you, Mrs. Mozinski," Jenny said, giving her a quick hug. For a moment, Allie felt a flash of angry jealousy that her mother was hugging the tutor. The tutor. She never hugged any of their teachers back in Cleveland, and honestly, this was the same thing.

"Ellington, I know there's a lot to talk about. Would you come downstairs?" Mom asked.

"Nope," Ellington said and headed back to his room.

"He is such an asshole," Allie muttered.

Her mom reached out and gently put a hand on the side of Allie's head. It felt nice. "Oh sweetie," her mom said. "He isn't."

The vaulted ceiling and tiled floor made the entryway look and feel cold and sterile, but the acoustics couldn't be beat. Allie muttering "He is such an asshole" echoed right up the stairs. Ellington heard it. He was used to having Allie call him an asshole. That was pretty much all she knew how to say, considering she was such a bitch. Living with just their dad made it seem like calling each other "asshole" and "bitch" several times a day was normal. Hearing Allie say it in front of their mom seemed strange. For the space of an eighth note, it made Ellington feel embarrassed that he and Allie couldn't even stop fighting for two seconds during their mother's homecoming. The feeling passed as quickly as it arrived, because they shouldn't have even needed a homecoming, because she never should have left in the first place.

His father had bought a conga because he claimed Ellington should branch out musically. He sat in front of it now and started to play. Sometimes it seemed like he was born with drum sticks in his hands, so when he first sat down with the conga, hitting the drum head with his bare hand felt awkward. By now slapping the conga with his hand felt as natural as tapping the snare with a stick. He was in his room practicing when his mother knocked and poked her head in the room.

"Hi Ellington," she said. "Could we talk?"

"We *could*. But we won't," Ellington replied without missing a beat. The notation of "Calypso Blues" hung in the air above his head because the old Nat King Cole tune was the first song he could think of that featured a conga.

Undaunted, his mother walked right into his room and leaned against the edge of Ellington's little-used desk. He was glad she didn't try and sit down next to him on the bed. That would be too close, especially after 10 months.

"Ellington, I owe you an apology and an explanation," she said after moment. "You know that Viola...didn't quite fit in on the show. The only way I could think of to help her was to get her away from the show. I never wanted to hurt you or your siblings, and I'm so sorry that I did."

"So, you traded the rest of us for her," Ellington said. "Awesome." He kept the rhythm going, not rushing it but hitting the drum heads a little bit harder.

She let him play for a moment, long enough that adding the extra oomph every time his open hand hit the drum head started to seem stupid, and he lightened his touch. "I deserve all your anger," she said finally.

For the past 10 months, Ellington had not read his mother's letters and mostly managed to avoid talking to her on the phone. He didn't go to see her at Christmas, and this was the first time she'd come back. Even so, he had had a hundred conversations with her in his head. Sometimes she cried. Sometimes he yelled at her and told her what a crap mother she was. Sometimes she begged for his forgiveness. In none of these imaginary conversations had his mother said she deserved his anger. It kind of made him wonder what to do next. He stopped playing and looked at his mother for the first time. She looked a little bit older than he remembered. Tired. Too bad for her. "Well, you have it. You have all my anger," he said.

"I accept that. I can only say that I'm sorry for leaving the way I did. Viola needed..." she paused for a second, like she was trying to find the right word.

When his mother said "saving," Ellington scoffed. "Saving from what?"

"From being continually forced to try and do something she can't do and be something she isn't. It pains me to say it, but you know she's not a musician. Viola is who she is, with a ton of other talents. She has a lot to offer the world, but she would never get a chance living in the shadow of the five of you. I'm not saying that everything was perfect for you or your other siblings. I know it wasn't — isn't — especially with you and your dad. But Viola needed help right then. And the only way I could see to help her was to get her away from the show and the expectation that she should be part of it."

Ellington was still angry. He also hated that everything his mother said was true. "So what if *Viola* needed you? The rest of us needed you too."

"I'm so sorry, Ellington. I should have taken all of you. I know you weren't happy, but you weren't in crisis. Please know that if your life ever depends on it, I will drop everything to be there for you." Ellington didn't bother responding to this. "Crisis" and "life depending on it" seemed like a big exaggeration. "Sweetie," his mother continued, "did you know that Viola cried every night before bed because she couldn't read music and couldn't make it through her Birthday Solo without making a mistake? Do you remember how skinny she was? She stopped eating from fear."

"I didn't know that. It's not like we hung out that much."

"I understand. You're nine years older than she is — you don't have much in common. Although I remember how kind you were to try and help her with the John Cage solo."

Suggesting that Viola play 4'33" had been less to help her and more to piss off Vincent. Ellington figured his mom knew this, but just in case she didn't, he merely replied, "Thanks."

"Viola needed me then. If you need me now or ever, please ask. I will always be here for you."

"I don't need anything, Mom."

Ellington's mom looked at him like she knew he was lying. It sucked that she could go away for 10 months and come back and still seem to know what he was thinking. "I heard you dropped out of school. May I ask why?"

"I don't need it. I haven't used one thing Jenny taught me in show school."

"You will."

"When? I'm not gonna go out and like build bridges or program computers. I'm only ever going to play music."

"Ellington, you're 18 now and technically an adult. I can't tell you what to do, but I will ask you to at least get your GED for your own sake. You should learn enough math to make sure your royalty checks are correct. And enough history so you know when it starts to repeat itself. And learn enough literature to give you something to write about in your own songs." She stopped and gave him a sheepish smile. "Sorry for going on like that. You are so important to me, but your future is just that. Yours. Please know that I will always, always support you on your path."

Just to mess with her, Ellington asked "Even if I vote Republican?"

"Except that," she replied with a smile. His mom stood up from where she'd been leaning against his desk, walked over to him, and gave him a hug. Against his better judgement, Ellington accepted it. "Ellington, I love you so much and I am so, so sorry for leaving you," she said. "I hope you can understand why, and I hope someday you can forgive me."

Ellington noticed she said she was sorry for leaving "you." For leaving him. For once, it was nice to be singled out. Everything was always about The Musical Mozinskis or The Mozinski Brothers. No one ever talked just about him, they were always lumping him in with everybody else. It was kind of nice to have his mom talk to him about his future without mentioning the rest of the family. "Maybe. I'll try," he replied. Suddenly he had an idea. "You know, I think I'm going to start a band. My own band."

"Really? That's exciting," his mom replied. She sat down next to him on the edge of his bed. "What are you thinking?"

"Well, first Bix was all into, like, having The Mozinski Brothers be a power trio, but then Theo moved in with you, and he never really cared anyway, so whatever. Bix keeps saying he and I should find a new bass player, but he's more into Rush and The Police. He wants to get all arty and shit. That's not me, you know? I want more of an edge, more metal."

"Have you talked to Bix about it yet?"

"No." It felt stupid to say that he had gotten the idea for his own band right then while they were talking.

"You'll find the right time."

"Yeah, I guess so." He paused for a second. "Why did it take you so long to come back? And why'd you come back now?"

"First, I needed a little time to think. Then you were all out on tour. Then your grandma had knee surgery. Then we moved up to Cleveland. Then..." She sighed. "Then your father sent me divorce papers. I thought I should return them in person."

Ellington had figured they'd be getting divorced. His dad had been going out with Patty for a few months. Actually, he wasn't really sure when they started dating. "Why'd you move out of Grandma and Grandpa's house?"

His mom smiled. "Would you want to live with me when you're 47 years old?"

"Good point."

"And, confidentially, Viola was getting picked on at school. Because of what happened with the show," she added.

"I don't mind that the show got cancelled. I was getting tired of it anyway."

"That's understandable. The good thing is, you're free now to choose your path."

When his mom left the room, Ellington wasn't sure if he was still mad at her or not. It seemed easier to be angry. He knew anger. Vincent had raised him on it, encouraged it. If he thought about it, Vincent had been consistently shitty to him his whole life, whereas his mom had done one huge thing wrong. But he could almost see why she did it. She wanted to get Viola away from Vincent. That he could understand. Some days he just wished she had taken him with her, too.

GROOVY TWOSIE (REPRISE)

Going to music school was like paradise. Sure, there were egos and drama and general education requirements in things like history and literature, but those were manageable. Clara would go so far as to say that the classes were fun. Every waking hour was devoted to music, specifically the harp. There were no cheesey arrangements of old pop songs, no ugly costumes, no half-baked plots or poorly written scripts. It was like preparing for a Birthday Solo every day, and Clara loved it. Frankly she'd be fine if she never picked up a bass again.

Her mother, Theo, and Viola lived near campus. Close enough that Clara could walk there — even in the snow. She didn't mind coming back to Cleveland winters after four years in California. When she graduated from the Institute of Music, she had a boxy Volvo station wagon that could carry her harp to gigs and a small, steady income from her trust that paid the rent on an apartment in a building with an elevator because she was not going to hump the harp up and down stairs and risk damaging it. She found gigs and harp students, and she was busy and happy. She dated here and there, mostly other musicians. Once in a while she'd meet a guy who knew nothing about music. Although it would seem refreshing at first, after a while they'd realize they had nothing in common. After the way her parents' marriage had turned out — a marriage that was supposed to be of like-minded equals — she wasn't too keen on long-term relationships. Honestly, if Grace and Vincent Mozinski couldn't make it, who could?

Clara was fine with her life as it was. When she saw that The Hi-Tones were playing in Cleveland, she told herself and her mother she wanted to go for old times' sake and no other reason. Her mother had given the band a few more songs over the years. One of them, "Ask Me If I Care," had cracked Billboard's Top 100, which meant some nice royalty checks for her mom. There was a postcard with a photo of the St. Louis Arch from Eddie Gibson on her mother's refrigerator, so it wasn't surprising when her mom said she had two comps to The Hi-Tones show for her.

"What about you?" Clara asked. "Don't you want to go?"

"You go with a friend. They're here for an extra day, so Eddie and I are getting together for lunch. Did you know he and Harrison have an aunt who lives in Akron?" her mother replied. Clara did not know this. It made her wonder what other things her mother knew that she didn't. She was pretty sure her mother knew she had a crush on Harrison Melond when she was younger, although in retrospect, she hadn't been all that subtle. She chalked it up to having been 16. Going to see them now would confirm that she had gotten the puppy love crush out of her system.

Clara asked her best friend, Fiona, to go to The Hi-Tones show with her, but Fiona was unenthusiastic.

"You said they play like R&B? I'm not really a fan. And since when do *you* like R&B?" Fiona asked.

"Since always. Since I played with them when I was 13 and again when I was 16."

Fiona flopped back onto the futon in Clara's living room that doubled as her sofa. "Ugh, I keep forgetting you were a child star." She said "child star" as though the words themselves were afflicted with some sort of pox. Fiona played violin and was prone to exaggeration.

"Trust me when I tell you I've also tried to put it out of my mind. To no avail."

"Yeah, it must have sucked being on television every week and making all sorts of money..."

"And having no life of my own and being with my siblings 24/7...It was absolute paradise. But can we get back to the subject at hand?"

"We have been friends for nearly five years and in all that time, you've never once told me one good story about growing up on television. Why is that?"

"If you go to the library and find some old copies of *People* magazine, you can read about my family to your heart's content. I had no desire to relive it."

"It can't have been that bad. Your mom and Theo and Viola are great and mostly normal."

"To all outward appearances. Did I mention I have comps to The Hi-Tones show?"

"If I don't have to pay, I'll go." They were no longer students, but Fiona had held onto her student mentality towards money. "But in return, I want one juicy story about life on the set of *The Musical Mozinskis.*"

A dozen potential stories flashed through Clara's memory. The problem with talking about her past was that every story either required scads of exposition, or it sounded like bragging, or it might make Fiona think differently about her. For instance, she couldn't talk about performing on *The Tonight Show* at age 13 without explaining that it all came about because she and her younger siblings were musical prodigies and her father an opportunist. Although being a former child prodigy hadn't been a liability in music school, it wasn't a career path. And trying to explain why the family performed so well together would require explaining about seeing the music, and who would believe that? If she was ever going to find someone who saw music the way she did, music school seemed like the best place to look. In recitals and practice rooms and classrooms, she used to watch her contemporaries to see if any of them appeared to be seeing the music the way she saw it. She even asked open-ended questions to see if anyone took the bait. No one ever did. The only people Clara knew who could see and experience music the way she did were related to her. And not all of them could. But talking about that would also require talking about Viola's deficiencies and how her family broke up. It was just easier not to talk about her past or her family at all.

One of the best things about moving out of her parents' house had been the opportunity to hang out with people her own age, who weren't her family and weren't in television. She looked up a few of her old friends from elementary school when she started at the Institute, but they were either in college out of town or seemed like strangers when they met up. Clara had met Fiona in their first year at the Institute, and was the closest friend she had ever had. And that friend was waiting for an answer. Plus, she didn't want to go to see The Hi-Tones alone. "Okay, fine," she said. "Umm, when my parents first moved our family out to California, my sisters and brothers and I were disappointed because the house they bought in Altadena was really small and it didn't have a swimming pool. My mother said she bought a cheap house just in case the show got cancelled."

Fiona looked at her blankly. "Perhaps we should have a semantical discussion of the word 'juicy' in the context of stories," she said.

"I'll work on that," Clara said.

She didn't. Even thinking about the more pleasant memories just seemed like it would dredge up painful ones too. Clara didn't think about it again until the night of the show when she and Fiona were waiting in the will-call line at the Cleveland Agora. "Okay, I'm here, going to the show with you," Fiona said. "Where's my story?"

"Oh, you were serious about that?" Clara replied as she tied her sweater around her waist. It was midfall and bound to be chilly when they left, but why bring a coat that would get in the way while you're dancing?

"Yes."

"Why is it so important to you to hear a story about my childhood?"

Fiona gave an exaggerated sigh. "Because you had an unusual child-hood, and I like unusual stories. Because you're my best friend, but you keep things from me. I've told you tons of stuff about growing up in Tennessee. Why is it so difficult for you to talk about yourself?"

"It just is."

They were at the front of the line now, and Clara gave her name to the dreary-looking girl with purple hair and raccoon-like eyeliner working the ticket window. The girl looked through a box of paper-clipped tickets separated by alphabet tabs.

"I don't see your name," she announced.

"Could you double check, please?" Clara asked. "It's 'Mozinski,' 'M' as in monkey, O-Z-I-N-S-K-I."

The girl looked annoyed. "There's nothing under that name."

"But the tickets are supposed to be here."

"They're not. You can go to the other window and buy some," the girl added with a nod of her head to the other window, which had a line that snaked to the lobby doors.

Fiona muscled her way in next to Clara at the window. "Do you know who this is?" she asked. "Clara Mozinski has played gigs with The Hi-Tones. She's an old friend of the band and there are supposed to be two tickets waiting for her. Now who do we have to see to get this settled?"

Clara had been muttering "Please don't, please don't..." during Fiona's rant. They didn't have to go or they could buy some cheap seats in the balcony. "It's fine," she said. "Maybe there was a miscommunication."

"They're not with the will-call tickets," the dreary girl said, as though that should settle everything. She looked like she was ready to call security to remove them.

Fiona wasn't going to back down so easily. "Is there any other place where two comped tickets might be hiding? Like maybe a different box?" she asked.

"Please?" Clara asked. "If you could just double check?"

The girl sighed as though this was the worst encounter of her young life. "Hold on," she said and got up.

"I like how you're doing good cop to my bad cop," Fiona whispered. "Smart move."

"I wasn't. I was trying to be polite," Clara whispered back.

"What the hell is taking you so long?" the guy behind them in line said.

"Hold your horses," Fiona snapped. "We're just trying to get our tickets."

"So am I!"

The girl came back to the ticket window looking as dreary as before but with a slight hint of respect. She handed them two plastic badges attached to black lanyards. "Here," she said as she handed them to Clara. She didn't look at Fiona.

"Thank you," Clara replied, trying to stay cool. "Sorry for the bother."

As they stepped away from the window, the guy behind them sang "Finally!" in the same falsetto Danny Daley used on the chorus of the song by the same name. Clara burst into laughter as she pulled Fiona away from the line.

"Don't start a fight," she stammered between giggles.

"I won't. And what's so funny?"

Clara considered her closest friend. "Okay, here's a story. I lost my virginity to that song."

"To 'Finally'?"

"As it was being sung to me by Danny Daley."

Fiona screamed. "You lost your virginity to...whoa! I will need details, but between that and the backstage passes, I think our friendship is back on solid ground."

"Glad to hear it."

They filed into the auditorium, which was starting to fill up and getting noisy. Clara tried to stay calm, but the idea that she was going to see Harrison — not just watch him perform but probably talk to him — was making her heart pound. They walked down the side aisle leading towards the stage. It was so noisy and crowded that she couldn't even turn around and talk to Fiona, but she felt Fiona's hand gripping her shoulder so they wouldn't get separated.

Just behind the speakers lining the right side of the stage, they came to an open door being guarded by two men, one white, one black. If not for the fact that they were both wearing Cleveland Agora T-shirts, they were each large enough to be mistaken for a brick wall. Clara started to say hello, but they took one look at her and Fiona's passes and waved them in.

"Nice..." Fiona muttered to her.

They walked up five steps, and there they were, backstage. It had been a long time since Clara performed with her family, but standing in the wings and looking at the opening act's equipment on stage took her back. For a moment, she was a teenager again, getting ready to go onstage. She half expected to see Bix and Ellington punching each other or farting around with one of the roadies.

"Are you okay?" Fiona asked.

"Yeah, sorry."

A pot-bellied, middle-aged guy with mutton chops and carrying a coiled electrical cord moved past them. "Excuse me, ladies. Are you supposed to be back here?"

Clara half held up the backstage pass that was hanging around her neck. "Yeah, I'm an old friend of the band, actually."

The man paused, as though weighing whether he believed her and how much he cared. He shrugged. "They're in their dressing room."

"Thank you," Fiona said brightly. "This is fun, we can go anywhere we want. Let's go say hi."

Clara led her as far out of the way as she could, all the way to the black-painted wall. "I should probably say that my first-ever crush was on Harrison Melond, the lead singer of The Hi-Tones."

"Not Danny Daley? Why, you little minx."

"It was before I met Danny. I was 13 the first time I met The Hi-Tones."

Fiona's face scrunched into a delighted *oohhhh*. "That's so cute. Did anything ever happen between you two?"

"No! I was a teenager."

"You're not a teenager now," Fiona said pointedly. "You're 24 years old. A bona fide adult. How old is he?"

"Maybe...30?"

"That's no longer an insurmountable age gap. Do you still like him? What am I saying — of course you still like him. That's why you're freaking out. You're pretending you don't still have a crush," Fiona said as though she had solved some great mystery. "Come on. We're going to see him."

Having Fiona with her made the whole thing feel like a game, not like she was stalking Harrison. There was only one other door besides the one they had just come through, so they walked through it, trying not to laugh and trying not to look like groupies. Random roadies and techies passed them but ignored them once they saw the backstage passes. It felt a little sleezy to ask where the dressing room was, so they just kept moving as though they knew where they were going. They came to a well-lit, wide set of stairs leading down.

Fiona held up her backstage pass like a talisman as she headed down the stairs. "Just think, without these, we'd be no better than groupies."

"On our last tour, my brother Ellington used to ask one of our roadies to send girls with big boobs backstage."

"Oh my God, you're spilling everything tonight."

"Not everything," Clara said as she reached the bottom of the stairs. There was only one way to go. She could hear voices, familiar voices. The last time Harrison had spoken to her was after The Hi-Tones played on the show. At the end of the taping, he'd given her a hug and said, "I hope I see you again someday, Clara." During her teens, she had replayed those words a hundred times, wondering if he was just being nice.

An older black man was walking down the hallway towards them. He was big in height and in girth. Clara had a vague memory of meeting him during the taping, but that was eight years ago. The man didn't look happy to see them. He stopped a few feet in front of them and said, "I'm sorry, young ladies, but you are not allowed to be back here. I'm gonna have to ask you to leave." His voice was higher than you might expect for a guy that size — tenor rather than bass. That confirmed it. She had definitely met him before.

Clara had never used her name to her advantage, but in this instance, it seemed like the best course. "Hi," she said, extending her hand. "I'm Clara Mozinski. I think we might have met a few years back when The Hi-Tones were guest stars on *The Musical Mozinskis.*

The man cocked his head slightly as he shook her hand. "Curtis Conway. I remember that. Which one did you say you are?"

"I'm Clara. The oldest. I played bass."

"Oh yeah..." The man gave her and Fiona a quick once-over with what her mother always called "elevator eyes" as he said, "Look at you, all grown up."

"We just wanted to say 'hello' real quick and thank Eddie for the passes."

"I guess that couldn't hurt. They got a few minutes." Curtis led them down the hall and then stuck his head in an open door on the left. "Ya'll got a visitor from the Mozinski clan," he said loudly. To Clara and Fiona, he said, "Go on in."

For a second, Clara wished she had brought her mother, because she always seemed to know what to say and what to do in any social situation. She did her best to channel her inner Grace Mozinski, walked to the dressing room door, and said "Hello."

AT LAST

Even though everyone in the family had ostensibly gotten over the divorce, Theo could never shake the feeling that lines had been drawn and sides taken. He, his mom, Viola, and Clara were in Cleveland. His dad, Ellington, and Allie were all firmly in and around Los Angeles. Bix was in the demilitarized zone in Chicago. There had been times when he wanted to blame everything on Viola, like maybe if she could have gotten it together to read music or just plink out that stupid *Ode to Joy* then they might all still be together. But he had left too, he chose his mom over his father, so maybe it was partially his fault, too.

El was playing with a band called Skutch that played hard rock. They weren't quite metal because they didn't wear a lot of black leather. And they weren't a hair band, because Ellington still called any guy with long hair a fruit or worse. That was one of the reasons Theo was glad to have moved in with his mom. He sometimes saw a Skutch video on MTV, which was always a little surreal. Watching Ellington on MTV didn't feel like watching his brother. It was just somebody he knew. Most of the kids at the Bellflower School listened to obscure alternative bands on college radio. They were barely impressed by the music Theo had created, much less an older brother in a second-tier rock band. If Ellington showed up for a family function or holiday, Theo said "Hi," and they sometimes talked. One of them always managed to beg off whenever someone — usually Vincent — suggested a family jam. Just because he and his brother could see each other's music didn't mean they could see eye to eye. Bix was still Bix, always in that aggressively pleasant mood. Theo was starting to wonder if maybe it was an act. The three of them hadn't played together since they recorded The Mozinski Brothers album. Then there was Allegro, who was just scary. She took the GED at 16, enrolled in UCLA, and finished her B.A. when she was 20, all while still performing as a guest artist all over the place. Theo was about to graduate from high school and had no desire to go to college. It was hard not to compare himself to Allie, but really, who could compete with her?

Looming above all of them was his father. They talked on the phone maybe once a month or every other month — usually because his mother told him and Viola that they needed to call. He and Viola still got shipped out to their father in Los Angeles for a couple weeks every summer and alternating holidays. His father and Patty ran off to Las Vegas and got married. Mr. Karpenko said it was nice. He was the only person Theo knew who'd been invited.

Pretty much everyone he knew and a bunch of people he didn't know were going to Clara and Harrison's wedding in the fall. Whenever Clara came over to dinner, sooner or later they always ended up talking about the wedding. Theo didn't mind too much, because it took the pressure off talking about college and why he didn't want to go. Plus, he liked Harrison. He and Clara were staying in Cleveland instead of moving to Detroit, where Harrison was from. Having him around was like having another brother, one who wasn't an asshole or a fake. Most of the time they talked about music. It was still the family business even if they weren't exactly one big happy family anymore. Sometimes Theo felt bad for Viola because she never took part in those conversations. She listened and nodded, but it wasn't like she could really be part of it because she didn't know music — didn't experience music — the way he and Clara and their mom did. Everything Theo thought he knew about Viola changed when she hung up the painting.

Viola had done a watercolor at school that turned out really nice. She even matted and framed it by hand because teachers at the Bellflower School were big on DIY. The painting was all these brown and yellow swirls that reminded Theo of one of the banana and chocolate Fudgsicles he used to buy from the ice cream truck. The colors were one thing, but somehow Viola managed to make it look like the swirls of color were dancing together. Every time Theo looked at it, it seemed like the colors were in motion. He had always liked Viola's artwork, but there was something about this new watercolor that drew him in. It was the type of thing he could imagine seeing in a gallery. The first time Clara and Harrison came over and saw it hanging in the stairway leading up to the second floor, they immediately asked about it.

"I did it," Viola said. "I matted and framed it too. By hand." She took the painting off the wall and turned it around so Clara and Harrison could see the back. It was pretty badass that Viola could turn some random pieces of wood into a frame.

"Wow, that's impressive," Harrison said.

Clara turned the painting back to the front. "It's gorgeous..." she murmured.

"Thanks."

"What was your inspiration for the painting?" Harrison asked.

Theo was sitting in the living room, half listening to the conversation and half doing American government homework. Their mom was in the kitchen. This was a question Theo had never thought to ask Viola, or anybody really. Art came from within and sprang out. Who the hell thought about things like inspiration? That sounded like those idiots who thought they had to wait for the muse to hit them before they could paint or write or compose. He wondered if Harrison had to wait around for inspiration to strike before he wrote a song. About the only thing of value Theo could recall learning from his father was the knowledge that art comes through work and practice and perseverance, not inspiration. You had to do it over and over and over.

"Actually, it's um...it's the two of you," Viola said. "The first time you played together over here."

"Cool, so it's sort of like symbolic art?" Clara asked. She sounded a little puzzled. From his spot in the other room, so was Theo.

"No, it's representational."

Clara and Harrison were silent for a moment, as though they didn't know how to respond. Theo suddenly remembered a conversation he and Viola had had ages ago, back in show school, and gave up on his homework. He stood up and walked across the living room to the staircase where his sisters and Harrison were still standing with the painting. "Viola, is this like how you once told me my voice was purple?" he asked.

Viola looked a little relieved, like maybe she wasn't sure how to talk about all this. "Yes. You're purple. Well, your voice is purple — well, violet — and Clara's is that shade of yellow, and Harrison's is the brown..."

"So you assign colors to people?" Harrison asked.

"No, that's what it looks like when you sing or when you play."

"It looks like that?" Theo asked, pointing to the painting.

"Yeah." Viola looked confused, like maybe she had said something wrong. "Isn't that what you see?"

Theo didn't mean to say "No" in stereo with Clara, but he did. This was too weird. Then he added, "We see the *music*."

"I know. That's the music," Viola replied and sort of held up the framed painting as she said this to indicate that the music and the painting were one and the same.

Harrison turned to Clara and asked, "What do you mean, you *see* the music?"

Theo had never talked to anyone about being able to see the music, and from Clara's expression, she had never told Harrison. "Can we talk about it later?" she said to Harrison.

"It really seems relevant to the conversation."

Clara looked over at Theo for a second, as though she thought he might help her out. It wasn't his issue to sort out. Harrison wasn't *his* fiancé. "Everyone...almost everyone in my family sees music. It looks like musical notes in the air," she stammered.

"Really?"

"Kind of like in *Peanuts* where Schroeder is playing and the music is above the piano."

"That's kind of what it looks like for me," Theo said, "but the notes are all around. It's kind of like being in a tunnel." He wondered why he had never had this conversation with any of his siblings before.

"Whoa, cool. Can you still read it?" Clara asked.

"Yeah, I see the whole notation. Even if it's improvised."

"Me too!"

"Wow, that's...that's wild," Harrison said finally. "I don't see anything."

"That's not what I see," Viola said. "I see this," and she held up the painting.

Harrison and Clara loved the painting so much that they asked Viola to design their wedding invitations using the watercolor as the basis. It seemed appropriate. Somehow word got around to the rest of the family that Viola could see, well, something. Theo noticed at the wedding that Allie and Bix seemed to look at her a little differently, maybe with a bit more respect. But maybe that was just because everyone was on their best behavior. Even Ellington showed up sober.

Theo and Viola weren't allowed to bring dates to the wedding. Viola didn't have a boyfriend, but Theo thought by now Clara knew that calling Christopher his best friend was euphemistic at best. It would have been nice to have him to talk to during the reception instead of Mozinski and Klinefelter relatives he didn't remember and Melond relatives he'd probably never see again. Since Viola was in the same boat, they spent most of the wedding weekend together, primarily dishing about their siblings and parents, because there was a lot to talk about.

The wedding itself was nontraditional, which delighted Theo and seemed to scandalize most of the older folks, which was even more delightful. Clara and Harrison didn't have a traditional wedding party, so they held a rehearsal barbeque the night before for immediate family. Plus, they got married outside instead of in a church. They still had a minister and made all the standard promises to love and cherish each other for the rest of their lives, so all the old-people-finger-wagging seemed like a waste of time.

The entire family hadn't been together in the same room since that last day in the television studio eight years earlier. Theo couldn't remember the last time his parents were even in the same city. Plus, one of his siblings was always missing. Ellington or Allie would be on tour, or Bix would spend the holidays at the home of whatever girl he was dating at the time. Theo had liked Eileen. Bix obviously had too, since he moved all the way from Los Angeles to Chicago for her, but then they broke up. Now he seemed to have a rotating door on his bedroom because every time Theo talked to him, Bix mentioned a different name. Bix and someone named Carrie drove in from Chicago for the rehearsal barbeque and the wedding. Carrie seemed nice enough, but how much could you really tell about a person when they're on their best behavior at a cookout?

"Frankly, I'm not impressed," Theo said at the reception. They had been seated at a table with Bix and Carrie and two of the guys from The Hi-Tones and their wives. Now that dinner was over, the adults had moved to the bar and the dance floor. He and Viola pushed their chairs back from the table and surveyed the room. Theo loved to dance but only in controlled situations. Weddings where he would give the old folks a heart attack by dancing with another guy were not controlled situations. Growing up with Ellington and Bix in the house and ever-present cameras outside the house, he had perfected the art of passing, of appearing to be what he was not. It was easy to pretend to be a guy who doesn't dance. Plus, Viola didn't want to dance.

"I wasn't either, but maybe she was just nervous yesterday," Viola replied. "You don't bring someone to a family wedding unless you're serious about them."

"You're saying you think Bix is serious about her?"

"Yeah. Well, Bix-level serious. He gave Carrie a ring, but she said it isn't an engagement ring, more like a pre-engagement ring."

"How do you know this?" It was inconceivable that Viola could have gotten this sort of inside information before he had.

"She told me in the bathroom."

Theo inwardly cursed his gender's general lack of bathroom camaraderie. "Bix gives girls rings like he's passing out Halloween candy," he scoffed. The band was doing a respectable cover of Stevie Wonder's "Uptight (Everything's Alright)," and Bix and Carrie were grooving on the dance floor along with a few other couples. Dinner had just ended, and the party portion of the reception was getting started. The wedding band was made up of friends of Harrison and Clara, plus half the guests were musicians. Even the finger-wagging, tradition-loving old folks would admit that the music was top-notch.

"True," Viola said. "So far, I like Carrie okay."

"You can't really judge someone's character until you've seen how they behave around an open bar."

His younger sister considered this for a moment. "That's actually not a bad assessment tool," she replied as her eyes scanned the dance floor. "By that measurement, Carrie seems like a decent person. Ellington on the other hand..."

"I'm gonna stay away from that one."

They were silent for a moment, then Theo caught sight of Allegro heading their way. "Allie at 10 o'clock," he said.

"She's already seen us. There's no escape."

"Where's what's-his-face?"

"Probably robbing more cradles," Viola said, then Allie was upon them.

"Hi Allie," they said unison.

Allie was wearing a slinky dark green dress that seemed to be made of some ethereal fabric that Theo longed to touch because nothing so shiny could possibly be comfortable. Then again, this was Allegro. Comfort wasn't as great a concern as appearance. "There you both are," she said, as though they hadn't seen her an hour earlier, as though they weren't still sitting in the same spot. She leaned closer to be heard over the music. "Dad wants us to play a song or two later. Everybody," she added, looking at Viola.

"Last I checked, it was Clara's wedding, not Dad's," Theo said.

"Apparently, lots of people are going to sit in with the band. And you know it's not a wedding unless Vincent Mozinski sings 'At Last.'"

"Of course he *has* to do a solo."

"Mr. Karpenko said he even sang it to Patty in the chapel in Vegas," Viola added.

This was news. Theo was once again impressed by Viola's dirt-gathering ability. Maybe she ought to go into journalism instead of art.

"Be that as it may, Dad wants to have the entire family play together."

Something about the request triggered a wave of protectiveness in Theo. "Does that include spouses?" he asked. "They're family. Is Ken going to play?"

"We aren't married yet."

"Okay, how about Patty? Is Patty going to play with us too?"

Allie sighed as though she was dealing with a very slow three-year-old rather than a sarcastic 18-year-old. "No. Patty isn't a musician."

"Neither am I," Viola said as she stood up and walked away. It looked like she was headed towards the cake.

"Honestly, can't she just pick up the stupid tambourine and stand there and smile to make our father happy?" Allie said this as though she actually thought Theo would agree with her.

"It's not like he ever did much to make her happy."

"Theo, any of us could say that." Theo inwardly disagreed, but said nothing. "You're playing," Allie added, and it was less of a question than a statement.

"Do I have a choice?"

"Not really. I'll see you later."

It had taken a moment for Theo to register what his older sister just said. He stood up as she took a few steps away from him. He practically had to yell and gently put his hand on her back. It would have been easier to touch her shoulder, but the dark jade dress was strapless. Touching Allie's back meant he could touch the dress fabric. It was satin. Soft. Of course. "You said you and Ken aren't married *yet*. Are you engaged?"

"Yes, but don't say anything. I don't want to steal Clara's thunder."

"He's your agent."

"Agent and manager. You'd be surprised how many people are married to their manager."

"He's like 50 years old!"

"Forty-two."

"It's a big age difference."

"You know, you could have just said congratulations."

Theo opened his mouth but really didn't know what to say as he watched Allie walk away from him and head back to the bar. Later in the evening, when they were huddled near the side of the bandstand with the rest of the family, he whispered a hasty "Congratulations," followed by "Sorry."

"Thanks," she said as she adjusted the strap of the electric guitar one of The Hi-Tones had lent her. Everyone else brought their own ax, because that's what you do when you go to a wedding of musicians. Theo hadn't planned on sitting in, but his mother put his saxophone and her trombone in the trunk of the car anyway. Sometimes at home he and his mom would play, or he'd jam with Harrison when Clara brought him over. But having his entire family together, knowing they were about to perform together for the first time since he was a little boy, felt surreal. And though he didn't want to admit it, kind of fun. They were all gathered there by the side of the stage except for Viola. His dad, Ellington, and Bix were standing together. Ellington's eyes were bloodshot and he kind of reeked of stale booze. Theo kept his distance. "If Viola refuses to be on stage, then we'll do 'Let The Little Girl Dance.' She can dance," Vincent said.

"She's not five anymore, Dad," Bix said at the same time Theo said, "She doesn't want to."

"Fricking drama queen," Ellington muttered, but it wasn't clear if he was referring to Theo or Viola. Theo didn't ask.

The bandleader, whose name Theo hadn't gotten, was at the mike, introducing them as they walked up the two steps to the bandstand. "We have a special treat for you right now. Yes, that is the lovely bride, Clara Mozinski Melond, taking the stage on bass along with her amazing family. Ladies and gentlemen, for the first time in — how long?" he asked, looking over at Vincent, who was settling in behind the keyboard.

"Eight years!" Vincent yelled back with a broad smile.

"Playing together for the first time in eight years, I give you The Musical Mozinskis!"

Bix looked over at their father, shook his head "No," and immediately went into the iconic Chuck Berry riff. Theo had been too young to play on the "Back in the U.S.A." single, but he knew the song intimately. The original arrangement had backup singers, not a horn section. Instead of singing the "Oh yeahs," he and Grace played them. It gave the number more pop. Given the reaction from everyone on the dance floor, this was a much better choice than "Let the Little Girl Dance."

He knew after this song, his father would "slow things down" to sing his obligatory favorite wedding song. He knew Harrison and The Hi-Tones would play later. He even thought about sitting in some more, just jamming to celebrate Clara and Harrison. He scanned the dance floor. It looked as if every single wedding guest was out there except Viola. She was standing slightly off to the side, alone. Theo wanted to go to her and tell her everything would be all right, but he couldn't leave the stage in the middle of a song. Then he saw Mr. Karpenko lumber over. He must have asked if she wanted to dance because she shyly shook her head No. Karpenko motioned to the stage and said something to her. She sort of shrugged and smiled. Theo watched Viola and big, hairy Mr. Karpenko walk onto the dance floor. Karpenko was surprisingly light on his feet. He twirled Viola around as she laughed. Theo thought she looked free.

Playing the saxophone had always made him feel like a human exclamation point, punctuating the rhythm and the vocals. He could see the music swirling around him and his family, the notes rushing out, bobbing and swirling. He had made music virtually every day of his life, and seeing the notes dancing above and around him never failed to amaze him. There was a magic in it that he still didn't fully understand even though he was part of its creation. He had a sudden urge to ask Viola what she was seeing.

HEART-SHAPED BOX

Ellington was well into his 20s before he realized that most people had had multiple jobs in their lives. He'd only ever had one job: musician. Even with the girls and ample drugs, there was a lot of down time on tour, so he and Scab and the rest of the guys talked a lot, especially on the bus. Sometimes they talked about weirdo jobs they'd had. Scab worked at a Dairy Queen in high school, where he'd give cute girls an extra twist of ice cream on their cones. "I got so much pussy doing that," he'd say longingly as somebody, usually Ellington, would throw something at him and call him a liar. Before he moved to L.A., Charlie waited tables at a family restaurant in Pennsylvania that was frequented by Amish. He said they were surprisingly good tippers. Matt poured concrete for six years — from the time he got out of high school until Lost Dog got its first recording contract. Roger, the tour manager, was a little older than the rest of them, and had dug graves at a cemetery for two summers when he was in college, which was the most metal job of any of them.

When they asked Ellington what his first job was, he said "playing drums." He never had a paper route, never worked in a restaurant or a store, or had an internship, or worked a nine-to-five. Music was the only way he'd ever made money, even though he and his siblings never actually got paid until they were 21. This news was typically greeted with a "Dude, that's messed up," as though the speaker thought it would have been a good idea to give a 15-year-old Ellington Mozinski unlimited cash.

It was also a revelation that most people didn't spend as much time with their family as he did unless they grew up as members of a religious cult. Ellington joked that it balanced out because he hardly saw them at all now. Sometimes that joke made journalists and girlfriends ask him if he hated his family. The most annoying one about it had been Tammy, who asked straight out, "Why do you hate your family so much?" She didn't ask, "Do you hate them?" She just assumed.

They were in a hotel suite somewhere near Portland, Oregon, lying in bed the morning after a show. Ellington woke up first. A-hole Vincent had made them wake up early every day when they were kids to have more practice time. It's like his body was programmed to wake up early, no matter what time he went to bed or how hard he'd partied the night before. It was nine-thirty in the morning, and he was painfully, miserably awake. In a couple hours, Roger was going to be pounding on the door to make sure he was still alive and hadn't wandered out to a party somewhere in the middle of the night. Moving the band from one city to another without losing anybody was Roger's raison d'être.

Tammy was lying next to Ellington. She was all twisted up in the sheet, and her long, light brown hair was splayed out across the pillow and over part of her face with just her nose sticking out. Ellington thought she looked like some cute, hedonistic, woodland creature, except for the little flecks of coke that were still crusted around her nostrils. That wasn't so cute. He looked at her for a moment, debating whether he felt like playing with her tits and maybe messing around before they left. She had her half of the sheet wrapped around her like a mummy. While he was trying to extricate Tammy's left tit from the twisted sheet, she woke up, which sort of ruined the element of surprise.

"What the hell?" Tammy said, wrapping the sheet back around her as though she didn't parade around naked in front of him any chance she got.

"What's the problem?" Ellington asked as he reached for her again.

Tammy just made the hurt little *tchaw* sound she always did when she was upset, and then she got out of the bed. The *tchaw* sound was always in B-flat, and the tied note hung in the air as Ellington watched her perfect heart-shaped ass make its way to the bathroom. He ordered room service and grabbed the television remote.

Half an hour later he was still in bed, finishing off a room service omelet while Tammy ate her dainty little fruit cup, and out of nowhere, she asked him, "Why do you hate your family so much?"

"What are you talking about?" he asked without looking up from the television.

"You never talk about them or see them. We've been going out nearly three months, and I've never met any of your family. And don't some of them live nearby?"

"One, I talk to them. Two, they don't live anywhere near here, babe," he said, and took another bite of omelet. If he was chewing, it should indicate that the conversation was over. And he threw in a "babe" to let her know there were no hard feelings.

"I've never heard you talk to them."

"You don't need to know everything I do."

"I'm just saying I'll bet your mom would like to see you," Tammy said, as though she knew the desires of a woman she had never met. "It's not like we couldn't afford to fly over and see her."

This crossed the line. Ellington knew he could afford to hop on a plane and go anywhere he wanted. He could afford go to Cleveland, or Hawaii, or Hong Kong, or wherever the hell he wanted. Tammy couldn't afford to go down the street on her own. When he first met Tammy, she'd seemed great — a hot chick who could party hard. She was cute and all with fabulous tits, but she was still just a glorified groupie. Saying "*we* could afford it" sounded like she thought they were a permanent couple and she was claiming half of all his stuff. That was not cool.

Ellington didn't answer her. He made a deal with himself. If Tammy shut up now, if she could just drop it, he'd keep her with him the rest of the tour. He was pretty sure it was only a couple more months. Instead of shutting up, she whined, "I just want to get to know you better. I just want to be closer to you."

"If you want to be closer to me, come over here and sit on my face," Ellington replied. He knew it wasn't the nicest thing he'd ever said, but she was really starting to annoy him.

"Ellington! How dare you!"

"Come on, it's not like I said 'come over here and suck my dick,'" he replied, even though she had done that the night before.

Tammy stood up abruptly and started moving around the room, getting dressed and gathering up her things. "You know what? I'm sick of you treating me like crap. I'm leaving," she said. Ellington watched her and calmly ate the last bite of his omelet. Every few seconds, Tammy glanced over at him, like she was waiting for him to stop her. Ellington didn't say anything. She had to have known this wasn't going to be a long-term thing.

He kept one eye on the TV and one eye on Tammy to make sure she didn't take any of his stuff for a souvenir. She'd probably sell it. They had done some blow the night before, and there was still at least a gram left in the vial. Plus, a baggie that had either Ecstasy or some benzos. All of that was still sitting on the table in the other room. He got out of bed and walked naked into the other room and took the baggie out of her hand.

"Nope. Mine," he said and reached down and palmed the coke too.

"Come on, Ellington! I scored that."

"With my money. Get out. Tell Roger I told him to get you a plane ticket home."

Tammy bitched and even slapped him on the face like she was some chick from an old black-and-white movie. It wasn't worth the energy smacking her back. Instead, he took one of the benzos from the baggie and swallowed it. "See? Mine, not yours," he said. He could tell it pissed her off. It was kind of fun. Just for shits and giggles he took another one out of the bag and dry swallowed that one too. "Also mine. Now get out of here."

She finally left. For a second it seemed unnaturally quiet in the suite. They'd been together for two months and while he wasn't in love with her, he'd gotten used to having her around. The hotel suite was the standard living room/bedroom set up like a thousand other ones he'd been in. There was half a glass of whiskey still sitting on the table next to the sofa. He forgot Roger had hung out with them last night. Roger always drank Cutty Sark on the rocks. They'd both been drinking it. The two benzos were kind of sticking in his throat so he downed the rest of the whiskey, since he knew it'd be half water anyway. Then he went back to bed to watch TV.

Ellington had joined the band when Lost Dog lost its bass player and drummer. Ellington used to see Lost Dog flyers in Tower Records and stapled to telephone poles. At first, he wasn't sure if it was a band or legit somebody missing their dog. When Ellington found out that Charlie called it Lost Dog so he could put up flyers pretty much anywhere, he introduced himself after one of their shows. Lost Dog was like most of the other garage bands from the early '80s — kind of okay, but not great. Ellington needed a band. Charlie needed a drummer. Having Ellington Mozinski as their drummer got them a recording contract. They changed the band name to Skutch and put out their first record. Charlie called him Midas, because it was like the band turned gold, went gold, when Ellington joined. He never bothered to mention that Ellington couldn't put together a decent band on his own. He'd been playing with Charlie and whatever band he had for 11 years. It wasn't exciting anymore. Ellington wondered if this was how people who went to the same job every day felt.

The *Barney Miller* rerun he'd been watching was over, so he flipped around a few channels and saw a Nirvana video, "Heart-Shaped Box," which Ellington always thought was a better song than "Smells Like Teen Spirit." Skutch was great, but they didn't have the loud-quiet-loud modulation of Nirvana or the Pixies or any of the other bands Ellington admired. Skutch was straight-ahead power chords all the way. He loved Nirvana's sound, but kind of hated them too, mainly because Kurt Cobain could write circles around him. Maybe he should have listened to his mom way back when she told him to learn enough literature so that he'd have something to write about. Maybe he wasn't meant to be a songwriter, the same way Viola wasn't meant to be a musician. Viola was doing something with art, so he guessed she found her thing. He had found his thing. It seemed like it. He was a musician. Only ever a musician.

The video was over, and he was about to change the channel because it was the news, but then he wondered why were they playing Nirvana videos on the news and then the announcer said that Kurt Cobain had killed himself.

"Shit..." Ellington whispered. He sat through the news report, which wasn't much of anything, then flipped around until he found another station playing a Nirvana video. He'd never met the guy in person. He tried once, asking Roger to put out feelers, but no dice. When you've been on national television wearing stinking bell-bottoms and playing a cover of Abba's "Waterloo" at age 14, most other musicians your age think you're a joke. Even now, he'd meet people who thought it was funny to bring up the old *The Musical Mozinskis* TV show, like they thought Ellington was still that kid performing with his family. Stupid Theo was out in Seattle, playing with some grunge band. Rumor had it that Nirvana had asked him to play cello for their unplugged show, but Theo couldn't make the rehearsals. That whole story was probably a load of crap.

Ellington always thought Cobain had it good, better than good, and then he goes and offs himself. *You never know...*Ellington thought. It all started to feel like too much. The benzos were starting to kick in but not fast enough. He didn't want to feel anything for a while. The coke was still sitting on the coffee table in the living room. He did two quick lines and poured what was left of the Cutty Sark into the glass. The coke hit fast, the way he liked it, but it didn't last long enough. He did another line and thought about calling Bix, but he couldn't remember what time it was in Chicago or what Bix's number was. Ellington's heart was beating faster, like someone had set his internal metronome to 196. Somewhere he remembered that tempo was called prestissimo. Probably his mother had taught him that, since Vincent didn't know shit about classical notation.

He took two more of the benzos and washed them down with the rest of the whiskey because he wanted more and because his brain hadn't turned off yet. He was still feeling things, still thinking too much. Not just about Cobain but about Tammy and the band and whether he still loved being a musician and how screwed up his family had been, even though everything that came after the show and after his family came easily to him because of the show and his family. He couldn't have one without the other. Lost Dog wouldn't have gotten a recording contract if it wasn't for him. Basically, he wouldn't be where he was now without being who he was.

"Who the hell am I?" he said out loud, even though there was no one to hear him except the talking head on the TV still talking about Kurt Cobain. He was feeling a little dizzy, and it was kind of hard to breathe, so he laid back down on the bed. That's where Roger found him.

PICTURES AT AN EXHIBITION

Viola's senior show was the culmination of four years of exploration into the theory and practice of fine arts, at least that was the way the course selection book described it back when she started her BFA. Academic achievement and final grades aside, everybody knew that gallery owners, collectors, and art brokers checked out shows like this. The chance to make good connections was why she had spent the previous 10 days measuring and hanging and rehanging the show so that everything would be perfect. She told Bix, "I want to give the show a unified flow while still allowing each individual piece to stand on its own as a discrete viewing experience."

They were sitting at a small table in the back of one of the school galleries eating the sandwiches Bix and his new girlfriend Aimee brought so Viola would take a break and eat something. Viola had loved getting to know Bix as a brother and a friend during her four years in Chicago. The eight years between them wasn't the obstacle it had been when she was a little kid.

"Did you just say 'discrete viewing experience'?" Bix said. He didn't appear to make any effort to hide his amusement.

"Yeah. You got a problem with that?" Viola replied. She was too tired to deal with Bix making fun of her.

Aimee gave Bix a little flick on the arm with her left hand. "Not at all," Bix said quickly. "I'm just not familiar with art terms. Thanks for teaching me something."

"Nice save," Aimee said. "Don't be mean to your sister. She's under a lot of stress."

This was the first time Viola had met Aimee, but she liked her immediately, especially after Aimee said she did competitive gymnastics all through elementary and high school, which kept her from watching much TV as a kid. She had never seen *The Musical Mozinskis*, didn't know who Bix was when they started going out, and consequently had no idea who Viola was. It was refreshing to meet someone with no preconceived notions of their family.

"I'm the nice brother. Come on, who brought you food in your hour of need?" he added to Viola in mock protest.

"Eh, it's a toss-up between you and Theo for the nice brother award."

Bix threw a potato chip at her. "She's lying," he said to Aimee. "I'm her favorite."

Even when Bix wasn't funny, he could make Viola smile. He always had. "I don't play favorites. I'm not *Dad*," she replied.

"You guys make me wish I had a big family," Aimee said. "I just have one sister. It seems like you all had so much fun."

"Fun is a subjective term," Viola said.

Bix actually looked surprised. "It wasn't that bad."

"It was fine for you..."

"Seriously, our dad didn't really play favorites..." Bix said to Aimee. "He just gave some of us a more difficult time than others."

"That's the diplomatic way of saying it," Viola replied. "So has Bix made you watch the box set yet?" she asked Aimee.

"On the contrary, he asked that I never watch any portion of *The Musical Mozinskis*."

"So you have, right?"

Aimee giggled. "A couple episodes," she said. "I had to figure out who I was dealing with after I met you."

"You're dealing with a boy whose big brown eyes and enviably curly hair made young girls everywhere tune in to get their Bix Fix," Viola said, adding just enough faux drama. "At least according to *Tiger Beat*."

Aimee was laughing so hard she could barely stammer "Oh my God, they wrote about you in *Tiger Beat* magazine?"

"Hey, look at the time!" Bix said, half standing. "We should let you get back to work."

They went on joking like this for a bit longer until Bix really had to leave so he could get cleaned up and go to his regular piano gig at a pricey bar/restaurant over in Lincoln Park. "I can help you tomorrow," he said as he was putting on his jacket. Early April in Chicago was still cold. Aimee was kindly cleaning up from lunch so they had a moment to themselves.

"Thanks, but Antonio is coming in a little bit to help me finish," Viola said, trying to sound nonchalant. "I'm doing a walk-through with my thesis advisor tomorrow morning, and then Mom flies in, and the opening is tomorrow night."

"Aahhhh...the infamous Antonio," Bix said with a smile. "The guy you talk about but haven't introduced to the family yet."

"You're one brother. You aren't the whole family."

"I'm a stand-in for the rest of the family."

"He's coming to the opening."

"So he gets to meet me, Mom, and the Clara contingent at the same time?"

"I think he's disappointed he's not going to meet Theo. He's a big Elephant fan."

"You're dating an Elephant fanboy?"

"Yes. But he didn't know Theo was my brother when we met," Viola added quickly, even as she realized she sounded defensive. "He also asked if you were going to play for the opening."

Bix snorted back a little laugh. "You know I would if you wanted me to..."

"It's fine. I'm playing a CD. *Pictures at an Exhibition*."

"Mussorgsky. Totally appropriate."

"It's probably totally pedestrian and lowbrow."

"It'll be fine. Don't worry so much about what other people think."

"Are you going to introduce Aimee to Mom?" It was easier to change the subject.

"Yes, I am," he replied without a trace of hesitation. "I'm glad you finally got to meet her." Viola was glad to see him so happy and grounded; it seemed like whatever he had with Aimee was substantial. She already liked Aimee more than any of the other girlfriends Bix had introduced her to over the years.

After Bix and Aimee left, Antonio showed up — a bit late, as usual — and helped her finish hanging the show, although all he really did was tell Viola everything looked great. Antonio was Viola's first real relationship. Even though she couldn't say she was in love with him, she liked him, enough to support him when he showed his senior film but perhaps not enough to stay in Chicago with him after graduation. And even though she longed to find someone of her own, she certainly wasn't ready for the responsibility of asking someone to move to Cleveland for her sake. Antonio was Mr. Right Now, and she could live with that.

The next day, Viola woke up anxious about the art opening that night and excited that her mom, Clara, and Bix would all be there. Theo was on tour, and Allie was performing in Vancouver but sent flowers to her apartment, which Viola ranked in the top five list of kind things Allie had ever done for her. Everything was going the way it should — she had breakfast with Antonio, met with her advisor, who had glowing things to say about her exhibit, then went back home to her studio apartment in the South Loop to wait for her mom to arrive. She had hated growing up on television but was grateful for the trust fund that helped pay her rent each month. Small as it was, having her own place instead of living in the dorm was heaven.

She turned on the news while she waited and saw that Kurt Cobain had died. Killed himself, which was beyond horrible. Theo had met him a few times and said he was a troubled but good guy. She wondered how he was taking it or if he'd heard since Elephant was on tour. Viola flipped around on the news while she waited for her mother. Every minute she expected a phone call saying she'd arrived or a taxi pulling up in front of her building to deliver her mom. Instead, there was nothing. Finally, her mother called saying that Ellington had OD'd but was alive, and instead of going to Chicago, her mom was on her way to a hospital in Portland to be with him.

Her mom kept apologizing on the phone, as though deciding between the nearly died child over the senior show child was an actual choice. Viola said all the correct things: "You have to go." "I'm just glad he's going to be okay." "Tell him I love him." Inwardly, she couldn't help but think stupid Ellington probably wouldn't even know or care if their mom was there not. Then she felt guilty for thinking that way.

As much as she didn't want to admit it, she was worried. She hadn't lived with Ellington since she was eight, and he'd never done her any favors, but he was still her brother. By the time evening rolled around, they'd gotten word that Ellington was stable, and Viola was feeling slightly better. Antonio met her at the gallery early and held her hand as she told him about Ellington. A group of friends from the art department arrived promptly at seven to make the gallery opening look busy. This is what they did for each other. Viola had done the same thing for one of them the week before.

Her mom wasn't there, but she had Clara and Harrison, who drove in that day from Cleveland, plus Bix actually took the night off from his regular piano gig and was there with Aimee. Antonio seemed to spend half the night making sure the wine and cheese hadn't run out and occasionally checking on the gallery's temperamental sound system, which was known for eating CDs but hadn't been replaced because it was low priority, and the other half of the night hanging out with Bix, who was subdued, talking about Ellington while putting on a cheerful front for Viola's sake. She appreciated it, but she knew he was hurting. More than once, Bix said, "I'm sorry if I'm raining on your parade," to which Viola replied, "You're not, it's fine." Because everything was fine in its own messed up way. She had learned to make do with what she was given way back when the family moved to California when she was four, and she'd been doing so ever since. Tonight, at her art opening, what she had been given was a pregnant sister who had to leave early due to nausea, a sad and sullen brother, and an increasingly tipsy boyfriend.

It wasn't like she had much time to talk with her family during the opening anyway. Her advisor had told her to circulate, introduce herself, and be open and engaging with any patrons who wanted to talk about her art. Frankly, she would rather run naked through the student commons than talk about her work. Viola tried to concentrate on the moment, on her show. There were people there she didn't know, actual strangers who had inexplicably come out to see a student art show. It was hard to think of herself as an artist — as *the* artist — rather than the one hanging out on the sidelines with a tambourine.

The anchor of her show was a series of seven canvases, hung close together, each representing one of her family members. The pieces weren't titled with the person's name but with the name of the piece they'd been playing when Viola first sketched it. A trio of well-dressed older women were standing in front of the family canvases, clearly discussing what they were seeing. Viola inched towards them and lingered nearby, waiting for a natural break in the conversation so she could introduce herself.

"Very nice to meet you," one of them said. "I'm Carol Hubner." She looked like the ringleader. Her well-tailored black pants and shirt were paired with slightly funky, brightly colored accessories, making Viola think she might be a collector or maybe a college benefactor, or both. She did her best to sound professional and engaging as she gave her prepared explanation of her work. Telling people she painted what she heard only caused confusion. Instead she usually said, "It's a visual representation of an auditory experience."

"Can you tell me a little bit more about this one?" Carol asked, pointing to the painting titled "Lazy Day." The predominant color was the pale yellow of her mother's singing voice, but instead of Viola's usual swirls, the bursts of color appeared more as fireworks or the tops of flowers. When she and her mother first moved to Cleveland, before Theo lived with them, her mom would sing "Lazy Day" as they worked in the garden or cleaned the house.

"It's named for a song my mother used to sing to me when I was a little girl," Viola said. She had learned not to reveal too much too soon.

One of the other two women, the heavy-set one with the short gray hair and absolutely perfect complexion asked, "Miss Mozinski, are you related to the violinist Allegro Mozinski?"

It never failed. "Yes, she's my older sister." Viola replied.

The woman nodded. "I heard her play last year. She's marvelous."

Viola forced a smile that she hoped looked genuine. "Yes, she certainly is." She almost said, "Thank you." But why? The woman was complimenting Allie, not her.

"You have a very talented family."

The third woman put an index finger to her lips and said, "Oh! If that's your family, that means your mother actually wrote 'Lazy Day.'"

"Yes," Viola said even though she wasn't entirely sure the woman was asking this as a question or not. For a moment, Viola wished she was anywhere else in the world but there and doing anything but talking about her stupid family yet again.

"It definitely adds another level of significance to the piece," Carol said to her friends, who murmured their agreement. To Viola she said, "You must be very brave. Or a bit of a rebel," she added with a smile.

This was starting to feel very awkward. "Not really," Viola said.

"What I mean is, you didn't go into the family business. That takes some courage."

"I never really thought of it that way."

"Maybe you should."

The other two women had moved on to another canvas. "It was lovely meeting you," Carol said. "And I like your work. You definitely have something."

This time Viola said, "Thank you" and meant it. She paused a moment in front of the family canvases, thinking about the people who inspired them, even though most of them weren't there and some of them she didn't even particularly like. Part of her felt like she'd wasted her time with the series. Taking a quick look around the gallery, she saw a younger couple she hadn't spoken to yet. Each time she introduced herself to someone as the artist, it got a little easier, a little more relaxed. As the evening wore on, circulating and talking to strangers about her art started to feel more natural and less like she was pretending to some sort of legitimacy as an artist. Near the end of the night, Viola walked by the set of family canvases and saw that "Lazy Day" had a red sticker next to it. It had been sold. So had a few other pieces. She was legit a working artist.

DON'T LET ME BE LONELY TONIGHT

B ix was glad Ellington went to rehab and got clean because it meant
he still had a brother on this side of the daisies. For the first few
months, he didn't mind being on call, but Ellington had been out
of rehab for two years and the near-daily phone calls at odd hours had
become a pain in the ass. The first time Ellington called him in the middle of the night, Bix panicked, thinking something was wrong. Now he
knew it was Ellington before he picked it up. Ellington always seemed
to forget what time zone he was in versus which time zone Bix lived
in. Sometimes he'd call in the evening just as Bix was leaving for a gig.
Most of the time, he'd call early in the morning after having been up all
night. When Bix was still with Aimee, she didn't like sleeping at his place
because of Ellington's calls. He would always have to get up and freeze
his tail off in the living room so he wouldn't keep her awake. She used
to say that Ellington was abusing their relationship, but she had never
almost lost a sibling. She didn't know what it was like to worry so much
about a brother. Bix always talked to Ellington. He could never shake the
feeling that the one time he might ignore a call would be the one time
Ellington OD'd again.

Now that Aimee wasn't around anymore, Bix could at least stay in
bed when he answered an early morning call. It was the only upside to
their breakup.

The web of family communication was complex at best. Even being
scattered in four different cities and half the family not talking to the
other half, everybody still knew everyone else's business. Bix was the
only one Ellington talked to regularly. It was kind of like El saved up all

of his family phone calls and funneled them to one person. Ellington was on speaking terms with their parents but wouldn't initiate contact. Allie didn't call anyone except their mother. Their father never called anyone except Allie, and that was only because Allie had local grandchildren. Bix got close to Viola when she went to art school in Chicago. Even after she moved back to Cleveland, they still talked regularly, but she never spoke to Allie or El. Bix traded emails with Theo and Allie every so often, but they were always superficial. Clara was Clara. Somehow, she managed to stay above the tangle of family drama. Everybody still talked to her.

Ellington's current obsession was doing an unplugged Mozinski Brothers show. "Maybe in L.A. Maybe New York. Maybe both. What do you think?" he'd ask excitedly on the phone. Bix tried to point out that they hadn't sold enough records as The Mozinski Brothers to warrant an unplugged concert. After all, they only recorded one album under that name, and that was nearly 15 years ago. No matter what Bix said, Ellington wouldn't let the idea die.

When Ellington called early one morning in February and asked, "Hey, Bix, what are you doing May 23rd?" Bix readied himself for another onslaught of energy. Ellington was speaking very fast in the quasi-manic way he sometimes had that made Bix wonder if he was using again.

Bix didn't have the heart to look at the alarm clock. He just knew that it was the middle of the night. He stretched and yawned as he replied "I have no idea. If it's a weekend, I'm probably playing a gig."

"It's a Friday, and you are playing a gig because we're doing The Mozinski Brothers unplugged at the El Reye Theater in L.A. I just got back from a party with some people and we talked and they liked the idea and they booked it. Boom, boom, boom. We're there."

Bix was lying flat on his back, phone to his ear, listening. Fat Brubeck was curled up next to him, purring away. One of them was now most definitely awake, and it wasn't the cat. "Wow, that's some news. Have you talked to Theo about this?" he asked.

"This just happened like an hour ago so no. And you should probably talk to Theo since you get along with him better than I do."

Ellington's lack of self-awareness was frequently impressive. Theo didn't hate Ellington, but it was no secret he avoided him. "I can ask,"

Bix replied. "I don't know if his band is touring then. And I'll have to look at my schedule."

"It's only one night. Fly out, stay at Dad's, fly back the next day."

"The three of us haven't played together since we were teenagers. When would we rehearse?"

Ellington made a sound somewhere between a laugh and a curse word, which looked to Bix like a big fat E-flat hanging above his bed. "Vincent made us rehearse our whole lives. We could do this in our sleep," Ellington said.

Bix scratched the back of Brubeck's head. "I know what you mean about Dad, but I don't think this would be that simple," he said absent-mindedly, and realized that sounded like he was agreeing to do the show. "If it even happens," he added.

"It'll happen. It's got to. I gotta do this. It's my Jesus year."

"Your what?"

"My Jesus year. Jesus was 33 when he died. You're supposed to do something important and meaningful when you're 33. Live like it's your last year on earth, you know? I mean I'm not gonna do the full-on Jesus Christ thing where you die and all that, okay? Been there, done that."

"Glad to hear you aren't taking it to the extreme." Whenever Ellington talked like this, Bix felt like he had to tread carefully. It was like dealing with Brubeck. Most of the time, the cat was affectionate and would let Bix rub his belly, but once in a while he would arbitrarily decide Bix had gotten too close and claw him. Five minutes later Brubeck would be back purring and lovey as though he hadn't just drawn blood.

"Okay, I gotta go now. Talk to Theo, okay? G'night." It had long ceased to bother Bix that conversations with Ellington usually ended abruptly. After he hung up the phone, he lay in bed for a moment, eyes closed, trying to fall back to sleep. It didn't work. Admitting defeat, he turned on the lamp on the nightstand, got out of bed, and threw on the pair of sweatpants hanging over his closet door. It was too early and too cold to go for a run, but playing the acoustic always helped him relax. As he was walking across the bedroom floor, he stepped on something hard.

"Dammit!" he said as he reached down to see what he had stepped on. It was tiny with a sharp edge. He brought it over to the nightstand

and held it under the light. It was a silver earring back. Aimee's. It was too small and inconsequential to return. She probably had no idea it was missing. Even so, he gently placed it on his dresser for safe-keeping. He liked the idea that an object that had been attached to Aimee's body was still here in the apartment. "Do not knock this off of here," he said to Brubeck, who was now sitting on the edge of the bed watching him, and added "Please," just in case the cat cared.

Bix walked down the short hallway from his bedroom to the living room. The clock said it was 3:27 a.m. He liked his apartment building, but sometimes he wished he had a house so he could play music whenever he felt like it. His all-time favorite guitar, the Martin six-string, lived on a stand in a corner of the living room. Usually all he had to do was start playing to make a date fall for him. The thing that always stood out about Aimee was she liked him before she ever heard him play. They had kept running into each other at the coffee shop down the street. A smile and nod turned into "Good morning" turned into small talk turned into a longer conversation turned into a date with someone who didn't really know who he was. It felt like what he thought being normal must feel like, and he liked it. And he liked her.

He picked up the Martin and sat down on the sofa, but didn't play. Without weighing whether it was a good decision or not, he picked up the living room phone and called Ellington back. It felt good to be the one who didn't say hello. Instead, he merely said, "I'll talk to Theo and I'll do the unplugged show."

Ellington's voice sounded slightly muffled and far away on the phone. "Bix, that's great, man. But you know, I just fell asleep. You woke me up."

"That sucks, doesn't it?" Bix replied. "I'll do the unplugged show, I'll make sure Theo does the unplugged show. In return you have to promise not to call me in the middle of the night ever again. No calls after midnight or before 10 a.m. central time. Take it or leave it," he added, just to make sure Ellington understood the deal he was trying to cut.

"When is that my time?"

"Not after ten o'clock p.m. your time and not before eight a.m. your time."

Ellington gave a chuffed sigh. "Yeah, okay."

"Thanks. I love you, El, and I will always be here for you. Just please don't call me in the middle of the night."

"And then you'll do the unplugged show?"

"Yes."

"Cool."

After they hung up, Bix put the phone down and just sat quietly for a moment, holding the Martin and having a staring contest with Brubeck, who had followed him to the living room and was sitting expectantly on the arm of the sofa. "I have to play quietly," he said to the cat. "Any requests?" Brubeck continued to stare at him. "James Taylor? Good choice," he added as he began to play.

DANCE THIS MESS AROUND

Grace still lived in the house she bought 18 years earlier when she and Viola moved back to Cleveland. Since then, she had cultivated a life that made her happy on her own terms. At some point over the years, each of her children had referred to her departure as when she and Viola ran away. Grace preferred to think of it as a rescue, but didn't quibble over semantics. She left because it was the only way Viola would have anything resembling a normal life. In spite of everything, she never regretted leaving.

There were the odd moments when she considered moving back to Los Angeles. Her career as a songwriter would certainly be easier if she did. Of course, going back to L.A. would mean she'd be in the same city as Vincent. Los Angeles was a sprawling metropolis of nearly 12 million people, but the music business was smaller and more insular than one might think. She'd see him. She didn't hate her ex. Truth be told, she only thought about Vincent in relation to their grown children or the new grandchildren. That didn't mean she wanted to live near him. Swapping Cleveland for LA would also mean swapping living near Clara and Viola for living near Ellington and Allegro, and neither of those two were the type to visit often. It was hard to imagine Allie or El coming over to hang Christmas lights, as Viola was doing.

"You're really going all out with this," Viola said as she surveyed the yards and yards of coiled tiny white lights. "You do realize that if we hang all of these, your house will be visible from space."

"So be it," Grace replied. "I want this year to be extra special."

"Are you really that enthused about the new millennium?"

"Technically, the year 2000 will be the last year of the old millennium and no, that's not why. It isn't every day that Theo brings someone here for Christmas."

"True. That's happened exactly...zero times?"

"You understand. Now get up that ladder."

Viola scurried up the ladder with the coiled Christmas lights in her left hand. "I wonder if Theo's going to introduce Matt to Dad and what's-her-name?" she said as she hung the lights onto one of the nails they'd hammered into the edge of the porch overhang. Then she carefully handed the coiled Christmas lights to her mother and climbed down the ladder.

"I'm sure he will at some point," Grace said, "Also I believe your father's wife is named Marilyn."

"Right, right, Marilyn," Viola replied lightly.

"I don't know her well, but she seems nice enough. Maybe if you got to know her, you'd remember her name."

"Why bother? He'll probably have a new wife next year anyway," she said.

Grace gave a little sigh and took a couple sideway steps across the porch as Viola moved the ladder. "That's his business. He's free to do whatever he wants," she replied.

"Why did you ever marry him in the first place?" Viola asked as she climbed back up the ladder.

"I thought that anyone who played and composed as beautifully as he did must be very deep and soulful."

Viola snorted back a laugh. "Wait, we're still talking about Vincent Mozinski, right?"

Grace handed the coil of lights up to Viola, saying "Maybe I misjudged. But my music trusted him."

"What do you mean?"

There were rare moments like this where Grace forgot that Viola didn't experience music in the same way she did. "My music...You know that when I'm playing, I can see the music that I create. And my music reacted to him. It...trusted him."

"That's why you shouldn't trust music."

"Sweetie, I know you and your father haven't always seen eye to eye..."

"Understatement of the year."

"He may be more shallow than I thought, but he isn't a bad person."

"No one said he was."

"It's just that you still seem so angry..."

"Can we change the subject?"

"Sure." A thought occurred to her that she'd never asked. "When you sing, do you see your own voice as a color?" Grace asked.

"I don't sing," Viola replied firmly.

"You've said that before, but everybody sings once in a while. In the shower maybe or in the car?"

"I don't."

"That's a shame. I wish you would."

Viola stopped what she was doing and looked down at Grace from her perch on the ladder. "Mom, can we please change the subject?"

"Again?"

"This all seems like the same topic to me."

Grace had a lot of experience changing the subject with Viola. Sometimes her youngest wanted to talk. Sometimes she'd clam up. Conversations about Vincent inevitably ended with her clamming up.

Grace's old friend Evelyn always said, "You're only as happy as your saddest child." Most people assumed that Grace's saddest child would be Ellington. There was a time when that was true. Grace had stayed with him in the hospital and then later in L.A., after he went AWOL from rehab, sitting in rooms with him while he ranted and sweated and vomited through withdrawal. He still drank too much, but he was stable. Even as a child, even before the show and the fame, Ellington hadn't been carefree. Happiness is relative to the individual. Ellington was as happy as he was ever going to be.

When Grace walked out of the taping and took Viola home all those years ago, it had taken them 17 hours to get to Youngstown, including a four-hour layover in Chicago in the middle of the night. By the time they got into Cleveland, rented a car, and drove the 75 miles to Youngstown, Grace had been awake for 36 hours straight. The only thing that had kept her awake and moving was Viola. Somewhere in that journey, she started to truly see her youngest child. It always seemed as though Viola was being outshined by her older siblings. In the middle of five burning-hot spotlights, who could see a flickering little candle? Away from her siblings, Viola had her own light, but sometimes she still couldn't see herself. Each of Grace's children had taken their turn being her saddest, but Viola was the default, the one who never seemed to fully turn the corner to happiness.

Viola had the honor of picking up Theo and Matt at the airport because Grace didn't want to go anywhere near the airport a week before Christmas, and Clara was absolutely not taking two small children to the airport on her own, and Harrison was on tour with The Hi-Tones until the 22nd. Viola kind of liked being called upon to do the job no one else wanted to do, even for something small like an airport run. She was of the opinion that art was a necessity, but still, painting pictures wasn't as necessary as, like, being a teacher or firefighter or farmer. It always felt good to be needed in a more concrete way.

She stood by the gate, standing on the outskirts of a mass of people waiting for the direct flight from Seattle to arrive. Between being a moderately successful musician and the trust fund, Theo could afford to fly first class, but Viola knew he wouldn't, just as she knew he would travel light, with no checked bag. She waited as the folks from the front of the plane exited, adding to the chaos. *Just keep moving, people...*she thought as she scanned the crowd. Then she caught sight of Theo's dark hair, long enough now that he had it back in a ponytail. He was walking with a tall guy with short dark hair and a complexion so pale she wondered when the last time was he'd seen the sun. That had to be Matt. Theo wasn't as tall as Bix or Ellington, and had always been on the slight side. At first, he and Matt seemed like a mismatched pair. Then Theo caught her eye, smiled, and said something to Matt, who gave her a broad smile and waved to her with a sweet abandon that reminded her of Forrest Gump. They made their way through the crowd, and she hugged them both with a moment of sudden recognition that she was hugging the guy her brother was probably going to spend the rest of his life with.

Viola had visited Theo in Seattle a few years earlier and drawn a pen-and-ink promo poster for one of his musician friends as a favor. That led to another band poster and another until, four years later, she had a unique sideline that sometimes threatened to keep her from painting. The best things about doing the band posters was having people who'd never set foot in an art gallery tell her how much they liked her work and not having people ask why she wasn't in the band. Matt had seen some of the posters and liked them, which was another point in his favor.

All through the next week and a half, her mother kept saying it was the best Christmas they'd ever had. She said that every year, but this year it was kind of true. Seeing Theo happy with sweet, smart, goofy Matt was awesome. Bix and Aimee were in town with baby Rosie, who really deserved to be referred to toddler Rosie at this point. Clara and Harrison's kids, Miles and Stevie, were at the perfect age to be into Santa Claus. Allie even emailed a video message on Christmas Day with her and Ken, little Jacqueline, and her very pregnant stomach. It took eight minutes for the video to load through her mother's dial-up AOL account, by which time Miles, Stevie, and Rosie were off to run rampant through Grandma's house, but it was still an uncharacteristically sweet gesture on Allie's part.

"Must be the pregnancy hormones," Clara quipped. "It's softening her up."

Viola doubted that Allegro would ever soften up, but kept that thought to herself because why bitch about her sister on Christmas? She had better things to do, such as going out with Theo and Matt practically every night between Boxing Day and New Year's Eve. They went to hear some local bands, and Theo sat in on a gig with an old friend from high school on what Matt dubbed "New Year's Eve Eve."

"Viola and I get to be your entourage, babe," Matt said in the car.

"Don't we have to be more than two people to be an entourage?" Viola said. She was driving and only glancing over at Matt in the passenger seat sporadically. Theo was sprawled out in the back, legs spread wide, arms over each of the seat backs, playing rock star.

"Engage your multiple personalities," Matt said.

"I don't have any."

"That's true," Theo chimed in from the back. "Viola's only ever been herself."

"I'm not sure how to take that statement." She was pretty sure Theo and Matt had gotten stoned in Theo's old room before they left. It amazed her that Theo managed to track down a nickel bag when he'd only been in town for eight days, but that was the thing about Theo, about all her siblings, really. Things were handed to them because of who they were. Theo and Matt hadn't asked if she wanted to join them. Not that she would have — she rarely got stoned anymore and didn't want to be messed up if she was driving. She had learned to drive in the snow, but that didn't mean she enjoyed it.

"It was supposed to be a compliment, sweetie!" Theo said. "You've just always been you. No pretending to be somebody else."

"And look where that got me."

"I know I don't know you that well," Matt said, "but it seems like being yourself made you a successful artist. That's pretty cool."

"See?" Theo practically yelled from the backseat. He seemed a little overexcited to be sitting in with a group called Fictional Indie Band, led by a guy named Deni who had gone to the Bellflower School with them. He pronounced his name "Deh-ni," with the emphasis on the second syllable. In high school, someone told her that Deni had changed the spelling and pronunciation of his name back in the fourth grade, which seemed awfully young to be so pretentious. She'd done a few band posters for him and had to admit the band name at least had a certain appeal.

The gig was in a converted Irish social club on the near west side, not too far from her apartment. The location was good, because if it got really late, they could always crash at her place. They got to the club while the opener was playing, a trio of scruffy kids who didn't look old enough to drink legally. She, Theo, and Matt stopped and listened politely for about two minutes. Viola couldn't say much for the music, which rolled off the stage in lazy, translucent clouds of faded pink and yellow, with all the shape and substance of cotton candy. The band played in what had obviously been the social club's dance hall. The best part of the room was the Depression-era murals along the top third of the walls depicting rural Irish life, replete with ruddy-faced lads and lasses and green hills. The hall was only a quarter full at this point. Fictional Indie Band had a decent local following, so there'd definitely be more bodies in an hour or two, but Viola wondered why Theo was even bothering to sit in.

She followed Theo and Matt along the back of the hall and through a set of open double doors to the bar. There were almost as many people in the bar as in the hall, and Viola felt a little bad for the opening band. Deni was sitting at a table with two guys and girl, but he jumped up and yelled "Theo Mozinski!" the second he saw them. It seemed a bit like overkill. Deni was wearing the tight black jeans, retro T-shirt, and black beanie that seemed to be the uniform for hipster dudes. She'd already counted four other guys with the exact same look and they'd only just got there. Theo was wearing his same old casual black sweater and blue jeans that weren't too baggy and weren't too tight. He never seemed to try too hard to dress to impress.

Even without Deni yelling his name, Viola suspected a lot of the people in the bar would have recognized Theo. His old band, Elephant, had been pretty big by indie rock standards, part of the wave of Seattle bands from back in the early '90s. Elephant broke up two years earlier, and Theo said he'd been writing material for a solo project. When she thought about it, it started to make sense for him to start playing out here and there, reminding people he was still around.

Deni was acting like it was old home week, giving Theo the one-armed guy hug and then hugging Viola even though they had never so much as shaken hands the times she'd met with him to talk about band posters. Deni had asked her out once, but Viola turned him down, not just because he was pretentious, but because he was forever turning the conversation to her family. He always wanted to know if Theo or Ellington were going to be in town, dropping hints about going to see whatever iteration of Skutch was touring. He always seemed more interested in her family than her. It was like Antonio all over again. She was glad when Deni and his band went to what passed as the backstage.

They had some time to kill in between bands, and it was nice to hang out and talk with Theo and Matt without the rest of the family around. The fewer Mozinskis in the room, the freer one was to share her true feelings. The sound system in the hall was playing what Theo termed "full-on, old-school, indie-rock crowd-pleasers" like the Cure, Violent Femmes, and Bowie. It just seemed like background noise, but clearly not to Theo. He named every song that trickled in from the hall.

While Matt was telling Viola about the courses he was taking to become an EMT, Theo murmured, "London Calling..." as though he was thinking out loud.

When Viola was answering Matt's question about how she got started doing band posters, Theo quietly said, "Dead Milkmen. Nice segue."

"You hear everything," Matt said to him softly.

Theo looked like they'd just woken him up from a nap. "Sorry, can't help it," he said. "Everyone in our family is like this."

"Not *every*one," Viola said.

"Sorry — almost everyone. I know, it's an annoying habit."

"No, it isn't," Matt said as he gently put a hand on Theo's forearm. "Music is who you are."

It seemed like Matt already knew everything important about Theo, so Viola thought it was safe to ask, "Does the music look different to you if it's recorded versus live?"

"Yeah, it does. Live music looks like a tunnel of notation all around me. Recorded it's just kind of there. It's like a shadow, just not as vibrant. What about you?"

"What about me?"

"The rest of us see the music as the notation, on a staff," Theo said to Matt, "Viola sees it as colors. Isn't that cool?" he added as he took one last pull on his beer bottle.

"Oh, you're synesthetic?"

It was a little embarrassing to admit that in her 26 years on the planet, no one had ever given Viola a name for how she saw things. "I guess so, yeah," she replied.

"It's pretty rare, I think. I mean, I don't know that much about it, but it's a real thing."

"I can't believe you never told me that this exists," Theo said. "So our whole family is syne-what?"

"Synesthetic. I don't know if the whole seeing musical notes is part of it, but there are definitely other people who see sound as color."

Theo smiled at Viola from across the tiny, sticky bar table. "So you're the normal one," he said.

It felt like a small but significant weight had been lifted off her back. "And the rest of you are the freaks," she said and felt slightly triumphant.

"I knew it." Theo tilted his head to side slightly and absent-mindedly said, "Oh, B-52s." Almost immediately he apologized.

"You don't need to apologize for naming every song," Matt said.

"Thanks." Theo glanced up at the clock above the bar. "I should probably go backstage and meet the rest of the band. I'll find you two later?"

"Yes. Have fun," Viola said.

"Looking forward to hearing you play, babe," Matt said. He and Theo held each other's gaze just for a moment. Viola thought that it wouldn't be too bad to go through life with someone who looked at her the way Matt looked at Theo. After Theo left, Matt asked if she wanted another beer.

"No thanks. I'm your designated driver, remember?"

"You're responsible. I admire that," Matt replied with a nod. He listened for a second. Viola could vaguely hear the B-52s playing from the hall. Matt stood up and said, "Let's go dance this mess around while we wait."

"What? No, I don't dance."

Viola realized she was actually holding her hands up in front of her chest, as though she was facing a mugger. Matt leaned down so his face was near hers. "Theo's told me all about what it was like when you were a little kid."

"Great, so you know I had a messed-up childhood. Congratulations. It's all on video."

"The best thing either of us can say about our unhappy childhoods is that they're over. It doesn't define you. Now would you please come dance with me before the song ends? I love the B-52s."

Matt straightened up and extended his right hand to her. Viola stood up. "Okay, I'll dance. But don't make me hold a tambourine," she said.

"Never."

LOTUS BLOSSOM

Allie didn't kid herself that being her father's favorite made her special. It wasn't as though he loved her more than he loved, say, himself. Being the favorite among her siblings was a relative position. She just pissed him off less often than the rest of the family pissed him off. Vincent routinely annoyed her, but he and Marilyn were reliable babysitters. She and Ken had a lot of evening engagements, and sometimes Mariana wasn't available. Giving the nanny ample vacation time meant she would stick around longer.

There were downsides to being the favorite. When Dad and Patty got married, he told only her. It was her job to tell everyone else in the family. It was the same when he and Patty got divorced. Same when he signed on to be the music director for a television series or to do some arrangements for a film. Same when he announced he was getting married to Marilyn. It wasn't so much a question of him being too modest to talk about his accomplishments as it was him being too lazy. And he seemed to think he and Allie had a special bond, which meant he could ask her and Ken for favors. Her father found plenty of work during the '80s and into the '90s. As time went on, his fame faded and the entertainment industry changed. Fewer and fewer television shows used theme songs. Film scores turned into soundtracks. There was less and less work for an aging composer/arranger. Vincent was never destitute — she'd never let her father hit rock bottom, no matter how tiresome he was — but she asked Ken to have a client throw her father some work more than once. One of the things she loved about Ken was how much he loved her. He would literally do anything for her, and he let her do whatever she wanted. Some people thought her marriage to a man 21 years her senior was a little weird, but some people could buzz right off.

The thing most people didn't know was that she had pursued him. Back in the day, she had a couple of short-lived, insipid teenager romances that were ultimately tremendous wastes of her time. Boys took her away from her music. Ken was her agent and later her manager. He was always around. As time went on, Allie came to value that reliability. On her 20th birthday, she kissed him. He kissed back. After a month of ending every encounter with a make-out session, she asked him point blank, "Are we going to consummate this or what?"

They consummated.

After 20 years together and 17 years of marriage, she was genuinely happy, even if some parts of her family still didn't like Ken, but honestly, who cared what Ellington thought? And while she didn't have anything against Theo or Viola, it's not as though she had meaningful relationships with either one of them. Viola at least sent cards and presents to Jacqueline and Glenn on their birthdays and Christmas. So did Clara. When Allie toured in the summer, she sent her kids out to Cleveland to spend a couple weeks with Grandma Opera, so named by Jacqueline at age five. If her children were with her mother, she knew they'd practice and do more than simply watch television. Ken was competent in many areas, but he had no business taking care of children on his own. When the kids spent the day or the night at Grandpa Vincent's, there was just a lot of television and sugar. Her father didn't hold his grandchildren to the same practice standard she'd been held to as a child, which was probably just as well. Her children were talented, but they weren't going to grow up to be musicians. She had learned to accept that. Her father and Marilyn babysat when she needed it. She and Ken sent some work her father's way when he needed it. It was a symbiotic relationship.

She and Ken and the kids were at her father's house on Memorial Day when he told her he was dying. Fortunately, he didn't lead off with that news. They had the obligatory picnic on Vincent and Marilyn's back patio, and then her father suggested that Marilyn and Ken go play croquet in the backyard with Jacqueline and Glenn.

"Croquet, Dad?" Allie said. "I had no idea you played."

"I got a croquet set special for them. It's in the carport."

"I might sit this one out, Vincent," Ken said as he leaned back in his deck chair and stretched out those long legs of his.

Something about her father's tone made Allie realize this was not a suggestion but a request for a private conversation. Sometimes her husband's emotional intelligence was lacking. "Actually dear, I think it's time to put your superior putting skills to good use," she said.

"I don't want to play either," Glenn said. "Croquet is stupid."

Allie quickly ran through the best approaches to dealing with a recalcitrant nine-year-old and went with competition. As the younger sibling, he was always trying to one-up Jacqueline, who had the blessing and curse of doing just about everything well with very little effort. "Croquet actually requires great amounts of skill and strategy. I can see why you might not want to play against your sister. She's more experienced."

Glenn immediately puffed up. "Just because she's older doesn't mean she can beat me."

"I don't need to be older to beat *you*. Just better," Jacqueline said.

"Oh, it's on," Glenn said as he stood up like a preppy WWF fighter. "Let's go."

"You're dead meat," Jacqueline said as they walked across the patio to the carport.

When Marilyn stood up and cheerily said, "Let's go have some fun!" to Ken, Allie's suspicion was confirmed. This was planned, and her father definitely wanted to talk to her alone.

"Let's go inside," he said and cleared his throat. "I need another drink."

Allie pretended she didn't suspect any ulterior motive, just said "Sure," and followed him inside. She immediately started going through her mental rolodex, trying to remember if she heard about any projects that might need her father's talents. At 72, her father was still working wherever and whenever he could. Most of the gigs were nostalgia gigs, playing piano for other silent generation retirees who still liked straight ahead jazz and the Great American Songbook. He didn't seem to want to retire. Honestly, she wasn't sure if he could afford to retire. There had been some tax issues in the past, and he had long sold off most of the instruments he accumulated back when she was a teenager. She still had the Stengel. And she was always glad to see that the great room of his and Marilyn's home in Irvine still held the baby grand he bought when they all first moved to California more than 30 years ago.

Instead of getting another drink, her father led her through the kitchen to the living room. Allie always thought of his house as one long room, because the kitchen opened up onto a dining area which fed into a great room that took up half the footprint of the house. When he and Marilyn bought the house 10 years earlier and ensconced the piano in one corner of the living room, she wondered if her father would miss having a separate composing room. She had heard Marilyn call it the music corner more than once, which seemed dismissive considering music was what had purchased the house.

Her father walked past the sofa and divan in the middle of the room and headed straight for the piano. Truth be told, if there was a musical instrument in a room, Allie always gravitated towards it too. In spite of herself, she half smiled at how similar she was to her father.

It had taken less than 90 seconds to move from the patio to the piano — essentially the length of the house — yet her father seemed slightly winded as he sat down on the cushioned piano bench. She spoke first to give him time to catch his breath. "I can't imagine we came all the way in here just to avoid a croquet game," she said. "But I was thinking, Ken knows an independent film maker named Lydia Krause who's looking for someone to score some incidental music for her next film. I've seen some of her other work and she has a sort of midcentury classic-film aesthetic that I think you'd mesh well with."

"That's nice of you, Allie, but that's not what I wanted to talk to you about," he replied. Her father absentmindedly laid his hands on the keyboard and played a B-flat major chord. Then a D-flat. Instinctively, Allie looked up so she could watch the notes floating in the air just above the piano.

"I remember standing by the piano with Bix when I was little and seeing who could call out the name of the chord first. We weren't allowed to look at the keyboard, so we just looked at the notes in the air," she said.

"That's how your mother and I figured out you see what we see."

"Clever."

"Those were magic times," he said as he started playing a slow waltz in B-flat.

Allie had watched her children closely when they were younger and first learning music. She even asked them separately, quietly, if they could see the music. Jacqueline had looked at her strangely and said, "Am I supposed to?" Glenn simply said, "No." She tried not to let it disappoint her.

The piece her father had started playing was melancholy and gorgeous. "How do I not know this song?" she asked.

Vincent cleared his throat. "Because you don't know *everything* and because you didn't pay attention when I tried to teach you about jazz," he said simply. "This is called 'Lotus Blossom.' Written by Billy Strayhorn. And if you don't know who Billy Strayhorn was, I will disinherit you."

At age 40, Allie was over her father's bad jokes, plus she knew her net worth was 10 times his. She politely replied "Yes, I'm well aware of him and his career."

Her father continued to play as he spoke. "Duke Ellington played it in concert often, but never recorded it. After Billy Strayhorn died, Duke Ellington and the band were in the studio making a tribute album to him. They were packing it in for the night when Duke sat down at the piano and started playing 'Lotus Blossom.' Fortunately, the tape was still rolling. Some people think of the recording as Duke Ellington's eulogy for his friend."

"That's a beautiful story..." Allie began, then she stopped. The combination of the story and the melancholy tune and the mention of death and eulogies caused a sudden wave of dread as she realized there was more going on than her father had said. "Wait, what's going on? What's wrong?"

Her father gave a little sigh but kept playing, the cascading chords of the lilting melody hanging in the air above them. Allie ignored it and focused on her father. "An awful lot, as it turns out," he replied.

"Dad, I need you to tell me what's wrong."

"You know I've had this cough for the past couple years..."

"That's why you quit smoking."

"Mmm-hmm. Well, I guess I didn't quit in time."

Allie took a breath and tried to mentally regroup. "Are you saying what I think you're saying?"

"It's the big C. In my lungs," her father said, as he added a delicate arpeggiated chord sequence to the end of the phrase he was playing.

Allie's throat tightened. "Oh Dad, I'm so sorry..." she stammered. "This is probably the first time in my life where I'm a loss for words."

"That's okay. This song doesn't have words either," her father replied and kept playing.

CRY ME A RIVER

Back when she was a teenager, Viola and Theo had been sent out to visit their father every summer. Her father was always nice enough, but there had been too many times when they would smile awkwardly at each other in silence during a meal or across the living room. Viola never knew what to say to him, and it was obvious he didn't know what to do with her either. They spent a lot of time going out to eat. Her father said it was because having her and Theo visit was a special occasion, but she suspected it was a way of killing time. Whatever wife her father had would try to talk to her about clothes and shopping and hair while her father and Theo talked music. It was a relief when she turned 18 and no one could force her to visit. As she got older, she saw him less and less. Every few years, he'd pass through Cleveland and she'd see him, but she had negative desire to go out to Los Angeles. There were times when she almost forgot she had a father until the day Allie called and told her he'd been diagnosed with lung cancer.

"Shit," Viola said. It wasn't necessarily a reaction to their father having cancer. "Shit" was the first word that came to mind whenever she heard anyone had been diagnosed with cancer. It just seemed appropriate.

Even delivering bad news, Allie sounded completely in control. "Yeah, it's terrible," she replied in a tone that could also be saying it was terrible that it had been raining all day. "Let me know when you want to come out. You can stay with me and Ken if you'd like. I completely understand if you don't want to stay with Dad and Marilyn."

It was tempting to ask Allie what, exactly, she completely understood — feeling like an afterthought for her entire childhood or being repeatedly set up for failure or being benignly ignored? She held her tongue and merely replied, "Thanks for the offer. I'll let you know."

"Honestly, you probably shouldn't wait too long," Allie said, as if she knew Viola was thinking of not making the trip at all. How someone as emotionless as Allegro could still see right through her was equal parts annoying and surprising.

Clara and Harrison and their kids all went out to L.A. for a visit as soon as they heard the diagnosis. Bix, Aimee, and Rosie traveled from Chicago to see Vincent too. Even Theo and Matt went down. Viola didn't make any plans to visit her father. Instead, she concentrated on finishing a series of canvases for a show at a new gallery that had her really excited.

"He hasn't been part of my life for years," she reminded her mother. "What am I losing? Nothing."

They were sitting in a booth at Tommy's, Viola's favorite restaurant. Even though she had moved to the Tremont neighborhood on the west side because it was cheap and had a lot of art galleries, she still made regular visits back to the old neighborhood to see her mother and share a milkshake. "Those are harsh words," her mother said.

"Please don't give me the 'He's still your father' line."

"I wouldn't dream of it." Her mother took a sip of her peach shake, the color of which reminded Viola of old Mr. Karpenko's singing voice, which she had heard occasionally growing up. It always surprised her that such a big, loud person would have a pale, subdued hue to their voice. "Mmm...," her mom added, "it's amazing he's been making these for decades and they are still the best milkshakes on the planet."

Viola just nodded, aware that her mother was likely planning her next verbal volley. They'd been talking through this for three weeks. She didn't want to be convinced to visit her dying father — the phrase itself reeked of melodrama — but privately she had to admit she didn't not want to be convinced. She waited. Her mother met her eyes and gave a little questioning smile. "What?" Viola asked.

"I didn't say anything."

"But you were thinking something."

"Was I?"

"Aren't you trying to talk me into going out to see Dad before he dies? Isn't that the whole point of this lunch?"

"I thought the point of this lunch was I love seeing my daughter and Tommy's milkshakes are too big for one person."

"Mom, you're being infuriating. Everybody in the family has been trying to guilt trip me into going to see Dad, and I honestly don't want to."

"Then don't."

"I won't. I don't see how any of them want to see him. I mean, he calls Clara's kids his 'schwartze grandchildren' and she still went to see him. What the hell is that?"

"I can't speak for Clara, but maybe she understands and accepts that your father is not always the most sensitive man around..."

"No kidding," Viola replied as she picked up her falafel and took a bite.

"We all make decisions about relationships. You choose what you can put up with and what you can't."

Viola swallowed and asked, "What couldn't you put up with with Dad?

"The way he treated you kids. I'm tempted to add his self-absorption, but I guess that went both ways."

"You mean leaving?"

"Yes. It almost cost me my relationship with your siblings. I've worked every day for years to repair those relationships."

"Well, he's never made that effort with me." The whole conversation was starting to irk her.

"You said that you don't want to go see him because you won't be losing anything when he dies."

Viola took a French fry and sort of stirred it around in the ketchup "Okay, you're right, maybe that was a little harsh," she admitted.

"Is there anything you might gain by seeing him?"

Viola was silent for a moment, wondering if she had everything backwards. She hadn't considered the possibility of gain. "I have some questions," she replied.

"Then maybe it's time you asked them. Because there are some things only he can answer."

That was how, against her better judgement, she found herself sitting on the back patio at her father and Marilyn's oversized ranch house in Irvine. She hadn't seen her dad in nearly three years, and it took all her self-control not to gawk at how thin and, well, sick, he looked. He wasn't the suave crooner who had charmed the panties off a lot of women who weren't her mother. If Bix was to be believed, some of that charming took place while their parents were still married. She was grateful Theo had decided to make a second quick trip to L.A. while she was there. It felt like she had an ally.

She was staying with Allie and Ken, but had spent three of the previous four days awkwardly sitting on this very same patio, listening to her father and whatever sibling was there swap musician stories and talk about life on *The Musical Mozinskis* set like they had all spent four television seasons in heaven.

On her last night in California, it was her, Theo, and Allie at her father's house along with Mr. Karpenko, who apparently still had a standing dinner invitation once a week. There were rumors that Ellington might even make an appearance, since he happened to be in town. Her father was in rare form this evening, saying whatever came to mind, and everyone else was eating it up. Even Theo, which felt like a betrayal. "Favorite episode — Season 3 finale," he said. "Sitting in with the Tookie Talbot Trio was one of the high points of my career. The man is a legend."

"Oh, I love that one. We have the box set of all four seasons on DVD," Marilyn explained. "You played 'Cry Me a River' with them, right?"

"Yes!" Vincent wheezed with delight, as though Marilyn had just demonstrated great insight. Viola took a deep breath and held her tongue. It's not like her father got that excited over anything she ever said.

Mr. Karpenko was still big and bushy, although Viola noticed that his salt-and-pepper beard was pretty much entirely salt at this point. "I was so happy when we get him for the show," he said.

"No one was turning eight that year, so there wasn't a Birthday Solo debut," Allie added. "They needed a big name for the finale."

"Also true," Mr. Karpenko laughed.

"The story was Tookie and the guys have car trouble right outside our house," Vincent said as though the rest of them had no idea about the episode. "They come in to use the phone to call a tow truck and we end up jamming together. Oh, it was so good."

"The key change right after the bridge made it," Theo said. "Incredible."

"And Fritz kept saying nobody was going to watch if we had a jazz act on."

Mr. Karpenko gave his signature "Eh," and added, "The ratings were just okay. Not as good as a Birthday Solo."

"The big thing I remember from that episode were Ellington and Bix getting pissed off because they weren't allowed to sit in," Theo said.

"Your brothers were good at that age, but they weren't good enough to hang with those cats," Vincent replied with a laugh that turned into a cough. Marilyn was up and by his chair in an instant, asking if he was okay. "I'm fine...fine...Yeah, the Tookie Talbot episode was great, but you're right, Gregor. The kids and the Birthday Solos. That's what made the show."

"What were your favorite Birthday Solos?" Marilyn asked.

"I don't know, probably my first one, Bach's Prelude No. 1 for solo cello," Theo replied, then added, "In G Major."

"I'm going to go with my last one, Season 4..." Allie began.

"Tartini. *Devil's Trill*," Mr. Karpenko said.

Allie looked genuinely shocked. "You remember?" she asked.

"It was...transcendent."

"Wow, thank you, Gregor," Allie said.

"You're welcome."

Viola had never seen her sister look so touched, even a little vulnerable. Instead of feeling tender, it made her angry and envious. "What about my Birthday Solo?" Viola asked. This wasn't exactly the way she had planned on trying to find some answers, but once she said it, she was glad she had. "It got the show cancelled — doesn't get much more memorable than that," she added to her family's wide-eyed looks.

Theo was sitting next to her and gently placed his right hand on her forearm. "Viola, come on..." he whispered.

She ignored him. Speaking up felt good, liberating even, so she kept talking. "My one and only Birthday Solo was so impressive they didn't include it on the Season 4 DVD. Instead, it's just all of you playing *Ode to Joy* without me. Which is what it should have been in the first place." Viola looked directly at her father, willing him to listen to her for once. "Why did you keep trying to make me do something I couldn't do?"

"I thought you were a late bloomer," her father said in a voice that sounded so smooth it had probably convinced her mother that he wasn't cheating.

"Did you really believe that?" Viola looked at all of them — her father, Allie, Theo, Mr. Karpenko. "I was never going to be as good as the rest of you. Why couldn't you have just left me out of it? Why?"

"It would have been cruel to exclude you like that," Allie said.

"Hey, if anyone knows about being cruel, it's you."

"That's enough!" Vincent said sharply but then he erupted into another cough.

Marilyn again went over to Vincent. "Viola, you're upsetting your father," she snapped.

"I've been upset for years. Now we're even," Viola replied. She scanned their faces looking for even the smallest glimmer of understanding. "Forget it," she said as she stood up. "I'm gonna go. I'll get a cab home."

"Viola, don't go," her father said as he tried to stand up, but Marilyn seemed to think he needed help getting up. Allie and Theo started talking at once, telling her to stay. Mr. Karpenko stood up and said, "I'll drive you to Allegro's house. Is on my way."

Viola didn't know Los Angeles very well, but she knew that Allie's home in Brentwood was a good 30-minute drive past Mr. Karpenko's house in Torrance. Allie and Theo and Marilyn kept talking over each other. Viola opened the sliding glass door that led from the patio to the kitchen and saw Ellington walking towards her. She couldn't believe her father actually gave El a key to his house. Theo had nominal contact with Ellington through the indie band grapevine and said El was still clean, at least as far as he knew. He might have been clean, but Viola could see that he was definitely not sober. They hadn't seen each other in years. She knew that Skutch broke up in the late '90s or early 2000s, and now he did...something, played somewhere.

"Oh, hi," he said.

"Hey," Viola replied. Allie was right behind her, saying, "Don't leave," but stopped short when she saw Ellington. Their greeting seemed even more awkward than hers had. Viola had a sudden flash of memories — Allie and Ellington arguing, fighting, but also their father endlessly berating Ellington, punishing him more often and more harshly than anyone else.

Ellington asked, "Is he out there?" in a voice that sounded like he might be afraid of their father, except El had never been afraid of anyone. He was the one everybody else feared. This was all a little too much.

"Yep, in full regal mode," Allie replied at the same time Mr. Karpenko slid the glass door open, saying, "Okay, Viola. We go." He added a hearty "Ellington!" upon seeing him, leading to another flurry of greetings and exhortations to stay and polite declines and goodbyes, then Viola was in Mr. Karpenko's electric blue Lexus on her way back to Allie's house.

They drove in relative silence for a few minutes. It started to feel uncomfortable so Viola said, "Thanks again for giving me a ride."

"My pleasure. My God, a cab would cost enough to buy a car," Mr. Karpenko replied. Allie actually called him "Gregor" now, which sounded odd to Viola's ears. It was a little ridiculous. She was almost 35 years old — a grown-ass woman — but she still couldn't call Mr. Karpenko by his first name.

"Sorry about all that back there," Viola said.

"All that what?" Mr. Karpenko sounded genuinely surprised. "You have a right to be angry. Honestly, I should apologize to you."

"Why?"

"Your father and I...we have been good friends for years, decades. I think he might have listen if I say 'Hey, do not make Viola play. Let her be little girl.'" He sighed then added "I could have helped, and I didn't," in a tone that tinged his normal peach-colored voice with a darker hue. "I'm sorry for that."

"Thank you for saying that, but it wasn't your responsibility. You didn't do anything wrong."

"Neither did you," Mr. Karpenko replied. He was quiet for a moment, accelerating around a truck and a few other cars. It was almost as though he was deliberating letting her stew on this thought for a moment, long enough to make Viola wonder if he'd been talking with her mother. It was definitely one of Grace's tactics. "You remember what I say to you at Clara's wedding? Before we danced?"

Viola smiled at the memory. "You said. 'Don't let your family stop you from having a good time,'" she said. "They haven't. I have a great life. I'm having a good time, I promise."

"If you are still angry, I think perhaps you could be having a...better time."

"It's not like I'm *consumed* with anger..."

"Consumed, no. But you are angry." He sighed, then said "I think you do not really know your father."

"You can say that again."

"I tell you a secret. Your father tried very, very hard to be successful musician. For years. Then he become successful through all of you children. I think he was maybe, eh, a little jealous?"

"That's no secret. So far, this all tracks."

Mr. Karpenko laughed his big bushy laugh. "Here is the secret. Vincent is a simple man in disguise as a complicated man. He only knows music."

"I'm not a musician. Thus, we have no relationship."

Mr. Karpenko glanced in the sideview mirror and merged into the left lane. "Pretend," he said.

I'LL BE SEEING YOU

With the exception of Allegro, whom he called weekly, Vincent didn't call his children except on Christmas. He always told Marilyn "If my kids want to talk to me, they'll call." Sometimes they did. Clara did. Theo, once in a while. The other ones didn't, but who had time to keep track of that? Before his diagnosis, he still had a career, still played out occasionally. He had a gorgeous wife and a nice house. Grace was still in Cleveland and didn't bother him about anything. He'd been in show business long enough to know that having an ex-wife who didn't ask you for anything was a gift. Even after the diagnosis, life was pretty good because it made all the kids call him. They even came out to see him. It got messy here and there, but they were still his kids.

The last time Viola ever called him was a Tuesday. For some reason, he remembered that. A Tuesday afternoon. She said, "Hi Dad, it's Viola," as though he might not recognize his own child's voice, even though he had seen her two months ago. The way things were going, he realized that was the last time he would ever see her.

"Hello," he said, feeling a little cautious after what had happened when she visited. "Everything okay?"

"Yeah, everything's fine." Her speaking voice sounded a little like Grace's now, a rich contralto. He'd never noticed it before. "I just wanted to check in and see how you're doing," she said.

"I got up this morning."

"I'm glad you did," she replied, and her words sort of thawed him out, melted him. "I just wanted to share something fun with you. My friend Sarah got married last weekend. You might have met her once in Cleveland."

"Wasn't she one of your little friends from when we lived there?"

"No, Dad, I was four when we moved to California. I know her from high school. Anyhow, I met her new husband's parents — Bob and Janice Goldblum. They said you played their wedding way back in 1971 at Shaker Country Club."

"Ah, the Goldblum wedding!" Vincent said. He couldn't pinpoint one gig from 37 years ago out of the thousands he'd played, but he liked the idea that there were still people back in Cleveland who remembered him when. And he liked that Viola thought to share it with him.

"They went on and on about great you were. It was pretty wild."

"Wild that I was great?" He could hear himself wheezing as he said this, and cleared his throat.

"Oh stop," she laughed, "you know what I mean."

"Did they happen to say if it was with the trio or the band?"

"They called it a big band."

"It was a sextet, but when people see a couple of horns onstage, it's suddenly a big band," he said with a chuckle. For a space of a sixteenth note, it felt like he was talking to another musician instead of Viola. She gave a little laugh as though she understood. She knew how a band worked, even if she'd never be a part of one. Maybe she couldn't play, but she was still a Mozinski.

"She also said she swooned over your singing. Her words."

"'At Last' gets them every time."

"Surprisingly, she didn't go on about 'At Last.' She said you sang 'I'll Be Seeing You' for the father of the bride dance, and that it was her father's favorite song."

"Aw, that's sweet. That's such a pretty song. I wish I wrote it."

Viola laughed. "For the sake of writing a classic tune, or for the royalties?" she joked.

"Both."

"Mrs. Goldblum got a little teary-eyed talking about it. I guess her dad died shortly after the wedding, so the dance meant a lot to her. You gave her a really beautiful memory."

"That's my job."

They were both silent, which was okay because it gave him a chance to catch his breath. He wondered if Viola could hear him breathing.

Marilyn said sometimes he wheezed. He and his youngest had never had much to say to each other, but she was his daughter. His daughter the artist. It occurred to him he'd never asked her the one thing he'd been wondering about since she made the invitation for Clara's wedding. "I have a question for you," he said.

"Okay..."

He coughed a bit as he chuckled, "Nothing bad. I was just wondering, when I sing, does my voice have a color?"

"Yeah," she replied after a moment. "It's blue. It's always been blue."

"Huh," he said half to himself. "A dark blue or a light blue?"

"Sort of a cerulean blue, like a cloudless sky just before sunrise."

"That sounds very nice."

"It is. It's gorgeous."

Vincent stopped for a moment, breathing in the idea that the music he created was also his favorite color. The realization that he wasn't going to live long enough to learn if this was a coincidence or not gave him a wave of sadness so suffocating that he had to gasp for breath. "Well, thanks for telling me about the Goldblums. It's a small world."

"Tiny. It's good to talk to you. Take care of yourself."

"You too. Love you," he said.

"Love you too."

"I know I wasn't always good at showing it, but I'm proud of you."

For a second, Vincent couldn't hear Viola, and wondered if maybe she had already hung up. Then he heard her quietly say, "Thank you."

After they said goodbye, Vincent turned off his phone and put it down on the sofa next to him. Marilyn was at the grocery store, so he had the house and the silence to himself. For a moment he considered getting up and going to the piano, but that seemed like too much effort. Instead he leaned back and softly sang the first line of "I'll Be Seeing You." He didn't have the breath support he used to. Back in the day he could fill a room with just his voice, no microphone needed, and the music would linger. At the end of the night, the notes were still hanging in the air, as thick as cigarette smoke. Now the music above his head was faint, ethereal, like it would be gone any moment. He wished Viola were here to tell him if it was still blue.

Musical Mozinskis Discography

Back in the U.S.A. (single)
Groovy Twosie (B side)
Released November 18, 1976

The Musical Mozinskis (LP)
Released April 26, 1977

> Back in the U.S.A.
> Groovy Twosie
> ABC
> The Loco-Motion
> Come Go With Me
> Let The Little Girl Dance
> Snap It Up
> I'm Happy Just to Dance with You
> Black and White
> A World Without Love

Lazy Day (LP)
Released November 14, 1978

> Lazy Day
> From the Bottom to the Top
> One Fine Day
> When Are You Coming Over?
> I Should Have Known Better
> Give Me Once More Chance
> Lookin' Out My Back Door
> Mother and Child Reunion
> Indeed I Do
> One Green Shoe
> Hopscotch

Music Factory
Released February 5, 1980

> Music Factory
> When You Went Away
> I Know That You Know
> Through with Love
> Somewhere, Sometime
> Don't Wake Me Up
> Mama Told Me (Not to Come)
> Better Together
> I Hear You Knockin'
> The Music Inside You
> Uptight (Everything's Alright)

The Mozinski Brothers
Released April 27, 1982

> Let Me Stand Next to Your Fire
> Better Wait
> Side Two
> The House across the Street
> I'm the One
> Goin' Back to Indiana
> City
> The Middle Brother
> Walking on the Moon
> Wipe Out
> She's Not There

Acknowledgments

The actual writing of a book may be a solitary pursuit, but nearly everything one has ever experienced comes into play somewhere, sometime. With that in mind, thanks to my parents and siblings for keeping 2939 full of music, art, and literature. It wasn't all good, but the good parts stuck. Particular gratitude to my brother Mike — from dueling typewriters until now, you've always been a great sounding board. Thanks to Marge Adler and Greg Neiman for their thoughts on the Chuck Berry riff. A shout out to Erin Hill, Toni Thayer, Catherine Donnelly, and Jean Cummins who read this back when it was a short story. Thanks to Lou Aronica for his editorial know-how and eternal patience. And as always, many thanks to my family for putting up with me. Living without you wouldn't be nearly as much fun.

About the Author

Susan Petrone lives in Cleveland, Ohio, with one husband, one child, one cat, and far too many dogs.